S H I F T E R
PLANET

D.B. REYNOLDS

Entangled Publishing, LLC
2614 South Timberline Road
Suite 109
Fort Collins, CO 80525
Visit our website at www.entangledpublishing.com.

Select Otherworld is an imprint of Entangled Publishing, LLC.

Edited by Allison Collins and Candace Havens
Cover design by Sara Eirew
Cover art from Deposit Photos

Manufactured in the United States of America

First Edition October 2015

Chapter One

Amanda Sumner shifted her weight slightly, trying to ease the pain in her right thigh without letting her opponent see she was injured. He caught the movement anyway and grinned. Amanda bared her teeth in response. She wasn't a small woman, but Chief Petty Officer Angel Falzone was a very large man. He had a hundred pounds and at least three inches of height on her. She was faster. Or she had been before he'd delivered a side kick that would have broken her leg if they'd been fighting for real.

She saw his next attack coming and stepped into it, shifting her weight onto her sore leg, swallowing a groan as the muscles screamed in protest. She turned her body, letting gravity do her work for her. She felt the momentum shift and grinned, knowing she had him.

"Lieutenant Sumner!"

Amanda found herself flat on the mat, crushed beneath more than 250 pounds of sweaty male, and desperately trying to breathe. Her chest spasmed, trapping her scream of pain in lungs that no longer wanted to work. She pushed frantically at Falzone, whose eyes widened in dismay as he realized what was happening. He levered himself up onto both arms, and her chest expanded slightly, permitting the first hiss of precious air. Falzone rolled completely away, and Amanda squeezed a second breath through unwilling bronchial tubes, concentrating on the next one and the one after that.

A hand appeared in her field of vision, and she grasped it automatically, coming briefly to her feet before leaning forward to rest her hands on her knees. Her chest wheezed with every sucking inhalation, and the ship's recycled air had never tasted so sweet.

"Bad form, Sumner." Master Chief Jansson's barking voice broke through her pain. "If you can't concentrate when someone calls your name in a gym, how the hell are you gonna be able to focus in a combat situation? You think everyone's going to stop what they're doing so you can have a quiet conversation? Do I need to bust you back, Lieutenant? Teach you the basics of hand-to-hand all over again?"

"Sorry, Master Chief," Amanda wheezed. "No, Master Chief." She gave all the right responses, and hoped he'd keep talking long enough for her to catch her breath before she actually had to assume an upright position and pretend that nothing hurt. She swiped a quick hand across her eyes, wiping away tears that had nothing to do with pain and everything to do with her body's automatic response to a lack of oxygen. Or so she told herself.

"—briefing with Admiral Leveque."

Amanda caught the master chief's final words and straightened too quickly, nearly stumbling as she widened her stance to keep from falling over and embarrassing herself any further.

He gave her a disgusted look. "Do I need to repeat myself, Sumner?"

"No, Master Chief," she said quickly.

He shook his head and walked away, already intent on drilling a new asshole for some other unfortunate soul who'd had the temerity to schedule gym time during his rotation. Technically, Amanda outranked Master Chief Jansson. No way would she remind him of that. Not on his gym floor, and not in this lifetime.

"Sorry, Amanda."

She looked up at Falzone and gave him a weak smile, shaking her head. "It was a fair throw, Angelito." The nickname was a joke between them—*little Angel,* hah! "Thanks for the match," she said and started for the exit before turning back to ask, "Uh, you didn't happen to catch the time of that Leveque briefing?"

He laughed. "You got less than ten minutes."

"Fuck!" Amanda swore and ran for the exit. She ripped off her T-shirt as soon as she hit the locker room door, then grabbed a bottle of water and poured it over her face and shoulders as she headed to her locker. Drying herself quickly, she jammed the wet shirt into the laundry chute, zipped her lightweight uniform jacket directly over her sports bra, and dashed for the lift, punching up Deck 5. Her fingers shook slightly as she ran them through her long hair, re-braiding it as neatly as possible in the space of the one-minute lift ride. When the doors opened, her heart still raced with an adrenaline rush that was only partly due to her headlong dash from the gym.

The fleet had taken up orbit around an uncharted, uninhabited planet three days ago. Except that the planet turned out to be neither of those things. No sooner had they dropped out of warp speed than they'd picked up the loud squawk of a distress beacon, shouting its message with all its puny power. It was an ancient design, engineered to last hundreds of years, and used primarily by the first wave of old Earth colony ships, usually in a last ditch effort to let someone know where they'd gone down.

Admiral Nakata had ordered the deployment of an unmanned probe, and Amanda had already spent hours devouring the data it had sent back before being mysteriously destroyed. These probes weren't designed to last forever, but this one had burned up rather spectacularly shortly after entering atmosphere. Fortunately, it had managed to record quite a bit of information during its short life. And that information was beyond exciting. There were *people* living on this planet—human colonists who'd had no contact with Earth in almost five hundred years. That meant a specialized First Contact team would be going down there, followed by a full science contingent. And Amanda wanted to be among them.

Unfortunately, Admiral Leveque was pretty much in charge of deciding who would get to go. And she was about to show up stinky and late for his meeting.

The guard standing outside the admiral's conference room gave her a quick once-over when she approached, followed by a miniscule nod of approval as he murmured into his throat mike and tapped the door controls. Amanda breathed a sigh of relief.

"You're the last one, Lieutenant," the guard said in a low voice. "Better pick it up, though. The admiral's walking through the door."

She smiled her thanks at him, and stepped into the back of the crowded conference room just as Vice-Admiral Randolph Leveque strode in from his adjoining office. Everyone stood to attention while Leveque took up a position at the head of the table. He scanned the twenty or so people assembled, finally focusing on her, and taking in every detail of her appearance with pursed lips.

"Good of you to join us, Lieutenant Sumner. Be seated," he added to the room at large.

"Thank you, sir," Amanda replied, taking the nearest chair.

"Perhaps we'll leave the door open," Leveque said, with a delicate sniff. There was humor in his smooth voice when he said it, and there was nothing specific to indicate he meant her, but her face burned with embarrassment. Leveque hadn't liked her from the moment they were introduced, though she'd never figured out why.

Forcing herself to relax, she clasped her hands on the table and waited, watching the admiral peruse the several reports his aide was calling up on the two separate datapads in front of him. Another aide hovered nearby, making a ritual out of pouring tea into a delicate cup with the Leveque family crest. The aide finally set the cup on the conference table at the admiral's elbow, sighing with relief as if she'd delivered his firstborn son instead of a stupid cup of tea.

Leveque ignored the woman with the ease of someone used to having servants around, then looked up and smiled, his perfect white teeth gleaming against an equally perfect tanned and handsome face. "You've all heard about our lost colony, of course."

Amanda's heart skipped a beat as she joined her voice to the general chorus of "Yes, sir," that responded.

"Lieutenant Sumner, perhaps you can summarize what we know. In fifty words or less," he added.

Everyone laughed dutifully. It was well-known that Leveque's knowledge of anything scientific was exceeded only by his lack of interest in same. He'd been with Nakata's fleet less than a year, and both his exalted rank and his position on this ship had more to do with his family's fortune than any singular achievement on his part. The fleet was in search of profit, and no one understood profit better than the great industrial families of Earth.

"Yes, sir," she responded, trying to figure out how to compress countless terabytes of data into a single paragraph. "The colony ship was launched out of the old European Union, a Spanish and Irish joint venture, with no name designator. Data download indicates they made a critical landing approximately 485 Earth years ago after a general system failure, cause unknown. Comm has made repeated attempts to contact the colony via various bands with no success. There is, however, a definite human, colonial presence, and a fair level of development using what appears to be a solar power source."

Leveque raised his eyebrows, as if surprised she'd managed to be coherent. "Solar," he repeated. "Its use is a function of the electromagnetic anomaly we've detected, I assume.

The same anomaly which caused the probe's destruction?"

"That's our working assumption. Yes, sir."

Leveque scanned a few more pages on his datapad, before looking up. "Unfortunately," he said, "this planet offers nothing in the way of natural resources." He tossed the datapad onto the conference table. "Which I shouldn't need to tell you is the primary mission of this fleet."

There was a general intake of breath when he said this. Ancient law, going back to the wet navies of Earth, required all aid and assistance be rendered to any ship in distress. And that certainly included the so-called "lost" colonies, even if they didn't have anything profitable to offer. Surely the admiral wasn't suggesting they move on without contact?

Leveque was clearly aware of the reaction, and he paused long enough to rake the room with an arrogant glance. "Nonetheless," he continued, "Fleet Admiral Nakata has decided that we will pay them a visit. Daylight over the main settlement is in two hours, at which time First Contact will drop for a meet and greet. Let's hope the locals are early risers. Commander Wolfrum will be heading up that team. Barring complications, we'll drop the science contingent a day later, and that's all of you, ladies and gentlemen. You have forty-eight hours to prepare. Dismissed."

Chapter Two

Rhodry Devlin de Mendoza stared at the piece of fine writing paper, and read the few lines of elegant script for the third time. Or maybe the fourth. It didn't matter which, because no matter how many times he read the words, their meaning stayed the same.

Cristobal Martyn, the Ardrigh and current ruler of Harp, wanted Rhodry in the capital. It was phrased formally, a summons to serve in the Ardrigh's guard, which was the duty of every man on Harp. The formal language wasn't even half the story.

"It's those damn Earthers," his cousin Aidan said from across the room. He stood glaring out the window, as if expecting an Earth invasion to drop from the sky at any moment.

"Probably," Rhodry agreed. It had been only yesterday

that he and Aidan, along with almost everyone else, had witnessed the fiery passage of the Earth fleet's unmanned probe through Harp's sky. Rhodry and his mountain clan had barely accepted the fact of Earth's rediscovery of their small planet, and now this summons from the Ardrigh had arrived, calling him away.

"Cristobal only wants me," Rhodry observed, reading the letter once more. "He's pretty clear about that. No cousins are welcome."

Aidan snorted. "As if he could stop us from coming. He hasn't the power or the right. You're the de Mendoza clan chief. We're not going to let you visit that place with no one to guard your back."

Rhodry didn't say anything. He shared his cousin's concerns. On the other hand, he understood Cristobal's reasoning, too. Being the de Mendoza clan chief meant something on Harp. While the Ardrigh's city might hold the larger population, the fiercest warriors on the planet came from the five mountain clans. And of those clans, de Mendoza was the largest by far. They might squabble among themselves, but when push came to shove, they all looked to de Mendoza for leadership.

Cristobal Martyn wanted to greet these Earth visitors — or invaders, depending on your perspective — with a united front, and the might of the clans at his back. He wanted Rhodry to stand with him as a symbol of that united front. He did *not*, however, want a critical mass of clansmen to come along with him.

The de Mendozas had ruled all of Harp for generations before the Martyns took over, and there were some who had never abandoned the possibility of a de Mendoza on the throne once again. Rhodry himself had no desire to take up the Ardrigh's crown. It was a largely bureaucratic position, and involved dealing with far too many of Harp's most difficult citizens. Rhodry was willing to let the Martyns have it. Although not everyone agreed with him. And not everyone believed him, either. Which gained him distrust from *both* sides of the political spectrum.

As it stood, however, he had no qualms about standing with his Ardrigh in confronting these Earthers. Separately, they were Martyns and de Mendozas—together they were all men of Harp. And all of Harp would have to stand together if they were to weather this new and largely unwelcome development. They would need one face, one purpose, to deal with these unexpected visitors and, most importantly, to ensure that Harp's secrets remained just that.

"I'll leave within the hour. The hover that brought the summons is waiting to take me back to the city."

Aidan turned from the window to stare at him unhappily. "He's eager to get you there, isn't he?"

There were only two of the solar-powered hovercraft on all of Harp, and they were reserved for only the most necessary travel. Harp was a small planet, with a small population, and only one major city. Traveling with a few companions and moving fast, it would have taken him just two days to reach the city. Cristobal didn't want to wait that long.

"The Earthers must have made contact already." It was the only explanation for Cristobal's urgency in getting him to the capital.

"Aye, well, I don't care what Cristobal Martyn says, you're still not going to the city alone."

"There might not be room on the hover for more than

me, what with the escort he sent."

"You mean guards. Let's call 'em what they are. And I don't care if one of them has to stay behind and walk himself back to the capital to make room for me. I'm going with you."

Rhodry grinned at his cousin, feeling more than a little relief. He was fully capable of watching his own back if he had to, but he wouldn't mind having a friendly face there instead. "You're just curious about the Earthers."

Aidan shrugged cheerfully. "You never know, Rhodi lad. There might be a pretty female or two wanting to test the virility of their long-lost cousins. Can't leave them to those city dandies. They'll give Harp a bad name."

"If the Earthers send a landing party — "

"You mean *when*."

"*When* they send a landing party," he agreed, "it will be a scientific mission. I suspect brains will count more than beauty among its members."

"Nothing says you can't have both. They might just surprise you."

Rhodry frowned. He wasn't looking for any surprises, whether they came wrapped in pretty packages or not. The Earthers brought danger to Harp...danger not only to its people, but to its very survival.

Chapter Three

Amanda barely noticed the brief interlude of weight-lessness as the shuttle slid through the big, open doors of the launch bay and into the black of space. Maneuvering thrusters kicked in with a jolt and gravity was restored. She'd been born in space, had grown up on one ship or another, moving every few years until finally her mother had been named chief medical officer for Admiral Nakata's expeditionary fleet. They'd taken up residence on the admiral's flagship, the James T., and there they'd stayed for just over ten years now.

She'd begun dropping down to explore planets long before that, however. When she was eight years old, she'd persuaded one of her mother's medical residents to take her along with his landing team. She'd been a lowly gofer on that trip, and the team's assignment had been no more dangerous than attending a major scientific conference on a highly developed and well-settled world. But she'd been as excited as if they'd been setting out to explore the raw unknown. Planetary life *had* been unknown, at least to her.

Since that first time, she'd begged landing berths at every opportunity, graduating from gofer to whatever else they needed as she got older, even when it was only a strong back to haul equipment. Her mother had indulged her obsession, considering it nothing more than a childish whim, an idiosyncrasy Amanda had inherited from her planet-bound father and one she would soon outgrow.

Despite Elise Sumner's best efforts to coax her daughter down a different path, however, Amanda had been interested in only one thing, and that was the job she now held, the coveted position of landing team specialist. She didn't want to explore space. She wanted to explore planets. And someday she fully expected to find the right one and stay there forever.

The shuttle pivoted smoothly on its axis, giving the passengers a perfect view of Harp. A gray-green ocean spread out just below them, a wide stain across the visible surface, broken by streaks of mineral color where it touched the bluish-white shadow of a massive glacier. The ocean slipped behind them as the shuttle crossed over the planet's frozen pole, its ice cap rendered effectively permanent by an axial tilt that left it nearly sunless year-round. In contrast, the sunward latitudes were a vast desert, dry and burned to a sere beige by constant exposure to the system's volatile red dwarf.

As intriguing as they were, it wasn't the poles that interested her. What drew her attention, and that of every other person onboard the shuttle, was the emerald green band in between the two extremes, a vast forest where human colonists had survived to build a home nearly five hundred years ago. Trees, lush with fresh growth, towered over a temperate zone that, according to fleet sensors, was teeming with life. That green swath spoke to something deep in her soul, some genetic memory of the Earth she'd never seen, something buried in her DNA long before humans had taken to space all those centuries ago. It conjured images of water running fresh from a spring, cold and biting, of warm soil beneath bare feet, and cool shade on a summer's day.

"They call it 'the Green,'" said a voice to her left.

Amanda glanced next to her at one of the scientists who'd been with the First Contact team.

"The forest," he clarified. "It's not very original, but certainly apt, don't you think?"

She nodded. "It's beautiful. Did you get a chance to explore?"

The scientist shook his head. "Not yet. The locals say it's too dangerous to go beyond the city limits without an escort. We're trying to set something up with them to take a team out there."

"Can anyone join?" Amanda asked.

"Sure. Check with Wolfrum. He's running a list."

The three-toned note that they'd all been waiting for sounded at that moment, a warning for everyone to get settled and strapped in. The ride down to the planet would be fast and furious. She leaned back and closed her eyes as they built up speed, feeling the ache in every muscle of her still-sore chest as she was pushed back against the thick crash padding. Heat shields snicked shut over the windows just before they hit atmosphere, blanking out the sight of the planet and its forest.

And she heard something begin to sing.

Amanda's eyes flashed open. The singing continued. She glanced around the compartment—no one else seemed to be hearing anything unusual. The crew members closest to her leaned back in their seats, eyes closed, mimicking pretty much everyone else onboard. She frowned and concentrated on the sound, trying to isolate it from the general noise of the shuttle's descent. Her first thought was that the flight crew were indulging in a little musical interlude, but the overhead speakers were silent as usual. She scanned the compartment once again, thinking someone's personal recorder was malfunctioning. That wasn't right. The sound wasn't coming from inside the shuttle at all. In fact, it wasn't coming from outside the shuttle either.

It was inside her own head.

A quick spike of adrenaline had her heart tripping, and she forced herself to assess the situation rationally. She'd visited many different worlds over the years, from planets to moons to deep-space stations. The possibility of some sort of telepathic communication wasn't exactly a shock. The only real surprise was that she seemed to be the only person onboard who was hearing it, and that it had manifested before they'd even made planetfall. And now that she thought about it, there'd been no mention of any telepathic phenomenon in the First Contact team's report, either.

Her curiosity growing, she listened more closely to the singing which only she seemed to be hearing. It was a lovely sound, multilayered and harmonious. And it seemed to maintain a constant decibel level, which pretty much ruled out human origin. The human voice lifted in song could be a beautiful thing, but it tended to ebb and flow with words and rhythm and eventually stop altogether. More simply, humans needed to breathe. No one could hold a note forever.

This was considerably steadier than any singing she'd ever heard, like a constant flow of sound from a computer, only more musical. She'd heard something similar on Delby Seven, but the screaming corals of that planet were far more likely to induce nightmares than this pleasant perception of welcome. Because that was definitely what she was hearing—a warm, almost joyful sound, as if… Well, as if the planet was welcoming her home.

And that made no sense at all. The logical, scientific part of her brain dismissed the whole thing as some weird physiological response to their rapid descent, perhaps a function of the atmosphere itself, or maybe Angelito had hit her harder than she'd thought back in the gym.

This defied logic. Despite everything her brain was telling her, there was some deeper part of her that responded to that song, as if she really was coming home.

The shuttle slowed, going in for a powered landing. Apparently the shields had held, and the engines were still with them. Amanda smiled absently, her thoughts focused almost completely on the voices in her head. They were no longer singing so much as whispering, a thousand voices at once and all saying the same thing, though she didn't know what it was.

The ground hovered below them as the pilot performed a perfect vertical landing. The engines died, and she unbuckled and stood with everyone else, the weird voices pushed to the back of her mind as she waited for the hatches to open, for that first breath of unfiltered air which would tell her so much about this new planet.

Vacuum seals hissed, and warm, humid air rushed in, and, oh gods, it was wonderful. Dirt and flowers and trees… bitter, sharp and sweet all at once. And the voices! They were so loud now that Amanda was having trouble hearing the people around her. She forced herself to remain calm and steady, when what she wanted was to push her way through the crowd of excited scientists, and rush out to experience the forest for herself. To find the source of the voices in her head and finally understand what they were saying.

One of the crew finished deploying the ramp, and Commander Guy Wolfrum appeared in the door almost immediately, blocking the hatchway with his considerable bulk. Wolfrum had led the small First Contact team earlier. He was head of the entire science section and as such outranked everyone on the shuttle, civilians included.

"Ladies and gentlemen," he said loudly, drawing everyone's attention. "I trust you've all read the initial First Contact briefing by now." There were nods all around, accompanied by scowls at the unexpected delay. *Of course*, they'd all read the damn briefing. They were professionals.

"Just to remind you," Wolfrum continued unfazed. "The local language is trade common, for the most part. There's been some degradation over the years, and there's a sprinkling of Earth native tongues, nothing most of you on this shuttle haven't encountered before." He paused and raked a stern glance over the anxious team. "Now, listen up, people, and listen well. The so-called magnetic anomaly that brought down the probe is a natural resonance produced by a certain species of trees here on Harp. Because of this resonance, the on-planet government has imposed an absolute embargo on any kind of powered weaponry, and Admiral Nakata has agreed. This includes personal lasers no matter how small or for what purpose. I cannot emphasize this enough. Use of any such device has the potential to produce catastrophic results. Pulsed weapons and/or devices *will* explode if used on the planet's surface. Anyone found harboring such, assuming he or she is alive to suffer the consequences, will be ordered off-planet and face severe discipline, including possible reduction in rank. This is deadly serious, people."

He paused briefly, glaring around the shuttle compartment to make his point. "Be advised, there is no need for weapons as long as you remain within the city itself. However, if you plan to explore beyond the city's perimeter — something I strongly discourage without a local guide — you may carry edged weapons only. In fact you are encouraged to do so, as many of the native species are distinctly hostile.

"Please check your belongings before leaving the shuttle, and deposit any embargoed items in the bin here on your way out." He pulled a disposal bin out from the shuttle wall.

"Other than that…" He smiled. "Enjoy your visit to Harp."

All around Amanda the various scientists were patting pockets and checking backpacks. Not for weapons, she imagined, since they *had* all read the briefing and it had specifically mentioned the weapons embargo. They were checking for laser instruments, which were so commonplace on the ship that they might easily have been packed automatically.

With no such concerns, she moved quickly to the ramp and out of the shuttle, then stopped to stare in wonder. She'd seen some great forests in her life—the blue hibideons of Zara 12, the unexpected beauty of the rain forest on Charos. She'd never seen anything like this. Trees soared all around and as far as the eye could see. To her left and behind her was dense forest, the trees so closely packed together in some places that even in daylight one would have to walk carefully.

Ahead of her and to the right, the ground sloped gently upward, with the forest thinning just enough to accommodate a small city. Even here, trees lined the streets and seemed to fill every available space. She couldn't see much else from this distance, only flashes of tan stucco, and the occasional gleam off a bright blue solar array on a rooftop. She could also make out the slight thinning of greenery that marked a road climbing up to where a single bare cliff of jagged rock stood out from among the trees high above the city. And nestled up against the gray rock was a stone building that looked as if it had been carved out of the cliff itself. It had the look of a government center, grand in size and design, although she'd certainly seen more ostentatious buildings in her travels.

"Lieutenant Sumner!"

Stifling a groan of dismay, she plastered an expression of mild interest on her face and turned to find Commander Wolfrum waving her over. "Commander."

"Come with me," he said and started off through the crowd, offering no explanation.

Amanda gritted her teeth. She had no choice but to follow as he made his way toward the edge of the landing field, gathering a few other scientists on his way. Amanda hung back, already thinking of ploys she could use to get away from him, when she finally glanced up and got a clear look at where Wolfrum was leading them.

Her reluctance vanished.

The three men were locals. Even if it hadn't been obvious from their clothing, she would have known, because there was no way men that gorgeous could have existed anywhere in Nakata's fleet without her knowing about it. Wow. Two blond, one dark, all tall and broad-shouldered, each with his long hair tied back. Two of them were younger and clearly bodyguards for the third, whom Wolfrum was even now introducing to the others.

"And finally, your highness, this is Lieutenant Amanda Sumner."

She snapped to attention automatically.

"Lieutenant," Wolfrum said, "it is my honor to introduce Cristobal Fionn Martyn, Ardrigh of the planet Harp."

Ard-ree, she repeated to herself as she stepped forward. Wasn't that Irish Gaelic for king or something, some old-Earth title? That would make sense since half of the colonists had hailed out of Ireland, and the other half from Spain.

She held out her hand to the Ardrigh, as she'd seen the others do—shaking hands was apparently the accepted custom on Harp. Customs varied from planet to planet. She was only glad that the form here didn't include curtseying, which was a pain in the ass and looked stupid when she was in uniform.

As she held out her hand, she wondered why Wolfrum had included her in this little ceremony. Certainly there were higher ranking officers and more distinguished scientists in their group. And, besides, the trees were calling to her, urging her to join them in the cool shadows beneath their branches. Her eyes widened in sudden realization. That was it! It was the trees who were singing to her.

"A pleasure, Lieutenant. Welcome to Harp."

Amanda jerked her attention back to the Ardrigh and managed a polite, if slightly distracted, smile as she shook his hand briefly. She noted in passing that his palm and fingers were rough and calloused, not at all the hand of a pampered royal.

"An honor, your highness," she said. In her experience, it never hurt to say she was honored to meet just about anybody. Although, at this point she was having trouble focusing on much of anything. Gods, couldn't anyone else HEAR that?

The Ardrigh smiled as he released her hand, and there was a definite twinkle in his eye that made her wonder if he knew exactly what she was thinking. Damn. Maybe that's what those voices she was hearing were all about. Maybe they were all telepaths here. She hated when that happened.

She lingered a polite few minutes while the Ardrigh spoke with Commander Wolfrum and the other scientists, just waiting for a chance to slip away unnoticed. One of the guards eyed her rather intently as if he knew what she was doing—the darker one with the black hair and a brooding expression. She smiled in a friendly way and tried to look innocent. He didn't smile back, which was unfortunate, because he probably had a killer smile to go along with that killer body. And also because he probably *did* know what she was planning, and would stop her if she tried.

She waited until his attention was drawn elsewhere by someone's question, then slipped away, quickly losing herself in the crowd. She paused once, to glance over her shoulder, then stepped off the hard-packed dirt and in among the tightly clustered trees. The forest swallowed her almost completely. If she turned just so, she could still catch glimpses through the trees of the shuttle and its crowd of people, could still catch the burned metal smell and crackling sound of the cooling engines.

All of that disappeared as she moved deeper into the forest. It was as if the trees were gathering around her now that she was finally here, as if they were swaying ever closer in their curiosity, as eager to study her as she was them. She had no sense of danger. She felt no fear. She was mindful of Wolfrum's warning about leaving the city limits, but she was armed with a knife and was confident in her own abilities to protect herself. That's what being a planetary specialist was all about. It was more than just her degrees in xenobiology and chemistry. It was the ability to survive the challenges of uncharted territory. It was the real reason that she loved her job.

She took a moment to breathe in the air, closing her eyes and tasting the scents and flavors of this new world. The voices in her head had quieted, as if now that she was here, they were willing to give her the time she needed to adjust.

Finally, she opened her eyes and walked over to the largest tree she could find, a giant that was nearly twenty-five feet around, towering so far overhead and with growth so thick that she couldn't lean back far enough to see beyond the first few branches. Curious, she reached out a hand and touched the tree lightly, pressing harder as the sensations multiplied beneath her fingertips.

It was warm and rough, with deep creases of age in the bark that were so wide in places she could have slipped her entire hand inside. There was life flowing just below its surface, an awareness that washed over her as she flattened both hands against the crinkled surface. It started with a trickle and quickly became a flood, spreading outward from this single tree to encompass the entire forest, spanning the width of the planet, overwhelming her with details of not just the trees, but the lives of every creature that dwelt among them, from the tiniest vole to the huge, dagger-toothed predators at the far edge of the ice cap, bombarding her with... too much!

She pushed away with a cry, falling to the ground and cradling her head in both hands as she tried to make it stop spinning. Huddled at the foot of the great tree, she fought to keep from throwing up, even as she was laughing with delight like a crazy person. Tears of pain and joy filled her eyes to overflowing, dripping down her cheeks and soaking into the leaf-covered ground.

"Are you sick?"

Amanda jerked upright and stared over her shoulder. Through a blur of tears, she saw the Ardrigh's guard staring down at her, the same one who'd been watching her so intently. He was a big man; at several inches over six feet, he was just slightly taller than the other two locals had been, and probably close to three hundred pounds of pure, gorgeous muscle. The severe way his black hair was tied back made his sharp cheekbones and almost pretty mouth stand in stark contrast to one another.

But it was his eyes that drew her attention, that sucked away her breath, and made her want to stare. She hadn't noticed their color in the sunlight of the landing field. Here in the shadows under the trees...they were pure molten gold, surrounded by thick, black lashes. They were the most beautiful eyes she'd ever seen, definitely not the human norm. And they were currently regarding her with a hostility that belied his concerned question.

She forced her emotions under control. She was supposed to be a professional, one of the fleet's best. "I'm fine. It's…" She waved a hand around to indicate the forest. "I don't drop to a planet all that often, and this forest is so beautiful."

"You shouldn't be out here," he said, staring at her with such focused attention that it bordered on something sexual.

Her entire body flushed with pleasure, but she managed to keep her voice only slightly breathy when she asked, "Why not?"

He stared at her a moment longer. Long enough that the blatant desire in his eyes faded into puzzlement, and finally disappeared altogether behind a wall so blank that Amanda couldn't be sure they'd ever shared that moment of intense heat.

He straightened to his full height, his posture as unyielding as his expression when he growled, "Because it's not safe. Your advance team must have warned you of this."

Amanda almost interrupted him to disagree. It was perfectly safe out here *now*. There'd been a whole pack of some monkey-like things earlier—now they were long gone, and there was nothing in the immediate vicinity that posed any threat to her at all. She opened her mouth to tell him so. And shut it just as quickly.

Maybe it wasn't a good idea to admit that the trees were talking to her. She knew very little about these people or their culture. They might be human—okay, they obviously were *mostly* human—but humans did all sorts of horrible things to each other. For all she knew, they burned people like her at the stake on this planet.

"You should go back with the others," he was saying, his voice cool and reserved. "I think the Ardrigh has plans to invite several of you to dinner at the palace this evening." He gave her a quick once-over, though he was careful to avoid meeting her eyes. "You'll want to change clothes first."

Well, well, sexy *and* insulting. Who could resist?

"Really, de Mendoza," a new voice drawled. "You'll give our visitor a bad impression of us." Amanda looked up to find the other guard, the blond one, strolling in from between the trees. She took the opportunity to stand up, using the tree for balance, and had to stifle a laugh at the little rush of warmth beneath her hand when she touched the rough bark. The new arrival was watching her, his gaze traveling up and down her body in a blatant appraisal, which had Mr. Sexy—whose name was obviously de Mendoza—bristling in disapproval. She held out her hand.

"Amanda Sumner," she said.

Unlike de Mendoza, Blondie had no difficulty smiling, a slow, lazy grin that lit up his already handsome face. He bowed slightly before taking her hand.

"Fionn Ignacio Martyn, at your service," he said. He straightened, giving de Mendoza a sideways look. "I apologize for my fellow guildsman, Amanda, but he's right. The forest is no place to wander alone. The rest of Harp is far more welcoming to visitors, and may I say that *I* think your presence will be a lovely addition to the evening's festivities, no matter what you wear."

De Mendoza snorted his opinion of Fionn's blatant

flattery, and some perverse part of Amanda, still stinging
from his comment about her clothes, decided to get a little
of her own back. Giving Fionn an appraisal every bit as bold
as the one he'd given her, she asked, "Will *you* be there?"

Fionn laughed out loud. "Yes, indeed. I will most
certainly be at my father's little get-together this evening."

Amanda joined his laughter. "Then so will I." But it was
de Mendoza's golden eyes she met when she said it.

A manda slumped against the lift wall, stifling a groan as
her body protested too many days of too little sleep.
She'd been riding an adrenaline high ever since they'd taken
up orbit around Harp, but that high had peaked to a painful
intensity with today's discovery that she, apparently, could
commune with trees. At least on Harp.

And what the fuck was that about? Her first thought had
been that it was a hallucinogenic in the air, possibly a spore
cast off by the trees themselves. Although that couldn't explain why she was the only one who experienced it. Or rather, the only one from the ship.

There was no doubt in her mind that de Mendoza and
Fionn had both known exactly what was happening to her
and why. And that they were determined to keep her from
exploring it any further. The two men had entirely different
ways of trying to control her—de Mendoza's stern bossiness
compared to Fionn's charm. Their end goal, however, was
exactly the same. They wanted her out of the forest and,
ultimately, off the planet as soon as possible.

What were they afraid she'd discover if she stayed?

Neither of them understood that trying to keep her from doing something was like throwing down the proverbial gauntlet. It was a challenge, and she could never resist a challenge.

She thought about the two men. Fionn Martyn was the Ardrigh's son. Did that make him the heir apparent? Was the position even inherited? Fionn had let that piece of information drop casually, and she was sure he'd done it on purpose. He'd wanted her to know, either hoping to impress her, or... Well, there was no *or*. She knew guys like Fionn. They were handsome, charming, and easygoing—at least on the outside—and they needed to hustle every woman they met. His charm wouldn't keep her from what she wanted to do on Harp, though if she'd been looking for a casual fling, sex with Fionn Martyn would certainly have been no hardship. It wasn't Fionn who was occupying her thoughts, however. For some reason, her mind kept returning to de Mendoza. Did the man even *have* a first name? He hadn't shared it, whatever it was. And he hadn't been particularly friendly *or* charming.

And yet, there'd been that flash of something when their eyes had first met, an almost physical snap of energy. She just knew that if they'd touched at that moment, it would have crackled between them like a wild electrical charge. He'd felt it, too. No matter how thoroughly he'd shuttered it over. He'd seemed almost angry after that. As if the very possibility that he was attracted to her pissed him off for some reason.

Amanda scoffed at her own reflection in the lift doors. So what if she'd felt a surge of desire for the man? His ego needed to be knocked back a measure. She wasn't exactly drooling over the idea of a relationship with him either. Broody bastard.

The lift doors opened and she headed down the wide corridor to the three-room suite she shared with her mother, which was far more comfortable than anything Amanda could have secured on her own.

She stuck her thumb into the biometric entry lock, and slipped through the door before it fully opened. From the main room of the suite came the gentle clink of crystal and silver and the low timbre of a man's voice, followed by her mother's soft laughter. Her mother was home, and she had company.

This wasn't unusual. Elise Sumner was an intelligent and beautiful woman, and she frequently had friends over. Occasionally that meant a single male friend, although she'd never dated any one man for very long. The two of them rarely discussed Amanda's father, but his presence, or absence thereof, was a constant in their lives nonetheless.

Since she felt like crap, and figured she probably looked like it too, she skipped the social niceties and went directly to her own room, thankful for a layout that permitted her to slip in discreetly. Stripping off her clothes, she thought wistfully of a long, hot shower followed by several hours' sleep, but there wasn't time. She'd have to settle for a short, tepid shower and a stimulant tab.

Without warning, her door whisked open and her mother stood there. Completely ignoring Amanda's half-clothed state, she zoomed right in on the vicious bruise left over from her sparring bout with Angelito. "What happened to your leg, sweetling?"

Amanda was struck as always by Elise's beauty…and by

how utterly different the two of them were. Her mother was small and delicate, with rich brown eyes and black hair that turned her pale complexion into the most fragile porcelain. She was in her fifties, and thanks to the advances of modern science she would remain youthful in appearance well into her seventies. Youthful or not, however, she would always be beautiful.

Amanda, on the other hand, took after the father she'd never known. She was nearly six feet tall, with blond hair, dark blue eyes, and golden-brown skin that even the sunless confines of the ship couldn't reduce to anything less than a healthy glow. She was attractive enough—fit, graceful and athletic, which somehow, next to her mother, made her feel like a huge, clumsy thing. This was all in Amanda's head, because her mother had never made her feel anything but beautiful and loved.

"You've got company," she said, arching an eyebrow.

Elise smiled, seeing the comment for the distraction it was, or at least was trying to be.

"A friend," she dismissed. "Now, what happened to your leg?"

Amanda grabbed a robe and slipped it on, trying to conceal the damaged appendage. "Nothing," she said. She sat on the bed to avoid towering over her petite mother. "A sparring accident."

Elise frowned, but thankfully let it go with a simple, "You should ice it." She wandered farther into the room, letting the door close behind her. "Randy tells me you'll be spending considerable time down on that planet."

Every planet was "that planet" to Elise Sumner. She'd never forgiven Amanda's father for choosing to remain rooted on his home planet rather than follow his pregnant lover back into space. He was perhaps the only man in history she hadn't managed to win over to her view of the universe, and, apparently, the only one who'd ever really mattered.

"I was down there with the science team most of the day, and I'll be heading back in just under two hours," she said with a glance at the clock on her bedside. "It's a fancy reception of some kind, which means dress whites, so I really need to shower."

"What you need is several hours' sleep."

"I know, but that's not—" She frowned. "Randy?"

"Admiral Leveque," her mother said, brown eyes sparkling with mischief.

Fantastic. She's dating Leveque.

"Don't look at me like that. He's a lovely man, quite intelligent. Besides, he's an old friend."

Amanda's eyebrows shot up in surprise. *An old friend? Leveque? Since when?*

"Okay," she said, drawing a deep breath that did little to erase the image of her mother and *Randy*. "I'm keeping you from your, um, guest, and I really do need to get in the shower. I'll need to do something with my hair, and I'm not sure my dress uniform is—"

"I could get you out of it, you know," her mother said thoughtfully. "Not the party, that might be enjoyable, I mean the rest of it. Wandering around down there for days…in the dirt. I could get you reassigned shipside. The leg injury alone would be enough."

She didn't even flinch, just gave her mother a quiet look. "It's a lost colony, Mom."

"Yes," Elise agreed archly, drawing out the word. "Nearly five hundred years lost and only one major settlement to show for it. One shudders at the genetic possibilities. You should advise the male members of your party to beware of friendly women bearing small specimen cups at this so-called party tonight."

She laughed. "I'll tell them to be careful. Can I please shower now?"

"Of course." Her mom leaned over and kissed her forehead. "Big night," she said, with wide eyes and a dramatic quiver of her slender shoulders. Then her eyes met Amanda's in a moment of perfect sincerity. "Stay safe down there, my child."

"I will. And you enjoy your evening."

Elise pressed the door control and turned back to give Amanda a teasing look before stepping out of the room. "Oh, I will. In fact, I'll see you there. Randy is taking me to the party." Her delicate laughter drifted back as the door slid closed.

She stared at the door for a few minutes and then shuddered. Her mother and Leveque. Fuck.

Chapter Four

Rhodry Devlin de Mendoza stood in perfect stillness and surveyed the field, his eyes always moving, never resting for more than the space of a single breath. This wasn't where he'd have preferred to be tonight, but Cristobal had given him little choice.

His gaze slid to the big double doors leading to the main entrance hall, where the guests had been arriving all evening, from both Harp and the Earth ship. His focus sharpened at a flash of brilliant white, which turned out to be yet another high ranking fleet officer, with rows of colorful bits of ribbon on his chest, and the occasional flash of gold. This one had a blond woman on his arm. But she was a civilian, and she wasn't Amanda Sumner.

He cursed softly and looked deliberately away. He told himself he was only looking for her because of the unique threat she posed to Harp. He didn't completely accept the idea that she could tap into the voice of Harp's trees, yet if it was even a possibility, they had to keep an eye on her. She obviously hadn't reported it to her superiors yet, but the more she learned, the more likely that she would. So, it was in all their interest to keep her away from the forest.

Which was why *his* only interest in her was official.

He found himself scanning the open doors again, and forced his attention to the growing crowd on the ballroom floor instead.

"Who is she, Rhodi lad?"

Rhodry gave his cousin Aidan a dark look. "Who's who?"

Aidan laughed. "Whatever fair lady you've set your heart on. Or is it only your balls that are set on her?"

"Could you be more crude? Besides, I haven't had time to meet a lady, fair or otherwise."

"That's not what I heard. I heard you and Fionn were giving a certain blond Earther a tour of our very fine forest."

"Trying to keep her out of it, more accurately."

Aidan laughed, his blue eyes dancing with wicked amusement. Rhodry smiled in spite of himself. Cristobal hadn't been happy to see his cousin at his side when he'd arrived in the city. He hadn't seemed all that surprised either.

The truth was that he'd mostly grown up in the Devlin household of his father's family, and every one of his numerous Devlin cousins was like a brother to him. Except for Aidan. Aidan was more. They were night and day in looks—Aidan's blue eyes to Rhodi's gold, his blond hair to Rhodry's midnight black. They'd been born only minutes apart and raised together, sharing a cradle and a wet nurse. They'd been inseparable from their first breath, and it was a fact of the Devlin household when they were children that where you found one, you'd find the other.

"I'm thinking I might stay on in the city a bit," Aidan was saying. "Some of these ladies are fairly fine."

"If you can stand the perfume."

Aidan laughed again. "Take them outside in the fresh air, and it's not so bad."

Rhodry grunted. This was yet another way they were opposites. Aidan had the Devlin charm and an eye for the ladies, which the ladies returned in full measure. He, on the other hand, had spent too many of his earliest years under the tutelage of his de Mendoza grandfather, who'd insisted a clan chief must exhibit a seriousness bordering on dour. He'd also convinced his young grandson that everyone— man or woman—would want something from him. So, while Rhodry garnered his share of feminine attention, he rarely returned the favor. It was too easy to see the ambition in their eyes, to wonder if they were after the clan chief, instead of the man.

A new flash of white drew his gaze to the entrance again, and this time it stayed there. Amanda had finally arrived. She wore the same blindingly white uniform as the others, although it looked good on her, with the jacket cut to fit her very feminine curves, while still remaining properly military. Had he given it any thought, he might have hoped for a skirt and a glimpse of leg, but the tailored slacks certainly did justice to her firm thighs and nicely rounded ass.

"That's her, is it?"

He glanced over and caught a very speculative look on his cousin's face.

"Don't bother yourself, cousin."

Aidan grinned. "So that's how it is. Excellent. I'll have to introduce — "

His words were interrupted as the doors at the opposite end of the ballroom opened and Cristobal appeared. There was no fanfare, it wasn't the Harp way. It was curiosity that had every eye in the room swinging in that direction, not for the Ardrigh, but for the Earthers who accompanied him.

"Well, now, there's a beauty," Aidan said appreciatively.

He followed his cousin's gaze to a small, dark woman, her petite figure shown to fine advantage by a deep coral dress that managed to hug her curves while still giving the appearance of modesty. She was lovely, but not to his taste. He preferred women who looked like they could walk the forest with him without screaming. Women like Amanda. Fuck!

Forcing Amanda out of his head, he studied the officer next to the beauty. He was tall and lean, his uniform fitting as if it had been tailored specifically for him. Which it probably had. His name was Randolph Leveque and he was the scion of one of Earth's wealthiest industrial families.

Rhodry had been briefed, along with all of Cristobal's guard, on Nakata and his officers. Everything they'd managed to gather so far anyway. Some of it had been gleaned from conversations with various members of the landing party, and much of it had been offered freely by the fleet's Commander Wolfrum and his First Contact team. He'd learned enough already to know that the Earthers hadn't come all the way out here looking for lost colonies. The rediscovery of Harp had been pure happenstance. The Earth fleet was after treasure — minerals and metals, anything they could send back to their home planet for a profit.

"She appears to be taken," he told his cousin, noting the way Leveque kept one hand low on the dark-haired woman's back, clearly staking his claim.

"Just means more of a challenge, lad."

Shaking his head in amusement, his focus narrowed as he scanned past the admiral and his party to fall on a familiar figure. Amanda was conversing animatedly with Leveque's companion, as if they knew each other well. She should have looked mannish in her uniform, compared to the petite beauty and her elegant gown. Instead, she looked even more attractive to him. Graceful and strong, feminine, and irritatingly sexy.

He scowled at his own thoughts. Lieutenant Amanda Sumner was trouble. He could feel it in his bones. She was too interested in the trees of Harp, for sure. Even more, she was trouble for *him*. His position on Harp was complicated enough, between those in the city who suspected him of dynastic ambitions, and his own clansmen who resented the fact that his de Mendoza grandfather had skipped an entire generation in order to name Rhodry as heir and clan chief.

He didn't need the complication of an affair with any Earther, much less *this* one, with her unexpected, and unheard of, connection to Harp's forest.

"So what's she like?" Aidan asked.

"I don't know the woman, but she looks like Leveque's, so watch your step."

Aidan laughed. "I meant the Earth lieutenant you can't take your eyes off of."

He shrugged. "She doesn't know what's good for her. She wasn't on the ground five minutes before she was off into the Green, lost in thought, without a care for what might be coming after her."

His cousin nudged his shoulder. "And you've taken a shine to her."

"Hardly," he lied. "I'll be glad when they've all gone back to their ships, and I can get back to the mountains where I belong."

"You think Cristobal will let you go?" he asked doubtfully.

He turned to regard his cousin. "Why not? He doesn't want me here; none of them do. And I don't want to be here, so we're all agreed."

"Aye, but he's *got* you here now. And he's made it clear that I'm not welcome to stay. Maybe that's what he had in mind all along, and our visitors just gave him a convenient excuse. Maybe he wants to keep you here in the city where he can control you. Far away from your own people." He frowned. "It won't work, lad. The Martyns could lock you away for years and we'd never forget you. You know that."

Rhodi flashed a quick grin. "You'd never leave me locked away for years in the first place."

"Well, no, I wouldn't. But I was making a point. I don't like leaving you here on your own."

"Go home, Aidan. No need for both of us to be miserable."

Aidan's glance lifted beyond Rhodry's shoulder, his eyes taking on a speculative gleam. "Our fine Fionn seems to like your woman, cousin. He's sniffing around her like a poohbear in heat."

His laughter at the comparison of the elegant Fionn to one of Harp's rotund and golden-haired mountain bears died when he turned and caught sight of the other man chatting up Amanda. He was moving before he knew it, before thought caught up to action. Long strides took him across the ballroom to where she was still laughing at whatever fake charm Fionn was ladling upon her.

She looked up when Rhodry joined them. "Good evening, Mr. de Mendoza."

"Ah, Rhodry," Fionn said smoothly. "Can I trust our lovely guest to your care for now? My father requires my presence."

Rhodry gave him a dry look. "I doubt the lieutenant needs your protection."

Fionn ignored him to take Amanda's hand in both of his. "Save me a dance, Amanda."

He swallowed a growl, keeping a distrustful eye on Fionn as he moved off into the crowd.

"That's not what you said in the forest this afternoon," Amanda said.

His gaze swung back to her. "What?"

"About me needing protection."

She gave him a half grin, and he studied her, trying to figure out if she was teasing him. "The Green is a dangerous place, while this…" He didn't finish his sentence, simply gestured at the crowd of mostly smiling people. "Are you enjoying the welcome party?"

"I am," she said, smiling. "And does my choice of apparel meet with your approval?"

His eyes narrowed as he definitely noted a spark of mischief in her blue eyes. "The white is—"

"Aidan Devlin," his cousin said, shoving him aside before Rhodry could say something offensive about the uniform. As if he would. She looked beautiful. Rhodry scowled as Aidan took her hand and raised it to his lips with a small bow. "I'm Rhodi's more charming cousin. A pleasure, Lieutenant."

She laughed. "Call me Amanda, please. There's no need to be formal is there?"

"Of course not, Amanda," Aidan assured her. "Harp is usually a very informal place, although tonight the Ardrigh and his lady seem determined to prove me wrong."

She turned and surveyed the gathering as Rhodry had done earlier, seeming to study her fellow fleet officers in their starched whites, the Harp officials in formal black, with the colorful ladies scattered in between. "It is all a bit stuffy, isn't it? I'm sure you'd rather be outside. I know I would," she muttered, then cast Rhodry a glance over her shoulder. "If it's as dangerous as you say, you probably don't go out into the Green at night very often, do you?" she asked with what he would have sworn was wistfulness.

"Only at need," he said sternly. "Which you don't have."

Instead of being properly warned, she gave him a wicked grin, then leaned over to Aidan and said, "Your cousin is upset because I didn't ask permission before trekking out there today. Tell me, is he always this strict?"

Aidan laughed along with her, which earned him a disbelieving glare from Rhodry. "Not at all, lass. You've just got to catch him in the right mood. Why I've seen our Rhodi—"

"Yes, that's fine, Aidan. Thank you," he said, cutting his cousin off, then turning to Amanda. "My concern is for your safety, and that of your fellow officers. Our earliest forefathers learned of the Green's dangers the hard way. It was decades before the colonists were able to achieve a measure of safety on the planet. I'm simply trying to spare you a repeat of their rather painful learning experience."

"Of course you are," she said with blatant insincerity. "Tell me something. What's the guild?"

He scowled. "What guild?"

She bared her teeth in what might have been mistaken for a smile. Yeah, right. He knew a challenge when he saw one.

"When Fionn joined us out there this morning," she reminded him, "he referred to you as his fellow guildsman. I assume that means there's a guild."

He cursed silently. She wasn't only lovely, she was smart, too. And fucking Fionn needed to concentrate more on minding his tongue and less on charming the ladies. The existence of the Guild came too close to the one subject they definitely didn't want to share with their Earth visitors.

"There's a Rangers Guild," he admitted, parsing the truth. "Most of us serve for a time, patrolling the forest around the city, chasing away the worst of the predators. We escort hunting parties and student groups, that sort of thing."

"Oh! Can anyone join a hunting party? I'd love to explore some more, and I'm not without skills."

The sparkle in her blue eyes made him want to say yes. He could picture her in the deep forest, the joy on her face as she made new discoveries, the dappled sun playing on her hair, the scent of the loam beneath her feet... The destruction her fellow Earthers would leave in their wake.

"Unfortunately, they don't go out frequently," he heard himself say. "I doubt you'll be here long enough. How long do you think your fleet will remain in Harp orbit anyway?" he asked, knowing he was being rude, but for some reason she brought out the worst in him. Probably because he wanted her, and knew he couldn't have her. Or at least, he *shouldn't*. Damn it. He nearly choked on the snarl of frustration that tried to crawl up his throat, but she didn't seem to notice. In fact, she was giving him a delighted smile that told him her next words weren't going to make him happy at all. And she was right.

"Haven't you heard?" she asked. "Your Ardrigh and Admiral Nakata just agreed to build a shuttle base on Harp. Congratulations, de Mendoza, you're about to become part of Earth's trade route."

He bit back a curse. What had Cristobal been thinking in granting the Earthers that kind of access?

Amanda was giving him a very speculative glance, as if she'd noticed his reaction and was determined to figure out why he was so opposed to the fleet's presence. Which was not a path he wanted her going down.

It was Aidan who jumped in to change the subject, however. "What of your Earth, Amanda? I've seen several old images of your planet's great forests. Are they as spectacular now as they were then? And how do they compare to our Green?"

She turned to Aidan and shook her head, saying, "I don't know. I've never been to Earth."

Rhodry was startled enough that he stared at her. "But your fleet is—" he began.

"The fleet is Earth-based," she finished for him. "And many of the crew, civilian and military, were born there, including my mother." She nodded in the direction of the lovely, dark-haired woman who'd arrived with Leveque. "I'm ship-born. I've never spent more than a few weeks on a planet, and never on Earth."

He didn't know which revelation was more stunning. That she'd lived her entire life on a spaceship, or that the black-haired beauty was her mother. They looked nothing alike. He struggled for something to say.

"Beauty runs in the family, then," Aidan said gallantly.

She blushed. "She is beautiful, isn't she?"

Rhodry thought Amanda was far more beautiful, and definitely more intriguing, and it bothered him that she clearly didn't think so. He had the idiotic thought that she needed defending, that he should jump in and tell her exactly what he thought of her. Until reason prevailed.

"Leveque is your father?" he asked instead, thinking that explained the differences in appearance between mother and daughter, and prevented him from making a fool of himself.

"No," she snapped immediately, then visibly swallowed her irritation and explained. "Admiral Leveque is my mother's escort for the evening, nothing more."

A hot flush of color crept over her high cheekbones. She didn't like Leveque, and yet, he was not only her superior officer, but was also, apparently, dating her mother. He had a moment's unwanted sympathy for her, and so did something he'd never intended.

"Would you care to dance, Lieutenant?" He held out a hand, studiously ignoring the smug look on his cousin's face.

She looked up and met his eyes, then glanced out over the dancers before shifting her attention back to him once more. "I don't know the steps," she said, frowning.

He couldn't help it. He smiled at her. "I'll teach you."

She reached out and placed her hand in his, and when she looked up at him this time, she was laughing…and every bit as lovely as her mother. A welcome warmth flooded his chest, as if he could fill his lungs again after too long holding his breath. As if everything had changed because Amanda had shared that joyful laugh with him. It was so unexpected that he froze for a moment.

She didn't give him any more than that moment, however, tugging him onto the dance floor, while his cousin chuckled his ass off at Rhodry's expense.

She stopped on the edge of the crowd, her hands clasped beneath her chin, her watchful study taking in the couples moving rapidly over the center floor in one of the clan's set dances. City folk on Harp might disdain and distrust the clans, but when it came to dancing, no one did it better.

"So it's Rhodry, is it?" she asked, her eyes following the dancers as they flowed and shifted in the complex pattern of the dance.

He glanced over, but her focus was on the dancers, not him. "It is," he agreed. "And you're Amanda."

She smiled, eyes still on the dancers, her body shifting in time with the music, almost vibrating with the need to join them.

He couldn't resist the happiness rolling off of her in waves, couldn't stop the grin that split his face. "Well, now that's out of the way," he said. "Are you ready to dance?"

She turned to him, her eyes alight with excitement. A wild laugh escaped as she reached for his hand again, and Rhodry braced for the same unexplainable reaction. This time, when their fingers touched, there was a shock of heat so intense that it was like touching a live flame. He yanked his fingers away reflexively, only to look up and see her staring back at him, equally stunned. Their eyes locked in silent acknowledgment of what they'd both felt.

He opened his mouth to say something… What would it be? That he'd never felt the like with any woman? That she was his, and he wanted to drag her away somewhere he could throw her down and fuck her senseless? Shit! He couldn't say that! Where had that thought even come from? It had to be the electro-static shock because of all the dancers swishing about. That sounded idiotic even to himself. And it wasn't true anyway. Shit again.

His cousin was now eyeing him strangely, so Rhodry reached out and gripped her hand again, her fingers squeezing his nervously, as they both waited for whatever might happen. When there was nothing but the normal warmth of their joined hands, they both sighed in relief, and he pulled her across the floor.

Putting them in position at the very end of a long double line, he said, "Watch and learn, Earth girl."

Three dances later, Amanda practically fell through the open patio door, laughing when she ducked under Rhodry's arm as he held it for her. The mild evening air was refreshingly cold on her overheated skin.

"Are all your dances like that?" she asked, crossing the broad porch to where a stone balustrade overlooked the city down the hill.

"You mean the dance itself? Or the Ardrigh's event?" He leaned next to her, his back against the balustrade and the view.

"Both, I suppose. I'm guessing from your tone that the

parties are usually less grand."

"That's one way of putting it," he acknowledged. "Everyone wanted a chance to see our visitors tonight. Did you feel like you were being watched?"

"Only every minute. I think they got tired of me after a while, though. Admiral Nakata and the others are much more interesting."

"You don't give yourself enough credit. Dancing is important on Harp. And you can dance, Earth girl."

She flashed a grin. "I told you, I've never been to Earth, so I'm no more an Earther than you are."

He snorted. "Your mother was born there. That makes you a few centuries more Earther than I am."

"Hmm." She rested her arms on the balustrade. She didn't feel like arguing. "It's beautiful out here."

He glanced over his shoulder at the view, but didn't comment.

"You don't like it?"

"I don't like the city. I prefer the mountains."

"We didn't get readings of any population centers other than this one. Are there many people in the mountains?"

"Not nearly as many as the city, but there's enough. We're more spread out than here. There's also a small settlement further south, near the desert. It's a mining operation, with a transient population. No one lives there full-time. Entire crews rotate in, work a month or two, then rotate back out."

Amanda nodded. "Is that all of you? No other cities?"

"There aren't that many of us."

"Enough for a viable population base," she pointed out.

"The founders included a number of genetic specialists."

She considered following up on that. Did he mean they

still had the kind of research capabilities necessary to maintain the stability of the population? It was the kind of data her mother would definitely be interested in. Fortunately, this was a party. And she was much more interested in the man next to her.

"Why don't you like the city?" she asked, coming back to his earlier comment.

He pursed his lips thoughtfully. "Different reasons, some political. The mountain clans and the city folk haven't always gotten along."

"Clans?"

"The colonists were mostly Irish and Spanish. It was the Irish who settled in the mountains, hence the clans."

"That would be Aidan's Devlin branch of the family, I'm thinking," she said, smiling at the thought of his charming cousin.

"The same, although more than just the Irish live there. We're an independent lot, and it's too crowded in the city."

"Crowded," she repeated thoughtfully. "You should live on a ship for a week."

He smiled faintly. "No, thanks. So how long before your fleet breaks orbit?"

She straightened away from the railing, grinning. "I think you're trying to get rid of me, de Mendoza."

He seemed to pause for a moment, his face completely solemn as he studied her. He looked away with a shrug, and said, "I've studied the background files you've sent us, and heard people talking. You're after profit. Once you build your shuttle base, there's nothing more for you here."

"Except the trees," she said deliberately, testing his reaction.

He surprised her, though. He huffed a laugh, as if she'd said something ridiculously naive. "I think you'll find the Green far less profitable than you think."

She blinked. The most unique forest for light years around, and he wasn't the tiniest bit worried that it might be despoiled.

"I think you're probably right," she conceded, feeling as if she had to redeem herself for even suggesting otherwise. "I love your trees, though. I'm hoping to get out into the Green as much as I can while we're here. Maybe do some camping."

"Not without an escort you won't. It's not safe."

"I've trekked through worse."

"I doubt it. Trust me on this."

"You'll just have to go camping *with* me, then."

"Or you could limit your explorations, since you won't be here that long anyway."

"Again with the kicking me off the planet. I might stay just to piss you off."

He studied her solemnly, then closed the small distance between them and rested one hand on her hip, his expression the determined look of a man facing his doom. He left his hand there for a heartbeat, then sighed, and gave her a smile of such relief that she knew he'd been steeling himself for the kind of jolt they'd both felt earlier, when they'd held hands.

She could have told him they probably needed to be skin-to-skin for that kind of heat, but since she didn't know quite what to make of it either, she let him enjoy his relief.

"You don't want to piss me off, Amanda," he said, his voice soft and deep.

She raised her eyebrows in surprise. Had she ever known a man whose moods shifted so easily? She looked up at him, and had to brace herself with one hand on his chest. It was that or fall over. His eyes gleamed in the low light of the patio, untamed and dangerous. It was more than their unusual color. They were the eyes of a wild thing, a predator sizing her up for dinner.

Some women might have been intimidated, frightened even. Not her.

Her heart sped up, but it wasn't in fear. She'd never met a man so intensely masculine. It called to everything feminine inside of her and, suddenly, she didn't give a damn if she got burned. She wanted him.

"Rhodry," she whispered. "Do you—"

"Amanda!" Fionn's happy cry interrupted whatever she'd been about to say. She wasn't sure herself what it would have been. It died unsaid as Fionn's voice hit like a splash of cold water. Rhodry stepped back immediately, his expression closing down tighter than it had been all evening. He was back to the glowering Rhodry of the landing field when she'd first arrived.

"What's this, de Mendoza?" Fionn said cheerfully, strolling over to join them. "Hogging the beautiful women?"

"I doubt there's a shortage in the city," he said coolly.

"I already know all of *them*. I don't know *Amanda*." He drew out her name playfully, coming close enough to drape an arm around her shoulders. He was much easier with casual touching than Rhodry was, but it wasn't him that she wanted.

"Come on, darling," Fionn persisted, tugging her back toward the ballroom. "You've spent all your time dancing with Rhodi here. You have to dance with *me* now. It's only fair."

She glanced at Rhodry, caught the flex of muscle in his jaw as he stared at Fionn's arm.

"It's awfully late," she protested, but he wasn't listening, and Rhodry wasn't saying anything.

Fionn opened the glass-paned door to the ballroom and drew her inside. "One dance. You're supposed to make nice with the locals, right? One dance."

She sighed. He was right. "One dance," she agreed. The too warm, perfumed air of the ballroom hit her in the face, and she looked back over her shoulder, searching the cool night shadows. Hoping Rhodry would wait for her.

He was nowhere to be found.

Chapter Five

The détente between Nakata's fleet and the people of Harp lasted two days. Since being summoned to the city by Cristobal, Rhodry had spent all of his free time down at the Guild Hall. It wasn't the same as living in the Devlin family compound surrounded by his cousins, but at least it was a place for people who shared his love of the Green and its wild nature. And the hall's location at the forest's edge made it more convenient than the palace when it came time to run patrols, or when he simply needed to run among the trees and try to forget Amanda.

This morning, he was running a training hunt for some of the younger hunters. Everyone born on Harp learned the basics of survival in the Green, and this particular group consisted mostly of teenaged hunters who hoped to pass the rigorous trials necessary for Guild membership. The Guild served a critical role on Harp, in some ways making life here possible. And as a result, they dominated almost every aspect of Harp society. Even the Ardrigh was always a Guild member.

The teenagers training with Rhodry today hoped to join that rarified group. First they'd have to pass a trial that was designed to weed out all except the strongest candidates. Their ability to survive on their own in the deepest part of the Green, where no one but experienced guildsmen ever went, would be key. And that meant they needed to learn every trick there was to hunting on their own.

Rhodry was one of the best hunters on Harp. Even his enemies would acknowledge that. Though they would probably refuse to admit the wider truth that *all* of the best hunters were clansmen. Be that as it may, the powers that be in the Guild Hall were taking advantage of his forced presence in the city to run these training classes on the finer points of the hunt.

It was mid-morning when he dropped from a thick tree branch high above the forest floor, with the ease of long practice. He bit back a grin as one of the students tried to copy his move and nearly broke his leg in the landing. The kid had courage, though. His leg wasn't broken, but it had to be hurting him, and still he managed to gain his feet and limp over to sit down without whining about it. He made note of the young man's name. He'd check on him later, and remember him for future hunts. Most hunting was done in teams, and a good team was only as strong as its weakest member.

One by one the rest of his class dropped down into the clearing, though none of them tried to imitate his maneuver. When all seven of them were seated in a group, ready to hear his assessment of their performance, he eyed them silently. There was a gap of a few years between the oldest and youngest. The younger ones probably wouldn't attempt the Guild trials for a few years yet, while the oldest no doubt intended to sign up at the end of the month. The trials involved a lot of preparation followed by written exams, and practical tests of skill and survival. The young hunter who'd tried to mimic Rhodry's graceful landing was right in the middle of the group. Not quite old enough to go this year, almost certainly a candidate in next year's trials.

"Okay," he said, crouching down to their level. "Overall, this was a good run. The best yet for this group. You still need to work on coordinating as a team, but I know some of you"—he nodded at the two older teenagers—"are more concerned with solo survival during the trials, so we'll—"

His head came up, nostrils flaring a full second before the forest went dead silent around them, and two seconds before an enormous explosion shook the ground beneath them. Almost as one, the students jumped to their feet, eyes wide, staring around the clearing as if looking for the enemy.

"Down!" he roared. His voice sounded even above the rolling thunder of the explosion, carrying such authority that his students dropped to their bellies where they stood. That instant obedience saved their lives when the shock wave rolled through the forest, tearing trees from their moorings and sending them flying through the clearing like kindling.

His heart nearly stopped beating when he tapped into the trees' song to find out what disaster had struck, and heard nothing except dead silence. He sucked in a horrified breath, and before his lungs had finished filling, the voice of the planet was back in a discordant wail of pain and rage.

"Damn them," he muttered, and shot to his feet.

"Arlo," he snapped, addressing the student who'd tried to imitate his maneuver, "you get the others back to the Guild Hall and tell Orrin Brady or whatever elder you can find that I've gone to the site."

He turned to the two oldest students, the two he thought would be running their trials in the next few months. "Bain and Savion, you're with me."

"Rhodry"—Arlo's voice was shaking, but his gaze was steady—"what was that?"

"That was our Earth friends ignoring the laws of Harp. Unfortunately, they're not the only ones who will pay the price," he added bitterly. "Now get going. I'm counting on you to see everyone back safely."

"Yes, sir."

Rhodry cast a quick glance over his shoulder. "I'll be moving fast," he told the two going with him. "Try to keep up, but I won't stop."

Before they could acknowledge his order, he was gone, racing faster than he ever had in his life, dreading what he'd find when he got there.

He smelled the horror before he saw it. The stench of incinerated wood and flesh blew past him in the wake of a flood of animals racing from the blast site. The ash was next, a gray powder that choked the air, making it so difficult to breathe that he climbed to the highest treetops where the air was fresher. He paused long enough to be sure his young companions had followed his move, then tore onward, traveling the thick, interlocking branches overhead, crashing to the ground with more haste than grace when he saw the sunlit gap ahead which told him he'd reached the blast site.

He hit the ground and fell to his knees, weeping unashamedly at what lay before him. The forest's song of pain was an ache in every nerve, every muscle of his body. He knelt on the edge of a near-perfect circle of destruction, an ash-filled crater of annihilation that stretched at least a hundred yards across.

A crashing noise told him his students had arrived, a moment before they sank down beside him.

"What did this?" Savion asked, his voice cracking in shock.

"Earthers," he said dully. "The last image I picked up from the trees…they went hunting with plasma rifles. They panicked when a pack of banshee took after them, and all of them fired at once."

"Do you think they're dead?"

"If I'm right…they're all dead, Savion. The Earthers, the banshee…and everything else."

He spotted movement around the ash-filled clearing and stood, assuming some other guildsmen had arrived. A flash of fleet blue caught his eye and he jumped up.

"Stay here," he ordered, then took to the trees again, racing around the disaster zone. It was faster than crossing it, even if he'd been willing to step into that circle of death.

He approached carefully, remaining silent until he was no more than five yards away.

"Come to see the damage you've wreaked?" he asked, his tone rough and unabashedly hostile.

The Earther spun around, blue eyes wide with surprise. He froze. "Amanda?"

"Rhodry." She stared at him, eyes wide with shock. "There's so much pain," she said, her voice cracking with emotion, her face wet with tears. "Can't you feel it?" She closed the distance between them and fisted her fingers in the loose fabric of his tunic, lifting her eyes to his in entreaty. "What can we do? I can hear—"

She broke off on a sob. He pulled her closer, comforting her automatically, even as he struggled to make sense of everything. He'd expected a stranger, someone who would be defiant, even callous in defense of the damage the Earthers had done. He'd never expected Amanda, and he'd never expected this reaction from her. The trees had been telling him for days that she heard their voices, but this was the first time he'd truly believed it.

His arms tightened around her, and she dropped her hands to his waist, resting her forehead on his chest, her tears soaking the thin fabric of his shirt.

"The forest will survive," he reassured her absently. "The grandfather is still alive out there." He looked over her head to the center of the burned-out clearing. The remains of an ancient tree, what Harpers referred to as a grandfather tree, stood in the almost exact center of the devastation. It was little more than a raised stump at this point, but he could feel it reaching out to the rest of the forest, drawing strength and life. In a matter of hours, there would be green shoots emerging from the ashes, in weeks, the clearing would be filled with young growth, interlaced with trees and plants that would encroach from all sides. There was no such thing as empty space in the Green, at least not for long.

"I don't understand," she said, shaking her head as she looked up at him. "What did this?"

He frowned. "You don't know?"

She shook her head. "No," she said, giving him a puzzled look, as if wondering why he'd expect her to.

"It was your own people. They ignored our laws, smuggled plasma rifles onto the planet, and then panicked when they were attacked. This is the result," he finished bitterly.

"My—" Her face cleared of all expression as she dropped her hands from his waist and stared up at him. "That's why you said… You think *I* was a part of this? That I'd condone bringing weapons out here? That I'd risk this? You bastard." She put both hands on his chest and shoved hard enough that it pushed him back a step. She was stronger than she looked.

He didn't have a comeback to her accusations. He could have told her the truth, that he hadn't known it was her when he'd said those things, that he'd never have said it otherwise. Because he *didn't* think she'd had anything to do with this disaster. No one whom the trees chose to favor with their song could ever do something like this.

Someone from her fleet had done it, though. The Earthers had brought death to Harp, just as he'd feared they would. He ached with the confused pain of the grandfather tree that was just now coming back to awareness, and he hardened his heart against whatever personal feelings had made him want to believe anything else of their visitors. The Earthers had no place on Harp, and neither did Amanda.

It would be better for everyone if this disaster forced them to leave sooner, if some good could be salvaged from tragedy.

He didn't explain, didn't apologize, didn't try to make her feel better about him. He simply hid behind the remote expression that was second nature to the child who'd spent too many years in his grandfather's joyless house.

"I need to inform my Guild of what's happened. And I imagine you have your own report to make."

Her blue eyes flashed with anger. She wasn't hiding behind anything. She stared at him as she swiped away her tears, and stiffened into a formal posture.

"As an officer of the United Earth Fleet, I offer my apology for today's events. Admiral Nakata will be informed at once, and I have no doubt that he will contact the Ardrigh personally."

Her eyes met his in a final defiant glare, then without a word, she spun on her heel and headed into the trees at a run.

He watched her go, thinking he'd never see her again, ignoring the pang of loss that stabbed his chest at the thought. If nothing else, the explosion would probably signal the end of crew visits from Nakata's fleet. He knew he should be happy about that.

So, why wasn't he?

Cursing, he lifted his head and gave the piercing whistle that would call his trainees to his location, and together they took off for the Guild Hall. Cristobal would need their firsthand accounts before Admiral Nakata called.

Chapter Six

Two days later Rhodry stood at Cristobal's side as Admiral Nakata offered an official apology on behalf of the entire United Earth Fleet for the recent tragedy. Amanda was in Nakata's party, standing stiff and formal, two steps behind her leader. She didn't say a word, didn't so much as glance in his direction.

Cristobal listened somberly, sitting on his throne-like chair and not stirring until Nakata finished speaking. And then he rose, took the single step down from the dais and waited until the Earth admiral came forward and offered his hand. They shook solemnly and to all appearances that was it.

He knew what others didn't, that Cristobal and Nakata had already met privately before this public display that was so necessary. Every person on Harp was reeling from the damage that had been done, but none more than the guildsmen who felt the forest's pain as if it were their own. It took a concentrated effort to shunt it aside enough to focus on other things. And all of Harp was agitating for blood from the Earthers. The Green was a part of all of them.

Cristobal and Nakata's earlier meeting had focused primarily on the details of the fleet's departure. Neither of them wanted to repudiate the earlier agreement regarding the shuttle base and Harp's inclusion in Earth's regular trade route. Both had agreed that some acceleration of the time-table was in order. They'd agreed that Nakata's fleet would break orbit within the week, with a small team of techs remaining behind to finish installation of the computer center and train Harpers in its use and maintenance.

He wasn't thrilled with that last part. No Earthers on Harp would have been better. The still-raw wound in the Green was evidence of that, if nothing else. But no one had invited his opinion, and even he couldn't deny the benefits the new computers would bring to the planet.

With the formal ceremony complete, Nakata gathered his people, including Amanda, and departed without fanfare. A suitable Guild escort was waiting outside to make sure they got safely back to their shuttle and off the planet. The *safely* part applying more to the planet's well-being than to any threat to their visitors.

He watched them go, happy to see the back end of the fleet, wishing he and Amanda had parted on better terms. Or that they'd had more time together before she left. Maybe it was better this way. In a few days, she'd be light years away, and that would be it.

Cristobal spun on his heel as soon as the big doors closed on the Earthers. "Fionn, Rhodry," he snapped, "with me."

He shot Fionn a questioning look. The returning shrug

said he didn't know any better than Rhodry what his father wanted.

"Close the door, Fionn," Cristobal said when they joined him in his office. He sat behind his desk, his chair pushed back, one hand on his belt knife which bore the Guild insignia. Rhodry had one just like it.

Fionn sank into one of the big chairs in front of the desk, draped over it like a big cat, while Rhodry remained standing. His gut was telling him that whatever Cristobal had called them here to discuss wasn't going to be welcome news.

"You know we signed an agreement with Admiral Nakata," Cristobal said without preamble.

He and Fionn nodded.

"Harp gets added to the Earth trade route," Fionn supplied.

"Which means little since we've nothing to trade," Rhodry added.

"True," Cristobal agreed. "But we *are* getting the new computer facility, and that will be to our benefit. Nakata's people will also be downloading their rather substantial scientific and historical databases. Our science and tech types are thrilled."

He wondered what the hell any of that had to do with him, then reined in his impatience. If it mattered to Harp, it mattered to him.

"You may also know that some of Nakata's people will remain behind."

"A very few, to finish the installation and train our own people," Fionn recited, letting his own impatience show.

Cristobal gave his son a long look before continuing.

"This morning, Admiral Nakata provided the roster of personnel who will be remaining. And guess who's on it?"

He didn't have to guess. The sinking sensation in his stomach was already telling him. "Fuck," he swore, even as part of him growled his satisfaction at the news.

"The trees *like* Amanda," Fionn said, sounding all too pleased, which he didn't like at all.

"Maybe that's why she needs to go," he said quietly. "She'll dig into things no one is supposed to know, least of all someone not of Harp."

Cristobal shrugged. "I agree. Unfortunately, I couldn't object to her without giving Nakata a damn good reason. Without it, the objection itself might make him take a closer look. She clearly hasn't shared her unique talents with any of her own people, which I find curious. It also makes me think better of her. Besides, Fionn's right. The Green wants her here."

"She's going to be a problem," Rhodry said glumly, thinking mostly of himself, although he didn't say so.

"Oh, come on, Rhodry. She's delightful," Fionn said, leaping up with animal grace from his slouch over the chair.

"She may be delightful, Fionn," Cristobal said sharply, "but Rhodry's right. She's a complication, and I don't want her left alone. We all know the trees like her. What we *don't* know is *why*. And until we do, I don't want her going out there alone. I don't care what she does in the city, but when she goes into the Green, I want one of you two with her at all times. Tell her it's for her own safety, tell her whatever she needs to hear, just keep an eye on her."

"She's not going to like that."

"As much as I hate to agree with Rhodi here," Fionn

said with uncharacteristic seriousness, "I must. She'll fight us at every turn."

"Then I trust the two of you will figure something out. See to it."

He and Fionn stood side by side as Cristobal left without a backward look.

"He's met Amanda, right?" Fionn asked.

"Apparently not," Rhodry said.

"I'm sure I saw them shake hands."

He snorted a laugh. "I think it takes more than that."

Fionn sighed. "Well, you're going to have to find a way to convince her it's in her best interest to let us tag along."

"Me? I think you should do it. She likes *you*."

"It wasn't me she was dancing with."

"I just happened to be the one standing there. She was a guest."

"You spent the whole evening with her. You must have gained some insight."

"Yeah, enough to know I'm the last person she'll want following her around. And that she will *never* go along with us babysitting her every time she wants to leave the city."

Fionn slapped his shoulder, as if they'd reached a decision. "So, we won't tell her."

"Right. We'll simply ignore the Ardrigh's orders."

"I didn't say we wouldn't watch her. We'll do it from the trees where she can't see us, and we'll get a couple of the lads to help us out. She'll never know we're there."

He nodded in agreement. Although, privately, he didn't think Amanda was going to make it that easy.

Chapter Seven

Amanda walked down the familiar corridor of the flag-ship, noting as she never had before the path worn into the royal blue weave of the carpet, testimony to the hundreds, probably thousands, of feet that had passed this way since the deck's last retrofit. Her own feet were responsible for a good part of that wear, rushing in triumph or dragging with exhaustion. Funny how everyone seemed to walk the same few inches of carpet right down the center.

She was dragging her feet today, analyzing carpet wear instead of facing what she knew she had to do. When the door to the suite she shared with her mother presented itself, she thumbed the lock with reluctant determination. The door slid open.

"You're leaving?"

Amanda looked up, dismayed to find her mother waiting

for her in the hallway. She must have come directly from Sick Bay, because she still wore her pristine white lab coat, her long dark hair tucked into a neat twist behind her head. Equally dark eyes regarded her in silent accusation.

Amanda cringed. She'd hoped to arrive at the suite before her mother, hoped to have everything packed, so she could make a clean getaway after what she'd known would be an uncomfortable and inevitable scene.

Coward. "Well, strictly speaking, I'm staying and *you're* leaving," she joked lamely.

"Amanda," Elise scolded.

"I'm sorry, Mom. I just found out for sure today, right before I shuttled down with Nakata for his meeting with Cristobal. How did you—"

Admiral Leveque stepped out of the living room to stand behind her mother, one hand going protectively to her shoulder.

"I see," Amanda said, giving Leveque a resentful glance.

He shrugged negligently. "I was in Sick Bay checking the status of some medical supplies for the colony and happened to see your mother."

She gave him a look that said she didn't believe him for one minute, and ducked into her bedroom without another word, closing the door behind her. She opened her closet doors with a snap and pulled down her single duffle bag, throwing it onto the bed as she surveyed the room. Not much to show for twenty-five years of living, more than ten of them on this very ship. A few mementoes from places she'd visited. A couple of images that she'd liked well enough to print out and frame, including one of her and her mother from two years ago when she'd made full lieutenant. One didn't accumulate many possessions living in space. There wasn't enough room for it, not even on the flagship of a fleet admiral.

She heard her mother's footsteps in the hallway a moment before the door slid open.

"Amanda."

She turned. Leveque was still there, hovering in the background, but Elise stepped away from him, crossing the threshold and letting the door close behind her.

Amanda felt a stab of satisfaction and pride. Elise Sumner had no need to lean on anyone, and most especially not when it came to dealing with the daughter she'd raised to be just as fiercely independent as she was.

"Talk to me, sweetling," her mom said, reaching up to smooth a stray hair back into Amanda's braid.

Tears threatened. Even though she desperately wanted to remain on Harp, she was going to miss her mother. Impatient with herself, she drew a breath to explain.

"We're installing a new computer facility on the planet with shields heavy enough to protect against the system's solar activity, which has been a major problem for the colonists up until now. Most of the fleet's databases have been downloaded, everything we can share anyway. A small team has to stay behind to maintain the facility and train the locals."

"And you volunteered."

"I did."

"Their science is centuries out of date," Elise objected. "It will take—"

"Their *natural* sciences are excellent, though. Fionn says—"

"Is *that* what this is really about, Amanda? He's a good-looking boy, but—"

"Mom. First of all, Fionn's hardly a boy. And it doesn't matter anyway, because you know me better than that. This isn't about him, it's about me. Harp is special, I can—" She cut her words off before she blurted out the truth about Harp, about how the trees *sang* to her. She didn't want anyone in the fleet to know, because she knew what would happen if they found out. Hordes of scientists would descend on the planet, prying into its secrets, shredding it down to DNA, and destroying the very thing that made it unique.

"I can't *breathe* up here sometimes," she said quietly, trying to explain something her mother would never understand.

Elise regarded her silently for several minutes, the look on her face a mix of fondness and something else. Something she'd never seen before. "You're just like him, you know."

"I know. I'm sorry."

"Don't be," she said softly. "Your father was a good man. I wouldn't have loved him otherwise." She stepped closer. "Sit down, sweetling. It hurts my neck to look up at you." Her proud smile took away any sting the words might have had as she sat next to Amanda on the bed.

"This," she said, shaking her head, "is proof of nature over nurture. How I managed to raise a daughter who despises ship living—"

"I don't despise it," Amanda protested instantly. "I loved growing up out here. I've witnessed amazing things and seen more of the universe than most people would see in a hundred lifetimes." She drew a frustrated breath. "It just gets to me sometimes. Recycled air, artificial light, the long corridors and silent doors. It's like it's all been sucked clean until there's nothing *real* to it anymore."

"I know."

She looked at her mother in surprise.

"Oh, I never feel that way," Elise conceded. "But I know you do. So did your father." Her glance fell on the open duffle, then she stood and began wandering the room much as Amanda had earlier. "I need to tell you something. About your father."

Her earlier surprise was doubled. They *never* talked about her father. Not since she was about eight years old when she'd finally grown tired of asking questions that were never answered.

Elise glanced at her, and then away, as if nervous. "He was an earth witch, you know," she said with studied casualness.

She stared. "A what?"

"That's what they called it on his home planet. Earth witch. On old Earth, they sometimes called it a 'green thumb.'"

She had heard of that in her studies as a child, and didn't understand why Elise was making such an issue out of it. "So, he was good with growing things," she said. "A lot of people are. Every member of the fleet's botany department, for example."

"It's a little more complicated than that," Elise said slowly, finally sitting down to face her once more. "He could make anything grow. Anything. He could coax a dead plant to life, could double the harvest in a single season just by wandering the fields. I doubted, naturally. I'm a scientist. Until I saw with my own eyes what he could do. There was no other explanation."

"Why didn't you tell me this before?"

"I meant to tell you, when you were older. Then I saw how much you loved going dirtside, how you never missed an opportunity to visit a planet. It didn't even matter which one. If it had dirt, you were there." She reached out and took Amanda's hand, squeezing her fingers. "And I was selfish. I was afraid I'd lose you, that you'd choose him."

"Mom, I'd never—"

"I know that. Mostly," she admitted, with a fleeting smile. "And yet here you are, leaving me for that planet."

Amanda stifled a dismayed sigh. She wanted to tell her mother the truth, to explain *why* she had to stay on this particular planet. But her mother was also Dr. Elise Sumner, Chief Medical Officer. And Dr. Sumner would never be able to resist siccing a whole team of scientists on such a rare phenomenon—even if it meant poking and prodding her own daughter.

On the other hand, this little history lesson might explain why *she* seemed to be the only one it was happening to. Well, the only fleet person anyway. She still believed Rhodry and Fionn, and probably some of the others, could hear and understand the trees a hell of a lot better than she did—the members of their so-called "guild" maybe?

"I have to stay, Mom," she said almost apologetically. "I *want* to. At least for now."

"For now," Elise repeated. "Well, that's something, I guess. If you're going to be living down there, though, I want to be damn sure their medical facilities are up to snuff. And from what I've seen, they're a few centuries out of date."

"The first few years here were brutal," she explained, feeling the need to defend them. "They ran out of almost everything, and they'd lost so much of their equipment and materials in the initial crash landing, not to mention people. Families and loved ones, specialists of all kinds. They had to prioritize. Simply surviving became everything."

"I know, sweetling. I understand." Her mother stood up and rested her cheek on top of Amanda's head, one hand stroking down the length of her braid. She straightened, then kissed her on the forehead and both cheeks before walking over to the closed door, where she paused with one hand on the control.

"You will write to me, Amanda," she said, looking back with her best stern mother expression. "At least once a month. And I will write to you. It may take months for the dispatches to wend their way through the various uplinks until we find each other, but we will do it anyway. Promise me."

"I promise," she managed to choke past a throat thick with emotion.

"I will not lose you," Elise said. She punched the door open and stepped into the hallway, and Amanda heard her mutter as she walked away, "Not you, too."

A manda stood on the landing field, watching as technicians loaded the last few pieces of equipment that were going back up to the ship. Everything the fleet was leaving behind was already secure inside the blocky, gray building the engineers had constructed to hold the new computer facility. The enclosure was functional, and ugly as sin. It stood out among the other buildings of the capital city like a troll among elves. She knew it was necessary, that the dull walls and reinforced ceiling carried heavy shielding to protect the delicate new equipment. But she couldn't help wincing guiltily every time she looked at it, as if she was somehow personally responsible for bringing this visual blight to Harp.

The people of Harp hadn't complained, though. Most of them seemed thrilled with the new facility, as well as the fact that the planet would now be on the regular trade route. In practical terms, that meant a supply shuttle would visit only once most years, twice on rare occasions. Cristobal Martyn had made it clear that Harp would not be open to tourism of any kind, and they didn't have enough exportable goods to justify any meaningful commercial traffic. No one on the planet seemed to mind that either.

Cristobal had issued a carefully worded statement on behalf of the Harp government, acknowledging the gift of the computer facility, and welcoming the renewed contact with Earth. And all while somehow managing to avoid even the tiniest hint of regret that the fleet was moving on, or that future contact would be brief and infrequent.

In fact, while the people of Harp had been kind, if not exactly welcoming, to Amanda and the rest of the team staying behind, she was convinced that they could hardly wait for everyone else to be gone. Rhodry had certainly made no bones about how he felt that day in the forest. He wanted them gone. And after that disaster, she could hardly blame him. Although, she'd wondered more than once if he knew she was among those staying. It was impossible to think that he wouldn't, but he hadn't sought her out. Nor had he said a word to her on the few occasions they'd been in the same room since.

She thought about all of this as she watched Guy

Wolfrum fussing over some last minute piece of cargo being left behind. He was dancing around the poor guys carrying it down the ramp, as though it contained his most precious possessions. Which maybe it did. She shook her head in renewed amazement. *Commander* Wolfrum was now just plain Guy Wolfrum, PhD. She'd found out just this morning that he would be remaining on Harp along with her and two computer techs. That would have been surprise enough, but apparently Nakata had objected to his decision, and so Wolfrum had resigned his military commission in order to stay.

Speculation was rampant that Wolfrum had found one of those friendly Harp women her mother had warned her about that very first day, and that he was staying behind for love.

She hoped the rumor was true, because the last thing she needed or wanted on Harp was a frustrated former fleet officer looking for someone to boss around.

"Lieutenant."

And speaking of bossy fleet officers... She spun around and snapped a sharp salute. "Admiral Leveque, sir."

"At ease, Lieutenant." He studied her face, squinting as if he thought he could discern who she really was if he stared hard enough. Or maybe he just thought if he squinted he could pretend she was someone else. Whichever it was, when he finally spoke, it was with obvious reluctance.

"I've made the Leveque corporate communications network available to Elise," he told her, radiating stiff disapproval. "It should be more reliable and faster than the military net, especially this far out. We maintain a considerable shipping presence along this galactic arm, and the ships bounce communications rather efficiently. It will make it easier for the two of you to stay in touch."

She concealed her surprise. "That was very kind of you, sir. Thank you."

He was silent a few more minutes, staring over her shoulder and pretending concern over some detail of the unloading process. Finally, he looked at her directly and said, "She deserved better."

She blinked. "Sir?"

"Elise. She deserved better than what your father gave her."

The main thing her father had given Elise was Amanda herself. She granted Leveque the benefit of the doubt, however, and assumed he was referring to her father's decision to let Elise go back into space without him, and to raise their child alone.

"Yes, she did." She wondered again at just how old the friendship between Leveque and her mother was.

It was his turn to be surprised. "You look so much like him, I assumed—"

She dared to interrupt. After all, in less than an hour, she'd be the last fleet officer left on the planet. "I am not my father, Admiral. I know I look like him, but I've never known him as anything except a blurry face on an old digital image from before I was born. My mother raised me, and it's always been just the two of us. Everything I am, everything I have achieved, I owe to her and her alone."

Knowing what she now did about her father, she realized that might not be true, but it didn't change how she felt about her mother. "She's the strongest, most determined woman I have ever met," she continued. "And I will miss her desperately."

Leveque frowned and stared down at his perfectly polished boots. He coughed nervously, then glanced up at her before looking away again. "You forgot beautiful."

"Sir?"

"You forgot beautiful. Your mother is beautiful."

"No, sir," she said with a wry twist of her lips. "I don't think anyone ever forgets beautiful when speaking of Elise Sumner."

He smiled at last, a quick curve of his lips that was there and gone. "Well." He nodded over her shoulder. "The shuttle seems to be ready at last. I'd better get on board." He gave her a brisk nod and started off.

"Admiral?"

He turned with an inquiring look.

"Take care of her."

He nodded again. "I will do that, Lieutenant. Never fear. Good luck."

She came to attention, snapping a salute as he did the same. She relaxed when he turned away, watching until he disappeared inside the passenger compartment, until the loading bay doors whooshed shut with the sucking sound of vacuum seals, and the engines powered up so that she had to step to the edge of the field to avoid the backwash. She continued watching until the shuttle was nothing more than a speck in the cloudless sky.

And then she walked away to begin the biggest adventure of her life.

Chapter Eight

Amanda drew her long knife with a hiss of metal on leather, legs bent, weight distributed evenly as she slowly backed away, her eyes locked on the snarling mass of fur and teeth in front of her. The trees had been warning her for the last several minutes, so she hadn't been entirely surprised when the unpleasant little beastie had come after her. And after weeks spent studying everything she could put her hands on when it came to the flora and fauna of Harp, she recognized her attacker as a Wyeth's badger. One who was having a very bad day, and determined to share it with Amanda. Roughly eighteen inches at the shoulder, the Wyeth was a compact bundle of muscle and attitude, with long, curved claws and a mouthful of very sharp teeth. The creature flashed those teeth now, letting out a scream reminiscent of tearing metal. Instinct told her to cover her ears against the noise; logic told her to keep the damn knife between her and the angry Wyeth. Logic won.

Holding the weapon in her right hand, she managed an awkward cross draw of her shorter belt knife with her left hand. With powered weapons not an option, she'd begun carrying the two knives with her everywhere she went. She was also putting in time training with them every day. She was already skilled in close-combat techniques, but knife fighting was new to her. Two weeks with even the best instructor—something Rhodry had quietly arranged, to her surprise—wasn't enough to acquire any meaningful skill, and it showed in her clumsy handling.

And speaking of Rhodry, it was his fault she was out here alone in the first place. He'd surprised her with the knife lessons, which was a really nice thing to do, and then he'd insisted that she had to be accompanied whenever she went into the Green. Which was ridiculous. She'd survived hazardous treks that would make him blanch. Fortunately, they'd underestimated her determination, her deviousness, and, frankly, her skill and discipline.

She reached for some of that discipline right now as she faced down a three-foot-long, yowling carnivore. The Wyeth took a crouching step forward, a steady growl rumbling from its chest, and saliva dripping from its lower jaw. Bristle-like hair stood straight up, adding bulk, and beady brown eyes gleamed with anger. She backed up blindly, hoping for the solid reassurance of the tree she knew was somewhere behind her. The Wyeth shadowed her every move, undeterred by either her greater size or her knives. She took another cautious step backward and cursed when her foot came down on a gnarled root, turning beneath her and throwing her off balance for a few precious seconds. She managed to avoid dropping the knives as her hands flew out reflexively to catch herself, but the brief stumble was all the opening the Wyeth needed.

It darted in low and fast, sinking its teeth into her leg, digging into the leather of her boot and hanging on, worrying at her calf like a meaty bone. She yelled and kicked out instinctively, trying to dislodge the nasty beast. The Wyeth only tightened its jaw as her boot gave way and sharp teeth sank into her flesh. She screamed, slashing down with her knife, catching the Wyeth on the hind leg, too afraid of cutting herself to aim any higher.

The Wyeth opened its mouth long enough to squeal in pain. She jerked her leg away, and struggled to her feet, waving both knives at it once again.

"That's right, you little bastard," she rasped, baring her teeth in a snarl. "I've got teeth too."

She was far from an expert on the local wildlife, but she was pretty sure Wyeths weren't supposed to be this aggressive. She'd probably surprised it, tramping into the clearing as she had, too busy being pissed and not paying enough attention to what the trees were telling her or where she was going—always a mistake no matter which planet you were on, and one she would be embarrassed about later. Assuming she survived.

Sweat rolled down her face, and she dashed her hand quickly across her eyes. The damn Wyeth should have turned tail and run when she hurt it. Nothing about this situation made sense. This animal was a male, bigger and darker than the female, and all alone. There was no reason for him to—

A high-pitched scream grated from somewhere above

her, and she twisted her head around in shock, her eyes traveling up and up to find the Wyeth's golden-haired mate perched overhead, her belly big with pups.

Well, fuck! Could this get any worse?

She spun away instantly, not wanting the enraged female directly over her head, and definitely not wanting to get between the mated pair. As she moved, she hoped against hope that the two of them would take the chance and run for it. A faint hope as it turned out. The female jumped as Amanda limped away, slamming into her back and shoving her to the ground once more, long claws slicing easily through the fabric of her tunic and into her skin. She screamed again and rolled, dislodging the female in time to see the male aim a running leap directly at her face.

Giving a wordless shout, she rolled once more, avoiding the male's leap. Sheer survival instinct got her back to her feet, barely managing to get both knives in front of her. The male made another dashing charge, this time at her injured leg, but she was ready for him. Drawing her good leg back, she delivered a vicious kick directly at the little bastard's jaw, all that martial arts training finally coming in handy after all. The male went tumbling over the dirt and she paused, certain the pair of them would finally run.

"Son of a bitch," she cursed as both creatures turned and renewed their attack, the female coming in low as the male bunched its powerful hind legs and leaped into the air from several feet away. She danced to the side, swiping her long knife outward almost blindly, the blade taking the male in the gut in an instance of pure dumb luck. The Wyeth let out its own scream of pain and dropped to the ground. Her longer weapon, still stuck in his gut, was jerked from her hand, leaving her with only the short belt knife against an outraged female.

Shifting the remaining knife to her right hand, she watched the pregnant badger take up a defensive position in front of her mate. The male lay in the dirt, unmoving, blood and intestines oozing from the obviously fatal wound in its belly. The female bared her teeth, eyes rolling with fear and rage as she divided her attention between Amanda and the male whom she didn't seem to realize was dead.

Amanda didn't know how much longer she could stay on her feet. Warm blood was pooling inside her boot with every beat of her heart, and she knew her leg wound was bad. More blood was seeping wetly through her shredded tunic, and her back muscles were seizing into a solid wall of agony as she crouched in readiness. Would the female run at last, protecting her unborn young? Or was her devotion to her mate stronger than death, stronger even than the instinct to protect her pups? She didn't know.

Without warning, a serrated yowl cut through the air, and she swore loudly. Apparently the day *could* get worse after all. Branches crashed overhead and a huge hunting cat dropped into the clearing, golden eyes sweeping her with a dismissive look as it stalked deliberately toward the female Wyeth.

It was a magnificent beast, shoulders rolling with muscle beneath thick, dark fur and saber-like fangs glistening between powerful jaws. The female badger squealed a protest as she was forced away from her dead mate, her pregnant belly scraping the ground as she paced backward. Amanda could almost see the calculation in the female's eyes as the huge, angry cat bore down on her, but the badger made the only choice she could. Driven by the need to protect her unborn pups, and seeming to understand finally that the male was gone, she gave a sorrowful howl of surrender and spun away. Sharp claws propelled her rapidly up the nearest tree where she paused long enough to give Amanda a final ear-piercing shriek of defiance and then disappeared into the thick foliage.

Amanda sank to the ground, staring at the big cat, grateful for the intervention, uncertain what her rescuer intended. She'd run into several of these monsters prowling the forest near the city, the first time when she'd walked into a clearing just in time to see one make a twenty-foot standing leap from the ground directly into the lower branches of a sizeable grandfather tree. She'd stood there like a fool, staring, but the cat had merely studied her lazily for a few seconds, before winding soundlessly up the trunk and out of sight. The strange thing was, she'd never felt threatened by the great beasts. It was more as if the cats were as curious about her as she was about them.

Like the one studying her right now, standing no more than a dozen feet away. She held perfectly still under that glittering regard, knowing she was losing more blood with every minute she delayed, wondering how long it would take her to get back to the city and if she could make it at all.

The cat's nostrils flared, probably taking in the scent of her sweat and blood. It stared a bit longer, then moved suddenly into a still crouch, muscles bunching. She tensed, fingers gripping her belt knife, knowing it wouldn't be nearly enough. The one time she could have used some protection from her ever-present babysitters, and they were nowhere in sight. And it didn't make her feel any better knowing that it was her fault.

She cursed Rhodry with what she figured was her last breath, hoping he'd feel guilty as hell when they found her body. And then she gasped.

It started gradually, a blurring of the air, like a ripple of heat on a hot day. She blinked, trying to clear her eyes, thinking it was the blood loss making her see things. As she stared harder, forcing her eyes to see, she knew it wasn't.

For a brief instant, the big cat seemed to disappear as its coloring altered chameleon-like to match the surroundings almost perfectly. A shimmery wave of nearly invisible movement, and then the air filled with the sound of joints and bones cracking and popping as dark fur flowed away to reveal golden skin, and suddenly the cat was gone and in its place crouched someone she knew. Tonio Garza, one of the Ardrigh's guards, crouched in front of her on all fours, panting slightly and completely naked.

He looked up into her disbelieving stare and swore. "Rhodry's going to kill me."

Chapter Nine

"You're bleeding," Tonio said sharply, and rushed over to her, swearing again when he caught sight of her torn and bloodied back. He bent to tug off her boot, but she jerked her foot out of his hands, almost kicking him in her urgency to get away.

"What the fuck was that?" she demanded breathlessly.

He ignored her, grabbing her foot again, succeeding this time in baring her foot and leg. "Shit, he broke the skin, we've got to get you—"

"Stop!" she nearly screamed, shoving him away again with her bloody foot. "What *was* that?"

His expressive face closed down completely. "I don't know what you're talking about."

"The hell you don't! What did you just do?"

"You're injured, Amanda; you're not thinking straight. I'm trying to—"

"Garza!" a deep, angry voice interrupted. She and Tonio

both muttered curses as Rhodry stormed into sight. "What the fuck are you doing? Jesus!" he swore when he saw her bloodied leg and the dead Wyeth. "How the hell did this happen?"

Tonio stood up, scowling. "What the fuck am *I* doing? What the fuck was *she* doing out here alone? I thought—"

"Shut it," Rhodry snapped and dropped down next to her. "*This* is why you're supposed to wait for me or Fionn before you go exploring. But no, you have to do it your way, sticking your neck out, making the rest of us work harder to protect you from things you can't possibly understand." He spoke in sharp, bitten-off words, even as he tore off his tunic and began ripping it into strips to bind the wounds on her leg.

She stared at him, feeling her heart pound and her breath grow thin with shock. "What did Tonio just do? What did I *see?*"

"I have no idea what you're talking about, and neither do you. I can stop the bleeding for now, but you'll need—"

"No," she whispered. "Get away from me." She pushed at him weakly, knowing she was losing too much blood, knowing he could overpower her with ease if he chose to, and still wanting him away from her until he told her the truth.

"Amanda, stop," he said quietly, then shot a glance over his shoulder at Tonio, who was still standing there naked. "Put some fucking clothes on," he snapped.

The other man snarled wordlessly back at him, then hurried away through the trees while she stared at the two of them in a daze of disbelief.

"Amanda," he said with surprising gentleness, drawing

her attention once Tonio was gone. "You're injured — seriously injured. We've got to get you back to the city. A Wyeth bite is nothing to fool around with. I'm going to — "

"Answer my question."

"What question, *acushla*?"

"Fuck you," she said, gasping with pain as she forced herself away from him, half crawling clumsily to the nearest tree. Ignoring her body's protests, she managed to haul herself up onto one leg. He reached out to help her, but she slapped him away, swearing when the effort only made everything hurt worse. "Don't touch me."

He made an impatient noise. "I'm not going to stand here and let you bleed to death to make a point. I can carry you — "

"I can walk," she insisted stubbornly, ignoring the tears of pain that she couldn't stop. She hurt so very bad. She took a single step and the ground rushed up to meet her. "Or maybe not," she said faintly.

It was the trees she heard first. Before she caught the soft patter of footsteps and the antiseptic smell that were the telltales of hospitals everywhere, the trees sang to her and she knew where she was. Keeping her eyes closed, she took inventory of her injuries. She ached all over, but that wasn't the worst of it by far. Her back felt like it had been flayed open, and her leg was a steady scream of hot pain. She heard a faint movement next to the bed and someone's indrawn breath.

"I know you're awake," Rhodry said drily.

And she remembered. Everything.

She opened her eyes and realized he was holding her hand. She took a moment to drink in the comfort that simple touch gave her, and then wrenched it away. "Leave me alone."

"A little gratitude would be nice. We could have—"

"You *could* have told me the *truth*. Asshole."

"Don't be such a child."

"No one's asking you to stay."

"Damn it," he hissed, then sucked in a breath, glancing over his shoulder as he remembered where they were. "Look, Amanda," he said tightly. "You were never supposed to see Tonio like that. The Ardrigh ordered—"

"How many of you are shapeshifters?"

"I can't talk about it," he insisted.

"Why not? I already know what you are, so what difference does it make?"

"It's not my decision."

"Is it everyone?" She waited for the answer as a different sort of pain made her stomach hurt. She'd begun to think of this planet as something special. The trees had sung only to her, not to anyone else from the ship. They'd told her she belonged here. But what if it didn't mean any of that? What if this was a planet full of shifters, and she was only the crazy Earther lady who thought she could hear the trees singing? Unwilling tears filled her eyes and she turned away, although not fast enough.

He swore softly. "Fuck. Look, it's *not*—"

"What the hell, de Mendoza. I'm gone five minutes and you've got her crying?" Fionn strolled into the room, letting the door whisk shut behind him.

"It's not everyone," Rhodry said in a quiet voice, staring at her intently. "It's not even most of us."

Fionn gave him a sharp look, but Rhodry ignored him as she studied his face, trying to decide if he was telling her the truth this time. She swallowed hard, letting anger replace the hurt. "You're not the first mods I've seen, you know. It's not like you're anything special."

Neither one of them bought that. They chuckled smugly, far too much the alpha males to deny their own superiority.

She curled her lip at them, which only made Fionn laugh harder. "Of course we're special," he said, then leaned closer, as if confiding a deep secret. "You are too, aren't you, Amanda? I won't tell your secret if you don't tell mine."

She jerked away, staring from him to Rhodry—who was giving Fionn a very unfriendly look—and back to Fionn. "What do you mean?" she asked, her breath tight in her chest.

Fionn laughed. "We know you can hear the trees," he crooned like a lover.

"You're crazy," she said, forcing a fake smile. "I don't know—"

"Now who's lying?" Rhodry demanded. "We've both seen you do it. Besides, the forest was fairly humming with it the day you arrived. We all heard it."

"We all who? What are you talking about?"

"Shifters, darling," Fionn said cheerfully. "Men who've been listening to the forests for generations, and who understand it far better than *you* ever will."

"Well, fuck you too," she came back, irritated.

Fionn just laughed again. "You *are* feeling better. Look, I know you'll miss me, but you'll have to settle for Rhodry here. By now, Tonio will have reported in, and my father won't be happy. I have to get back to the palace before he skins the lot of us and makes some nice rugs." He took two steps toward the door, then turned around, gave her a considering look, and came back. "They'll probably release you from here tomorrow. Will you go to the crew quarters at the science compound to recuperate?"

She scowled up at him. "No," she insisted. "I'll be perfectly fine in my own place in the city."

"Good," he said slyly, then leaned in and put his mouth next to her ear. "Leave your window open, darling," he murmured, "and I'll show you exactly what a shifter's capable of."

She started to push him away, but Rhodry grabbed him first, shoving him toward the door.

"Go brief your father, asshole."

"Touchy," Fionn said, shaking away Rhodry's hand with an amused look. He pulled the door open, but turned back to regard her, all humor gone from his face. "Leave Harp her secrets, Amanda. Forget what you saw today."

Rhodry scowled at the closed door as if waiting to be sure Fionn was gone, staring so intently that she wondered if he could actually hear the other man—the other *shifter*, she reminded herself—walking down the hall. Eventually, his face cleared, and he sat on the bed next to her. She wanted him to touch her, to hold her hand the way he had earlier.

Even more than that, she needed to *know*.

"How many of you are there?" she asked quietly.

He sighed at her persistence. "Not very many, just those of us in the Guild."

"The Rangers Guild?" She frowned. So, he'd lied about

that, too. It all made terrible sense now. Why he'd been so careful to brush aside the existence of the Guild as unimportant. She should have seen it. She'd been so focused on exploring the forest that she'd ignored the *men* all around it. And, damn it! Those big cats she'd seen prowling among the trees? The ones who were always around but who never bothered her? They were all shifters. Son of a bitch!

"Can all of you hear the trees?" she asked in sudden understanding.

He shrugged. "Of course. All of the *shifters,* I mean," he clarified.

"Of course," she echoed. "How? I mean, how is any of this possible? That colony ship was human."

He drew a deep breath, looking across the bed and out the window, to where a soft wind was causing the ever-present trees to sway gently. "What's the saying?" he said thoughtfully. "Adapt or perish? Well, the colonists were definitely perishing, and so they adapted. They took some Harp DNA and spliced it into a human…embryo, I guess. I'm not a scientist."

"Are you all cats, or are there others?"

"Just cats. The indigenous donor was a chameleon, a big cat who could blend in with his surroundings to become almost invisible." He gave her a brief smile. "When I was little and would misbehave, I used to think I could become invisible too, if I only tried hard enough. It never worked."

"Much to your mother's relief, I'm sure."

"My mother *never* saw me misbehave," he said, laughing suddenly.

And for a moment, she forgot to breathe. Even scowling, he was a handsome man. But when he laughed? He left merely handsome so far behind, it was a faint memory. He was beautiful. Unfortunately, it didn't last.

His gaze shifted back to her, abruptly serious. "Humans couldn't survive on Harp without us shifters. Not then and not now. We make it possible. No one knows the forests like we do, no one can hunt safely, or hear—" He stopped short, frowning. "Except you."

He didn't look very happy about that.

"No one? There's never been anyone before, someone who *wasn't* a shifter?"

He shrugged. "Not that we know of. There's no record of it at least. Don't worry, though," he added smugly. "Most of us don't believe you can do it either, or at least we don't think it will last. You just don't have the right DNA."

"But you said—"

"Fionn and I have both seen you do it, yes. And the trees sing about it. That doesn't mean you're hearing what we hear. It's pretty unlikely, but it doesn't matter anyway."

"What do you mean it doesn't matter?"

"You're not Guild, and that means the forest is still mostly closed to you. We're the only ones with free rein throughout the Green, it's just too dangerous, even for you."

"Does everyone in the Guild have to be a shifter?"

He gave her a dark look. "What difference does that make? No one but a shifter could possibly—" His beautiful eyes narrowed. "Don't even think about it. You could have been killed today, and that's just a small taste of the dangers to be found out there."

"But I *wasn't* killed."

"Only because Tonio and I showed up."

"You don't know that. I'd already killed the male Wyeth,

and the female was pregnant. She would have bolted soon enough."

"And how did you plan to get back to the city leaking blood the way you were? You'd have drawn every predator for miles."

She shrugged. And immediately regretted it as her back protested. "Maybe. And I'm grateful for your help. That doesn't mean I wouldn't have made it home on my own, and it definitely doesn't mean I'm giving up. If gaining admission to the Guild is the only way I can explore the Green, then that's what I'll do. I love a challenge."

"It's not a *challenge*, Amanda, it's what we were born to do. There are *shifters* who never make it through the Guild trials. You're a norm who wasn't even born on this planet."

"Norm," she interrupted. "You make it sound like a bad thing."

"It's not good or bad. It just *is*. And it means you don't stand a chance out there. There's a hell of a lot more to being Guild than hearing a few whispers in the trees. You're only going to get hurt. Or worse."

She had no comeback to that. He'd already made up his mind, but so had she. Rhodry thought the Green should belong only to shifters. He was wrong.

When she didn't say anything, he stood up, kicking the chair behind him. She thought he'd storm out — instead he regarded her for a long moment, as if memorizing her face. As if he didn't think he'd see her again. A slow look of resignation shaded his expression, and for a moment, he seemed almost sad. Then he drew a deep breath and said, "Goodbye, Amanda. We'll check on you later." And then he left, shutting the door behind him.

She stared at the closed door, her chest tight with emotion. Turning her head, she stared at the gently moving trees outside the window, opened herself to their song, then lay back and let it soothe away the pain.

"Don't have what it takes?" she said softly. "Don't put any bets on that, de Mendoza."

Chapter Ten

Amanda jogged through the early morning streets of the city, the system's sun barely a thought on the horizon. It would have been nicer to run under the trees, weaving in and out, listening to the forest come awake, but it was never a good idea to run in the Green, especially unarmed. It made you look like prey—and that was one thing you didn't want the beasts of Harp to think of you.

Somewhere beyond the trees, the sun crested the planet's edge and a shaft of light speared through the trees. She'd spent time on any number of planets in her twenty-five years and seen innumerable sunrises. And yet, three months after bidding good-bye to the fleet, she still wasn't immune to the beauty of a sunrise on Harp. There was just something magical about seeing it through the filter of thousands and thousands of trees. She couldn't see the horizon from here, the trees were too tall and too thick. She could feel the difference in the song of the Green, though. There was a rustling wakefulness to it when the sun rose, as if the giant trees were stretching their limbs after a long night's sleep.

She laughed at her own musings. That was an unforgivable anthropomorphism—comparing the trees to a waking human. It was fairly apt, however, because while Harp's trees were definitely not human, they *were* absolutely aware of their planet and everything that affected it. She didn't know exactly how yet, but she intended to find out, which was why she was jogging through the streets at sunrise.

She hadn't needed Rhodry's warnings about the physical demands of the Guild trials to know they'd be rough. She had only to look at the shifters she encountered almost daily, especially now that she knew what to look for. They were some of the finest male specimens that she'd ever seen, every one of them taller than human norm, big and beautifully muscled. And, yes, they were all male. No one had been willing to discuss it with her, but there were definitely no female shifters. Apparently, there never had been. She'd gotten that much out of a local shopkeeper, with whom she'd become friendly. He couldn't tell her much more than that, although it was obvious that the shifter trait was sex-linked. After all, they'd been created in a genetics lab for the sole purpose of defending the colony. A kind of super soldier. It would have made sense to make them male, given the greater potential for strength and aggression.

The Guild trials were designed to challenge even the physical perfection that was a shifter, but that didn't mean she couldn't do it, only that she'd have to try harder. Nothing motivated her more than being told she couldn't do something, and in this case she had an additional reason for pushing. She didn't believe it was random that the trees had chosen her to be the first non-shifter to hear their voices. There was a reason. And she'd never find out what that reason was if she was confined to the city.

Besides, Harp was her home now. The idea of leaving was...painful. And if the trees needed her somehow in order to defend their shared home, then she would do her best to make that possible.

She reached the end of the narrow street. It dead-ended into a dirt path that ventured into the forest. She paused briefly, bent over, hands on her knees as she caught her breath. She was going to need her strength for what came next. This was the tail end of her morning jog, and she was hot and sweat-soaked. It was early fall, but here in the planet's equatorial belt, the days were still warm. She started out every morning before sunrise, timing it so that by the time the city was really beginning to stir, she was back home and in the shower. She didn't need or want an audience for her runs. Regular Harpers—norms as the shifters called them—had found her morning exercise routine something of a novelty when she'd first started. They seemed to find the demands of everyday life enough to maintain their physical health. They didn't understand that Amanda wasn't running for health, she was running for strength and stamina. Two things she was certain she'd need during the trials.

The shifters around her hadn't said a word, for the most part, though their silence spoke volumes. She didn't understand why they were so opposed to her candidacy. It seemed a simple matter to her. If she could survive the trials, then she was an asset to the community. And if she failed, then she was the only one hurt by it.

Of course, she wasn't completely naive. The shifters

would have resented anyone trying to encroach on their sacred turf. Though it seemed unlikely she'd be starting a trend or anything. Norms weren't exactly breaking down the door to get into the Guild. In fact, in the nearly five hundred years that humans had lived on Harp, there hadn't been a single non-shifter who'd even attempted the trials, much less one who succeeded. She'd checked.

Despite the shifters' instinctive resentment, however, she still believed they would eventually come around to the idea of her candidacy—if only so they could be there to gloat when she failed. Not that she had any intention of failing. And so far, she hadn't done anything except check into the legalities involved, and find out everything she could about the trials themselves so she'd know how to prepare. Unfortunately, that was easier said than done.

The initial step was straightforward, nothing more than formally registering to participate in the trials. Sign-ups were held one day each year, and that day was today, with the first part of the trial taking place in five days. That would be a straightforward written exam to test the candidate's knowledge of the Green's life forms—not only the animals, but the plants. The candidate had to show near-perfect knowledge of each animal's characteristics and behavior, and in most cases how best to kill it, since almost everything out there would be trying to kill you first. For plants, it was identification, along with knowledge of any beneficial use, and a basic understanding of what was safe and what wasn't. The latter being a much longer list.

Her training had begun as soon as she'd been released from the hospital. Slowly at first, as her leg healed, but she'd been in excellent physical condition already and it wasn't long before she was training as hard as ever. It wasn't the physical demands of the trials that worried her, though. It was the enormous amount of new data she'd had to absorb in order to be ready for whatever she'd face out there, and for the written exam, too. Even for someone accustomed to dealing with the vast amounts of information that came into the fleet's science center almost daily, it was a lot to learn in a short amount of time.

And today was the day, the first step, and she was ready. She was also tired of waiting, which was why, instead of rushing home to shower this morning, she was going to swing by the Guild Hall and sign up first thing. If she missed today's registration, it would be another year before she could try again, and it had occurred to her that some of the shifters might try to stop her from putting her name on the list. She didn't expect anyone to ambush her on the pathway or anything physical. However, she wouldn't put it past them to make her jump through some bureaucratic hoops in hopes of delaying her registration until it was too late. She figured by getting there at the crack of dawn, she'd at least have all day to play their little games.

She straightened, stepped off the street, and started down the narrow dirt path that would take her to the Guild Hall. If the shifters had been decent about her candidacy, she would have made a point of showering first, and shown up looking and *smelling* all nice and proper. But she was still angry about a group of teenage shifters who'd expressed their displeasure in a very aromatic way when she'd first made her intentions known. She'd already moved her living quarters into the city, renting a two-room apartment on the edge of town above a busy clothing shop. The teenage pranksters hadn't dared pull their little stunt there, but her office was another matter.

They'd begun visiting the compound every day after dark, when no one was around to catch them, and using the ground just below her office window as their personal urinal. She'd stopped that practice short—quite literally. She'd installed a series of pressure plates along the outside of the building. The equipment was standard gear for planetary landings into unknown environments, usually part of a small perimeter set up to safeguard the human encampment against animal intrusion. The plates were designed to deliver a small, harmless, electrical shock, just enough to make the average indigenous life form decide it was too much trouble to keep going.

The sensitivity of the plate could be heightened, and the electrical jolt could be amped up, however, to accommodate larger and more dangerous animals. Put those two adjustments together and they were capable of producing a more, um…dramatic result.

She'd slept in her office the next night in order to monitor her security enhancements, and now she smiled, remembering the panicked shriek she'd heard when the first little pisser discovered his urine stream was highly conductive to electricity. The resulting arc had probably felt like his dick was being burned right off, and his yowl had given her the best laugh she'd had in a long time. Not that he suffered any permanent damage. She'd been careful about that. The asshole was probably peeing painlessly after just a few days. But not beneath her office window. Not anymore.

She left the shelter of the trees as the Guild Hall came into view, straddling the line between city and forest. Some of the trees here were far older than the building itself.

Others were newly grown as if trying to reclaim the slender strip of land the Hall sat upon. It was the oldest construction in the city, dating back to the landing itself. Originally, it had served the colonists as a little of everything—hospital, school, administrative offices—and that early utilitarian history was reflected in the many smaller out-buildings huddled around the main lodge like chicks to a hen. If one knew where to look, there were even parts of the old colony ship to be seen in some of the exterior walls.

The central hall was a sprawling and disorganized two-story structure, its ancient wood stained a dark, reddish brown from centuries of weather and use. It had been patched and modified over the years to add windows and a covered porch that stretched nearly the full width of the building. The core of it was still original construction, a testament to the determination of those original colonists to remain on Harp for generations to come.

As she crossed the clearing and climbed the stairs to the old-fashioned screened door, she mopped her face with the sleeve of her tunic and caught a whiff of herself. She grinned. Nice and stinky, just like she'd planned. And shifters had such *sensitive* noses.

R hodry came out of his room at the Guild Hall barefoot, wearing a loose-fitting pair of drawstring pants. He was leading a long-distance hunt today, and wanted an early start. One of the Green's worst predators, a long-haired primate known as a pongo, had been attacking the lumber camps throughout the forest. Pongos were big—as much as six feet tall when standing upright, and two hundred pounds of muscle. They were like banshees on steroids, but they usually traveled alone, and their favorite food was actually banshee meat. This pongo had killed a human, however, and that made him fair game for a hunt.

With the hunt's departure only minutes away, there was little reason for him to get dressed. He'd be going cat as soon as he reached the trees. Shifters were fairly casual about nudity—clothes were destroyed by the shift, and one could never guarantee there'd be something handy when changing back to human form. Many of the shifters living in the permanent residential areas of the Guild didn't even bother with pants, but Rhodry had been raised among the mountain clans in a house full of female relatives. He'd been taught early on that one did not run naked among polite company. Although calling the Guild Hall polite company might be stretching it a bit. Especially when he saw what was happening below.

Shifters lined the balconies. Some were sitting along the sturdy, wide railings in cat form, their tails switching with irritation. Others stood as humans. And they were all staring at the same thing—Amanda strolling over to the sign-up table for this year's Guild trials.

Rhodry stared along with the rest of them, not quite believing. He'd heard the same rumors everyone else had, rumors that only confirmed what she'd stubbornly insisted that day in her hospital room. She planned to try for Guild membership. He'd seen her many times out among the trees, walking along muttering to herself, taking notes on every little thing she came across, drawing pictures in that leather notebook she carried with her everywhere she went. Every shifter in the city had watched her at one time or another these last three months, always sitting high above her, hidden in the thick canopies where she couldn't see them. And if he had watched more than most, it was only because Cristobal had put her safety in his hands all those months ago.

She never acknowledged her watchers, and seemed unaware of them. That fact alone said she wasn't qualified for Guild membership, that they could sit up in the trees and watch her, and she didn't even know they were there.

Of course, it was possible that she *did* know they were watching and had decided to ignore them. That's what he would have done in her situation. Never let an enemy know you're aware of him. The shifters weren't her enemies. Not precisely. But if she could hear the trees as well as any shifter, and that was still a very big *if* in his mind, then she would definitely have known she was being observed from the treetops.

Rhodry had trouble wrapping his mind around that possibility. He had to admire her determination, though. Hell, he even had to admit that he'd been impressed with the way she'd handled that pair of Wyeth badgers back at the start of all this, when Tonio had made the mistake of shifting right in front of her. He'd never told her that, but it didn't seem to matter. That one event had set off a chain reaction in her thinking that had culminated in her ridiculous belief that she could qualify to become a member of the Guild. The other Earthers who'd remained behind on Harp kept to the city and spent most of their time in the science compound, but not her.

She was out in the Green every damned day, learning the forests as well as she could, he supposed, given her obvious limitations. The Guild wouldn't permit her to travel any farther than a quarter mile into the Green, not until she'd passed at least the initial exams. That didn't stop her from doing it, of course. It seemed to be in her nature to push boundaries. Shifters were set to watch her and had frequently stopped her from going any farther than she was allowed. On the other hand, he knew for a fact that she evaded her watchers sometimes and went where she pleased. Because he'd watched her more than anyone else, and while she'd given her assigned guards the slip, she'd never managed to evade *him*.

And it wasn't as if the restrictions only applied to her. Every norm on Harp, and even the teenage shifters applying for Guild membership, were subject to the same limitations. Although he acknowledged that young shifters were given much greater flexibility. As long as there were at least three or four of them in a group, they were permitted, from about thirteen years of age onward, to enjoy almost free run of the trees.

It was different for them. They were a part of the Green, a part of Harp down to their very DNA. More importantly, they'd been listening to the voice of the trees before they'd even left their mothers' wombs, and were equipped from birth with the fur and claws that made them shifters. Even if Amanda *could* hear the trees, she couldn't hope to match a shifter's advantages.

Raised voices drew his attention back to the scene down below. The shifter running the sign-up was arguing with Amanda, and she was arguing right back, quoting paragraph and line of Harp law at him—a law that gave every resident of Harp the right to enter the Guild trials. And she was a resident. She'd seen to that by moving into town. If she'd stayed out in the science compound with the others, an argument could have been made that she wasn't really a resident, since the compound was fleet territory and not under the sovereignty of the Ardrigh. That was now a moot point since she'd rented those two rooms and moved in.

He took a moment to marvel at the shortsightedness of the founders, that they'd written the law so that anyone could join the Guild, when the Guild had clearly been created to serve shifters alone. Not that he could blame the founders precisely. In all this time no norm had ever applied for the Guild. And why would they? Harpers *knew* this planet, knew how dangerous it was. They sure as hell knew better than to think they could take it on with their fragile bodies and deaf minds. That's what shifters had been created for.

The shifters around him grew still as Orrin Brady stepped up to the sign-up table. Orrin was one of the Guild's trial judges. The judges were older Guild members who were past their prime, but still strong and with the experience and respect necessary to resolve disputes among the fractious shifters.

"Interesting, don't you think, de Mendoza?" Fionn's voice announced his unwanted presence just over his left shoulder.

"Not really."

Fionn laughed. "I take it you don't approve?"

He turned his head and looked directly at Fionn. "It's not a matter of me approving or not. I worry for her safety. She may make it through the written exam. She probably will, given what I've seen of her. But what about the rest? She could die out there."

"I don't know," Fionn commented thoughtfully. "Amanda's rather extraordinary."

"You support what she's doing then?"

"I didn't say that. Simply that she's extraordinary. She'll do better than you think."

He gritted his teeth at the familiarity in Fionn's voice when he spoke of Amanda. He wondered if she'd succumbed, along with half the female population of the city, to the prince's charm; and then reminded himself that he had no say in whether she did or not. He'd made his decision; he had a simple plan. He was going to serve for as long as Cristobal insisted, and then go back to his life in the mountains. Amanda was a complication he didn't need.

Now if only he could convince his body of that, his life would be much easier.

A loud protest down below alerted him to the fact that Orrin had decided in her favor. She was signing her name to the register, just like the young shifters who jostled in line around her. He frowned as one of them shoved her roughly and then immediately apologized as if it had all been an accident. She simply regarded the boy like a badly behaved kitten, not at all intimidated by his size—which was already far greater than hers—or the number of his fellows crowded behind him. She had balls. He would give her that, too. Balls and determination. He fought a smile at the thought.

Ignoring the young shifters, she turned back to Orrin, said something Rhodry couldn't hear, then picked up her registration packet and spun away from the table with a triumphant grin. She glanced up as she went, spying him and Fionn standing together on the balcony. Her grin widened, and she winked.

Fionn laughed and clapped his hands together in applause. Rhodry could only try to keep his teeth from grinding together any louder than necessary.

The crowd broke up quickly after that, though there was plenty of muttering going on. He moved away from the railing, intending to go downstairs and out to the Green to get the hunt started, when Fionn put a hand on his shoulder.

"Message from the Ardrigh, de Mendoza," he said cheerfully. "He wants you at dinner tonight. No excuses."

"Why tonight?"

Fionn raised his eyebrows speculatively, and Rhodry knew he was debating whether or not to answer the question. After all, if the Ardrigh requested his presence at dinner, he'd be there regardless of the reason. Fionn shrugged negligently.

"Desmond Serna's in town. He's a cousin of yours, isn't he?"

He nodded, barely managing to keep his expression blank. "Distant cousin on my mother's side," he confirmed. *And about as trustworthy as a banshee.* He wondered what business Serna could have in the city this time of year.

"He escorted his mother to the palace," Fionn said, answering the unvoiced question. "I figured you'd be happy to have a fellow clansman around for a bit."

Not that *clansman.* "I'll be there, of course." He caught sight of his shifter patrol moving out the front door and nodded in their direction. "I've got a hunt to lead. I'll see you later."

As he loped down the stairs and out to the Green, he couldn't help but wonder what his cousin Desmond's true purpose was in coming to the city, and why Cristobal, who'd been so set on sending his cousin Aidan away, had instead invited his staunchest enemy to dinner.

Chapter Eleven

The shifters flowed silently through the trees, their long, sleek forms gliding from tree to tree and limb to limb, causing barely a ripple in the canopy of the forest. The red-furred pongo raced ahead of them, its eerie high-pitched squeals echoing back through the forest, both angry and frightened. It was intelligent for an animal, capable of calculation and viciousness in equal measure. Its normal prey were the banshee packs which so tormented the human residents of Harp, but this time the pongo had found the isolated human encampments too easy to resist. One logger was dead, two others injured. One of those injured was a boy who was barely more than a child, out with his father for the first time.

The shifters felt a certain empathy for the pongo, and an admiration for its hunting and tracking skills. But empathy was meaningless in the face of human survival. Shifters had been bred for this purpose, to keep the colonists safe by hunting the most dangerous predators on the planet. And in doing so, they'd become the greatest predators of all.

Rhodry took the lead as always, signaling the others with commands that were no more than snarls, using the song of the trees themselves to communicate. Every animal indigenous to the planet could tap into that song, but only shifters—with their shared human DNA—could use the information as a tactical tool. The pongo was in sight now, powerful arms swinging its massive frame through the trees with an effortless grace. But even as Rhodry caught sight of the animal, it changed its tactics.

Knowing it was trapped, surrounded by shifters, the pongo stopped trying to outrace its tormentors and turned to fight. It charged without warning, racing through the trees with amazing speed, bellowing its challenge and heading straight for Rhodry.

Rhodry bared his teeth in answer, his own razor-edged yowl ripping through the trees and setting the forest to trembling around them. He didn't wait for the pongo to reach him, but launched himself through the air, landing on the charging primate and digging in with his claws, swinging around to sink his fangs deep into the back of the animal's neck. Destabilized by the awkward weight, the pongo lost its footing and fell through the branches, Rhodry still clinging to its back. They slammed against branch after branch, blood flowing from a hundred cuts before they finally landed hard on a wide, main tree limb.

Using its arms to push off the thick tree limb, the pongo made a last, desperate leap. Back bowing with a mighty effort that lifted the nearly five hundred pounds of their combined weight into flight, the creature launched them both into the air once more. Pongo and shifter fell heavily through the canopy, forty feet or more, crashing through trees and vines until they hit the forest floor with a thunderous noise, sending ripples of sound and movement through the forest, shaking the surrounding trees and silencing the Green for miles around as every animal in the vicinity froze in terror.

Sound faded and dust settled, leaves drifting slowly down to land on the bloody mass of fur and fang. The pongo breathed its last breath with an agonized groan, collapsing into the pungent loam of the deep forest. Rhodry waited to be certain the pongo was truly dead, but finally relaxed his hold, his jaw aching as he opened it wide enough to free his fangs from the creature's neck.

Breathing heavily, still in his cat form, he stood on all four legs, every inch of him bloody and aching. He was alive, which made him the victor. But he'd lost nearly as much blood as his prey. No bones were broken, other than a rib or two, but those would heal. Shifters healed far faster than regular humans, a side benefit of the shift itself.

The greater danger for Rhodry was blood loss from the numerous deep wounds inflicted by both the pongo and the tree limbs as they'd crashed in a virtual free fall to the forest floor. It occurred to him that this would be a most opportune moment for his enemies to attack, and he wondered if any of his fellow hunters would stand with him if it came to that.

Even those who distrusted him for being a de Mendoza—those who still seemed to be waiting for the inevitable day when he would step out of line and betray the Ardrigh—even they followed him willingly enough into the hunt. Because he was the best damn hunter in the Guild, and everyone knew it. He granted that one of his own cousins might be able to best him, though it was a near thing. But one thing he knew for certain, and that was that none of those who called the city's Guild Hall home could hold a candle to him in the Green.

But the hunt was over now, and he was wounded and vulnerable. He lifted his head and opened his eyes, and found himself surrounded by his fellow shifters, some of them bloodied by the chase, all of them exhausted by the long hunt. His mouth opened in a fang-toothed snarl of victory, a reminder to them all who had won this encounter. And they grinned back at him. Rhodry permitted himself to relax, at least a little. They might hate him for who his grandfather was, might very well politick against him behind his back. But they were united in the hunt, and today had been a very good day.

Unfortunately, tonight was going to be a very bad night.

R hodry concealed a wince as he reached for his water glass. His ribs were still sore from the pongo hunt, and one or two of the deeper wounds had required bandaging. He should have been soaking in one of the natural hot springs that fed into the palace, instead of sitting here having dinner with people he disliked. He could picture it now. Steam billowing around him, the heat soaking into his muscles as Amanda massaged his shoulders. Her blond hair piled on top of her head, tempting tendrils trailing over her breasts.

He blinked in surprise, wondering where that image had come from, and hoping none of his fellow dinner guests had noticed his lapse. He drank deeply, thinking it was far more entertaining to imagine being in a tub with Amanda than to wonder what plot Desmond Serna and his mother, Isabella, were hatching now. It certainly wasn't chance that had brought the two of them to the Ardrigh's palace, and it sure as hell wasn't because either one of them had a burning desire to reunite with *him*.

He had a fairly good idea of what it *was* about, however.

Desmond Serna was a shifter, and the de Mendoza heir if something should happen to Rhodry before he produced a son of his own. There were plenty of clansmen who thought he was already the better clan chief, regardless of Brian de Mendoza's wishes, and not a few of those would have been willing to hurry Des's inheritance along by getting rid of Rhodry for him. It was enough to make a shifter aware that he had enemies, including dear cousin Desmond.

And yet here he was, forced to sit and watch with carefully concealed disgust as Des's mother, Isabella Serna, let loose with a girlish giggle that set his teeth on edge. He saw with relief that the staff had begun clearing away the remnants of dinner, preparatory to the final dessert course. There would be a brief lull while coffee was brewed and the various cognacs were presented on the sideboard, which was Isabella's opportunity to broach whatever it was that had brought mother and son to the capital.

Cristobal leaned back, as if stretching after dinner. It had the effect of drawing him away from Isabella's grasping hand, and Rhodry had to admire his tact. The Ardrigh knew as well as anyone that serious matters were about to be discussed, and he was separating himself symbolically from either party.

"So, Isabella," Cristobal began smoothly. "As delightful as this evening has been, I suspect there are other matters which brought you to the city."

Next to his mother, Desmond straightened in his seat and shot Rhodry a nervous glance. Isabella had no such qualms. She leaned forward earnestly, and would have placed a hand on the Ardrigh's arm again had he not casually moved it out of reach.

"My lord," she began. "You are astute, as always. As much as I value an evening in the company of you and your lovely Kathryn, we are here on a much more serious matter."

Cristobal nodded briefly for her to continue.

"As you know, my mother was Chief Brian de Mendoza's sister, his only sibling. There was also a younger brother who died as a child. So many did then," she added with a sorrowful and well-practiced shake of her head. "In any event, genealogically speaking, that would put my son"—she gestured at Des, as if everyone in the room didn't already know who the asshole was—"in equal standing with Rhodry in terms of blood link to the de Mendoza line."

His eyes narrowed to irritated slits. The woman was actually going to ask Cristobal to intervene in clan business. She had to be acting on her own, because all of the clans felt very strongly about outsiders and where they belonged. While there were those who disagreed with his grandfather's choice of heir, the one thing they *all* agreed upon was keeping the Ardrigh out of clan business.

"I'll not waste your time with pretty words," Isabella was continuing. "I'm here to petition for the Ardrigh's justice on behalf of the de Mendoza clan. We're asking you to grant Desmond the de Mendoza mantle—temporarily, of course—now that Rhodry is here with you in the city. He can't possibly see to the clan's needs from this far away, while Desmond, who surely has an equal claim to the title, sits in the heart of the de Mendoza lands and sees them suffering."

Cristobal's eyebrows went up at that. "I wasn't aware de Mendoza was suffering, Isabella. The latest reports I've seen show them to be doing quite well. I wouldn't have taken Rhodry away otherwise."

"Of course," she backpedaled quickly, not wanting to suggest Cristobal had acted against clan interests. "We only wish to ensure that the prosperity continues, my lord, to the benefit of the clans and all of Harp."

Rhodry sat in stiff disbelief listening to Isabella prattle on, painfully aware of the others at the table listening to every word. Did the woman have no sense of honor? And what about Desmond? Was he such a tool of his mother that he could sit there and listen in silence while she violated the very core of clan sovereignty? He risked a glance down the table and caught Fionn watching him intently. His eyes narrowed in distrust, while Fionn only grinned and gave a little jerk of his head toward Isabella, as if he was highly amused by the whole thing.

Rhodry wasn't amused. He was furious.

Aware that Isabella had finally ended her ridiculous bleating, he switched his attention to Cristobal, who was nodding thoughtfully. "A very serious matter, indeed, Isabella, and one that would have far-reaching consequences, I would think." He looked down the table and asked, "What do you think, de Mendoza?"

He held Cristobal's gaze, aware of Isabella stiffening slightly at the Ardrigh's deliberate use of his last name, which in this context was his clan title. As clan leader, he was "the" de Mendoza.

"What I think, my lord, is that this is a matter best left to the Clan Council rather than spread like dirty laundry for all of Harp to see."

"The Clan Council is overrun with Devlins," Isabella snapped. "Unable to see past their own interests to the good of the clan."

"Whereas you," Fionn murmured, "have only the clan's interests at heart."

Rhodry glanced at him, eyebrows raised, not having expected any support from that quarter. He turned back in time to see Cristobal shoot his son a quelling look.

"I'm not certain I understand, Isabella," Cristobal said. "Why would Rhodry require a surrogate for what is, after all, only a temporary absence? And in the capital city at that."

"Why, so that he can *remain* here in the city with you, my lord," Isabella oozed. "What with the Earthers knocking on our very door, you surely want your staunchest allies close at hand."

He waited. Cristobal was certainly not fooled by this clumsy bid for power. Once Desmond took over as *temporary* clan chief, he'd pack the council with his own cronies and Rhodry would be out permanently. Assuming they let him live that long.

Cristobal had been watching Isabella thoughtfully as she spoke, and he now smiled slightly. "Your argument has merit, Isabella, and I certainly bear no love for Brian or his political ambitions." The woman beamed in triumph as Cristobal continued, "Still, Brian was the undisputed leader of de Mendoza when he died. His wishes must be considered, as must clan tradition. It was my own grandfather's insistence on trying to bring the clans under the throne's power that drove Brian to rebel in the first place. I have no desire to repeat his mistake."

He smiled and lifted a hand over his shoulder, signaling the staff to begin the dessert course. "I shall consider your request. In the meantime, let us turn to more productive topics, like today's hunt, which I understand went quite well?"

Rhodry eyed Cristobal for a moment, trying to figure out his angle. He hadn't granted Isabella's request, though he hadn't denied it, either. And now he was bringing up the day's hunt which had clearly been a triumph for Rhodry.

Cristobal speared him with his turquoise stare and raised an eyebrow, inviting his response.

"It was a successful hunt," he agreed.

Fionn laughed. "You're too modest," he said. "Word around the Guild Hall is that it was the best hunt in years. Rhodi here had shifters flying through the trees."

The other shifters around the table shared a grin. They knew Fionn was being polite because there were ladies present. The hunt had been wild and bloody, a shifter's favorite kind. Even Des grinned.

"That's what I heard," Cristobal said with a laugh. "In fact, Des, as long as you're here in the city, you should stay a few months, join some hunts yourself. It will be good to have a few more clansmen at my side."

A few more clansmen as long as they're not Devlins, Rhodry thought sourly. He missed his cousins viciously, felt naked without them at his back. Still, he had to admit it was amusing to see Isabella's reaction to Cristobal's invitation, which, of course, Des couldn't refuse. Though, Isabella was already trying to convince Cristobal that she needed her baby boy to escort her back home.

"Nonsense," Cristobal was saying, waving his hand dismissively. "Des can take one of the hovers. He'll have you home and be back here within the day. In fact, I've a couple of younger shifters who'd probably enjoy riding along. It's good for them to see more of what's beyond the city's perimeter."

Rhodry kept his expression carefully blank as Isabella sputtered. His mind was roiling. Cristobal wasn't at all what he'd expected. Perhaps the clans had more in common with the city than he'd believed.

And maybe he would get out of this city alive, after all.

Chapter Twelve

On the morning of the Guild's written exam, Amanda cut across the still-empty streets of the city, walking, not running. She didn't want to arrive all sweaty this time, since she'd be spending the next several hours in a small room filled with young shifters. It wasn't concern for the other test takers that made her walk, though. She didn't care if they liked the way she smelled or not. She simply had no desire to sit there all sticky with sweat and smelling *herself* for the rest of the day.

She smiled and turned toward the main part of town, passing a long line of shuttered stores, most with second story apartments like her own. Beyond that were the residential areas which consisted of neat clusters of homes, frequently facing each other around short cul-de-sacs and occupied by members of the same extended family. As with almost everything else on Harp, the houses were constructed primarily of wood with a rosy gold grain. Every house had a blue solar array on the roof and several had eaves painted to match, gleaming through the gray mist of morning.

She took a shortcut between several houses, her nose tickling with the scent of herbs growing in home gardens. It still amazed her sometimes that the colonists had survived long enough to build all of this. And many of them hadn't. Their ship's captain, Thomas Harp, had perished during the landing, along with his executive officer, Jose Vaquero. The two of them had remained on the bridge, fighting to bring the crippled ship into some semblance of a controlled set-down. None of the people now living on Harp could appreciate what those men had gone through. None of them had ever been off the planet, much less flown a starship into the black void of space. She had. She'd read the histories and seen the compiled data on the system failures the doomed ship had suffered. She knew what it had been like on the bridge.

The surviving colonists—and most of them *had* survived the landing at least—had named the planet after their captain, and their city was officially Ciudad Vaquero, although most Harpers simply called it *the city* since it was the only one of any note on the planet. Captain Harp and his XO Vaquero had paid with their lives, but their success was written in the generations of Harpers who'd gone on to build a new life for themselves and their children here.

She turned onto a tree-lined path to the Guild Hall, listening idly as she walked along. The trees' voices were quiet this morning, only the low-level hum that was always present, and nothing like the buzz of excitement racing through her own veins. This was the beginning, her first Guild trial, even if it was only a written test.

She forced herself to walk slowly, strolling across the

clearing and around the main Guild Hall to the small blocky building where the exam was being held this morning. She wasn't nervous about the test itself. She'd pass, as long as no one tried to cheat on the scoring in order to keep her out of the running. She didn't think they'd go that far, though. Orrin Brady was overseeing the process this time around, and while he seemed puzzled by her persistence, he appeared quite ambivalent to her actual candidacy.

Stepping out of the weak morning sunshine, she found the room just as crowded with young shifters as she'd expected. Most of them were no more than sixteen years old, already big and tall, and seeming to fill every inch of the low-ceilinged space. They eyed her with the suspicion she'd come to expect from shifters as she looked around for a seat. And she wasn't surprised when chairs were shoved out of place to block her way no matter which way she tried to go.

She laughed privately at their antics. These babies had no idea whom they were dealing with. If she could survive a bout on Master Chief Jansson's sparring floor, she could survive a fucking classroom scuffle with a bunch of over-muscled teenage pussycats.

Their antics ceased abruptly, chairs suddenly finding their proper place as the baby shifters cast nervous glances at the open doorway behind her. She turned, expecting to find Orrin Brady. What she found was Rhodry de Mendoza scanning the room with his usual glowering disapproval.

At least this time it was aimed at someone other than her.

"Good morning, de Mendoza," she said cheerfully, mostly because she knew it would irritate him.

"Amanda," he growled.

"Are you proctoring the exam this morning?" she asked.

"I am. And there will be no favoritism shown for special needs. To anyone."

Amanda stared into his beautiful golden eyes, and just for a moment wished she would see her smile reflected back. It wasn't going to happen this time. Apparently whatever friendship, or more, that the two of them might have forged was history as far as he was concerned. She dug up a fake smile that felt like it was breaking her face and said, "Good to hear. I wouldn't want any of these hooligans to be coddled."

That earned her a scowl directed at her personally, which made her want to pat his handsome cheek. Her sense of survival kept her hands to herself, however. Rhodry wasn't a baby like these others. He was a fully-grown shifter. *A glorious, fully-grown and very male shifter*. She sighed wistfully, remembering the evening they'd danced and laughed together. It seemed like a dream she'd had long ago.

"You should take a seat now," he suggested in a tone that made it more of an order.

"Quite right," she agreed. She winked at him—again, just because she knew it would piss him off—then walked over and took the desk in the farthest corner of the room, with walls to her back and side. She preferred to keep even baby shifters where she could see them.

Rhodry watched Amanda cross the room and take the most defensible position available, the very seat he would have chosen in this situation. What was it about her that she took such delight in tormenting him? And more importantly, why did it work so well? He shook his head and moved to the front of the room. He had more important matters to deal with than the irritating ways of a certain blond Earther. Today's test was important, which was why he was here, despite it representing absolutely no challenge to his skills as a shifter. That would come in the spring. The candidates who succeeded today would have all winter to hone their weapons skills and to prepare for the most grueling trial of their lives.

He had no doubt Amanda would be among those moving on to the next phase, and wondered if she understood the full scope of the trials to come, the sheer physical strength and skill that would be required. This was far more than passing some test. Her very survival would be at stake.

Chapter Thirteen

Amanda stepped into the shower, hissing when hot water hit the scraped and raw skin on her forearms. The water ran pink for several minutes, swirling into the drain until finally she'd gotten through the blood and down to dirt and grime. She sighed tiredly and rested her forehead against the tiled wall, letting the water pummel her back and shoulders, pounding away the aches and pains which seemed to be her permanent companions these days. It wasn't long before she felt the water growing cooler and sighed once again. If she ever bought a house here, she was going to have the biggest hot water tank on the planet.

Washing the rest of her body quickly, she turned off the taps and stepped out of the shower. She was going to need bandages on her arms. And she'd have to wear long sleeves to cover the bandages. Either that or endure pointed comments about how her arms had been injured, which she wanted to avoid.

As far as she knew, no one was aware that she was practicing tree climbing. She made a point of practicing only when she was alone, with none of the shifter watchers who so often accompanied her trips into the Green. They probably thought she didn't know about them, because they stuck to the heights, but they didn't count on the trees. She could always tell when a shifter was near because the forest's song changed. It became happier. The Green liked the shifters a *lot*.

She dried the rest of her body, then pulled out the enormous first aid kit her mother had stocked for her. After a liberal application of antibiotic ointment, she layered non-stick gauze on her raw arms. Taping it in place, she walked out of the bathroom and into the small bedroom she'd effectively transformed into a large closet and storage room.

Her apartment was comfortable, with just enough space for one person who didn't like to mess with housekeeping. Amanda used the wide-open main room as both bedroom and living room, leaving the small bedroom for storage. It was convenient, though the real reason she'd chosen this apartment was the bathroom with its separate shower and huge, enameled tub. Normally, after a day like today, she'd have made use of that tub for a long soak. Not today, though. She had an errand to run. One that couldn't wait.

She was supposed to pick up her bow this afternoon, the kind every Guild member owned. It had taken a lot of time and persistence on her part to locate the weapons expert who made most of the hunting bows for the Guild. She'd never seen a shifter actually hunt with one of the weapons; she *had* seen the Guild members practicing and competing against one another.

She supposed the tradition went back to the early days, before they'd perfected their hunting techniques as cats, though it hardly mattered where it came from. It was tradition, and it was required, which meant it was a skill she'd have to master before being permitted to move on to the next phase of the Guild trials.

Shooting a bow was something she already knew. She'd even hunted with a compound bow a few times several years ago. The Guild weapon, by contrast, wasn't like any bow she'd used before. It was stubby, thick, and damned difficult to draw. Short for ease of carry through the trees and undergrowth, it had a hard pull that was designed for a shifter's considerable strength. She was going to need both time and muscle to perfect its use. Her upper body strength was already better than average, which wasn't enough. The bow required very specific muscles, so she'd begun working with the weight equipment at the science compound. The workout was helping with her tree-climbing, too, which was a little side bonus.

When she'd tried to practice with a bow itself, however, she'd discovered that no shifter was willing to lend her his bow for even an hour's practice. At first she'd thought it was another example of their resentment and dislike. She'd soon discovered that shifters didn't lend their bows to *anyone*. Apparently, they were very touchy about them, since bows were handed down from father to son to grandson and blah, blah, blah. So, she'd ordered her own, and today would be the first time she got to hold it in her hands.

She pulled a tank top over her bra, and added a long-sleeved tunic before braiding her long blond hair just like the shifters did. A pair of loose, warm pants, socks and boots, and she was ready to go. Grabbing her keys, she hurried out the door and down the stairs, suddenly eager for the feel of warm wood beneath her fingers.

Rhodry stepped into the weapons master's shop on a back street of the city. Normally, he wouldn't have gone to a city craftsman for any of his weapons. Fortunately, this man was a clansman. He and his then-young wife had moved to the city decades ago to be with her ailing father. They'd never intended to remain permanently, then the first of their children had been born, and eventually their grand-children, and the old clansman was still here. He was the most popular weapons master in the city, and the only one Rhodry would have trusted.

A small bell jingled overhead when he opened the door, and he could hear voices from the back room where the man did most of his work. So he waited patiently, examining a row of knives, picking up each and weighing it in his hand. They were fine work, too light for his use, obviously aimed at the city's non-shifter population. He heard footsteps, and then the owner's gravelly voice as he came back into the main showroom. It was the second voice that brought his head up. What were the chances? He turned to find Amanda following the old man. Beaming happily, she carried—he could only stare. It was a short bow. And not just any short bow, either. That was a shifter's bow. *Son of a bitch.*

"My lord." The weapons master hurried toward him, one hand fisted over his heart indicating his loyalty as a clansman. "I didn't know you were here. I have your arrows ready."

He looked over the man's head and saw Amanda eyeing him cautiously, clearly not any happier to see him than he was her. Their paths hadn't crossed much since that day in the testing room, and when they did, they both went out of their way to avoid speaking to each other. For his part, he carried some residual guilt over the way he'd handled things. In the final analysis, however, and despite many things he admired about her, she was still a complication, and he had plenty of those already.

She gave him a polite nod of recognition and returned her attention to the bow in her hands, drawing it experimentally. And didn't she look damn fine doing it, too? She had always been a beautiful woman, but the last few months of training had only made her stronger, more graceful in the controlled way that spoke of physical discipline. Still, he was surprised she could draw the bow at all. He ran his gaze up and down the curved wood and frowned.

He crossed the room in three long strides. "Amanda," he said, by way of greeting.

She looked up, her expression reflecting surprise that he'd approached her. "Rhodry?"

"May I?" he asked, indicating the bow. Her fingers tightened fractionally, and she met his eyes for a long moment before she released it to him.

"Of course," she said.

He had to fight back a smile at her forced courtesy as he lifted the bow and examined it carefully from tip to tip, then balanced it on the palm of one hand. He didn't say anything, just turned to the old weapons master who was standing behind him looking distinctly uncomfortable. The old man tried to meet his stare, and couldn't hold it. Instead, he hurried forward with a distressed look on his face and took the bow from Rhodry's outstretched palm.

"What is this?" the man said, fretfully. "No, this can't be right." He lifted it in both of his hands, bending it slightly, mimicking the bend of an archer's draw. "How did I not see this? Lady, I don't know what to say. I am desolate —" The man shook his head in a very convincing act of dismay. "Forgive me. One moment, please."

Rhodry watched the man scurry back into his workshop, then turned to find Amanda staring at him, one eyebrow raised cynically.

"I take it I was just about to be rooked?"

He shrugged. "You're a woman. He probably assumed the bow was a gift for a husband or a brother. Something to use on an annual hunting trip, maybe. It would have been fine for that."

"No." She shook her head. "I told him what it was for."

"Then he probably didn't believe you," he said drily.

She looked away. "Or he figured it didn't matter," she said on a sigh.

A shadow of exhaustion crossed her face, and he felt a tug of something more than just guilt. Sympathy maybe, or genuine care for her. Neither of which he wanted to feel. He was saved from having to respond when the old man emerged once again, bearing a new bow in his hands, this one made of a bronze wood that had been rubbed to a ruddy glow. It was a beautiful piece of work, sized for a young shifter. Like the other, it was too short for someone as big as Rhodry, which made it perfect for her.

The old man held it out to him, and he glanced at her for

permission. "Go ahead," she said resignedly, acknowledging his greater knowledge in this at least.

He took the bow, weighing it carefully. He bent the wood gently, then slipped on the gut string and let the bow grow taut. Turning toward the front of the shop, he drew it experimentally. Satisfied, he handed it to her.

Her eyebrows lifted.

"It is *your* weapon," he explained.

She tilted her head in acknowledgment and took the bow from him, repeating his testing motions. When she raised her arms to aim the bow, he saw a flash of bandages beneath her long sleeves, stained red with blood. He sniffed discreetly. The blood was fresh. He frowned as he watched her unstring the weapon and run her hands reverently over the gleaming wood.

"It's beautiful," she said softly.

"A perfect match," the weapons master said proudly. "As if it was made for your hands."

"Yes," Rhodry drawled meaningfully.

The old clansman pretended not to hear as he slipped the string off the bow end and let it slide loosely down the back. "I'll package those extra strings for you, my lady. And the arrows we discussed." He hurried into the back room once again.

"What happened to your arms?" Rhodry demanded in a low voice once they were alone.

She shied away from him, tugging her sleeves down. "It's nothing."

"It's not nothing," he insisted. "You're bleeding."

She blushed a dark pink beneath her tan, and he felt something twist in his gut once more. Definitely not sympathy this time. She gave him an angry look that he knew came at least partly from embarrassment.

"I'll take care of it," she insisted.

"You should see a doctor—"

"My mother is chief medical officer for an entire fleet, de Mendoza. I think I can handle a simple scratch."

He met her defiant stare, his mouth tightening in irritation. Whatever had happened to her arms, it wasn't a scratch, and it sure as hell wasn't simple. And why did he care? As she said, her mother was a damn doctor. If anyone knew the dangers of infection on Harp, it was Amanda. And besides, she wanted to be a Guild member, didn't she? That meant being capable of seeing to her own injuries.

"Fine," he said, with a tilted nod of his head.

"Fine," she repeated.

The weapons master hurried up to them carrying her new bow and a wrapped package which was the right shape to be a quiver and arrows, as well as a few extra strings. Amanda took the package, tucked it under one arm, slung the bow over her shoulder and, with a nod of thanks to the old man and another to Rhodry, she left the shop. The doorbell chimed merrily at her back.

He turned back to his fellow clansman.

"My apologies, my lord," the old man said, and he grimaced, his gaze casting about the store, as if hoping to find the words he needed among his many weapons. Finally, he just blurted it out. "She is a woman, and an Earther!"

"She intends to enter the Guild trials."

The old man gave him a look of disbelief. "So she told me. Surely she won't succeed!"

"And when she fails, do you want it to be because of the

bow you sold her?"

He looked away, unable to meet Rhodry's eyes.

"You've been too long in this city, old friend," he said gently. "You should visit your home in the mountains more often." He put his hand on the man's shoulder. "You didn't give her my arrows, did you?" he asked, lightening the mood.

The old clansman looked up at that, his eyes twinkling. "Of course not, my lord. I'll get them straight away." He hurried off, and Rhodry stepped over to the window, watching Amanda disappear down the street. He remembered what Fionn had said about her, that she'd do better than anyone expected. And he wondered if, in this case, the irritating prince might not be right.

Chapter Fourteen

Winter was coming. That's all anyone seemed to want to talk about lately. The fleet had rediscovered Harp in the middle of summer, with the weather mild and the days still long.

Now summer was gone, and fall was drawing to an end, and Amanda found herself sitting in an outdoor café, watching the people of Harp go crazy. At least that's what it seemed like. Harpers were normally friendly and easygoing, along with very hardworking. They'd made a go of it on the difficult planet and slowly progressed to the point where life wasn't a constant struggle. The absence of technology, which was enforced by their erratic sun and isolation from the rest of humanity, still kept life at a slower pace, however. And the city of Ciudad Vaquero rolled up the sidewalks when the sun went down, except in summer apparently, when restaurants and stores stayed open a whole hour later.

Which made it even more remarkable that tonight the

sidewalks weren't rolling up at all. It was the last blast before winter, an annual celebration that brought the population out in force. Every restaurant and bar, from the tiniest five-seater to the big restaurant on the edge of the Green was lit up like a laser array. Even the palace up on the hill was glowing. She figured the entire city must have been storing up solar energy all year just to power this one holiday. And that didn't count the candles burning on every table, carefully shielded within glass pillars in deference to the surrounding forest.

Everywhere she looked there was dancing, drinking and general merriment. The celebration had its origins in the early days of the colony, when winter had meant being cooped inside for months at a time. The fact that this was no longer true had absolutely no effect on the holiday spirit.

"Where's Fionn?"

She glanced over at Tonio who was sitting across the table from her. His pretty wife, Nadia, sat on his lap, her big pregnant belly dwarfing her diminutive frame. "He'll be here," Amanda said. "He's always late, you know that."

He snorted. "I don't know what you see in that guy."

Nadia laughed gaily and said, "That's because you don't have the right equipment between your legs."

"You've never complained about my equipment before."

She only laughed harder and placed a big wet kiss on his mouth. "I love your equipment, sweetheart." She placed her hand over his on her swollen belly. "Although if this one doesn't pop out soon, I might be less fond of it the next time."

"Fionn's only a friend," Amanda said quickly, wanting to set the record straight. When they both looked at her, she changed the subject. "Boy or girl?" she asked Nadia.

"A big shifter boy, by all that's holy," Nadia replied,

shaking her head. "I swear this child will weigh more than I do by the time he's born."

She smiled at the two of them, so happy with their baby shifter on the way.

"There's his highness now," Tonio said, nodding behind her.

She looked over her shoulder and saw Fionn walking through the crowd, trailed by the ever-present Nando. She knew the other shifter well enough. He was always friendly when Fionn was around, and politely cool when their paths crossed without him. He was a classic sycophant, and she wondered what Fionn saw in him.

She knew what Nando saw in Fionn, however. He drew the eye of every woman he passed and every man as well. It wasn't just his looks, it was his personality, and, of course, who he was and what he could do for them. He claimed to grow tired of it. She didn't believe him. Fionn came to life in a crowd. He loved the attention, regardless of how much he complained about it. She stood up to greet him, shaking her head as he was waylaid yet again by a small group of admirers. Looking around idly as she waited, she caught sight of Rhodry sitting alone at a table on the edge of the café. He had a glass of wine at hand and was reading a book. She glanced over at Fionn, who was still engaged in conversation, then turned quickly to Tonio and Nadia. "I'll be right back," she said and walked over to Rhodry's table.

"Happy whatever you all call this celebration, de Mendoza," she said in greeting.

He looked up, then tucked his book under one arm and stood, his golden eyes gleaming in the candlelight. He smiled slightly. "We don't call it anything. We just enjoy the party."

The waiter came by, and Rhodry handed him some money with murmured thanks.

"Are you still training?" he asked her.

"Of course. I have a lot of catching up to do."

"So you remain determined to enter the trials," he concluded, not bothering to mask his disapproval.

"Tell me something," she said impatiently. "Why are all of you so opposed to me even giving it a try? The worst that can happen is that I'll fail and prove all of you right. So where's the downside?"

"Maybe some of us are worried that you'll get hurt," he said, his eyes meeting hers solemnly.

She found herself caught in the grip of that golden gaze, unable to look away. Her heart raced, and it was suddenly hard to breathe. She took a step closer and rested one hand lightly on his broad chest.

"Is that why *you*—" she started to say.

"Amanda!" Fionn's voice carried across the crowds, cutting her off and drawing everyone's attention, which was probably what he'd intended.

Her head swiveled, her hand slipping away from Rhodry's chest. She waved. "I'll be right there," she called, and turned back...to find Rhodry was gone. If it wasn't for the faint, leftover sensation of his shirt on her fingertips, she might have thought he'd never been there at all. She searched the restaurant and the trees beyond. There was no sign of him, of course. There wouldn't be. Not if he'd headed into the forest, which he probably had.

"Damn that man," she cursed softly. Though, she might as well have been cursing herself. Why couldn't she let him go? Especially since she'd never had him in the first place.

It wasn't as if Harp had a shortage of beautiful men. So why did she have to go and fixate on the one guy with…*issues*? Whatever the fuck they were.

She sighed in disappointment. She'd hoped to at least thank him again for his help with the weapons master. She'd been practicing with her new bow, and even her unskilled hands could tell the difference between the one the old man had originally given her and the fine piece of craftsmanship she now owned.

And even if she hadn't trusted her *own* assessment, Fionn's stunned reaction upon seeing the new bow had told her everything she'd needed to know. Fionn, her good buddy who'd never told her about the master's shop, even though the old man had confided proudly to her that the Ardrigh and his son bought all of their weapons there.

Amanda had wasted all of two minutes being disappointed in him, and then moved on. Fionn was who he was. And so was Rhodry. Even though he disapproved of what she was doing, he'd stepped in to help her. She figured it had gone against his sense of fair play for the weapons master to cheat her. Just as he'd made a point of proctoring the exam the day she'd taken it. She wanted to believe he did all of these things because he cared about her. If only she could be sure that was it.

"Amanda." Fionn's voice was closer, impatient.

"That's my name," she said drily, as she turned to greet him. "You're late."

"I'm always late, and you love me anyway."

"Why is that?"

"Because I'm loveable."

"Not that, you idiot. Why are you always late?"

"You're in a mood. De Mendoza has that effect on people."

Expecting to hear another one of Fionn's charming excuses for his habitual lateness, she was only half listening, still brooding about Rhodry, and about what he'd said.

"Are you worried about me?" she asked Fionn abruptly, pulling him to a stop as they threaded through the crowded restaurant to their table.

"Worried about you how?" he asked in confusion.

"About the trials. Are you worried about me?"

"Not really. I'm convinced you'll come to your senses long before then."

"Great. Thanks."

"Come on," he said, giving her a hug that included rubbing his face against her neck like a big cat leaving his scent. It was typical shifter behavior for a lover, which he decidedly was not.

"Stop it," she murmured. He knew she didn't like when he did that. They weren't lovers and weren't going to be in the future, either. He just liked to show off in front of the crowd, letting them think he'd claimed her for himself. Not because she was desirable. Because she was one of a kind, the only Earther female on the planet. A rare collector's piece to be trotted out and showed off to strangers. She pushed him away firmly. She didn't want to embarrass him or herself any further.

"You *are* in a mood," he said, pulling her over to the table and urging her to sit. "Why don't I get us a drink. Sweeten you up a little." He didn't wait for an answer, simply gestured to Nando, and headed off toward the bar, while running the usual gauntlet of well-wishers to get there.

"That could take a while," Tonio observed.

"Why don't you help him," Nadia said, scooting off his lap and onto her own chair. "I could really use a fruit juice, and the waiter is nowhere to be seen."

"I think Nando can—" Tonio caught the look on his wife's face. "Sure thing," he said instead. "You want anything in particular?"

She shook her head. "As long as it's fresh. You know what I like."

"Besides me, you mean?"

"Go away."

Amanda tilted her head curiously at Nadia as he walked away. Nadia knew full well that the waiters would pay plenty of attention to them once Fionn sat at the table.

The other woman smiled at her. "I wanted a minute alone."

"I figured."

"Amanda…"

She braced herself for another lecture about why she should give up her pipe dream of Guild membership. It seemed a popular theme tonight.

"I know the guys are all after you to quit," Nadia said.

"Tonio doesn't say much."

"No, he wouldn't. He's a sweetie like that. I heard what Fionn just said to you, though, and I know he's not the only one."

She didn't say anything, just waited.

Nadia's hand stroked over her belly absently. "I just wanted you to know that there are some of us who applaud what you're doing. Women mostly. We don't want to join the Guild or anything. We also don't see any reason why you shouldn't be able to try. Does the possibility of one woman in their precious Guild threaten them that much?

It's ridiculous."

While it might have been nicer if Nadia hadn't felt the need to express her support in secret, she still took heart in knowing that not everyone was against her.

"Wait, you said *mostly* women. Are there shifters who agree—?"

"Oh, no," Nadia said quickly. "I mean, sure, one or two like Tonio who have a live-and-let-live philosophy in most things. I didn't mean them. There are a few non-shifter guys who'd like a chance, and they figure you're blasting through a door they won't have to open later on."

She had a moment of panic. This was exactly what she *didn't* want to happen. The few shifters who didn't hate her already certainly would if they found out there were other norms who hoped to follow once she'd forged the way.

"Look, Nadia, I'm not trying to change—"

"Good thing, darling," Fionn drawled, dropping down next to her. "Because my mind's made up. This is your first Harp celebration, and we're making the most of it. We've got drink," he said, setting a trio of glasses on the table. "Now we need food, lots of food. I'm starving."

"What else is new?" Nadia quipped. "You guys are always starving. My little guy isn't even born yet, and he's got me eating all the time."

Amanda sat quietly as her friends ordered the enormous amounts of food shifters routinely consumed. She had other thoughts on her mind tonight. Old worries and new. Mostly thoughts of the coming winter, and of the spring to follow. She had four months until the trials resumed, four months to prepare for the biggest challenge of her life.

And that wasn't nearly long enough.

Chapter Fifteen

Amanda leaned against the tree trunk, her cheek crushed to its rough surface, arms outstretched as though to embrace the ancient wood. It was warm against her skin and she closed her eyes, imagining the tree as the living thing it was—sap flowing like blood through its veins, its branches like arms stretched out to the sky, almost touching, always reaching.

"What are you doing, Amanda?"

She jerked upright, startled and embarrassed at being caught unaware. She pushed away from the tree, feeling her face flush. "What do you want, Fionn?"

His laughter drifted down from above, and she tipped her head back trying to find him in the dense clutter of the canopy. The foliage was thick enough, or he was traveling high enough, that she couldn't see him, and she hadn't been tuned in to the trees enough to pick up his presence.

"Just passing through, darling," he teased. "I thought you might have fainted."

"Very funny," she said, sitting down to rummage in her pack. There was no point in straining her neck trying to find him if he didn't want to be found.

"Shouldn't you be getting ready?" His voice drifted from somewhere deep among the trees. "Tonight's the big night."

He meant the Founders Ball. The annual celebration to recognize the men and women who'd survived that catastrophic landing, the ones who'd taken on the unknown planet and made it work. It was the rite of spring, a two-day festival that culminated in a huge elegant ball at the Ardrigh's palace. The ball was the most sought-after invitation of the Harp year, a chance for the ladies to break out their finery for the new season. There would be music and dancing, with servers and footmen and all the beautiful people. Her mother would have loved it. She, on the other hand, not so much.

"Amanda?" Fionn's impatient voice from above reminded her that he was waiting for an answer.

"You're the one who should be getting ready," she said. "Your mother's probably worried by now," she added in a mutter, knowing he'd hear it. Shifters had very good hearing.

"She knows I'll be there," he replied dismissively. "Besides, there's plenty of time for me to get dressed. It's you ladies who need extra time to primp."

She wasn't interested, although…she wondered if Rhodry was going to be there. He might be worth a little primping.

"Come on, everyone's going."

Would Fionn tell her if *everyone* included Rhodry? Probably not.

There was a crashing noise in the branches of a tree behind her, followed by the unmistakable sound of lethal claws on rough bark. The noise was intentional. Like every other shifter, Fionn could move through the trees in perfect silence when he wanted to. She spun around and waited.

Moments later, he strolled toward her—barefoot, wearing only a pair of baggy cloth pants that hung loosely on his narrow hips. His long, golden blond hair tangled loosely over broad shoulders, and turquoise eyes sparkled with laughter.

She sighed. There was no question that a half-naked Fionn was a lovely sight. So why was she far more interested in seeing a certain other shifter in all of his naked glory? Especially when the chances of that seemed pretty slim.

"So, you'll be there tonight?" he asked.

"Maybe. It's not like you'll be wanting for partners, and I need a good night's sleep. Tomorrow's the—"

"The trials," he interrupted with obvious impatience. "Gods forbid I should forget the precious trials. That doesn't mean you can't spend one damn hour dancing with me."

"Maybe," she repeated, not at all surprised by his attitude. Fionn would never understand why she was so determined to become a Guild member. After the months she'd spent training, he no longer doubted her determination, and he still didn't approve. Maybe it was what Rhodry had said, maybe Fionn was worried about her, too. He did care for her in his own self-centered way.

They both looked up as a sudden flurry of birds taking flight had the trees rattling violently. The distinctive eerie wail of a banshee followed, quickly answered by another and another until the forest was alive with the creepy sounds. It was banshees those fleet personnel had been hunting when they'd triggered the catastrophic explosion which had hastened the fleet's departure. The animals looked somewhat like an Earth monkey, with prehensile tails and long gripping toes. They also had the vicious, ripping teeth and long, knife-sharp claws of a carnivore and their diet was almost exclusively meat.

"Unusual to have a pack so close to the city these days."

She spun at the sound of Nando's voice. He'd come up so quietly behind her that she hadn't noticed, though Fionn would have.

"Amanda," Nando greeted her politely.

"Hey, Nando. Guess you guys are going hunting."

Fionn gave a scowling glance upward, and said, "We have to check it out. We're on perimeter patrol." He gave her braid a hard tug. A little *too* hard. He was making a point. "Be there tonight, Amanda."

Before she could protest, he was stripped and shifted, a golden blur of motion as he followed Nando, who was already out of sight. She heard a faint scrape of claws as one of them took to a tree and climbed rapidly, and then nothing.

She stared after them, envying Fionn's liquid grace, his shifter ability to climb trees as easily as she climbed stairs. She scolded herself for still dreaming the impossible and turned instead to a different dream, one that was about to become reality. So what if she didn't have a shifter's fur or claws? The Green spoke to her, and tomorrow she would become the first non-shifter, and the first female, ever to undertake the Guild's final trials. It was her big day. She had a lot to get done tonight before she slept. And none of it involved putting on a dress and dancing at the Founders Ball.

Chapter Sixteen

Amanda bounced out of her sleepless bed, and walked over to stoke the coals in her fireplace. She'd kept the heat to a minimum over the last few weeks, in order to prepare her body for the possibility of freezing nights during her trial. It would all depend on where she ended up for the final, and most arduous, phase.

She stood and headed for her oversize closet to check her supplies one more time, even though she knew everything was there. She should be sleeping. Tomorrow would be one hell of a day, and she'd need her wits about her. Good advice, if she hadn't been way too hyped for sleep.

She glanced up in surprise when someone knocked heavily on her front door. No one knocked on her door, not even Fionn. He usually came through the window, which was why she kept her shutters locked. She lifted her heavy robe from the hook and pulled it on over her panties, which was all she usually wore to bed.

It occurred to her to ask who it was before opening the door, but she had no enemies on Harp. None who were stupid enough to knock on her door before trying to kill her anyway.

She lifted the latch and opened the door, staring in surprise to see Rhodry standing there.

"Amanda," he said, smiling a little as he took in the bulky robe.

"Rhodry. Come in." She swallowed the *I guess* that tried to slip onto the end of that greeting. If she'd known he was going to pay her a visit, she'd have worn something else. And maybe at least brushed her hair.

"You didn't go to the Founders Ball?" she asked, struggling to find something to say as she made room for him to step inside, and closed the door behind him.

"I did," he replied, indicating the elegant clothes he was wearing. "It was boring."

That startled a laugh out of her. "No music this time?" she joked, thinking about that long-ago night when they'd danced, and done...other things.

He shrugged. "There was music, but you weren't there to dance with."

"Oh," she said softly, heat creeping up her neck. That was sweet. And very unlike him. What was he up to?

He glanced around her apartment, his survey lingering on her piles of supplies just visible through the bedroom door. "You're packing all of that?"

He walked over to her bedroom closet, and she followed, stepping carefully over the cluttered floor.

She looked around, trying to see it the way he might. "I'm just taking inventory so far," she told him, realizing it looked like *a lot* of supplies. "I want to be sure I don't forget to pack anything."

"Candidates don't normally carry backpacks," he said drily. "It's rather the point of the trial."

She narrowed her eyes at him. Was that why he was here? To talk her out of doing this? Or at least to try, because that ship had sailed long ago. She leaned over and grabbed the bedroll she'd prepared, then spoke without looking at him. "Do you think they'll at least let me take a bedroll? I don't have any fur to keep me warm, although I suppose—"

"The final phase will be no different for you than any other," he said with unexpected sharpness.

She turned and frowned up at him in surprise. "Of course not. I wouldn't expect it." Which was the truth, although perhaps not all of it. She *had* hoped the trial judge would permit some practical concessions to her human form, like a damn bedroll for warmth. Not that it mattered. She would do without if she had to.

"I don't like this, Amanda."

"Don't like what?" she demanded, letting a bit of anger sharpen her own words. "That I'm about to sully your wonderful Guild? Or is it because I'm an Earther?"

He tsked impatiently. "I don't care about those things, but I don't want you to get killed doing something you don't have to, either. This final trial is dangerous, and I'm not sure you appreciate just how bad it could be."

She regarded him unhappily. What would it take to make him understand?

"My father is an earth witch," she said suddenly. "I never knew that until recently. My mom told me when I decided to stay here."

He gave her a puzzled look. "What's an earth witch?"

"He can make things grow, even in the worst conditions. It's kind of like magic, except it's not. It's a gift, and it's unique to his planet. A very few people in every generation can do what he does."

"Uh-huh. Our farmers can do that, too. It's called fertilizer."

She gaped at him. "I can't believe you! You turn into a giant cat, and that's perfectly normal. But I tell you my dad has a green thumb, and that's too much? What the hell? You think shifters have a monopoly on amazing skills?"

He tipped his head to one side with a little smile. "You think I have amazing skills?"

She rolled her eyes. "You know you do, and you don't need me to flatter you. You get enough of that every day."

"Not as much as you think," he muttered. "So Dad's an earth witch. What's that got to do with your determination to get yourself killed?"

"I'm not—" she started angrily, then stopped. "What I'm saying is that I think that's the reason I can hear the trees. I inherited my dad's affinity for growing things."

He listened thoughtfully. "You might be right," he agreed. "But I don't see how growing things will keep you alive in the Green."

She gritted her teeth, wishing she could growl like a shifter. "Look. I've studied, I've prepared. And I've been doing this kind of thing for years, long before I came here. None of you seem to recognize that my life up to this point wasn't spent sitting around a library. Damn it, Rhodry. I thought you of all people understood that."

He studied her unhappily, then shook his head, as if

engaging in an internal conversation with himself. Finally, he said, "I'll leave you to it, then."

"That's it?" she asked, half disappointed and half pissed as hell. "You came over here in the middle of the night to give me this little *pep talk*, and disappear?"

He regarded her for a long moment, and she could almost see the conflict in his pretty golden eyes. She would even have sworn that he leaned toward her the tiniest bit. Would he bend his neck and his principles enough to give her a kiss for luck? A peck on the cheek at least?

The moment didn't last. He unclenched his jaw enough to say, "Good night, Amanda." And then he strode over to the door.

"Wish me luck?" she called to his back, trying to keep her disappointment from showing.

He reached for the doorknob, and stopped. His head bowed for a minute, and she thought she'd won. But then he straightened, and spoke without looking at her. "Good luck, *acushla*," he said, then yanked the door open and was gone, the door closed tight behind him.

"Well, great, Rhodry," she said to the empty room. "Thanks for whatever the hell *that* means."

And then she shoved all thoughts of him down deep where it couldn't hurt anymore, and went back to her preparations for the trials. Which were now less than two hours away.

Chapter Seventeen

Amanda took a last look at her various piles of supplies and began stowing them in her backpack. She had planned for this day so carefully, making and re-making lists, checking with Tonio Garza — who'd volunteered to help her — then starting all over again, uncertain which list was the latest version.

First up today would be the test for proficiency on the bow. It would be challenging, and even after months of practice, she didn't think she'd excel. She'd do well enough to pass, though, which was all that mattered.

It was the next and final part of the trials that had her checking supplies compulsively, while her heart pounded and her nerves twitched. Guild candidates were dropped into the Green, far away from the city, with only fur and claws to get them back to the city. She didn't have those natural defenses, and so had to make other arrangements. There'd been nothing in the rules against carrying a backpack, and although she knew that was because no shifter would ever *need* a backpack, she was going to make the oversight work to her advantage.

She'd be carrying everything she needed on her back. Knives, medicines, a tiny bottle of soap, even a small folding shovel. All of it went into her pack, along with an all-important first aid kit, and a supply of antibiotics. There were also plenty of natural remedies in the forest and she'd made a point of learning them all.

Of course, once in the Green, she'd have access to the same Guild caches the shifters did. In addition to clothing, there were durable supplies and foodstuffs that were placed at regular intervals for use by shifter patrols, and for the rare, occasional traveler. Amanda had also set up her own, somewhat limited, network of caches that were filled with supplies no shifter would ever need and no male would think to include.

With a glance at the time, she began to dress quickly, layering on shirts, socks and even two pairs of leggings. They were all clothes she'd brought with her from the ship, all made of lightweight fabrics that when layered together would keep her warm in anything short of a raging blizzard. They also made her look about ten pounds heavier, and who cared? This was survival, not a beauty contest. Staring at herself in the mirror, she picked up and contemplated her heavy cloak. It had been a gift from her mother, something Elise had found on one of her planetary shopping excursions and bought for Amanda because it was beautiful, rather than practical. Made of thick, sturdy wool, it was full-length and heavy as sin. The sensible choice would be to leave it behind, and she knew she might very well regret the extra weight after a few days out there on her own.

On the other hand, no matter how much her brain might be telling her the lightweight fabrics she'd layered on would keep her warm, there was something about the comforting bulk of the cloak that made her *feel* warmer.

She swore softly and shoved it into her pack on top of everything else. The hell with it. This was all about instinct and her instincts said to take it.

She tugged on her boots and stood up to tie a compact sleeping bag to the bottom of her pack. It didn't look like much—which was why she thought they might let her keep it, even though it was actually designed for much colder temperatures than anything she was likely to encounter. And then, she added one final item. Shifters could see as well in the dark as in full daylight. Amanda had excellent vision…for a norm, which meant her night vision was severely limited, and Harp's forests were full of dark places, even in daytime, when the sunlight sometimes had to fight to reach the ground through the thick canopy. As a result, she always carried a small flashlight, especially if she thought she might get caught out after sunset. Little more than a penlight, it had a halogen beam that was surprisingly bright for its size. She slung it around her neck on a leather string, pulled on her hooded jacket and shoved her gloves into a pocket. She was ready.

Settling the familiar weight of the backpack over her shoulders, she picked up the bow Rhodry had secured for her months ago. She'd put in hundreds of sweat-filled hours building the strength necessary in her arms and hands to use it effectively, and she had the scars on her fingers and forearm to prove it.

The weapon went over one shoulder. She did a final tug

of straps and buckles, and walked out to face the Guild.

When she emerged from her apartment, the sun was barely over the horizon. Up on the hillside, above the main town, the white stone of the palace gleamed gold in the first light of morning, its face so bright that for a few seconds, it was as if twin suns battled for dominance in the Harp sky.

The morning air was fresh and cool as usual, the streets damp from an overnight ground fog that still lingered between the buildings and amid the trees that grew everywhere. Moisture clung to her cheeks and hair, easing wisps of curl out of the tight braid along her neck and washing away the last tendrils of worry. She wanted to run down the streets and shout out her excitement, to wake the neighbors and share the glory of this very special morning. Instead, she slipped unnoticed through the quiet streets.

The science compound was visible from here, a squat, utilitarian building whose concrete walls almost disappeared into the gloom, making the large solar arrays on its roof seem to float in the dense fog.

She took the now-familiar dirt path to the Guild Hall, then stopped short, hanging back among the trees on the edge of the open yard, all of a sudden keenly aware that she was alone. Two shifters crossed the yard while she stood there, and as she watched them disappear into the depths of the hall, she realized how stupid this was. Here she stood, ready to challenge nearly five hundred years of Harp history, and yet too timid to walk into the building in full view. Great. A promising start.

Gathering the courage that had gotten her this far, she turned back toward the path, nearly shrieking out loud when Rhodry was suddenly standing in front of her. She fought to control her reaction. How such a big man could move so quietly...

"Where's Fionn?" he demanded.

She gave him a narrow look. "Well, good morning to you, too. And how the hell would I know where Fionn is?"

"He's your lover. He should be here to walk you in."

She stared at him impatiently. What was it with the men in her life? She didn't have *time* for this crap. "Fionn is *not* my lover," she said with forced slowness. "I don't *have* a lover. You're all way too much work! Besides," she said, trying to get around him. "He hates the idea of me joining your precious Guild, just as much as you do."

He stepped closer, blocking her from leaving. "Amanda, I'm afraid you're going to get hurt," he said quietly.

Her heart sighed at the sincerity in that deep voice. Which only proved that her heart was an idiot. He'd had *months* to have this little heart-to-heart, and suddenly he was knocking on her door in the middle of the night, and waylaying her on *this particular morning*? Oh hell, no. She shrugged, pretending to be unaffected. "A life without risk isn't worth living," she said, cringing inwardly at the trite words.

She waited for him to shut her out like he always did, for the mask to close over his face, and his eyes to go cold. And they didn't. *He* didn't. He just stood there looking so gorgeous, his golden eyes filled with concern. And suddenly it hit her. He was right. They were all right. This trial could kill her.

She dropped her pack to the ground, closed the short distance between them, then went up on her toes and kissed him. She half expected him to reject her. To push her away, or to stand there like a stone. What she didn't expect was for him to band his arms around her, and kiss her back.

It was a ravenous kiss, hungry, like he was a starving man—a starving cat—and she was the last piece of steak in the world. She reveled in the strength of that powerful body, her lips open in welcome, her arms tightening around his neck as the kiss went on and on…

A door slammed from the direction of the Guild Hall, and he broke away sharply, as if she'd suddenly sprouted horns. He stared at her, breathing hard, his massive chest heaving in and out. He licked his lips, and his eyes closed briefly, as if savoring the taste of her.

"You walking her in, Tonio?" he asked, and she spun around in time to see Tonio Garza step out from among the trees.

"You're not?" Tonio asked, seeming surprised.

"My presence won't win her any friends in there," he said, then stepped in close again, his body like a furnace in front of her. He stroked the back of his fingers over her cheek, and said, "Be careful out there, *acushla*. And make sure you come back."

He exchanged an alpha-manly look with Tonio, and then he was gone as silently as he'd arrived.

Great. She didn't know whether to be thrilled at what had been the best kiss of her life, or furious at his lousy timing. Damn him!

"He likes you, you know," Tonio said, with a half grin.

"Yeah? Well, he has a funny way of showing it. What was that about walking me in?"

Tonio strolled over, his long legs covering the ground with that uniquely shifter grace. He slung a friendly arm around her shoulders. "No candidate walks into the Guild

Hall alone. They're accompanied by at least one relative, a male relative obviously."

Rhodry's unexpected appearance took on a whole new meaning. He hadn't wanted her to walk in there alone. "What'd he mean about not winning me any friends?"

Tonio didn't bother asking who *he* was. "Rhodry's a good guy, a *great* hunter. Regrettably, his grandfather made some enemies a while back, and certain people have long memories. Where's Fionn?" he asked, changing the subject.

"You're the second person to ask me that this morning, and I *still* don't know, or why I'm even expected to," she said, grinding her teeth.

He swore beneath his breath. "I assumed that asshole would step up for once. Guess you're stuck with me, huh?"

She should have been pissed at Fionn. He'd known about the tradition, and hadn't cared. And she didn't care, either. His absence was more than made up for by Rhodry's appearance. Even if he wasn't the one walking through the door with her. She gave Tonio a quick hug. "Thanks."

"You ready for this?"

She drew a deep breath and nodded. "I am."

They crossed the clearing and quickly loped up the stairs to the porch. The wide front door stood open, and their soft-soled boots made barely a sound on the smooth planks as they entered the main building. And there her feet stuttered to a halt. She was surprised to find the big hall empty, silence echoing off the tall ceilings where giant tree trunks criss-crossed two stories overhead.

She realized with a start what that meant. Everyone was already outside, waiting for her. She closed her eyes and drew in a fortifying breath, catching the familiar combination of musk and spice that was shifter, and beneath it, the smell of varnish and old wood, slightly musty in the damp morning. Someone had prepared breakfast in the kitchen and her stomach growled. She'd been too nervous to eat anything this morning, making do with a tasteless protein bar, even though this was probably her last chance at a decent meal for days, if not weeks.

She opened her eyes and took in the faded tapestries, the mezzanine circling the second level, its wide bannisters scratched by generations of shifters, and beyond that, the long, dark corridors lined with door after door, marking the rooms where several of the younger shifters lived full-time. They probably had a full house today. The annual trials were a big deal. Visitors would have come in from the mountains and other outlying areas for the event.

She gulped…and started moving again, suddenly in a hurry to get through the silent hall. She stepped out onto the broad back porch, and was glad there was nothing more in her stomach than half a protein bar. The yard was filled with shifters—big, brawny shifters who were all staring at her.

She took the stairs slowly, feeling Tonio at her back, grateful for his support as she surveyed the silent crowd. She knew most of those gathered by sight at least, if not by name. Conversations gradually resumed as she made her way to the judge's table. Some of the shifters she passed acknowledged her. Most simply stared, and even among the friendlier ones, she saw no support for what she was about to do.

Fionn appeared out of the crowd, intent on getting between her and Tonio, but he refused to give ground, regarding Fionn with the thinly veiled hostility so common to interactions among shifters. Fionn's head lowered, his eyes narrowing, and she felt Tonio tense beside her. These testosterone games weren't unusual among the alpha male shifters. She even found them charming sometimes. Today, she had no patience.

She sighed, disgusted, and stepped away from both of them to approach the sign-in table, surprised to find no other candidates in line ahead of her.

"Missed the rush, I guess," she joked to no one in particular.

The judge sitting on the other side was Orrin Brady, the same older shifter who'd approved her initial application way back when. She'd seen him around the Guild Hall since then, but they'd never spoken. He finished whatever he was writing before looking up at her. "The others will come in a month or so. For now, we've just the one, and that would be you, I'm thinking."

She jolted a little in surprise. No one had told her she was being tested separately. She wondered how many had known. As far as she knew, this had never happened in the Guild's history, which fit, because *she'd* never happened before either. She kept a smile on her face with effort. "Well, then," she said. "I'm ready."

"You sure you want to do this, lass?" Orrin said in a low voice. "No one would think less of you if you didn't."

I would think less of me, she wanted to tell him. She kept that defiant thought to herself and simply shook her head. "I'm ready," she repeated.

"Very well," he said on a long sigh. He stood, towering over her, big like they all were, and still strong despite the gray in his braid that made him old enough to be her grandfather. One more genetic bonus from that long-ago ancestor—or maybe this particular gift had come from the science of their human creators. Shifters lived a healthy twenty or thirty years beyond their normal human counterparts.

Orrin lifted a tall ceramic jar from the table. Holding it with two hands, top and bottom, he shook it up and down, making a terrible racket and proving definitively that it wasn't empty. According to custom, the jar was filled with stones in four different colors, each color representing a direction on the map. He stilled the rattling, held the jar in the palm of one big hand and removed the lid with the other before holding it out to her. "Choose your path," he said formally.

She drew a deep breath, cast a wish to the winds in the treetops, and stuck in her hand. She didn't waste time fishing around, just grabbed the first smooth stone her fingers touched, curled her hand into a fist, and pulled it out.

Orrin moved methodically, replacing the lid on the jar, setting it on the table, and then finally stretching out his open hand to her. She held her closed fist over his palm for a beat, and then opened it, watching fixedly as a black stone tumbled out. Orrin closed his fist over the stone in turn, glanced at her quickly, then displayed the stone in two fingers over his head for everyone to see, and said a single word.

"Darkward."

R hodry's jaw tightened almost painfully when he heard that fateful word. All around him, the clearing erupted in a low mutter of speculation, while his eyes remained fixed on Amanda. He'd been watching her from the moment she appeared on the back porch with Tonio Garza looming behind her. He'd seen the brief hesitation in her eyes and in her stance when she'd first stepped outside. He'd also seen her chin lift defiantly before she'd marched directly over to the table as if she had every right to be there. And now she stood calmly, seeming completely unaffected by what anyone else would consider a piece of truly foul luck. It made him wonder if she understood the full ramifications of drawing the black stone.

The format of the final Guild trial was simple. Every candidate chose from the jar of stones, which determined the direction of their trial. Using one of the solar-powered hovercraft, they were escorted deep into the Green until they reached a site that the escort considered sufficiently remote and challenging. Every trial was different, depending on the individual, his weaknesses and strengths, the weather conditions and the luck of the direction chosen. Only one thing was certain—once the candidate was abandoned, he was on his own. Not even the shifters on patrol would help him out, unless it became a matter of life or death. And if it reached that point, the trial was a failure anyway.

Rhodry had been to other trials—his own, of course, and those of his many cousins. And he knew the Hall was usually a lively place while everyone waited for the candidates to straggle back in. Guild members would come and go, food and drink would be plentiful, and betting was not uncommon. It was more spirited than usual with Amanda's trial, which the powers that be had apparently decided to single out from the others. Even shifters with homes in the city were hanging around.

The betting odds against her would skyrocket now

that she'd drawn the least favorable of the four possible directions. Darkward meant north toward the glacier.

Cold, inhospitable and, depending on how far north one traveled, never feeling the warmth of direct sunlight, the glacier was buried beneath a layer of ice deeper than anyone had ever bothered to measure. She wouldn't be going as far as the glacier itself; the trial candidates were always dropped inside the Green, since the goal was to test them, not kill them. Nonetheless, it would be much colder and far more challenging than it would have been if she'd drawn another direction.

He eyed her woefully inadequate clothing. High-tech fibers or not, she'd need more than what he could see if she was going to stay warm.

His thoughts were interrupted by the sound of movement, as shifters shuffled to form a rough circle around her. He'd seen shifter candidates quail at this point. Not Amanda. She raised her chin and forced a smile onto her face, meeting their scrutiny without flinching.

"Darkward it is," Orrin said from behind her.

"Should have fattened up a bit, lass, keep you warmer. You're with the big boys now," someone taunted. The others laughed and she laughed with them. It was all part of the ritual, subjecting the candidate to insults and verbal challenges before he—or for the first time, she—set out. "Will you put ribbons in your braid then, little girl?" someone else shouted.

Rhodry frowned at the foolishness of their so-called insults. They expected her to fail, and their taunts reflected that. He knew Amanda better than they did. She wouldn't cave after the first cold night, she'd push herself until something truly catastrophic happened, and by then it might be too late.

"Do the trees sing to you?" he demanded. It was the only question that truly mattered. The one that could mean the difference between life and death, and it dropped into the crowd of shifters like a stone, spreading an uneasy silence rippling outward. It was the issue on everyone's mind, the one never before raised in a trial, because every shifter could hear the trees from the moment his heart first beat in the womb.

A manda recognized Rhodry's voice, and her stupid heart raced when she found his face in the crowd. He stood there watching her with those beautiful golden eyes. The shifters she'd met all had some trace of the cat's gold in their eyes when in human form, usually flecks or streaks. She'd never met another shifter with eyes that were pure gold like his, eyes that were staring at her, waiting for an answer. And she didn't flinch.

"They sing to me in strong voices," she responded, loudly enough for everyone in the yard to hear her. "Before I ever set foot on the planet, from the moment I hit atmosphere, they sang their joys and sorrows. They sing to me now, calling me to join them."

Those golden eyes never wavered, his closed expression telling her everything she needed to know. He *knew* she could hear the trees, and he still doubted she could do it. That infuriated her more than anything he could have said, more than any imagined hurt that his reluctance might have caused. She stared back at him, daring him to challenge her.

"How about your claws, Amanda? Show us your claws." Tonio's familiar voice broke the standoff, and she blew her breath out in a long release, unaware until then that she'd been holding it. She glanced to the right, smiling. "I've claws enough to handle you, Tonio," she said, to loud guffaws of laughter.

"Forget the claws, I'd like to see her fur," someone muttered loud enough to be heard, and an entirely different sort of male laughter filled the clearing.

"Better check with your wife first, Nando." That was Fionn, and his voice had a hard edge to it. He was still angry from his earlier confrontation with Tonio, or maybe just not happy at the sexual suggestion in Nando's jest. Whatever the reason, it silenced the crowd of shifters for good.

"A weak effort, lads," Orrin chided. "Let's get to it."

The circle opened up until the only thing between Amanda and the trees was dirt. She dropped her pack to the ground and swung her bow around, sliding a single arrow from her quiver with the same motion. Orrin looked at her in question and she nodded, nocking the arrow in preparation.

The shifters standing at her back grew perfectly still as the judge drew his arm back and then threw it forward in a powerful motion, releasing the small black pebble to fly toward the trees.

It was a tiny missile, the black difficult to see in the misty light. She'd practiced endlessly for just this moment, figuring out a way to compensate for her less than shifter reflexes. Concentrating on the likely target area rather than trying to follow the pebble itself, she narrowed her field of focus, and almost panicked, finally catching sight of the black just before it hit a middle-aged conifer. Its base was a good twelve feet around, which made for a nice fat target. The only challenge would be to hit at or very close to the actual spot where the rock had impacted the bark. And every shifter in the yard knew that spot within a quarter inch.

Never taking her eyes away from the tree trunk, visually marking the barely discernible gouge of pale wood where the black rock had hit, she drew in a breath and held it, then drew the arrow back until her fist brushed her cheek. Someone coughed loudly, trying to break her concentration, and Orrin growled his unhappiness.

She ignored them all, hearing only the soft movement of morning fog through the leaves as she trained her sights on the distant target.

She let her breath out slowly and released. Her arrow flew across the yard, quills whisking the air, the trajectory arching slightly as it passed through the surrounding trees to hit the target dead on. Spontaneous cheers erupted from the gathered shifters, and she heard Tonio shouting her name in triumph. Even those who opposed her were unable to restrain their reaction to the perfect shot. Money changed hands as bets were paid with equal measures of laughter and chagrin.

She sagged in relief, not looking at anyone, feeling her shoulders twitch with adrenaline as she unstrung her bow and slipped it back over her shoulder.

When she finally raised her head, Orrin met her gaze with a smile. "Nice shot, lass," he said.

She grinned. "Thanks."

He gave her a short nod and shouted, "Let's do it, lads." The yard filled with purposeful movement as the shifters detailed to escort her clambered up the stairs and back inside the Guild Hall to gather up their weapons and gear.

Having nothing to do other than wait at this point, she leaned back on the table and stared at her own boots, trying to seem cool and collected when what she really wanted was to jump up and down with excitement. That shot had been perfect, everything she'd dreamed it could be. She could still see the arrow flying across the yard to the target as if connected by a wire.

There should have been someone with her, someone with whom she could share the absolute exhilaration of this moment. Someone like... She snuck a glance in Rhodry's direction, curious about his reaction, and saw the big, golden-eyed shifter facing off with several others, including Fionn. They were all yelling at each other, occasionally gesturing in her direction, and she thought for a moment they would come to blows, until Orrin intervened, snapping a few words that broke up whatever had almost happened. Fionn slanted a look her way with no expression and disappeared into the trees. He was carrying his gear, and she wondered if he was on her escort detail. Not that it mattered either way. He wouldn't do her any favors. He'd made that much perfectly clear.

"Last chance," Orrin said from behind her.

She stood and turned. "No, thanks," she said sincerely. "I've waited for this a long time."

"Your choice then." He nodded at someone over her shoulder.

She didn't spin quickly enough to see who it was. The needle slipped smoothly into her arm through layers of clothing and she collapsed into the judge's waiting arms.

Chapter Eighteen

Amanda woke with a start, rolled over, and retched violently. She bit back a groan when bile came up to burn her throat and nose, while doing nothing to relieve the unbearable nausea roiling her stomach. It was the drugs causing it, the ones her shifter escort were using to keep her sedated while they flew her out to the drop-off point. The journey so far had been a matter of days, rather than hours. She'd expected that. The hovers weren't all that swift, and even shifter candidates—who could travel much faster than she could—often took a week or two to make their way back to the Guild Hall.

She'd also expected them to take into account her human metabolism when choosing which drug to sedate her with. As awful as she was feeling, it seemed likely that they'd chosen the drug that would make her as sick as possible, rather than the opposite. She'd tried to tell them on their first stop for the night. They'd only laughed and asked if she wanted to quit. It was Fionn's good buddy Nando who'd laughed the loudest, and who'd gone so far as to suggest she'd gotten herself pregnant, and was looking for a convenient excuse to bow out of the trial.

It was such an asshole thing to say—and something of a surprise coming from the shifter who'd always been polite to her. No wonder they'd wanted Rhodry off her escort team. He'd never have gone along with something like this, no matter how much he opposed what she was doing. She wished he was here now, so she could point out to him just how *honorable* his fellow guildsmen were. Maybe she was just what they needed. A little dose of reality to remind them that they didn't, in fact, rule the entire universe.

Regardless, however, she'd stopped talking to any of them after that, suffering in silence, eating and drinking as little as possible, and then only foods she thought would stay down, vomiting discreetly when nothing did.

Orrin Brady had shown up at some point, his eyes full of kind sincerity when he asked if she was perhaps truly sick and did she possibly want to delay her trial. She hadn't been tempted even a little. Maybe if they'd played fair with her, she would have taken Brady's offer and gone for a second try. She simply couldn't let them get away with cheating. Besides which, there was no guarantee she'd get a second opportunity, no matter what Brady said. And even if she did, her failure this first time out would be held against her for the rest of her life, and they were likely to pull the same trick on a second trial. She didn't know what they were giving her; she *did* know that there were plenty of drugs available that wouldn't have made her so sick.

She fell back on the hard ground and lay perfectly still,

staring at the sky visible through skeletal branches overhead. There was a faint breeze blowing. It was cold, and wonderfully fresh. She sucked in a deep breath and had to roll over again as she began to cough uncontrollably, her face buried in her arms. Dry leaves and dirt scratched her nose, shifting slightly as she experimented with slower, shallower breathing. That helped. Eyes closed, she listened to the world around her, trying to locate the shifters of her escort. What little light she'd seen was pale enough for morning, which meant they'd probably already cleared the campsite and were sitting back waiting for her, laughing at her wretchedness. She was only surprised they'd given her this extra time to recover.

She frowned and listened harder, hearing only the steady pounding of her own pulse, throbbing in time with her aching head. She turned on her back again and opened her eyes, squinting against the sun, which was almost directly overhead. She froze, staring for a moment before the realization hit her.

This was it. Her escort was gone, and the bastards had left her lying unconscious, vulnerable to whatever creature happened to pass by.

Her heart raced. She sat up slowly, pulling her legs up to her chest and resting her head on her knees. She was grateful to be alone at last, even if she was so sick that all she wanted to do was curl up in a ball and let the world go away for a few hours. Unfortunately, she didn't have that luxury. If she was on her own, she didn't have a few hours. She needed to get her act together right now, figure out where she was, and get moving. Night fell early in the north.

Squinting blurry eyes against the thin light, she spied her

gear stacked a few feet away, leaning up against the trunk of a spindly yearling tree. She'd be able to think more clearly once she got rid of the awful taste in her mouth.

Standing was beyond her wobbly legs at this point, so she crawled slowly and carefully over the dry, scratchy ground. It was icy cold beneath her bare hands almost as if...

She sat back on her heels and took a good look around for the first time. And then she used every filthy word she'd ever learned to curse Nando Vaquero, his shifter buddies, and then just shifters in general for good measure. Even Rhodry. The land stretched out around her, flat and barren, except for a few clumps of scruffy trees, their limbs almost completely bare of foliage. Trunks were bent and bowed toward the ground, permanently deformed by the gale force winds blowing off the glacier...which was where they'd left her.

Her escort hadn't only taken her northward, they'd taken her all the way to the glacier and left her there. The ground she was sitting on was cold because it was frozen nearly solid most of the year. Even now, little pockets of icy snow that never melted lay in the hollows between the tree roots where the sun never reached. Looking further north, there was ice and snow as far as her eyes could see. To the south, she could barely make out a dark band of trees between the pale horizon and the sky.

An unfamiliar quiver of concern pinched her stomach. That distant band was the Green. She wasn't in the Green, she was well beyond it. There weren't even patrols out this far, because there was no reason for them. She had no idea how long it would take on foot to get back to the city from here. Several weeks probably, especially traveling alone and with no supplies.

Her first instinct was to be angry, no, *furious*. She'd read every account she could find of the Guild trials and there'd been nothing about a candidate being dumped this far away, and never on the glacier. Any lingering expectations of fairness she might have had with regard to her treatment during this phase of the trial disappeared, replaced by a steely determination. She'd spent months getting ready for this, sacrificing every other aspect of her life, following all of their arbitrary rules, competing in a system where every single test was weighted against her.

She stared at that distant tree line. *Fuck 'em*. If that's how they wanted to play it, then fuck every one of them. If they owed nothing to her, then she owed nothing to them either. She'd pass their stupid trial, and she'd do it on her own terms.

She twisted around to her backpack, and found they'd left it sitting right on top of the flare given to every candidate in case of emergency. Hold it up, pop the cap and it would send up a signal visible for miles. A signal that would write her failure across the sky.

"In your dreams, assholes," she muttered, then crawled over and tossed the flare aside with a derisive snort.

Snagging the strap, she pulled the pack closer and felt her heart sink into her toes. She could tell by the weight, and by its nearly flat aspect, that the pack was almost empty. After all the time spent planning and packing everything just right…she felt a weary sort of resignation as she flipped it open.

The first thing she saw was her cloak. She pulled the familiar brown cloth out and buried her face in it, letting the scents of home soothe her. Then she put it down and took stock of her remaining gear. Her sleeping bag was still there, tied to the bottom of the pack, its thin aspect apparently fooling her shifter escort into believing it was useless. Either that, or they'd left it for the same reason they left the cloak. Maybe leaving her to freeze to death crossed some inexplicable line for them. Drugging her, dumping her on the glacier, that was all okay, but not freezing. Assholes.

Back to the inventory... Her bow and the quiver of arrows remained, and her belt knife was still in its sheath. Everything else was gone. Everything. She lifted her head and stared into the empty distance for a few minutes, thinking, then slapped her hands on her thighs decisively and said, "Right. Let's get started then."

Dropping back onto her butt, she pulled off her boots, first one, then the other. Tucked into each, in a specially made sheath, was a knife. She was surprised at the *extent* of the shifters' perfidy; she was not surprised that it happened. They'd been playing games with her for months. She'd expected some sort of trickery and had planned for it.

The two knives hidden in her boots weren't quite as good as the long knife she'd had in her backpack, but they were each far better than the short belt knife which was all they'd left her with. Leaving one of the two blades in its sheath, she tucked the other into a loop on the outside of her pack, then rolled down her socks.

"Hello, baby," she said, and reached down to rip away the tape securing a supply of antibiotic capsules and a small tube of ointment to her lower right calf. She winced slightly as the tape pulled at her dehydrated skin, and was reminded that finding water had to be her first priority. She had some... She frowned and reached for her canteen, which was still tied to her pack right where she'd left it, along with her collapsible metal cup. Her fingers were weak, so it took longer than it should have. Eventually she loosened the leather ties and pulled the container away, shaking it experimentally. She heard and felt the reassuring slosh of water and breathed a sigh of relief. That was good. This close to the glacier there was little run-off and what there was would be heavy with minerals. Apart from the unpleasant taste, glacier water could cause all sorts of unpleasant reactions in humans, especially this time of year with the fresh melt. By the time it reached the forest streams and the city, it would have been filtered a few hundred times by the rock and soil it passed through to get there. Directly off the glacier where she was, it would be pretty harsh. She made a face at the thought and twisted the cap off her canteen, lifting it to her mouth for a careful sip.

Some sixth sense kicked in at the last minute and she hesitated, pulling the container away from her lips, and raising it instead to her nose for a quick sniff. Drugged. They had put drugs in the only water she had. That was a new low, even for them. And unfortunately, there were no smuggled packets of water taped to her body anywhere.

Amanda permitted herself a moment of despair—she was in the middle of nowhere, exhausted, half sick, hungry and dehydrated. She wished briefly for a radio to call for help…and a planet on which a radio would actually work… and someone to call on that radio. Although, Rhodry would probably come if she called him. Even if it was only to point out that he'd been right. She sighed and hung her head, eyes closed against the sight of all that bare earth. She deserved one fucking minute of self-pity, damn it! And then she drew a deep breath and forced herself to think.

Ice could be melted and she could rig some sort of filter system. It would be slow... She had a sudden thought and grabbed the pack frantically, breathing a sigh of relief to find her flint and striker, and a small box of wooden matches still tucked safely away in a waterproof side compartment. They'd probably just lifted the pack and dumped everything out, not even noticing the zippered pocket, which also contained a small sewing kit with needle and thread. Well, okay, that wasn't going to help much unless she had a sudden urge to darn her socks for entertainment.

She dug her fingers into the narrow space and found an ancient bouillon cube and a wax packet of honey drops, which she grabbed with a crow of delight. They were sticky and softened with age, more formless blob than lozenge. She didn't care. She popped one into her mouth and let the sweet flavor wash away at least some of the leftover sour taste. While it didn't make up for the lack of water, it was definitely a start.

Sucking noisily on the candy, she packed her few possessions into the nearly empty pack and stood up. It took her a few minutes, leaning heavily on the tree while her body distributed its blood to all the right places, before she took her first step, and then the next, and she was on her way. Her journey back to the Guild Hall had begun.

Chapter Nineteen

The dried out husk of a tree was barely big enough to shield her from the bitter wind. Amanda clung to its meager support and drew a deep breath. Either all of her senses had gone mad or, after hours of walking, she'd finally found water. She sucked in another breath, testing the air. The biting scent of piñata fern stung her nose and throat, and she closed her eyes in relief. The piñata was a hardy bluish-green frond that was almost synonymous with water on Harp.

With her goal reliably within reach, she found herself abruptly and completely exhausted. Her pack and everything else slid off her shoulder and hung to the ground as she leaned forward, hands on her knees, her breaths hard and shallow. It was tempting to sit down and rest, even for a few minutes. Once she was on the ground, though, she might never make it up again.

The dregs of anger-fueled energy had deserted her

long ago, leaving sheer willpower to drive her forward. She shivered violently, more from exhaustion than cold, and her head spun as she tried to focus on the near horizon and the setting sun. She figured there was less than an hour of sunset gloom left before total night descended, and then nothing. Banba, the smallest of Harp's three moons, would linger for a short time tonight, its cool, dim light offering more to poets than to weary travelers. And once it set, the sky would be utterly black, the tiny pinpricks of stars too distant to offer more than reassurance that there was light somewhere in the universe. Somewhere other than here, that is.

The smell of fern sharpened as she stumbled closer to the trickle of water, her footing more unsteady with every step. The ground around the small stream was littered with rocks and dirt mixed with old, dried sticks of branches and the skeletons of small animals. In a few months, at the peak of summer, this bare trickle would become a fast-moving wash of water, pushing detritus ahead of it as it sped out of the distant mountains at the height of the glacier.

Going to her knees, Amanda cupped one hand in the icy liquid and touched it to her lips. It was heavy with minerals and so cold it made her teeth ache, and she'd never tasted anything better in her entire life. Mindful of her uncertain stomach, she limited herself to small sips with an effort. She scooped up double handfuls to splash like rain against her parched face, while permitting only the barest sips to roll down her throat. Eventually she sat back on her heels and drew in the moist air over the stream, opening herself to what was only the thinnest song of the Green this far from the deep forest.

It was enough to remind her of why she was out here,

starving and sore, all alone on the precipice of a cold, dark night. She didn't care about the shifters and their petty jealousies. She didn't care if they mocked her clawless fingers and furless skin, or if they never let her dine in their ancient Guild Hall. For whatever reason, whether it was her earth witch dad, or something else, the Green had claimed her for its own and that was the only thing that mattered.

She rose on weary legs and set about making the best camp she could. It wouldn't be much. On the other hand, she had water, and there was plenty of fuel for a fire. And she wasn't throwing up. Good enough.

The next morning, Amanda woke slowly. She'd been dreaming, although she couldn't remember about what. Not a good dream though. She knew that much.

She groaned like an old woman when she rolled over and sat up. The aches in her back provided a detailed map of every single pebble on the hard ground. Morning necessities were taken care of at a suitable distance from camp, behind a straggly bush—after first checking the area to make sure there was nothing that would bite her on the ass. Because that wasn't just an expression on Harp.

The small fire she'd managed to light last night had gone out, so she gathered several more pieces of dry wood and used another of her precious matches to light it. The flint and striker were beyond her skill this morning, her hands too clumsy with cold and hunger. It was everything she could do to fill her cup directly from the stream and set it over the fire without burning herself.

While waiting for the water to boil, she forced herself to stand and stretch out stiff and sore muscles. As she moved, she gauged her body's response. She had no significant injuries, which was good. Everything ached, though, which she mostly attributed to the toxin in whatever drugs they'd given her. It left her feeling as though she'd gone a round with a band of banshees.

Her stomach, on the other hand, was completely empty, so empty it didn't even have the energy to growl. It just lay huddled next to her backbone, mewling softly. She dug out the lone, ancient bouillon cube she'd found in her pack and dropped it into the cup of hot water. She needed meat, which meant she needed to hunt. Even out here on the seemingly barren glacier, there was more than enough game to keep a solitary human alive.

Drawing her gloves back on, she picked up the hot cup of broth and sat cross-legged in front of the fire to consider her next steps. Logically, she should take a straight line back to the Green before veering west toward the city. Once within the forest, her situation would improve significantly. It would be warmer for one thing, and palatable fresh water and food were easily had for someone with her survival skills. On the other hand, the Green was also far more dangerous in terms of things that might want to kill her. The glacier was too barren for most of Harp's native life forms. That didn't mean there weren't any threats at all, only that they were either too small to pose a danger, or big enough that she would see them coming over the flat landscape. In the dense lushness of the Green, dagger-sharp death could and did come at you from all sides with little or no warning.

She took another sip of hot liquid and felt its warmth all the way down her throat, even as her gut grumbled its reaction to the meager broth. She almost smiled as she pursued her earlier train of thought.

Dangerous wildlife or not, a straight line back to the forest belt was the obvious course for her to take. Death might lurk behind every tree in the Green, but the benefits outweighed the risks, and besides, she was completely unfamiliar with life on the glacier, having never been this far north before.

The more she thought about it, however, the more doubts she had. Sure, it made sense for her to chart a path directly for the Green…which was exactly what the shifters would expect her to do. And the same shifters who'd left her out here in the first place might be waiting for her to do just that.

More than anything else, that decided her. She'd stay here and rest for the day, and then instead of heading straight for the Green, she'd parallel it for a few miles, tracing the edge of the glacier before finally veering south into the deep forests. That would take her off the most logical route, and put her behind any reasonable expectation of schedule. It would also make her harder to find—just in case anyone was looking to cause trouble.

She drank down the remainder of the broth, then took her canteen over to the stream and rinsed it thoroughly, leaving it suspended upside down to dry out. She caught a slight movement out of the corner of her eye and turned in time to see the dirty brown blur of a rabbit before it disappeared into a tangled burrow of dead, twisted roots. She smiled. Roasted rabbit was tasty.

She pushed up her shirtsleeve and snapped off the thick-braided bracelet which snaked around her forearm. A quick twist and it shook out into a long, very thin cable. Shifters had a lot to learn when it came to sneaky weapons. And *she'd* learned long ago that a snare was every bit as good as claws when it came to catching rabbit.

By the time the sun was retiring from its quick passage through the sky, there was a plump rabbit spitted and roasting over the fire. She had no herbs or vegetables, not even a packet of salt to season the meat with, and it didn't matter. The spring rabbit was fat and juicy and as good as anything she'd ever eaten—which probably had more to do with her empty stomach than her cooking skills. It was hot and filling, and there was enough left over to make a good breakfast before she set off the next day. She licked grease off her fingers, thankful no one was around to observe her manners, then tidied her small campsite, wrapping the leftover rabbit meat in the now empty waxed packet from the honey drops. Her decision to stay put and rest for the day had been the right one. Food and fresh water had gone a long way to getting rid of the drugs in her system, and tomorrow's exercise would do the rest. She slipped into her sleeping bag with the last of the sunshine and watched lazily as another rabbit ventured down to the stream, its long cord-like tail twitching nervously.

When humans had first arrived on Harp, they'd catalogued the local wildlife, using designations drawn for the most part from Earth. There were rabbits and bears and squirrels, just to name a few. Sometimes the names made sense and the indigenous animals actually resembled their Earth counterparts. Just as often, they'd been assigned as some sort of practical joke by the colonists, the meaning of which was completely lost on their descendants.

A breeze came up suddenly, blowing directly off the glacier, and she lifted her face, enjoying the fresh air even while grimacing at its icy bite. She knew she should be concerned about that wind. Spring or no, this far north, she could easily be overtaken by one of the glacier's fierce storms and she wasn't really equipped for that kind of weather. And yet, instead of being worried, she found herself laughing out loud. The little bit she'd done today had left every muscle trembling with fatigue. She was lying alone on the hard, cold ground with a rock digging into her hip that would only add to the landscape of bruises covering her body. And yet she'd never felt more exhilarated in her entire life. The only thing that could have made this day better was if Rhodry had been snuggled into the sleeping bag behind her, his furnace-like heat lulling them both into sleep.

She shook her head at the ridiculous image, then drawing a last breath of the bracing air, she snuggled down into her sleeping bag alone, zipped it all around, pillowed her cheek on her cloak and fell into a dreamless sleep with a smile on her face.

Chapter Twenty

Rhodry stood at the edge of the balcony, his knees almost touching the short stone wall separating him from the steep hillside. Banba was making its short journey through the sky, and as he watched the small moon, he couldn't help thinking about Amanda, wondering how she was doing, and where they'd left her. Nando and the others should have been back by now, and it worried him that they weren't.

A footstep brushed softly behind him. "Cousin."

The voice only confirmed the scent he'd already identified. He let the other shifter come a few steps closer before glancing over his shoulder.

"Des," he acknowledged, keeping his voice carefully blank.

Desmond Serna came to stand next to him and stare down at the city, much as Rhodry had. "It's quiet at least," he said, echoing Rhodry's earlier thoughts with an eerie precision. They stood in uneasy silence for a few minutes before Des said, "Nando's back with the rest of the woman's escort."

He grunted dismissively, not wanting Des to suspect just how eager he was to hear this piece of news. "About time. They dropped her off, then?"

"So they said."

His attention sharpened. "You doubt it? Nando's no friend to Amanda, and he seemed determined to make sure no one else would go easy on her. Even Fionn was rejected from escort duty, and our prince wasn't happy about it, either."

Des shrugged. "For all Fionn and she are said to be close, I don't think he's too keen on her joining the Guild. I'm surprised Nando pushed him off the escort."

"He wasn't the *only* one who was pushed," Rhodry said bluntly.

"Ah. I'd heard there was a scuffle of some sort. You should be careful, cousin. If Fionn has claimed the woman… he's the sort to cling to his grudges."

"I'm not worried about Fionn Martyn or his grudges. I was only concerned about Amanda's safety, and I don't trust Nando."

Des nodded thoughtfully for the space of two breaths and said, "So, you favor her candidacy?"

"What?"

"The woman. You support her admission to the Guild?"

"It hardly matters what I think, but she's strong for a norm. Maybe even strong enough to make it." It was strange how he could admit that to Des, whom he hated, and yet not to Amanda, whom he… Well, he certainly didn't hate her.

The other shifter shuffled awkwardly, as if deciding

whether to say whatever was on his mind. Rhodry waited, only caring if it had something to do with where they'd left Amanda.

"I spoke to Nando just an hour ago," Des said finally. He hesitated, then said in a rush, "They dropped her on the glacier."

His eyes widened in disbelief, his stomach sinking, as he turned to stare at the other shifter. "Who told you that?"

"Nando admitted it to me. Actually 'bragged' is more accurate. I'd heard rumor that he'd made certain she couldn't make it back without help, and I was curious. So I asked him straight out. They took her beyond the Verge to the edge of the glacier, stripped most of her gear, and left her puking her guts from the drugs."

Rhodry tapped his fingers on the hilt of his belt knife. "When was this?" he asked tightly.

"Early yesterday morning, as far as I can figure."

"And no flare yet?"

Des shook his head. "No one's seen it."

"Where's Fionn?"

"Making himself scarce since that scene in the Guild yard."

"You think he's part of it? That he'd put her in jeopardy?" Rhodry might not be crazy about Fionn, but he didn't think the shifter would sink that low. Especially not if it endangered Amanda. If he had, and if she was injured because of it…

Des shrugged. "Maybe. You saw how it was in the yard. He's not happy with her choices."

"What about Garza?"

"Gone the same day as the escort, indefinite detail to

the south."

"And Amanda went north. That's convenient."

Des nodded grimly. "Nando's got friends and frankly, she doesn't."

Rhodry frowned. Amanda had friends. *He* was her friend. Though perhaps he hadn't been a very good one. He bit back the oath burning the back of his throat. "Why come to me with this?" he asked. "You and I aren't exactly friends either."

"Maybe not. We're both from the clans, though, and we don't leave women to die in the wild."

He let the oath come, giving voice to a suddenly urgent concern for Amanda's well-being. "What do you have in mind?"

"I say we schedule a hunting trip. You, me, and maybe one other I can trust. We take the hover out, and who's to say how far we go with it? If she's fine, then good enough. If not…" He shrugged.

"When?"

"First light tomorrow. If we go now, it'll draw too much attention. Where are you on the duty roster?"

"I'm free tomorrow."

"I'll make the arrangements, then, and see you at first light."

Rhodry nodded his agreement and watched the other shifter stride quickly across the patio and disappear into the darkened palace. He'd never considered Desmond Serna a particularly honorable man, although he hadn't given it much thought. It was possible the clansman was honestly concerned at the idea of a woman being left on her own like that. Rhodry, not being a complete fool, was wary. And he was going to go anyway. Because whether Des really was troubled or not, Rhodry was, and he couldn't leave Amanda out there alone. Not on the glacier, and especially not this time of year. Spring brought the ice bears out of hibernation and there was nothing a hungry ice bear liked better than the taste of human flesh.

Rhodry leaned back, stretching his long legs in front of him. His cousin sat in the front passenger seat of the hovercraft, next to Kane Daly, who was their pilot. He knew Daly by sight, the man's almost white-blond hair—and a correspondingly colored shifter pelt—was distinctive enough to be notable. Des had introduced Daly as a friend, someone he could trust. Des might trust him, Rhodry didn't. Of course, he didn't trust Des either.

The hover skimmed effortlessly over the trees, Daly following the dips and swerves of the landscape with practiced ease. Shifters could travel nearly as fast through the treetops, using the hovers for more distant hunts, or when it was necessary to transport either a non-shifter or someone wounded. They'd used the excuse this morning of a long hunt. The truth was they expected to find Amanda unable to travel and would need the hover to get her back to the Guild Hall.

Des sat hunched forward in his seat, peering through the wide windshield and searching the ground.

Rhodry frowned and said, "It's a little early to start looking. She couldn't have made it this far in from the glacier already."

"We don't know for sure where they dropped her," his

cousin responded over his shoulder.

He pursed his lips skeptically. It didn't hurt to look, even though he was pretty sure she couldn't have made it this far on her own. No matter how extraordinary she was or how hard she'd worked to get ready, she was still bound by the limits of her norm physiology.

Des pointed at something and caught Daly's eye with a sharp nod. Rhodry felt the hover swerve left and begin losing elevation, and he sat up to stare out the window, seeing nothing unusual in the surrounding forest.

Des twisted around in his seat. "I thought I caught a glimpse of something. We're going to check it out."

Rhodry abruptly doubted his wisdom in traveling to this remote location with Des and his *trusted friend.* He wasn't immediately worried. Once they were on the ground, he could always shift. And he was confident he could take one or both of them in his animal form.

He glanced at his cousin and shrugged. "I wouldn't mind some time on the ground."

There was nothing to find on the ground, which was exactly what he'd expected. His cousin and Daly had gone off into the trees almost as soon as they landed, looking for what he didn't know, except that he was pretty sure it had nothing to do with Amanda. And he was beginning to think this trip didn't either.

He'd pretty much decided to leave Des to his increasingly suspicious pursuits, and continue the search for Amanda on his own, when a cold wind ruffled the trees overhead. He raised his nose into the gust, inhaling deeply, scenting snow and ice. There was violence building less than a day behind that wind. If Amanda was out here, and if they didn't find her first, her only chance would be to dig in and wait out the coming storm. She claimed to have trail experience, and he hoped her weather sense was good enough to sense the approaching cold front. Of course, she could hear the trees—he did believe that, though for some perverse reason he'd let her think he doubted it. The question was, did she *understand* the trees' voice well enough to recognize a weather warning?

A particularly strong gust sent leaves skittering across the small clearing, and he realized he and the other two shifters might find *themselves* digging in if they waited much longer. The lightweight hover would be useless if the weather really closed in.

He took a long swallow from his canteen, swirled it around his mouth, and spit it out discreetly just in case Daly was watching. About an hour into their journey, the white-haired shifter had offered some homemade trail bars around. His grandmother's secret recipe he'd said. Rhodry had accepted the bar readily enough. His shifter metabolism burned energy like a fire burns paper, and trail bars were designed to be high in calories. The trail bar Daly provided had been cloyingly sweet, which was something he'd encountered all too often since he'd come to the city. Everything was either too sweet or too bland, nothing like the spicy, rich foods of his mountain home. He sighed, just one more thing for him to miss.

He heard movement high in the trees and looked up to catch a flash of white fur. What the fuck? He threw his canteen into the back and started around the hover. "Damn it, Des," he called. "We have to get to Amanda before that storm closes in. She won't stand a chance if she's still out on the glacier. And what the fuck is Daly doing up there?"

There was no answer, and no Desmond either. He frowned and felt his earlier unease coalesce into a stark warning in his head. He was out here in the middle of nowhere with two shifters he didn't trust, at least one of whom actively wanted him dead. And no one even knew he was here. Des had made the arrangements for the hover, and Rhodry had no friends in the city, so there'd been nobody to tell where he was going, just as there'd be no one to miss him if he didn't return. Fuck.

He headed for the back of the hover at a run, stripping away his gear on the way. Bow, quiver, and knife went into the back of the craft. If his cousin and Daly had shifted, his only chance was to face them in cat form. It would be two against one, but he wasn't the best hunter on the planet for nothing. He had no doubts about who was the strongest animal among them.

He was down to shirt and pants, and toeing off his boots when a soft growl spun him around. The two treacherous shifters crouched low in the nearby branches, teeth bared, eyes regarding him with hungry malice. He didn't wait, he reached for his animal and... Pain.

Every inch of his body screamed in agony as his cat fought to claw its way out, as muscles and bones, tendons and nerves strained to accommodate a shift that should have been as natural as breathing. He staggered backward, stumbling along the side of the hover, putting its bulk between him and his enemies. He was fighting to remain conscious, to figure out what was going on. Why couldn't he shift? He could feel the animal crouching beneath his skin, eager to come out and play, to prove who the true alpha here was.

Something was stopping him, he couldn't... The trail bar. The gods-be-damned trail bar had been poisoned!

Desmond and Daly launched themselves from the trees, Daly's claws scraping along the thin metal of the hover as he scrambled over the top. Rhodry spun to meet the attack, a roar of outrage pouring from his too-human throat as razor-sharp claws dug into his chest. Des came in from below, powerful jaws closing around Rhodry's hip, fangs sinking deep into his belly.

Rhodry fought. He was a big man, strong and smart, with an insider's knowledge of his enemy. He was also completely unarmed against a well-planned attack, with not even a belt knife to defend himself. His beast was screaming for release, draining his strength even as it strove to protect him.

They rode him to the ground, raking bloody rows in his chest and arms, his legs, as he punched and kicked, refusing to go down easily. At some point at least one of them shifted back to human, and he felt something hard and heavy come down on his head. His vision started to gray out as he caught the bright slash of a blade at his groin. He rolled enough to deflect its course, but not its lethal edge.

Blood ran warm over his skin, soaking into the dirt beneath him, and he wanted to believe some of it was his enemy's. He thought of his home in the mountains, of his mother and sisters. He thought of Amanda, who would die out on that glacier without knowing he cared. And as the darkness took him, he thought of his Devlin cousins who were closer than brothers, and he smiled, knowing his death would not go unavenged.

Chapter Twenty-One

Leaves scurried ahead of Amanda, blown on a cold wind with ice in its teeth. She hunched her shoulders against gusts that seemed to attack from all sides, chivying around her like small tornadoes, kicking up leaves and dirt and rocks.

Her guess about the weather had been spot on. This was her third day on the trail, and clouds heavy with moisture were racing across the sky, the trees groaning beneath the looming storm's advance. She'd changed her heading this morning, abandoning misdirection in favor of outrunning the weather. She was making a straight southerly run for the Green and already she could see, and hear, the difference. The trees were definitely more plentiful, their voices growing louder with every step she took, and full of warning. She didn't need the trees to tell her a storm was coming, though, just as she didn't need them to tell her what it would mean. Once the snow started falling, her visible world would shrink to a few precarious feet. She could easily find herself completely turned around and heading back toward the glacier with no warning until her feet felt the unforgiving ice beneath her boots once again.

Unfortunately, that wasn't the worst Harp had to offer her. She sighed, pausing long enough to twist the cap off her canteen and take a small sip, hearing the growing voice of the trees all around her. There was something muttering and uneasy in their song, something clearly audible despite their distance from the Green. It had started right after midday as a mild uneasiness, a feeling of being watched. In the last hour, that feeling of watchfulness had reached a point where she was spending as much time looking over her shoulder as ahead. Except that this wasn't the straightforward danger of a creature stalking her through the trees. It wasn't even fear so much as it was…betrayal.

She shook her head and kept walking.

By nightfall, the pall of dread hanging over Amanda had become a physical thing. Snow was falling in earnest, having settled in along with the darkness. Her tiny penlight was useless against the thick shadows, but she was too tense to remain still, too certain that something awful was about to happen.

The wind died all at once, leaving her in stunned silence. Clouds that had been racing across the sky with the storm abruptly hit an invisible wall and stalled out, piling one on top of the other. Something barely seen drifted past the corner of her vision and she twisted quickly, her eyes straining in the darkness. She pushed back the hood of her cloak to see and hear better, and caught the sound of a low, rumbling growl. Holding perfectly still, she listened. The snow muffled the sound, flattening it, taking away any resonance or distance. She closed her eyes, narrowing sensory input, focusing only on hearing. A second growl joined the first, followed by a distinctive high-pitched whine, and she shivered in sudden knowledge. Those were hycats—shaggy coated, hunchbacked predators who were fully capable of bringing down their own meat, and just as happy to scavenge someone else's. By the sound of it, they'd found something.

It wasn't her they were after. Whatever it was couldn't be too far, though, if she could hear their growls so clearly. By the sounds the animals were making, their prey was something big and not quite dead. Something so dangerous that even with their prey injured and near death, the hycats were afraid enough to hold off their attack.

There were only a few creatures on Harp capable of frightening the vicious hycat packs that much. She stood up and pushed her cloak all the way back, swinging her short bow off her shoulder and nocking an arrow, holding it ready in both hands as she started forward.

Hycats feared ice bears—huge, hairy beasts with thick, impenetrable coats of fur and skin and eight-inch claws. Hycats feared Harp eagles—black-feathered bodies that dove sleekly through the trees like spears, gliding between the trunks to snag prey from the ground before powering upward with a single snap of their broad wings.

But more than anything, hycats feared shifters.

She glided cautiously forward, her feet finding their own way through the trees, as if some instinctive sense had finally kicked in. The thick snow now became an advantage, concealing her in its all-consuming folds of white, muffling every soft footstep. The air was still and silent, no breeze to carry her scent, only the imperceptible fall of snow on the ground.

The animal noise grew louder as she approached, until she could no longer hear her own movements, quiet as they were. From the sounds, there were more than two of the big cats up ahead, a hunting party who'd scented a potential meal for the family group, and were willing to wait out its eventual death rather than leave the meat for some other scavenger to feast upon.

She had a feeling they weren't going to be happy when she took their dinner away. *Or maybe you're wrong, Amanda. Maybe they've just found a big old bear who had a heart attack on the trail.*

Yeah, right.

She slowed her steps, close enough now to hear the animals moving restlessly, carving circles around their prey, long tails swishing the snow behind them in agitation. A shrieking yip and a flurry of angry snarls split the darkness as two of the big cats tussled, eager for the meat, blood scenting the air so strongly that she could smell it even with her dull human nose.

Something groaned, little more than a murmur of sound. Maybe it was her weak-hearted bear after all. And then the creature gave a gasp of pain, and her heart jolted.

She raced ahead, following the noise of the pack, heedless of the treacherous ground underfoot. The trees ended abruptly in a small clearing and she skidded to a halt, barely stopping herself from barreling into the open. A quick look around told her there were at least three of the animals in the clearing, maybe a fourth. Their dark pelts stood out like smudges against the white snow, their gleaming yellow eyes giving away their positions. A pair of those eyes swiveled to glare at her, tightening into narrow slits as the hycat opened its mouth to snarl a warning.

Stepping deliberately from the trees' shelter, she aimed at those eyes and let fly with her first arrow before her foot hit the ground. She was sighting on the second cat before the first arrow hit its target, then she fired and did it again, falling back and rolling away as the third cat spun toward her with a furious yowl. She rolled completely, feeling her ribs crush against thick tree roots, jumping up to swing her bow over one shoulder and draw her belt knife, positioning her back against a sturdy trunk. Two animals remained that she could see, one seemed smaller, a young female learning the ropes, maybe. If she could kill the larger animal, the smaller would probably run, too inexperienced and too terrified to face the human alone. Even now the smaller cat hung back uncertainly, shuffling from side to side, a nervous yellow gaze slashing between Amanda and the older female, probably a mother or an aunt.

She had a choice. She could wait for the dominant animal to attack and hope the smaller one didn't join in. Or she could go on the offensive. She thought about her long knife, the one her shifter escort had taken before leaving her on the glacier. It would have come in very handy right about now. And wishing for a better weapon wasn't going to do her any good. She risked a glance at the body lying a few feet away, ominously still in spite of the racket being raised by the surviving cats. Wishing wasn't going to save that man's life either.

She let her bow slide slowly down her left arm until she was able to grip the smooth wood, never taking her eyes from the snarling animals. Sucking a long breath into her lungs, hoping the gods favored stupid humans who wanted to become Guild, she repositioned her knife in her right hand, let her breath out slowly and with a quick, underhand movement sent it slicing through the air toward the chest of the big female.

The cat leaped as soon as Amanda moved and her thrown blade took it in the belly rather than the chest. It was enough that the animal twisted in flight with an almost human scream of pain. Its claws missed her face by a hair's breadth, slicing instead through her layers of clothing to dig into the flesh of her arm as the animal flew past to land awkwardly to her right. She swore, and didn't hesitate. The cat was stunned, not out of the fight yet. Bringing up her bow, she sent an arrow into the brain of the injured female, then nocked and drew again, sweeping her sights across the clearing in search of the smaller cat. With a streak of gray underbelly, and the flash of a pale tail tip, the young hycat was gone, disappearing between the trees, lost in the thick snow as it crashed through the underbrush in its haste to escape.

Amanda let it go, her body thrumming with the rush of adrenaline, her heart pounding as cold air rasped in and out of her lungs. When she was confident the youngster was gone, she moved purposefully through the clearing, going from body to body, ensuring the three other hycats were well and truly dead. The only thing worse than a live hycat was a live, pissed off hycat. As it was, she had three dead animals and that was going to be problem enough.

Retrieving her knife from the dead cat, she hurried over to the downed man. Her first touch told her he was still alive. A gasp escaped her throat when she turned on her penlight and got her first good look at his battered body. He was lying on his stomach, half turned to one side, his left arm flung out as if to ward off an attack. His other arm was under his body and there was a wide, red stain on the frozen ground beneath it. He was more or less fully dressed, his clothes torn and bloodied. From the size of him, and the braid in his hair, she guessed he was a shifter, and also because no one else would be out this far from the city. It made her wonder why he was in human form, why he hadn't shifted to defend himself. Maybe the attack had taken him by surprise. Not an easy thing to do with a shifter. Weirder and weirder.

She ran her light over the ground and didn't see any weapons—no bow, not even a knife. If he hadn't brought his weapons, then he hadn't planned on remaining two-legged for long. His clothes—soft-soled boots, pants, a pullover shirt—were nowhere near enough for the cold weather, more proof that he hadn't intended to stay here very long. She shuddered trying to imagine something that could bring down one of the powerful shifters so quickly that he hadn't even had time to fight.

She did a quick scan of the surrounding trees, looking for stray hycats, then dropped to her knees next to the wounded man. His hair was long and black, most of it still bound in its braid, the rest flung loosely across his face and matted with blood. She touched his shoulder gently, not wanting to startle him. He didn't so much as shiver beneath her hand. Barely able to see, she held her flashlight between her teeth and tugged off her gloves, running her hands quickly and gently over his back and legs, his outstretched arm. He had several deep and bloody furrows on his arm, and his left shoulder was ripped open, but those injuries weren't enough to account for the blood she could see staining the white snow. Dread filled her at the necessity of turning him over and seeing just what had caused the frozen puddle of blood he was lying in.

She rolled him as carefully as she could, unable to stifle a groan of dismay at what she found. His chest and belly were in terrible shape, deep diagonal slashes gouged into his flesh, his clothes little more than shreds of cloth stuck in the thick, oozing wounds. The ground beneath him was nearly bare of snow, which meant the storm had hit after he'd been attacked. That might actually have saved his life, as the cold had slowed the bleeding somewhat, although she knew there were other risks that the cold brought with it. And now that she'd rolled him, several of his wounds had begun bleeding freely again. He was going to bleed to death right in front of her if she didn't do something fast.

She stripped off her cloak and her pack, propping the flashlight against the thick material to free her hands. "Hang on," she said, leaning closer to brush away his long hair. "Try to—" She caught a look at his face and felt a jolt of horrified recognition. "Rhodry," she breathed. She stared in disbelief as her heart crashed against her ribs, and then she swore softly and started working.

There was a sizeable swelling just behind his right ear. He moaned when her fingers probed further, his eyelids rolling up briefly in a flash of gold. The swelling was trouble enough, but the injury was mottled purple and red with subdermal bleeding and there was a dried trickle of blood from the ear itself. Even more disturbing was the soft depression at the center of the swelling, a feeling somewhat like an overripe fruit. She ran through the symptoms of a skull fracture in her mind, and hoped she was wrong, because there wasn't much she could do about it out here in the middle of nowhere.

Packing snow around the head injury to dissuade bleeding and reduce swelling, she reached for her knife to strip away what was left of his clothing…and stopped. These were the only clothes he had and, as torn up as they were, they were better than nothing in this cold. Hopefully, he wouldn't need them much longer, since, as soon as he regained consciousness, he'd shift. Or his body would do it for him before then. It was an autonomic response in the shifter physiology, one of the reasons they were so damn indestructible. The shift itself would repair most of the less serious wounds and begin healing the worst ones. It had something to do with the cellular reconstruction during the shifting process. And the science didn't matter right now. The simple fact was, the sooner he shifted, the sooner he'd begin to recover. It was a little puzzling that his body hadn't shifted on its own yet, and she hoped it didn't have anything to do with his head injury.

In the meantime, though, the temperature was dropping and it was snowing so hard she couldn't have seen ten feet in daylight, much less in the cave-like blackness surrounding them. She pulled the small roll of her sleeping bag out of the backpack and spread it on the ground, rolling Rhodry first one way and then the other until the insulated bag was between him and the cold ground. Repositioning the flashlight against a piece of fallen branch, she shook out her cloak and used that to cover him. It would be harder for her to work on him, but the heavy fabric would hold in his body heat and keep him from going any further into shock. And maybe prevent the extreme cold from damaging the raw flesh of his injuries.

Cursing the lack of a first aid kit—that had been among the supplies her escort had dumped out of her pack—she yanked off her parka, tugged her top shirt over her head and quickly put the jacket back on. She immediately felt the absence of the extra layer, and wondered how much worse it must be for Rhodry who was practically naked beneath her cloak. Using her knife, she cut her shirt into strips for bandages that were admittedly far from sterile. Fortunately, shifters didn't generally have to worry about infection, because it was all she had. The main thing was to stop the bleeding and get the hell out of this clearing. Three fresh kills was a feast in the forests of Harp. The smell of the dead hycats would draw scavengers for miles around, and she didn't want to get caught in the feeding frenzy.

Working under the cloak, trying to keep him covered as much as possible, she apologized silently, and began removing his shirt, tugging his arms out of the sleeves and pushing the stretchy material up until he was wearing the whole thing around his neck like some sort of bizarre muffler.

It was a grim and bloody task, though not nearly as grim as the thoughts in her head once she got a good look at the wounds themselves. The injuries were narrow and deep, made with something very sharp and hard as diamond. Something that punctured the skin in a familiar pattern of bloody holes dug into the meat followed by parallel rows of torn flesh. Something very much like the claws of a big cat. Her brain reeled at the inevitable conclusion.

A shifter had done this, had attacked one of his own

and left him to die. That just didn't happen on Harp. Shifters were combative and difficult, big powerful men with the high-strung personalities of their indigenous ancestor. They often fought with one another, inflicting wounds that would have killed an ordinary human ten times over. But there was also a bond among them that went beyond friendship, beyond family. Or there had been.

Her heart clenched with fear as she realized that only chance had driven her across Rhodry's path. If she'd headed straight for the Green that first day, if she'd stopped tonight when she should have, made camp before it got dark, before the snow started, she never would have known he was here. He would have frozen to death, or worse. She thought about the hungry hycats. A shifter would have thought about them too, would have known what could happen. Whoever had done this had deliberately left Rhodry out here half dead and unable to defend himself, fresh meat for the scavengers to dispose of.

It was unthinkable.

She shivered and looked around the small clearing, suddenly grateful for concealment of the snow and the dark, hoping his enemies wouldn't bother to check on the results of their handiwork.

Chapter Twenty-Two

Amanda winced in sympathy as she maneuvered Rhodry's arms back into his shirt, then tugged it carefully down over the makeshift bandages now bulking his broad chest. She'd done the best she could, focused only on stopping the bleeding. His shirt, even shredded as it was, was clingy enough to help hold the bandages in place and that was good, because it was critical that he not bleed for the next few hours. It wouldn't do any good to move away from the dead hycats if she left a blood trail in her wake.

Later, when they reached somewhere safe, she'd do a proper job, probably sacrificing another of her dwindling supply of shirts. Especially if Rhodry didn't shift soon. That was for later. Now was for running.

The trees had ceased their song of snow, replacing it with muttered whispers of creatures moving in the night, of blood and claw and tooth and the feast of flesh to come. Hungry animals would soon descend on the clearing, fighting over the carcasses, killing each other and creating more meat to fight over.

She dug into her bra and pulled out a small folded square of silver the size of a thick tissue. Yet another hidden fallback for her trial, in case she lost her sleeping bag. Ripping off the tab, she unfolded it completely until she had a thermal sheet big enough to cover an adult human, and yet so thin that she had trouble shaking it out enough to lay it flat. The tissue-thin material was incredibly tough and could maintain a body's heat almost indefinitely under optimal conditions—which these admittedly weren't. It would still provide several hours of protection, which was what Rhodry needed right now.

Moving with quick, economical efficiency, she lifted her cloak from the unconscious shifter, and gently rolled him off the sleeping bag and onto the thermal sheet. Unzipping the bag until it was flat, she then rolled him back, tucking the sheet around his body as tightly as she could before zipping the bag completely closed, pausing only at the last minute to lean down and whisper directly into his ear, "You're safe now. I won't leave you."

She didn't know why she did that, didn't know if he could even hear her. Hearing was supposed to be the last sense to go before unconsciousness, though. And the first one to return. So maybe somewhere behind those beautiful golden eyes Rhodry de Mendoza was aware of everything happening around him, and unable to let anyone know. She'd be terrified if that happened to her, especially if there was no one around to reassure her that things were all right. So she whispered in his ear, and gave his shoulder a final pat before closing the zipper. Feeling the minutes ticking away, she threw her few supplies into her pack and donned her now blood-stained cloak. Her knife went back into the sheath at her belt and her bow was slung back over her shoulder where she could get to it easily.

She pulled on her gloves, and quickly discovered they made it too difficult to get a good hold on the slick fabric of the sleeping bag. While a few minutes without them soon convinced her she was risking frostbite. So she pulled them on again, smoothing the worn leather over her fingers, then rubbed her gloved hands on the wound of a broken branch, coating the palms and fingers with sticky sap. They were her favorite gloves, worn soft in all the right places, hugging her fingers and palms perfectly…and she'd never get them clean after this. The sap would sink in and stiffen the leather into uselessness. She didn't hesitate. She got them good and sticky, because pulling the sleeping bag over the uneven ground would be difficult enough, without having to constantly fight for a firm hold on the bag.

Once she'd found someplace safe, or as safe as they were likely to get, she'd rig something better. A travois maybe, like she'd seen in books. Of course, she didn't have a donkey or even a dog to pull it. Maybe some variation on the theme. In any event, she didn't dare take the time to do it now. Standing up, she gripped the leading edge of the sleeping bag and pulled.

It took a while to get started. The ground inside the small clearing was churned up from the fight and littered with hycat bodies and blood. She had to bend almost to the ground to make any headway, but once she got going, momentum grew until she was moving quickly out of the clearing and back among the trees. As soon as she hit the new-fallen snow on the almost invisible game trail, Rhodry's shifter weight made for easier going as the top layer melted beneath the friction of the heavy, waterproof bag.

Unfortunately, if his enemies were still around somewhere, she was leaving a clear trail for them to follow. It would have been better to leave the well-traveled path and forge her own way through the brush, with its twisted tree roots and congested undergrowth. That was, of course, impossible while trailing an injured shifter behind her. Besides, the most important thing right now was speed, not concealment.

Twenty yards out, she paused, leaving Rhodry in the sleeping bag tucked under the snow-heavy boughs. Walking their back trail, flashing her penlight from side to side, she looked for signs of blood mapping their escape. As she'd feared, the bag itself was leaving a track in the new snow that a two-year-old child could have followed. The good news was that hycats and ice bears both tracked by smell, not sight. The bad news was that all the bags and blankets in the world wouldn't stop a predator from scenting their passage if the wind came up the right way. She was counting on the plentiful meat in the clearing to occupy any creatures who might think to follow, hoping they'd ignore an obscure scent trail in favor of the readily available, fresh and bloody carcasses lying out in the open for the taking.

She hurried back up the trail and paused long enough to press a hand to Rhodry's shoulder through the bag, letting him know she was still with him. Then she grabbed the bag once again and set off through the trees.

Chapter Twenty-Three

One foot at a time. That became her mantra as she plowed forward, back bowed and aching, gloved hands frozen into claws inside the stiff leather. She concentrated on her legs, on her knees pumping up and down. Her booted feet barely cleared the surface of the deep snow before disappearing again as she forged her way forward, slow step by slow step. Traveling in a haze of fatigue, aware of nothing beyond the next few feet of trail, it was several yards before she realized that something had changed.

She paused, waiting for her tired eyes to focus, staring, without seeing, at her thighs where they emerged from the knee-deep snow. She blinked. For the first time since beginning this hellish march, she could actually see that her leggings were brown beneath their crust of icy white. The sun had finally risen. She looked up to see little more than a blur of silver in the congested gray sky. Her relief was so great it almost drove her to her knees, almost succeeded in doing what the long hours of toiling in the pitch black night had not. She bit back of sob of utter exhaustion, rubbing away the tears before they could freeze on her cheeks, scraping skin left raw by the freezing air.

She had no idea how far they'd come, didn't know if they were even going in the right direction. More than once she'd looked up to find the barely-made-out rock formation or fallen tree she'd been aiming for had disappeared beneath a white sameness that made it almost impossible to navigate. She could have gotten turned around and doubled back on herself a dozen times without knowing. Her little penlight had been comforting, and of little real value—too cold to hold in her teeth and useless hanging on its strap around her neck and pointing downward.

She'd soon turned it off, choosing to save battery power instead. She'd forgotten how dark it could get in the forest at night.

In her worst fears about the Guild trial, she'd never contemplated traveling through a snowstorm in the dead of night with only her penlight, while pulling some three hundred pounds of injured shifter behind her. She was freezing, wet, tired, and sore down to the marrow of her bones. If kindly Orrin Brady had dropped out of a tree at this moment, and given her the option of quitting, she thought she might have taken it. Might have.

Bending her back to the task one final time, she took firm hold of the sleeping bag with its cargo of injured shifter and started walking again, riding a false burst of optimism that she knew wouldn't last. It helped get her moving, helped her persuade her legs to take one more step and then another. She needed food and water. She needed to get warm again, and she needed to sleep. And that meant she needed to find someplace safe, if only for a few hours.

With the last of her strength, she made her way toward a trio of fallen trees. They'd been blasted by lightning long ago and now lay collapsed on one another just below the crest of a small hill, their thick trunks blackened by fire and hard as stone after years of harsh weather. A dense thicket had grown in below them, sheltered in the pocket created by their collapse, protected from the wind by their bulk.

She lowered Rhodry to the ground, then dropped to her hands and knees and pushed her way past the prickly branches into the cave-like space beneath the huge trunks. It was high enough for her to sit almost upright, with sufficient width for them to stretch out fully, which would make it a lot easier on the injured Rhodry. She did a quick sweep with gloved hands, clearing away small stones and chunks of bark, then reversed her course through the thicket, grabbed hold of the now-filthy sleeping bag, and dragged Rhodry in behind her.

He was the lucky one. All wrapped up in his nice little cocoon while she'd had to endure the whip-thin sting of branches against the exposed skin on her face, the wet slide of ice down her neck as a clump of snow somehow found its way beneath her layers of clothing.

Clumsy with fatigue and cramped in the narrow space, she slipped her short bow over her head and let the straps of her backpack slide down her arms to the ground. Her overworked muscles immediately began to ache in earnest, as if now that she'd stopped, they felt free to protest her abuse. She stretched her back in a fruitless effort to relieve the strain of hours spent hunched over in the dark. Her brain was already beginning to shut down, her eyelids so heavy it was an effort to keep them open.

She roused herself with an effort, wanting to check on Rhodry before she slept, needing to make sure he was breathing and that his color remained good. A little voice in her head kept saying it didn't matter, that there was nothing else she could do for him anyway. It was a message she'd been ignoring for all the hours she'd already struggled to keep him alive, and she no longer heard it.

She unzipped the sleeping bag one more time, her blurry eyes seeing him better in the wan light of dawn through the thicket than she had since finding him.

"Hello, again," she said softly, talking to him as she'd done every time they stopped to rest during the long, endless night, letting him know she was here, that he wasn't alone, that he was still alive. "We made it, you know," she continued. "The sun's up. I can see my hand in front of my face. Or your face," she added, her fingers reaching out to stroke the fine arch of one dark eyebrow.

He had a good face, despite his perpetual glower—at least whenever she was around. His skin was a natural golden brown, with a broad brow and sharp cheekbones tapering to a strong chin. His lips were full and, she knew from experience, surprisingly sensuous. And now that he was sleeping instead of scowling at her, and those beautiful eyes were hidden behind closed lids, with long, thick lashes that lay against a cheek rough with stubble...

What the hell are you doing, Amanda? She snapped her hand back, staring at her fingers as if they belonged to someone else. She was tired, that was all. Tired and feeling protective of the man whose life had been entrusted to her care. It was perfectly natural.

She checked his bandages quickly, schooling herself to remain clinical and impersonal as she drew the stretchy shirt up over his chest. He was warm, not hot, a healthy warmth courtesy of that wonderful shifter metabolism. Her primitive bandages were holding well enough, soaked with blood that was dry and black, which meant for now at least the bleeding had stopped.

She couldn't trust herself to do anything more than check him right now. She was having trouble simply focusing her eyes, and as long as he was stable, they'd both be better off if she grabbed a couple hours' sleep first. Just a short nap. She was so tired, every muscle aching. Her eyes tried to close, and she forced them open one more time.

Pulling his shirt back down, she tucked the silvery thermal back around his body and pulled the sleeping bag over on top of him. She was reaching to close the side zipper when she paused in mid-reach, running her gaze down the length of the sleeping bag and back up again. She could wrap up in her jacket and cloak and be reasonably comfortable on the bare ground, especially protected from the wind as they were now.

On the other hand, he would probably do better if she slept right next to him, drawing both warmth and comfort from her presence. And the sleeping bag was designed to hold more than one person in a pinch, although he was far larger than the designers had ever intended, and it would be a tight fit with both of them. She surveyed the cold, hard ground and remembered his warm skin beneath her frozen hand. She looked up as the thicket trembled suddenly in a fresh gust of wind.

It was, after all, *her* sleeping bag.

Taking off her cloak and spreading it on the ground to dry, she scooted down into the sleeping bag next to Rhodry, careful to avoid jostling him any more than necessary. After placing her weapons where she could reach them easily, she pulled the top of the bag up over both their heads and zipped it almost completely closed. Lying on her side, her back to Rhodry, she finally let herself relax one muscle at a time, feeling the heat from his body seep into her frozen self. He didn't move, didn't acknowledge her in any way, either untroubled or unaware of her presence.

Most likely the latter. He's probably concussed, maybe in a coma. I should stay awake, check on him every hour, make sure...

Behind closed eyes, Rhodry's awareness stirred, sensing his own injuries, smelling blood, shifter blood. His blood. So much blood it was difficult to smell anything else. He reached instinctively for his animal self, for the shift that would begin the healing and return his strength.

Nothing. Not even pain.

His thoughts stuttered in confusion and he tried again, stretching out as he'd done a thousand times, ten thousand times over his life, feeling the glide of muscle over bone...

And still nothing. Fighting panic, he forced himself to concentrate, to take stock of his situation.

It was obvious that he was badly injured, much worse than he'd first thought. But he wasn't alone. Someone was curled up next to him, breathing evenly, sleeping. His own blood scent was too overwhelming for his nose to tell him who lay next to him. One of his cousins most likely, letting him know he was with clan, cared for, protected. His animal wasn't within reach, but it was still within him. He could feel it sleeping deep inside. So he would sleep too. And when he woke, he would shift.

Chapter Twenty-Four

Amanda froze, not understanding for a single terrified moment where she was, why she couldn't move, why there was no light. Memory returned and she stifled a groan, having hoped it was all just a horrible dream, a nightmare brought on by exhaustion.

Unfortunately, while the exhaustion was real, the nightmare was too. She was stuck inside a sleeping bag in the middle of freezing nowhere with a badly injured shifter who, when he wasn't kissing her crazy, pretty much hated her and everything she stood for. If that wasn't a nightmare, she clearly didn't know what the word meant.

She'd pulled the zipper nearly closed earlier to conserve heat, and now she fumbled blindly for the double pull, thinking her plan had worked a little too well. If she didn't get some fresh air soon, she was going to start screaming, probably not the best wake-up call for her current bedmate. Her fingers found the sturdy tab just in time and she yanked it down, taking a deep breath of the cold air that rushed in. She rolled out of the bag in a hurry and re-zipped it halfway, tucking it around the injured shifter, but leaving his face uncovered. If she'd been stifling, he probably was too.

Although not quite warm in their hideaway beneath the tree trunks, it wasn't really cold either. The scruffy thicket had been mostly bare when she'd pushed inside before, but it was now almost completely encased in a layer of snow and ice. Perhaps the wind had shifted or some critical mass had been met on the hillside above. Whatever it was, the compressed snow made a very effective insulator against the freezing temperatures. A little bit of light filtered through, enough to let her know it was still daylight, and the muffled quality of sound made her think the heavy snow continued outside. But they were warm and dry, and fairly well hidden in here. What Rhodry needed most, what they *both* needed most, was a place to hunker down and rest for a day or more. And while the storm trapped them in place, it also prevented anyone from coming to look for them. In most cases, that would be a bad thing, but when the people looking for you were your enemies, the very ones responsible for your predicament, that changed the calculus somewhat.

She studied Rhodry thoughtfully. Whoever had attacked him wanted him dead. There could be no question of that. As for her own situation, she didn't *want* to believe Nando had intended her to die out there on the glacier, but he certainly hadn't wished her well. It would have been a very close thing if she'd been as helpless as they seemed to have assumed she was.

She pulled her backpack over and began taking inventory of her few supplies. He was breathing steadily which was a good sign. If he'd had a serious concussion, chances were he'd be showing it by now, so she had to assume either his thick head had protected him, or his accelerated metabolism was working overtime to heal whatever injury there was. She remained puzzled that he hadn't already gone kitty on her to accelerate the healing. But at the same time, she was relieved to have woken up next to a man rather than a big, angry cat.

Not that she had anything against shifters. In fact, she rather preferred them. They were just so damn…masculine. It was hard for a regular human male to compete. She still marveled at the idea of an entire species of alpha males. There was some disagreement in Harp's scientific circles about which of the two forms was a shifter's natural state, but if you asked a shifter that question, he'd just give you a pitying look and walk away. In her experience, they were just as comfortable in one shape as the other. Fionn, for example, had lounged in front of her fireplace more than once, licking his paws like a big tabby.

But regardless of her comfort level with shifters in general, she barely knew Rhodry. No matter that they'd once danced all night and, okay, had kissed more than once, or that they'd slept together very intimately for the last several hours. Or that every time she saw him, she wanted to tackle him to the ground and force him to admit that he felt the same tugging chemistry between them that she did. If she ignored all of that, she had to admit that their few real conversations hadn't exactly been personal.

Sighing, she gathered a few handy sticks and branches and lit a tiny fire, then grabbed the thickest stick she could find and jabbed it up through a corner of their snow cave until she felt the brush of cold air on her face. Their shelter wasn't airtight—if it had been, they'd have suffocated by now—but she wanted to be sure the smoke had an outlet between cracks in the overlapping tree trunks. She spent a few minutes watching the smoke wind its way up and over the uneven ceiling to her makeshift vent, then packed her empty canteen with snow, and leaving the cap off, set it in the fire. This was why she always carried a metal canteen. It might get too hot to handle, but it wouldn't melt.

While waiting for the water to heat, she pulled the sleeping bag back to expose Rhodry's torso and studied her handiwork from the night before. She clucked unhappily at what she found, and knew she was going to lose another shirt—those bandages would all have to be replaced.

Good thing I wore three. She stripped off her two remaining tops until she wore nothing but her usual sports bra. As soon as Rhodry could travel, they'd have to head straight for the Green and warmer temperatures, because she was running out of clothes.

She eyed the two shirts critically. It was a toss-up as to which was less dirty—neither was clean—but at least the one she'd worn next to her skin wasn't streaked with blood and dirt. Her skin was already prickled with goose bumps by the time she yanked her remaining top and jacket back on, and she rubbed her arms vigorously before using her knife to cut the shirt into bandages.

She smiled, thinking someday she could tell Rhodry that she'd literally given him the shirt off her back. She hoped he had a sense of humor about it. Hell, she hoped he had a sense of humor, period.

When steam was puffing from the wide mouth of her

canteen, she started removing his bandages. "Oh, baby," she whispered in shock. "Who did this to you?" It had been too dark last night, and the timing too urgent, for her to get a really good look at his wounds. But this morning, even in the dim light inside the thicket, she could see how incredibly vicious the attack must have been. Whoever had done this had definitely wanted him dead, but not right away. They'd wanted him to suffer, to lie out there in the snow, dying slowly, aware of the hycats circling and the horrible death awaiting him when he became too weak to keep them away. Someone out there truly hated him.

Several of the wounds began bleeding almost immediately, and she winced, troubled by how little healing had taken place. She was hardly an expert in shifter physiology, but this wasn't normal. Some of the deepest lacerations hadn't even begun to close yet. On a human, the solution would be a few simple stitches to help the body along, but on a shifter? She had no idea.

She blotted away blood, trying to see better, and frowned. Shifter healing abilities being what they were, very few of them were trained in anything beyond basic first aid. Norms rarely traveled the Green, and if one happened to be injured, he or she was transported to one of the clinics in the city, which were now fully equipped, thanks to her mother. Amanda routinely included a small dispenser of surgical glue in her first aid kit, which had, of course, disappeared along with Nando and all the rest of her supplies.

Fortunately, her mother had always insisted that she learn how to make do with what was available. If she was set on venturing down repeatedly to uncivilized planets, her mother had said more than once, she needed to know how to put herself back together if she was injured.

Drawing a deep breath and letting it out, she considered her options. She was pretty sure a few stitches wouldn't hurt Rhodry, and she didn't see how his wounds could get any worse than they already were, anyway. She dug into the backpack's side pocket, and retrieved her needle and thread, then poured some of the hot water into the canteen's cup, set the cup in the fire, and dropped the sewing implements into the water to sterilize. Regardless of a shifter's normal resistance to infection, it went against everything she'd been taught not to take minimal precautions. Besides, if Rhodry had been reacting normally, she wouldn't be sewing him back together at all.

To her surprise, her fingers were perfectly steady when she threaded the still-warm needle. It was a regular sewing needle, not the sickle shape she'd learned with, and the thread was much thicker and coarser. The principle should be the same. Or so she told herself.

She leaned forward to stroke his forehead and cheeks, making sure he remained unconscious. The last thing she wanted was a pissed off shifter waking up because some idiot norm was sticking a needle in his chest.

"Are you in there, kitty?" she said softly. "This might hurt a little. Compared to everything else, though…" Her voice trailed off as her gaze ran over the horrific wounds. Shifter or not, he had to be in terrible pain. Her eyes filled with sympathetic tears and she dashed them away impatiently. "Okay," she said, swallowing hard. "Be tough." She didn't know if that last was meant for her or for him.

She started on the worst of the injuries, a deep gash across his left pectoral muscle. He had a nice chest. She knew that already. She'd admired his hard, smoothly-muscled body more than once, although this was the first time she'd seen that sprinkling of dark hair running in a diminishing line down past his ridged abdomen and over his perfectly flat belly, like an arrow pointing... She sighed.

"I finally get you half naked, de Mendoza, and you're bleeding all over my sleeping bag." She flushed guiltily then, once more feeling as if she were ogling an unconscious man. Rhodry apparently brought out the voyeur in her.

Bending to her work, she first cleaned away the blood and grit she'd missed last night, then chose the place she thought stitches would do the most good and started sewing.

She talked to him in a low voice as she worked, still going on the theory that somewhere inside his head, he was aware of her and what she was doing to him.

"I'm sorry about the needle," she said. "I know you're not used to this kind of thing, being a shifter and all. I've had my share of injuries, though. The first really bad one was when I was twelve. One of the planetary department guys I worked for, doing gofer stuff, gave me a knife for my birthday. I'd had a puny little pocketknife forever, but this was my first real blade. Anyway, it was a sweet little four-inch beauty with a steel inlaid handle, and I thought it was the most wonderful thing I'd ever seen. My mother almost had a heart attack. I ran next door to show it to Meredith before my mother could take it away—Meredith was my best friend at the time. Her parents left the fleet and went back to Earth that same year."

She snipped the thread on a stitch, cleaned the wound one last time and moved on to the next injury, which was a set of nearly perfect claw marks. The four bloody slices ran in parallel lines, following the curve of his ribs almost perfectly, as if it had been planned that way. All four gashes were nasty, and one had gone dangerously deep, exposing a flash of white rib.

Desperate to distract herself from the raw truth of what she was doing, she started talking again. "Where was I?" she muttered. "Right, new knife. Anyway, I ran over to show it to Meredith, tripped over my own feet and ended up slicing open my arm." She lifted her left arm and tugged her sleeve up with her teeth to show him a thin line of smooth white scar tissue marring the tanned skin. "See? My mom left the scar, so I wouldn't forget. The whole thing was pretty embarrassing, let me tell you. I didn't see that knife again for nearly a year, and even then I had to sneak into my mom's bedroom and dig it out of her drawer."

Remembering her mother's reaction, she shook her head as she tied off another stitch and moved on to the next. She kept doing that, talking about nothing, moving from stitch to stitch until she was nearly finished.

"Okay. Almost done. One more and I'll tuck you in and let you sleep in peace." She huffed a soft breath. "Lucky you. No rest for me. We need food, and I need to find out what's going on outside. I have a feeling I'm going to be digging some snow. Too bad you're not in better shape, because those claws of yours would really come in handy. As it is, I'm going to have to use my knives and fingers, because you guys wouldn't let me bring my camp shovel. Bet if you were awake, you'd be wishing I had it right about now," she added wistfully.

By then, she was sewing up the final wound low on his belly. She had to untie his pants and pull them down low over his hips. She stopped there, leaving him his modesty. Not that she thought he'd mind since she was…that's right, saving his life. She smiled and kept working.

When the sewing was complete, she washed his arms and torso again, using the remnants of her shirt and boiled water. Since he wasn't healing like a shifter, she decided he might not be fighting infections like one either. So she dabbed the wounds with careful amounts of her precious antibiotic ointment before applying fresh bandages—or at least fresher ones. She also carefully washed his head wound and cleaned the blood from his ear. She thought the swelling might be down a bit and the bruise was already starting to discolor. Maybe it wasn't as bad as she'd feared. If only he would wake up, even for a short while.

"Please wake up soon, Rhodi," she whispered into his good ear.

She'd already decided to stay put for a couple of days—they both needed rest, and, with any luck, Rhodry would regain consciousness before then. Food wouldn't be a problem. She still had her snare wire, and small game would be plentiful, especially once the storm had passed. And if the storm lingered? Well, there were always other things to eat. She wasn't exactly sure how far they'd traveled, nor how much of that distance had been toward the Green. Judging by the number and size of the trees she'd seen earlier, there should be plants around for eating, and for medicinals as well—for pain and fever and to help the body start rebuilding lost blood. Of course, after a big storm like that, everything would be buried beneath the snow. The herbs should still be viable, though, and she had used her time well these last several months. She knew where to look.

One other thing she knew. The sooner they could start moving toward the Green, the happier she'd be.

Satisfied with her nursing efforts, she straightened Rhodry's shredded clothing, covered him as much as possible, then tucked her cloak around him and pulled the sleeping bag closed, zipping it only halfway. It was warm enough where they were, especially with her small fire, and she thought the fresh air was probably better for him than rebreathing the air inside the bag. The thin foil blanket she folded into its small square and shoved into her jacket pocket. She'd take it outside and shake it out. And the next time, she'd leave him wrapped in it and take the sleeping bag instead. That way everything would get aired out eventually.

Drawing on one of her gloves, she picked up the canteen and poured a little of the melted snow into her cup. Waiting until both rim and water were cool, she leaned over and held it to his mouth, lifting his head enough to pour a little past his lips. She watched the muscles in his neck work as he swallowed reflexively, and took that as another good sign that he'd wake soon, that he was in some sort of deep healing sleep rather than truly unconscious. She tipped a little bit more water into his mouth, and then a third time before stopping.

It was good that he was taking water, but she'd have to figure a way to get something nutritious into him soon. She still had the little bit of rabbit from her last fire. It should be frozen solid, so it would be safe enough to eat. Or maybe she'd get lucky with her snare. Either way, if she boiled the meat, there'd be broth to drink and the meat would be soft enough to mash up or something.

"Or you could pre-chew it, and feed it to him like a bird,"

she muttered to herself. Things weren't quite that desperate yet.

She had to force her way through the ice and snow built up around the thicket, only to fall face first into several feet of powdery fresh snow. It took a moment to get herself right side up, and she was still spitting out snow when she finally got a good look at the sea of white surrounding them. Bushes, shrubs, anything shorter than five feet had become a lumpy white swell beneath a low gray sky. It was just good fortune that their hideaway was elevated by the slight hillside, or they'd have been buried along with everything else. The trees she'd escaped through last night stood all around them, spots of color in the otherwise colorless vista. Great drifts of snow had piled around the thick trunks, and the lower branches were so weighted down that they were nearly scraping the ground.

A light snow still fell from the curdled sky, while a brisk breeze set the airy flakes to dancing sporadically, kicking up flurries to skim along the surface, vanishing as quickly as they started. She lifted her face to the cold and laughed out loud at the flakes that clung to her cheeks. It felt good.

She waited a moment more, enjoying the fresh air and the weak sun on her face, then she closed her eyes and listened. The song wasn't as strong here as it would be in the Green. That didn't mean it wasn't there. The forest was still, not so much as a vole disturbed the perfect silence. Sinking deeper, she found the song beneath the quiet, the trees content in their blankets of white, accepting the freezing storm, as they would the warm thaw that came after, as part of the natural cycle. Each had a part to play in the pattern of life and death on Harp. Submersing herself in the flow of the trees' awareness, she searched for a threat—shifter or animal, both were the enemy for now—and found nothing. Everything that lived was hunkered down, waiting to see what the weather would bring next.

Rising slowly back to focus on her immediate surroundings, she pushed up her sleeve and unwound the coil of wire from around her wrist. With a final glance over her shoulder to the thicket where Rhodry slept unaware, she turned for the top of the hill and slogged through the thick snow to set up a snare. She had to be careful where she walked, an unwary footstep and she'd sink up to her thighs. Though it would be difficult to travel in these conditions, they couldn't stay here forever. She needed to figure out a better transport for Rhodry and put together some snowshoes for herself. She'd never made anything like a snowshoe before. She'd certainly seen pictures, though, and she understood the principle behind it. While whatever she came up with wouldn't be pretty, it would work.

Another day or two and the storm would clear. The intense cold would retreat back to the glacier that had birthed it, and the snow would begin to melt. Once that happened she and Rhodry would need to move fast. The others, the shifters who'd tried to kill him, might come back then to make sure he was dead. And when they didn't find his hycat-chewed bones, they'd almost certainly begin to hunt.

It was cold where he was, icy cold, and fresh with the scent of new snow. Rhodry loved the smell of fresh snow. It reminded him of the mountains and home. But he wasn't home.

The air around him stirred and he heard a voice. Amanda. It was her voice he'd been hearing for hours now, although it seemed as if he'd just remembered. She'd slept next to him, kept him warm, *protected* him. It was an odd thing to think of a woman protecting him now that he was fully grown, especially *this* woman. It was even more odd to have his memories suddenly appear in whole cloth, as if they'd been waiting just over the horizon for him to climb a hill and find them.

She'd been outside somewhere. Her voice brought with it the scents of forest and freshly cut wood. He smelled the bright spark of a match. And then nothing.

"I'm home," Amanda sang out gaily. She threw several pieces of wood ahead of her, then crawled inside and dragged the rest in behind her, one piece at a time. Finding the deadfall among the trees had been the easy part. Digging her way through several feet of snow in search of food, with only her gloved hands and her blades, had been a lot tougher. The rewards, on the other hand, had been great.

She glanced over at Rhodry. He didn't seem to have stirred while she was gone, though he seemed more peaceful than before, his face less creased with pain. Once again, she thought how much easier it would be if he'd wake up and take animal form like a sensible shifter. She was increasingly worried that he *couldn't*, that his injuries went beyond what she could see.

What would happen to a shifter who couldn't shift? She had a feeling there was only one answer to that, and it went counter to all of her efforts to save him.

"How about some dinner?" she asked, talking to him as she'd done all through the night. "I found some goldbud and stickberries. They'll help your head too, I think. And there's a rabbit roasting on the fire outside. You should be able to smell it soon." She was working as she talked, breaking up the deadwood into pieces she could use, cutting into the bark with her knife so the wood would burn more efficiently.

"The snow's a little lighter today, although it looks like there's more weather coming in. Maybe tonight. I can smell it on the air. Not that I mind so much. If we're snowed in, so is everyone else, including whoever did this to you, and I'd really rather have you on your feet before anyone finds us.

"By the way, I'd like to take credit for finding this perfect shelter. Honestly, though, it was dumb luck. When I dragged us in here this morning, it could have been an ice bear den, and I wouldn't have known the difference. You probably know all about snow survival, don't you? Coming from the mountains and all. I've never been to your mountains. Too busy getting ready for all of this. Someday, I'll get there."

She struck a match and blew the small flame into a fire. The wood was dry, and it caught quickly. She settled her snow-filled canteen into the flames, topping it off as the snow melted in what by now was a well-practiced routine. When the water was hot enough, she dropped some of the herbs and berries she'd found into the cup, covered them with water and set it aside to steep.

As predicted, the scent of roasting rabbit soon drifted in from outside and combined with the fragrant goldbud in the tea to fill the small space. It was surprisingly soothing, and Amanda found herself smiling as she ducked back outside to begin the unfamiliar task of constructing a pair of snowshoes.

Chapter Twenty-Five

Rhodry woke all at once, his brain suddenly alight with the knowledge that something was badly wrong. His body felt like he'd been run through a thresher, his head was throbbing, and he was weak as a kitten. Memories flashed rapid-fire. He'd been ambushed. Betrayed by shifters, by his own cousin. He'd fought back, and he'd been... He felt someone move against him and he froze. What the hell?

He inhaled, drawing in the familiar scents of the forest, along with another scent, this one known, and far less familiar. He cracked his eyes open slowly to the dim glow of a tiny banked fire, and saw Amanda fast asleep right next to him. She'd saved his life. He remembered now.

She stirred again, curling her legs up, her butt pushing against his thigh suggestively, tensing his body in a way that it could *not* follow through on, even if they hadn't been wound up together in some sort of... Where the hell were they?

He closed his eyes again and concentrated, letting his senses roam, hearing the soft drip of melting snow, the scratch of a squirrel's feet along a branch far overhead, the rush of wind through the trees. Closer in, there was the snuffle of a vole poking through some bushes, dry and crackling.

The smell of blood was strong, his own and, fainter, definitely there, hers as well. She'd been injured badly enough to draw blood, and like his own wounds it was at least a day old. Maybe more. Beneath the smell of blood was the musk of the vole he'd heard rooting nearby, the slightly dusty smell of dirt and old brush, and the fresh, welcome scent of new snow. A thicket of some sort, then. Sensible woman, she'd found a dry place to shelter them from the weather.

And knowing that, he realized they were in a sleeping bag. Hers, of course. She'd have needed one for the Guild trial, having no fur of her own, although he didn't remember seeing it. Her head was very close to his, her breath light and steady with sleep. As injured as he was, he knew it must have taken a tremendous effort on her part to get them to this safe place. What was it Fionn had said about her? That she was remarkable.

He lifted his head slightly, bending his neck to see her, his shifter eyes dilating to see in the near dark as he looked down the long line of her body, lying so close to him beneath the thin covering. A sharp stab of pain threatened to send him under once again, and he let his head fall back, closing his eyes.

"You should lie still," she said. Her voice was heavy with sleep and beneath that an uneasiness, maybe embarrassment. They were lying as close as lovers, and yet they barely knew one another. Survival demanded practicality sometimes.

She stiffened minutely so that their bodies were no longer touching with such intimacy, and he heard the rip of a zipper being undone. She rolled away and sat up, placing a cool hand to his forehead in the darkness.

"How do you feel?" she asked.

"Alive," he croaked, then coughed, surprised by the roughness of his voice. She put a canteen to his mouth, and he drank gratefully. The water was cool and soothing. "Thank you." He sounded pitifully weak to his own ears and he frowned. "How long have we been here?"

She didn't answer right away, focused instead on stoking the fire. He caught the scent of cooked rabbit and his nostrils flared with hunger. The flames jumped, then steadied, and she glanced over her shoulder.

"We've been here," she gestured at the cave-like enclosure, "for most of a day. It must be nearly midnight by now, and we crawled in a few hours after dawn this morning. If you're asking how long since you were attacked, I'm not sure. I found you soon after, I think. You weren't dead yet." She slanted a quick grin at him, then sobered to add, "The hycats were circling. It took me most of the night to patch you up and get us this far."

"I remember the cats. How did you get rid of them? They don't usually—"

She turned completely and gave him an expectant look. He stared back at her.

"You killed them," he said, not quite believing. "All of them?"

"I let the youngster run home. The three adults... I thought it unlikely they'd be willing to let you go otherwise."

"You really did save my life."

"Ouch, huh?" He could hear the smile in her voice, though she'd turned back to her fire, and he couldn't see her face. "What hurts worse, the bump on your head or admitting that to me?"

"A difficult choice," he admitted grimly.

She laughed, a carefree sound that was incongruous with their circumstances. "I bet," she said. "I roasted a rabbit earlier, and I made a sort of tea with goldbud and stickberries. You drank some of that already. If you're up to it, you should eat some of the rabbit. Your body needs more than tea if it's going to get better. Speaking of which, I'd like to check your wounds before we do anything else," she added.

When he didn't say anything, she gave him a quizzical look. "Do you mind?"

A manda met Rhodry's gaze, his eyes shining like hot, melting gold in the firelight.

"It's a bit late for modesty, I imagine," he said drily.

She stared, unable to look away. "You have the most beautiful eyes I've ever seen," she said, and felt her face flush. *What an idiot.* "Sorry, it just struck me. I don't think I've ever seen eyes like yours, not even on another shifter."

"They run in my mother's family."

She muttered a wordless acknowledgment, suddenly embarrassed, and scooted over to his side, thinking it was far safer to consider him a patient than a handsome man with beautiful eyes. She gave him a single warning glance, then flipped the covers back and began lifting his shirt up over the many bandages. He hissed, whether in surprise or pain, she didn't know. "I'm sorry. You were cut up pretty badly. I had to put a few stitches in."

He looked down at his chest, his scowl turning to alarm when she unfastened his loose pants and tugged them down toward his groin. "Stitches?" His voice went up a few octaves, and Amanda had to fight the urge to laugh.

"Stitches," she managed to agree somberly. She ran her fingers lightly over the wound high on his chest. "Don't worry. I'm well-trained and actually rather proud of the job I did on you, given the conditions. I've never sewn on a shifter before." She looked up to find him watching her. She blushed nervously and joked, "We've got to stop meeting like this."

He gave her a puzzled look, obviously unfamiliar with her mother's old movie collection, which only made her blush harder. "Never mind." She began pulling his clothes back into place, slapping away his hands when he tried to help. "Save your strength, big guy. You ready for something to eat?"

"I need to go outside."

"Sure. Maybe after you've eaten something. It's dark—"

"I need to go outside *now*."

Her eyes widened. "Oh! Right. Okay." She backed away toward the opening, cursing herself for not thinking about this before. Not that they had many options. "This is going to be a tight fit. You need to let me help you."

"I can—"

"Rhodry," she said, forcing him to look at her. "You need to let me help you."

His handsome face took on its usual scowl as he gave her a grudging nod of acceptance.

It was more than a tight fit to get him outside without ripping any of his wounds open or inflicting any new ones.

She reached down and helped him sit up, wrapping her cloak over his shoulders.

"Let's just rest here for a minute." She was panting nearly as hard as he was. "When you're ready—"

"I'm ready."

Amanda blew out a frustrated breath. Damn shifter pride. "Okay. I'm turning this on," she said and clicked on her flashlight, careful to turn it away from his eyes. "It's for me, not you. I'm blind out here. Now, the snow's deep, so I'm going to help you." She shoved her shoulder under the arm opposite his injured pectoral and stood up, taking him with her. It had to hurt like hell, and she gave him credit for doing little more than grunting, though she'd never tell *him* that.

Naturally, the minute they stood, he tried to shake her off, taking a determined step away. She grabbed his arm. "Watch your step and stay on the hill where the snow's not so bad. I've cut a path, so we'll go that—"

"I know how to take a piss in the woods on my own, woman, and I'm familiar with the concept of snow."

"Yeah? Are you familiar with the concept of falling on your ass? Because that's what'll happen if I let go of you."

He was breathing hard, his face already sweat-soaked with effort. His mouth tightened irritably, and he must have been feeling really crappy, because he let her help him, all the while grimacing in pain and, probably, disgust with himself. She wondered if he'd ever been helpless before. Big bad shifter.

When they reached the trees set beyond the top of the hill, she turned her back as a courtesy and pretended not to hear anything. She waited until she thought he must be finished, then looked over her shoulder cautiously. He was slumped against a wide tree trunk, his head thrown back on the rough bark and his eyes closed.

She hurried forward. "Rhodry? Are you all right?"

His eyes opened long enough to locate her, then shut again. "Yes. I needed the air, the open space. I miss this in the city."

"I understand. I feel the same way. I can't spend two days in the city without going back out into the Green. It's as if my lungs seize up and I can't breathe anymore. Too many people, too much noise."

"And the smell," he added.

"And the smell. Though it's probably worse for you." She watched him a while longer. "Can I ask you a question?"

"I owe you my life."

She smiled. She'd read enough Harp history to know that the mountain clans prided themselves on their somewhat rigid sense of honor and duty. "Nothing so drastic as that," she said lightly. "I was just wondering why you haven't shifted yet."

R hodry reached deep within himself, looking again for the shift, and uttered the most foul oath of his mountain upbringing, one his mother would have been horrified to hear him speak in front of a woman.

"Rhodry?" she asked in alarm.

"I *can't* shift," he spat. He caught her look of pity, and rage burned away the embarrassment.

"Is it the head injury?" she asked. "Because I'm sure that will—"

"Not my head. They fed me rockweed." It was in the trail bar, he knew that now. He'd wondered at the sweet taste, probably honey added to cover the familiar herb.

"Rockweed?" she repeated, then frowned in thought. "I remember that one from my studies; it's an anti-seizure medication. I didn't read anything about—"

"No," he agreed, hating the weak sound of his own voice. "You wouldn't have. It grows wild in the mountains. We use it to ease the transition through puberty for young shifters. In small doses, it—" He struggled for the right word. "It *dulls* the urge to shift to animal form."

She stared at him, her eyes growing wide. "Why would—"

"In larger doses, it prevents the shift altogether. They poisoned me so I'd be unable to shift and fight back or even heal myself afterward. They knew this storm was coming. They wanted me dead, and the evidence destroyed. And they would have succeeded, if not for you."

"Who are *they*?" she demanded. "And why would they do this? I thought you shifters—"

"Politics, woman," he cut her off, and saw her stiffen angrily.

"Look, de Mendoza," she snarled. "I may be only a woman, but I'm the woman who saved your mighty shifter hide, and I'm also the one who's stuck with you until we get out of this. I'm not going to pretend I know everything that's going on, though I sure as hell don't need *you* to tell me that those wounds were caused by another shifter. Maybe more than one. You've got defensive wounds on your hands and arms, so you put up a fight, and someone must have decided you were a little too lively, because they whacked you on the head for good measure.

"Now, I'd like to think that whoever did this is already dying a slow, painful death somewhere. Since that's unlikely, I need to know what the fuck is going on, or you can just lean against that tree for the rest of your natural life, because you'll never make it anywhere else without my help! And stop calling me *woman*!"

He studied her in the darkness, her features as clear to him in the clouded moonlight as they would have been in full sun. She was angry as hell, her fair eyes narrowed to slits, her plump mouth set in a tight line. And she was right. He wouldn't make it two steps without falling on his face. He did enjoy watching her temper flare, though. She was a lovely woman with smooth, even features and a lusciously full upper lip on her soft-looking mouth. And she was far too smart for her own good.

He smiled slowly. "You're right."

"I'm… What?" She'd clearly been all ready to lay into him some more. His agreement had surprised her.

"You're right," he said simply. "And I'm sorry. Sorry for being an asshole since almost the day we met, sorry for being rude, sorry you've been dragged into this mess, and sorry there's no getting you out of it. Not until we're back in that stinking city anyway." A wave of exhaustion swept over him and he closed his eyes again. "I'm tired. A few lousy steps in the snow and I'm tired."

"Let's get you back inside," she said immediately. She came to his side, slipping her shoulder under his once again, her arm around his waist. He let himself lean into her support as they started back down the hill, questions about traitorous shifters, rockweed, and everything else forgotten. At least for now.

Amanda took pity on him once they'd maneuvered down the hill and back inside their makeshift shelter. He was in such obvious pain, and his inability to shift had to be frustrating and more than a little terrifying. He didn't say anything to her as she settled him back into the sleeping bag—after making him wait while she took everything outside and shook it out in the fresh air. He was almost pale with exhaustion by then, and his hand when he raised it to cover his eyes shook visibly.

"How long before the rockweed wears off?" she asked quietly.

He answered without looking at her, without uncovering his eyes. "I can't be sure how much I ate. If I was stronger, I could do something physical, chop wood or climb a tree, hell, help my mother rearrange furniture—anything to use energy, metabolize the drug faster. Like this? Another two days, maybe more."

"Or maybe less," she said encouragingly. "I don't know how long you were lying there injured and fighting off those hycats before I found you. And while you're not chopping wood, believe me, your body is burning energy. You'll be back to kitty form in no time."

He rolled his head in her direction, and lifted his hand long enough to glower at her where she sat cross-legged by the tiny fire. She just smiled back, one elbow on her knee, her chin propped on a fist.

"I could stick some more needles into you," she offered. "That'd get the juices flowing."

He gave her a reluctant smile. "No thanks. I'll take my chances." His eyes closed heavily, and soon his chest was rising and falling in a steady rhythm. She thought he'd gone to sleep, until he said, "We can't stay here much longer."

"I know."

"You could—"

"If you're about to suggest I leave you here, you'd better remember who's still got her knife."

She saw his hand drop automatically to his waist where his belt knife would have been. "My weapons?"

"They must have taken them. There weren't any in the clearing where I found you. I checked."

"That bow was my father's."

"I'm sorry."

"Don't be. I'll be getting it back soon."

"Can I watch?"

Those golden eyes opened to meet hers again. "It's a date. So, Guild candidate Sumner, how do you propose to get us both out of here since you so foolishly refuse to leave me behind?"

"It *is* tempting. Unfortunately, Judge Brady might frown on my decision to abandon a wounded man." He just grunted and she grinned. "We'll leave as soon as the storm clears out. I'll put together a sled, kind of a travois—"

"A what?"

"Travois. It's a sort of three-point sled. I lugged you this far in the sleeping bag; we'll make better time with a sled. Besides, we need the sleeping bag in one piece, and while that material's tough, it's not that tough. If not for the snow, I don't think it would have held up.

"I've already started on the sled, though. I found some

long branches for the poles and I've cut the crosspieces. I'll finish tomorrow, assuming I can work outside. I'm making snow shoes for myself, too." She held them up, then immediately bristled at the doubtful look on his face. "Hey, they'll work fine. And, besides, what do *you* know about snowshoes, with your little cat feet carrying you light as a feather?"

"What do *you* know?" he asked with a meaningful look at the primitive contraptions.

She gave him a dirty look, then eyed the shoes she'd spent so much effort on and started laughing. "Okay," she managed. "So they're ugly. They'll do the trick. I should only need them for a couple of days anyway, and after that, they'll make fine kindling."

"Might as well get some use out of them," he muttered.

Opening her mouth to retort, she yawned hugely instead. "It's been wonderful getting to know you better," she said around the yawn. "A real treat. We should try to sleep now. Some of us have a lot to do tomorrow, so…" Her voice trailed off as she contemplated the sleeping bag, suddenly uncomfortable at the memory of waking up next to him. "Um, you go ahead and use the bag tonight. I'll—"

"Don't be a fool. We slept together earlier. This is no different."

"You were unconscious then, I mean you didn't even know I was there."

"I think my virtue is safe with you. Besides, it'll be warmer if we're together." He gave her a challenging look.

She wavered. It *would* be warmer with both of them in the sleeping bag. She banked the fire down to embers and stretched out next to his big body, keeping a careful inch between them, and leaving the zipper halfway down.

He chuckled. In spite of his weakness, it was a low masculine sound, and she was abruptly reminded that he was very much a male. "You're going to want to relax," he purred.

She blew out a breath and rolled onto her side away from him, feeling the heat of his shifter-enhanced metabolism burning at her back. Pillowing her head on her arm, she closed her eyes, convinced she'd never sleep. It had been a long, tiring few days, however, and she was soon drifting off.

"You're wrong, you know," he said softly.

"About what?" she asked drowsily.

"I did know you were here. I heard you talking to me. It helped."

"I'm glad," she said, and fell into a deep hole where the only sound was the steady rhythm of his heartbeat.

Chapter Twenty-Six

Rhodry braced weakly against a sapling too narrow to hold his weight, the little tree bowing so precariously that he'd swear he could hear its groan of protest. And he could sympathize. He would gladly have borne his own weight, but didn't want to embarrass himself any further by falling flat on his face. Bad enough that he was barely able to take care of his own necessities. The last thing he needed was Amanda coming to his rescue again, picking him up off the ground. It didn't get much more humiliating than that.

He looked down the few yards to the base of the small hill where she was working steadily, weaving strips of soft bark into a mat of some sort which she then planned to tie onto the triangle of branches she'd bound together earlier. He'd never seen such a sled. He had to admit it would probably work, though it would take a lot of effort on her part to pull it with him aboard.

Her long blond braid fell over one shoulder and she

flicked it back in a careless gesture when she stood up. She'd combed his hair for him this morning, then threaded it back into a traditional braid, and tied it off with a leather thong from her pack. It had seemed a far more intimate act than the two of them sleeping together, her strong, slender fingers winding through his hair, brushing against his bare nape.

His lips curved slightly as she muttered a curse down below, the sound carrying easily in the thin, cool air. She was strapping those ridiculous snowshoes on again.

Having grown up in the mountains, he'd seen plenty of snow in his thirty-five years of life, and plenty of snowshoes to go with it. She was right, though. Being a shifter, he'd never had to worry about them. His many norm cousins would have known how to put together a perfectly fine pair, he was sure. He thought now that it had been a mistake to rely so completely on his shifter abilities, and he promised himself he'd change that as soon as he got home. Assuming he did. While she'd let the subject drop last night, he had no doubt that Desmond Serna and his friend would be back to try again. Especially if he didn't make it back to the city before they discovered he was still alive. Their nightmare would be if he lived to testify against them.

Amanda gave a little shout, and he glanced up to see her treading more or less successfully across the snow pack, her primitive foot gear working just fine. She laughed and gave him a big grin. He lifted a careful hand in greeting, watching as she took a few more tentative steps, getting the feel for the shoes.

He didn't quite know what to think about Amanda. Oh, he knew what he thought of her as a woman. As weakened as his body was by the rockweed and his various injuries, he still wanted her. He had almost from the beginning. It was the other Amanda who still puzzled him, the one who'd been so doggedly persistent about joining the Guild. He'd been dead set against letting her undertake the trials, and certain she'd only end up injured, or worse. And she'd proved him wrong. She'd fought off a hunting pack of hycats all by herself, and saved his life in the process. No, that wasn't right. The *only* reason she'd dealt with those hycats had been to save his life. And she'd done it all without the benefit of fangs or claws.

It wasn't that he didn't know any strong women. His mother and sisters—hell, most of the women of his mountain clan—were strong females, tough-minded and no-nonsense. And none of them could have killed a pack of hycats using only a Guild short bow, or any other weapon, for that matter. Amanda had done it in the dead black of night, then dragged his useless ass through the forest in a damn sleeping bag, in a blizzard. That was more than strength—that was courage and unwavering determination.

She was down there now, wrestling with the sled frame, muscling it onto the snow pack all by herself, never asking for help she knew he couldn't give right now. Her jacket, worn over a single undershirt and heavy leggings, was warmer than it looked, but she still had to be cold. She'd ripped up her spare shirts for his bandages, and given him her wool cloak to wear over his clothes, which were little more than pieces of tattered cloth.

And that brought his thoughts right back to his inability to shift. It was galling to find himself as furless as a norm. He'd tried calling his animal again this morning, with no luck. Serna and Daly would pay for that. More than anything else, more even than for trying to kill him, they would pay for taking away his animal, even for only a few days.

Down below, Amanda cursed. She was trying to hold together the mat she'd woven, while tying it in place between the poles at the same time. Wanting to do something other than stand about, he gritted his teeth and straightened away from the tree, which snapped up in relief as if to push him on his way. The simple effort of standing left him panting for breath. He didn't care. He'd had enough of being an invalid, and was determined to overcome this humiliating frailty.

He made his slow way down the hill, leaning heavily on the thick branch Amanda had trimmed for him to use as a cane. She seemed to understand his need to remain upright, to do for himself where he could. Although he was pretty sure she thought it a uniquely male stupidity that he insisted on being upright at all. She'd stopped her work and was watching him now, just waiting to jump to his aid. And so, stupid male that he was, he kept going.

His chest ached as though steel bands were tightening around it, and the stitches she'd sewn into him felt like they were tearing him apart rather than holding him together. His legs wanted to wobble out from beneath him on the soft, thick snow and he covered their weakness by balancing on the cane with an obvious clumsiness as though it was only the slick surface making it difficult to remain upright. He stumbled slightly, and a knife's edge of agony slid through his groin as he tried to recover. He bent nearly double with it, and would have fallen if she hadn't shot up like an arrow to grab his arm.

It wounded him to take the help, although not as much as it would have to slide nose first into a snowdrift.

"Time to go back inside," she said. "That wind's kicking

up again, and it's damn cold."

He nodded, unable to catch his breath enough to talk, letting them both pretend it was the cold driving them back inside and not his plaguing weak body. In reality, the snow had pretty much let up by this afternoon. He'd even spotted brief patches of blue sky and sunshine in the short time he'd been outside.

When they reached the narrow entrance to their burrow, he tensed, waiting for the pain when he knelt down to ease his way through. It didn't disappoint him. His left thigh felt like it was on fire, like a hot blade was trying to cut away his leg from his body. He closed his eyes against it, forcing himself to keep moving so she wouldn't see.

"Rhodry?" she said behind him, her voice thick with worry.

"It's just the blood rushing to my head, damn it," he snapped and regretted it almost immediately. She didn't deserve his rudeness. And besides, she wasn't stupid. She'd know something was wrong.

He crawled on all fours over to the sleeping bag, pretty much collapsing as he fell onto it, barely managing to turn and lie back with his eyes closed. Her worried stare burned right through his closed lids, so he flung his arm over his face, hiding the pain written there.

"I'll make some tea," she murmured.

He heard her soft movements as she maneuvered in the cramped space, unzipping her jacket, stoking the fire and putting the water to boil. She didn't push him now, just as she hadn't pushed him on the question of who was behind the attack, although she had to be itching with curiosity. Hell, it was more than curiosity. For better or worse, they were in this together. He owed it to her to tell the whole story, to let her know what she'd gotten tangled up in by saving his life.

A manda heard Rhodry's breathing even out, becoming slower and deeper. She was worried. He should have shifted by now, rockweed or no. It was a built-in defense for shifters, part of the reason they were so dominant on the planet. Shifting was as much a part of their biology as the blood in their veins and, damn it, he *should* have shifted by now. Something was wrong besides the rockweed they'd fed him. There was something she'd missed. Something he didn't want her to know. And to hell with that.

"Rhodry?"

She kept her voice soft yet demanding, and she saw him jerk awake, probably unaware he'd even fallen asleep. "Sorry," he muttered. "Must be more tired than I thought."

"You may have overdone it today," she agreed. "And I'm a little worried you might have torn something in that last fall you took. Why don't you stretch out, and I'll take a quick look at your stitches, make sure everything's still all right?"

"I'm tired. Tomorrow's soon enough."

"No," she said firmly. "It's not. Don't be a baby, de Mendoza. Let me see some skin."

He scowled, and didn't resist as she peeled back the cloak and helped him sit up to remove the shirt. "Just stay that way for a minute," she said. He gave her a puzzled look, which she ignored. She wanted to get a good look at all the parts of his body she'd given only a cursory exam before.

She ran her hands over the smooth skin and firm muscles

of his back, admiring his strength even as she searched for some overlooked injury. He was such a big man, his shoulders broad and muscular above a strong back and narrow hips. She would have sighed with pleasure under different circumstances.

"All right," she said instead, tapping his shoulder lightly to indicate he should lie down. She waited until he was settled, then said, "I want to check—"

Her gaze shot to his face in surprise when he grabbed her hand and sat back up, preventing her from loosening his trousers.

Aha. "I need to check the belly wound, Rhodry."

"It's fine, no pain at all."

"That's good. Then maybe it's time to take out the stitches. Let me see."

He didn't release her hand. "It's unseemly," he said, sounding embarrassed.

He probably *was* embarrassed, because that was a stupid thing to say on so many fronts. Shifters were the least modest people she'd ever met. If they wore clothes, it was only for the comfort of others. "Rhodry," she said implacably.

"Damn it, woman, am I allowed no privacy at all?"

She just stared at him until he released her hand with a sigh, then lay back and flung an arm over his eyes again.

She unlaced his pants and tugged them down, careful to avoid rubbing against the belly wound, which was, in fact, healing quite well. "It's as I expected," she commented, pressing lightly along the line of sutures. "We'll wait a few more days with the stitches, though." She hooked her fingers in the loose waistband and tugged the cloth all the way down to mid-thigh...and gave an audible gasp as she sucked in a surprised breath.

He chuckled falsely without looking at her. "He's a fine specimen, though perhaps not that fine."

"What were you thinking?" she hissed furiously. No longer bothering with being careful, she yanked his trousers completely off and pushed his thighs open to reveal a deep wound on his left thigh. It was in a bad location, nearly in the crease between his testicles and his leg. The whole area was angry red and puffy, discolored with infection. And the wound looked like... She stared up at his face, meeting his angry glare.

"That's a knife wound," she breathed.

"Aye, they thought to end the de Mendoza line for good," he said bitterly.

"Rhodry." She felt tears of frustration burning her eyes. She'd worked so hard to take care of him, and he'd been concealing this the whole time. She couldn't understand why he'd done it. And she sure as hell wasn't about to let him die over it.

Swallowing hard, she pushed away the emotion. "I need to clean this," she managed to say in a matter-of-fact voice. "It's already infected, which is probably why you're still so fucking weak," she snapped, feeling helplessness trying to overtake her and substituting anger instead.

"Shifters don't get infections," he growled. "Besides, once I shift it'll be gone."

"If you live that long," she retorted nastily. "And maybe the whole infection thing is tied to your inability to shift, have you thought about that? What if you can't shift for a while? Are you just going to wait for the leg to rot off along with everything else?" She was shouting now, furious that he'd put himself in danger, that he'd put *both* of them in danger with his foolish pride. "What is your fucking problem? You think I've never seen a dick before?"

"They tried to castrate me!" he roared, trying to sit up. "Do you understand that?" He gasped with sudden pain and fell back weakly. "It wasn't enough only to kill me," he said more quietly. "They wanted to geld me first."

"So you decided to finish the job for them, is that it? You didn't even—" She closed her eyes and sucked in a calming breath. "You're an asshole. A stupid, prideful, ignorant asshole. And screaming at each other isn't going to help," she said with forced logic. "Whether you like it or not, we're in this together. So I'm going to save your precious manhood for you, not because you deserve to breed more fools like yourself, but because no one, *no one*, gets to die on *my* Guild trial, you got that? And that includes you, you pigheaded, prideful—"

"You already said that one."

"Well, it deserves to be said twice," she snapped, then twisted around to check the canteen and make sure there was enough hot water. When she rummaged in her pack and pulled out the contraband antibiotic capsules, he looked at her curiously.

"What are those?"

"I smuggled in some antibiotics so you bigoted, short-sighted shifters wouldn't take them away from me when you dropped me off. Just because you all can heal almost anything doesn't mean the rest of us can."

"I'm not taking—"

"Shut up. You've officially abrogated your rights to refuse medical treatment by virtue of being too stupid to live.

If we weren't stuck up here in the middle of nowhere, I could find some coneflower and make a poultice, and it would probably work better on your Harp metabolism than these capsules. Since we *are* stuck here, we'll have to make do with what I brought. You will take these pills, or I'll simply grind them up and put them in your food, and then you'll have to eat them or starve to death."

She looked up to see him watching her, his golden eyes half lidded, his full mouth twitching.

"Don't you dare," she snarled.

His mouth tightened against an obvious smile, and he gave her a look of total innocence. She snorted in disgust.

"This is going to hurt. A lot," she added sweetly.

The thigh wound had been every bit as bad as she'd feared. Another day or two and he wouldn't have had to worry about losing his testicles, because he'd have been too busy dying from blood poisoning. She washed the wound out thoroughly, trying in spite of her anger not to hurt him, and knowing she didn't succeed.

At one point, he sat up with a snarl and tried to push her hands away, muttering something about "cleaning his own damn balls."

Amanda gave him a look and a shove, and he fell flat on his back once again, golden eyes glaring.

"This is too serious for half measures, de Mendoza, and I've already seen your idea of wound care. I'm not impressed." She leaned forward again, pushing her braid over her shoulder impatiently. "Besides, I'm nowhere near your balls. If I was, you'd know it."

She smiled slightly at his disgruntled huff of breath, then frowned as she continued cleaning out the wound. In spite of what she'd said to him, Amanda was very aware of just how close his attackers had come to their intended target. And it was bad, very bad. A regular human would have been much sicker than Rhodry was, if not dead. Even without shifting, his enhanced metabolism had minimized the damage, and was probably already working to rebuild the muscle, now that she'd cleaned the worst of it.

She straightened finally, having done everything she could under their primitive circumstances. She hoped it was enough. He needed a proper hospital, not her small cache of pills and her dirty shirt.

He downed the first of the antibiotic capsules, grousing like a three-year-old, as she cleaned up, washing her hands with water as hot as she could stand it. Her back was stiff from working bent over in the cramped space, on top of already having spent much of the day struggling to weave together bark and branch that didn't want to be woven. And she thought her hands and fingers might never recover from the harsh treatment they'd suffered over the last week or so. She made a mental note to bring moisturizer the next time she was abandoned in the wild, then sighed wearily as she dragged his pants back up, leaving the ties unfastened. It would have been better to leave him naked from the waist down, but it was cold and besides, she had to sleep next to him again tonight.

He was already sound asleep, so she lay down and pulled the cover over both of them. She wanted to groan with pleasure at finally being able to stretch out, and she'd have given just about anything to be home in her big, soft bed, fresh and warm after a hot bath, with…

Her eyes flashed open in shock. In her fantasy, it had been Rhodry waiting for her in that big bed. Stubborn, pigheaded Rhodry. Rhodry, whose searing kiss in front of the Guild Hall had left her wanting him more than ever. She stared at the fading embers of the fire for a while, unwilling to close her eyes. Eventually her worn out body took away the choice.

It wasn't long before her dreams had his warm arm slipping around her waist and tucking her in close, and if she briefly woke up enough to wonder whether she was dreaming or not, she was too tired, and fell back to sleep too quickly, to worry about it.

Chapter Twenty-Seven

Amanda was unusually quiet when they rose the next morning—at least it was unusual in his experience. The one constant while he'd been struggling back to consciousness had been her voice, and she hadn't shown any reluctance since then to express her opinion. While she went about their morning preparations with her usual efficiency, she didn't say much of anything that wasn't absolutely necessary.

If she was trying to make him feel guilty, it was working quite well. He should have told her about the knife wound. He'd kept thinking he would shift soon, and everything would be fine. He'd never needed medical attention before, never seen a doctor, not even the time he'd broken his leg in a dare with his cousins over a leap from the rooftops. Although in that case the pain had certainly been real enough.

He looked up to find her regarding him silently. "What?" he said suspiciously.

She screwed the cap back on her battered canteen and stowed it in her pack. "I think we should get out of here today. The weather's cleared and we should take advantage of it while we can."

"Agreed," he said cautiously, knowing that wasn't all of what she had to say.

"I want to check your injuries before we leave."

He scowled, then lay back and pushed his trousers down, spreading his legs in lewd invitation. "I'm all yours," he said with a flat stare.

She didn't respond to his challenge, just scooted closer and ran her soft fingers over his chest and belly. "I've been thinking about rockweed," she said absently. "It stands to reason that a shifter's enhanced ability for cellular regeneration is part and parcel of the shift process. You are, after all, rapidly destroying some cells, while regenerating others every time you shift. A drug that suppresses the ability to shift would also be likely to suppress cellular regeneration. And *that* would affect your ability to heal injury and avoid sickness. Which would explain why someone like you—"

"Someone like me?"

She gave him a mild glance. "A healthy and strong shifter."

"Ah." He flushed, then stirred uncomfortably when her examination moved to his groin. It wasn't that he was shy. No shifter was shy. It was the sensuous feel of her fingers as they glided purposefully along the skin of his abdomen, her breath warm as she bent to check his wound, and the fact that he was definitely feeling better.

She straightened, her hand resting lightly on his naked thigh. "Very nice, de Mendoza," she said, and he would have sworn there was the first glint of humor behind her serious expression. "It's improved tremendously just overnight. If my theory's right, your recuperative abilities are returning. I wouldn't be surprised if you can shift again soon."

"Thank the gods," he muttered. "Can I get dressed now?"

She left her hand on his bare leg and gave him a lazy look that had him sitting up straight and pulling on his trousers before he embarrassed himself any further. "I'll just take a trip outside," he said, then rolled over to all fours and crawled out of the damnable thicket, wincing as his various injuries made themselves known. He hoped she was right about the shifting. It couldn't happen soon enough for him.

When Rhodry finally finished his business and made his clumsy way down the hillock, Amanda was already arranging things on the makeshift sled. He took one look at the sleeping bag all cozied up on the matting between the poles, and said, "I'll walk."

She turned and gave him a thoughtful look. "That snow pack's five feet deep, maybe more."

"We have the snow shoes."

A look of irritation crossed her face. "Only one pair."

His answer was a raised eyebrow.

She stared at him, squinting a little, because the morning sun was directly behind him. With an irritated grunt, she came several steps closer until she was standing close enough that he blocked the sunlight.

"Let me get this straight," she said. "You're going to

wear *my* snowshoes—which you thought were only good for kindling, by the way—and I'm going to ride in the sled while you, big strong shifter that you are, will be pulling. Do I have that right?"

Rhodry opened his mouth to respond, and she leaned forward suddenly, closing the small distance left between them. She had to tip her head back to meet his eyes because he was a good four inches taller than she was.

"I know this is difficult for you," she said in a low voice, though there was no one else to hear. "It's hard to depend on others when you're used to doing for yourself. We need to move fast, Rhodry. Someone tried to kill you—you don't want to tell me who, that's fine. It doesn't even matter who they are. We need to be gone from here before they come back. Please. Just a little bit longer."

Her eyes were dark blue this morning, like the shadows beneath the trees in summer. There were bruised-looking circles marring the fine skin beneath those eyes, and she was worn out, pale with exhaustion in spite of her cold-reddened cheeks.

Rhodry was abruptly ashamed. He brushed his thumb over the dark circles, and wished he could brush the exhaustion away as easily. "You're right," he said. "I'll ride in the damn sled."

Her eyes closed briefly. "Thank you."

"Don't thank me, Amanda. I'm feeling enough of an ass as it is." He pulled the sled around so he could climb aboard, feeling the pull in every muscle after days of inactivity. She was right. He knew it. Damn if he liked it, though.

"Thank you, anyway," she said.

It was quick work to get him settled, all wound up like

a piece of sausage. She patted his shoulder as she walked to the front and lifted the tow ropes. He felt the ropes grow taut as the snow tried to hold on, and then she gave a single grunt and they were moving.

They made good time, better than Amanda expected. The storm had dipped much further south than she'd guessed, leaving a snow-covered landscape over which the sled traveled easily. The next day would be more difficult as they gradually left the cold weather behind. Harp was a small planet with a severe axial tilt, and even a short distance could make a big difference in temperature. By tomorrow, the undergrowth would thicken, and tangled vines would begin to clog passage between the trees, making it increasingly more time-consuming to find a clear trail for the sled.

Fortunately, Rhodry's healing abilities seemed to be returning with a vengeance. By tomorrow morning, he wouldn't need the sled for anything except walking support. And by afternoon, they'd hit the Verge, which was a barren zone of rock and dirt. Dragging the sled over that would be almost impossible. Once they crossed it, however, it was a straight shot back to the Green, and just the thought of that cheered Amanda tremendously.

"We should camp here tonight," Rhodry said. He'd already spent the last hour walking next to the sled, instead of riding in it. "It's nearly sundown, and tomorrow will be rough going."

She blinked. "We only have to cross the Verge tomorrow," she said, and immediately regretted it.

The look he gave her was carefully blank, despite the smug smile she could see trying to fight its way onto his face. Clearly he knew something she didn't, and since he wasn't about to share, and she wasn't about to ask... Damn. He'd been much easier to get along with when he was unconscious.

"Right," he agreed with suspicious ease. "But if we camp here tonight, there's a small stream through those trees. And with a good night's sleep, I'll be able to walk all day so we'll make better time."

His alpha tendencies were creeping back, too. He didn't wait for her agreement, just started pulling the sleeping bag and other supplies from the sled, wincing only slightly when he reached too far. Although his shifter metabolism had finally kicked in with some healing, he still hadn't shifted. Maybe his system was spending too much of its energy keeping him alive and healing the various wounds. She didn't know that much about shifter chemistry—no norm did as far as she could tell, and shifters seemed to like it that way. Rhodry certainly wasn't willing to talk to her about it. Or anything else for that matter, since he still refused to tell her who had attacked him.

He'd already selected a campsite and was slowly clearing a space for their sleeping bag when she blew out an exasperated breath. "Sit," she ordered him. "I'll clear the campsite. You can clean the rabbits," she added, when he gave her an irritated look.

He laughed for the first time since she'd found him, his teeth flashing white, golden eyes dancing with amusement. And Amanda's stomach did a little flip as a familiar desire tightened her chest. Damn it.

"Just don't forget whose trial this is," she managed to

say briskly. And that was something she'd better not forget herself.

Amanda threw the last of the bones into the fire, wiping her hands on her already filthy leggings and thinking longingly of a hot bath. They had only a small fire going, enough to cook the two rabbits she'd snared, and to heat some water for tea. The sky was clear above the quiet trees, and on the horizon, the biggest of Harp's three moons, Fodla, was a thick slice of pale promise. There was no wind at all, and the air was mild enough that Rhodry had thrown off her cloak once they settled in. He lounged near the flames, eyes half closed, as he lay propped up against a downed tree trunk and looking quite comfortable.

"I'd kill for a piece of fruit," Amanda said suddenly. "I think there's actually a disease you can get from eating nothing except meat."

Rhodry's eyes opened, and he gave her a big cat's grin.

"Okay, not you, just us humans in general. You could probably live for months on rabbits and…I don't know, nuts from the trees or something."

"Not months," he corrected lazily. "And that doesn't mean I'd enjoy it."

She chuckled softly and settled back, propped up on one elbow. It was amazing, really, how easy they were with one another. Here they were sharing a fire and a sleeping bag with no problem. Although that sleeping bag *was* going to be a problem soon. She was already thinking of him more as a man and less as a patient who needed her help to stay warm.

"So tell me," she said, intentionally forcing her thoughts down a different path. "You weren't on the escort team that abandoned me out on the glacier. Even though I was pretty sick, I made a point of remembering every one of *them*. So, how'd you happen to be so far north of the Green? Coincidence?"

It was a question that had been bothering her ever since she'd found him. There were no regular patrols that close to the glacier, because there was no one out there to protect.

He studied her silently for a long moment, long enough that she thought he wasn't going to answer her…again. Until finally he said, "I was *supposed* to be on your escort. So was Fionn." He shrugged. "Fionn objected to me. I objected to Fionn."

"Why?"

"Why to which one?"

"Either, both, I don't care."

"I suspect the answer's the same to both anyway. I wanted him gone, he wanted me gone, because the two of you are lovers."

"We are not."

He shrugged. "I believe you. Fionn's another matter. He's let everyone think it's true, and he was acting awfully possessive at the Hall that day."

"Fionn's an idiot. A shifter idiot," she added. "Which is the worst kind. You guys are territorial about everything from who goes out the door first to who gets the last piece of fruit. Besides, what difference would it have made for Fionn to be on the escort, even if we *were* lovers? Which we're not," she repeated. "He doesn't think I'm qualified for the

Guild any more than you do."

Rhodry had the grace to be embarrassed. "I think it's safe to say my position on that has changed. If not for you, I'd be dead."

Amanda didn't say anything to that. What was there to say? It was true. "So why *were* you all the way out here then?" she persisted.

R hodry straightened away from the log with a wince of pain, and made a show of rearranging his legs. Nothing hurt, he just needed to give himself time to think. Should he tell her about Desmond Serna's supposed rescue mission? If he told her that much, he'd also have to reveal what he'd been told of Nando's plan to sabotage her trial, and he had only Serna's word on that. And while he sure as hell had no obligation to protect his traitorous cousin, he wasn't comfortable with the possibility of spreading false rumors. So, he told her the truth. Just not all of it.

"Fionn was pissed when I objected to his inclusion on the escort," he said finally. "We argued, so Orrin Brady stepped in and kicked us both off. I'm not exactly Mr. Popularity at the Guild Hall."

"What a shock."

Rhodry grimaced. "You don't know the half of it. Anyway, Desmond Serna approached me—he's a distant cousin on my mother's side. He told me that he and Kane Daly were going out to do some hunting along the glacier, and did I want to join them."

"So what happened?" she asked.

"I forgot my family history," he growled, angry at himself. "Serna's a cousin, like I said. A cousin from a branch that would benefit greatly if I died. I guess he got tired of waiting."

"Your own cousin tried to kill you?"

"I did say he was a *distant* cousin."

"Very funny."

"Families are funny things sometimes."

"I wouldn't know," she muttered.

"No family squabbles among the Sumner clan?"

"There *is* no Sumner clan. At least not for a few million light years."

"Ah. That must be…different, I suppose. I was raised with family living practically on top of me. My closest friends are all cousins. Devlin cousins, that is. Not the kind who try to kill me." He felt a pang of miserable homesickness when he thought about the many Devlin cousins he'd grown up with.

Over on her side of the fire, Amanda had fallen silent. She had a sad look on her face that made him feel guilty about lying to her. Not that he'd lied precisely. Not outright anyway. She had to suspect what Nando and the others had done, what they'd hoped would happen to her. She wasn't stupid, and she'd sure as hell defeated their plans anyway. If he hadn't slowed her down, she'd probably be halfway back to the city by now. He grinned privately, contemplating Nando's reaction when she walked into the Guild Hall on her own.

And then he frowned, thinking about the repercussions to Nando and the others if Amanda survived to tell the truth of what they'd done. Maybe it would be better if she wasn't *entirely* alone when she walked into that Guild Hall.

She sat up and began dismantling the roasting spit, dropping the sticks into the flames where they burned hotly for a few minutes before disintegrating.

"You want any more of this?" she asked him, holding out the metal canteen which they'd used to make tea.

"No, thanks," he said, starting to rise. "Give it to me, I'll take it—"

She pushed him back gently. "You go ahead and lie down. I'll rinse it out and refill it for morning."

He wanted to protest. He would have if every healing wound and aching muscle in his body hadn't been making itself known. The amount of rockweed necessary to keep him from shifting for this long, and under these conditions, took a toll on a shifter's body. That trail bar must have been filled with the stuff. He shuddered to think what might have happened if he'd eaten the whole thing. As it was, his body was fighting a constant battle, trying to do what was natural to it, while the herb continued to deny it.

He stood up and walked over to where they'd spread out the sleeping bag. He lowered himself carefully, stretching out on his side, his watchful gaze never leaving her trim form as she threaded through the trees. While he might be weaker than his normal self, he wasn't too weak to defend her if it came down to it.

Amanda walked through the dark trees to the small stream, her penlight providing just enough illumination to light her way over the uneven ground. She knelt by the water to rinse the canteen a couple of times, then filled and capped it for morning. Setting it to one side, she leaned down enough to splash her face and hands, wishing she had even a small sliver of soap.

She froze at the sound of movement across the water, then lifted her head slowly and found two pairs of bright green eyes glowing at her, one slightly higher than the other. Gyr-wolves. Not exactly friendly, not necessarily a threat to her either. They would have smelled the cooking meat and been drawn to the fire, where Rhodry's presence had kept them from coming any closer. There were very few creatures on Harp that didn't fear a shifter. And rightly so.

A slight yipping noise erupted from further back, and she saw two of the eyes disappear as one of the animals swung around to check out the disturbance. The other continued to regard her steadily, and Amanda understood. This was a mated pair, with their pups nearby. As long as she stayed on her side of the stream, they'd leave her alone. Especially with a shifter sleeping back at the campsite.

She met the wolf's stare, never turning away, until the second pair of eyes reappeared briefly, followed by both wolves moving away from the stream, probably taking their pups to a safer location. She picked up the canteen, then stood and made her slow way back.

Rhodry lay on his side, golden eyes following her return to the campsite. He scooted over when she knelt down, making the necessary room for her in the narrow sleeping bag. There was no real reason for them to sleep together anymore. It wasn't that cold, and she'd be just as warm wrapping herself in the cloak by the fire and letting him have the bag to himself. Besides, he'd probably welcome the room now that he was feeling better. His eyes followed her as she banked the fire to a bare ember and picked up her cloak. He shivered slightly.

"Are you cold?" she said instantly. She crawled over and touched his forehead. It was warm beneath her fingers, no more than the usual shifter heat, though.

He lifted the top of the sleeping bag, clearly expecting her to join him. She sighed and crawled inside, feeling the warmth of his body against her back as they settled into what was by now a familiar comfort.

"Gyrs?" he asked softly once she was stretched out next to him.

"Yes. A pair with new pups."

"It's that time of year."

Amanda nodded wordlessly, then yawned. "It's handy having you around. I'd have been awake half the night waiting for them to raid my camp."

"So glad to be useful."

She chuckled, feeling him relax into sleep as she closed her eyes, and knowing she'd sleep through the night undisturbed, just because he was there.

Chapter Twenty-Eight

Amanda had never seen the Verge before, at least not this close. From space, it looked completely barren—a wasteland of dirt where nothing grew, and where house-sized boulders lay tossed on one another like a giant's discarded baubles. Up close…

She swore softly. The boulders were there, and the dirt. What she couldn't have seen from four hundred miles up were the small stones littering every inch of ground between her and the distant edge of the Green. Millions of stones piled one on top of the other. It was going to be pure hell to walk across that. And, gods, she was tired of this.

Standing on the edge of yet another obstacle in their journey home, Amanda truly appreciated for perhaps the first time just how far out her Guild escort had dropped her. Maybe Nando and the others actually *had* wanted her dead. And what did that say about Fionn? Had he known what they planned? She knew he didn't want her in the Guild.

Would he have agreed to risk her life to prevent it?

Or maybe it was Rhodry she shouldn't trust. Maybe he'd known about Nando's plan, and gotten Fionn kicked off her escort because he knew Fionn wouldn't go along with it. She shook her head immediately. She trusted him. Especially after these past days struggling together to survive. As gruff as he'd been, as stubborn about her joining the Guild, and convinced she'd never make it, he'd always been upfront about it, and he'd always insisted that she have a level playing field, even when he'd been sure she would fail. Besides, if Rhodry had wanted her dead, she'd be hycat food by now.

She turned her back to the Verge and watched as he caught up with her. He was moving slowly today, and she could see what it cost him. No matter how much of the rest of his story was true, someone had definitely wanted *him* dead.

"You knew it was like this," she accused him when he was within earshot. "All of these fucking stones."

He shrugged.

"Why didn't you say anything?"

"You wouldn't have believed me. Deep down, you don't think there's anything you can't overcome. It's admirable. It also means you don't really trust anyone other than yourself."

She looked at him in surprise. "You don't know anything about me," she muttered irritably, unwilling to admit he might be right. Of course, he *was* right about the Verge, she'd never have believed him. She'd have dismissed his warnings, confident she could handle it. Was he also right about her not trusting anyone? She sighed and turned back to study the shadows cast by the giant boulders in the afternoon sun.

"We won't make it across in a day, will we?" she asked.

Rhodry shook his head slightly. "We'll get a good start, though, and camp in there overnight." His gaze wandered over the landscape. "There are caves in some of the larger rock formations. But after a storm like this last one, it'll be cold, though. Those big rocks hold onto the chill."

She shook the empty sled she'd been dragging most of the day. "We seem to have plenty of kindling," she said morosely.

He smiled gently. "Tomorrow night we'll be under the trees and back in the Green."

"Am I that obvious?"

He sighed. "I'm just as eager as you are to get there. So," he gestured ahead, "shall we conquer the Verge?"

Amanda drew a deep breath and started forward. Conquer, hell. She'd be happy just to make it across with both ankles intact.

As they made their way carefully onto the boulder-strewn field, weaving around the petrified remnants of ancient trees, she considered what she knew about the Verge. It had been created millennia ago, when the retreating glacier had shuffled back and forth over the same mile or so of latitude for a few thousand years before resuming its northward retreat to what was now the permanent ice cap. What it left behind was about a mile of dead zone between the Green and the greater glacial area.

Like everywhere else on Harp, the Verge wasn't completely dead. There were all sorts of rodents and reptiles living there. And for tonight, it would be home to a couple of humans as well.

The sun was sinking and the air was already noticeably

colder when Rhodry led her around a pile of huge stones that were crushed up against one another in a permanent battle for space. Together they formed a sort of horseshoe formation. At the closed end, jagged-edged boulders had fallen together in an imperfect fit to create a small cave, which faced away from the glacier, and so was protected from the coldest winds. Amanda tugged her flashlight from around her neck and walked toward the dark hole, to find that Rhodry was already there.

"Let me—" he began.

"I'll do it," she said, dodging quickly around him. She pulled out her knife, in case they weren't the only animals looking for a likely shelter, and dropped down to crawl through the low entrance. Once inside, she was able to stand almost upright, flashing her light over the uneven ceiling, the walls, and finally the ground. There was a desiccated Gilly bear skeleton in the very back of the cave. That skeleton, combined with the plentiful spoor scattered around, told her the Gilly had been the cave's last tenant, not some other creature's lunch. The bear had died peacefully in its own bed. Of course, it might also have been severely injured somewhere else and crawled home to die, which, call her a cynic, she thought was far more likely.

She emerged from the cave to find Rhodry already dismantling the sled. He straightened and gave her a knowing smile. Of course. His nose had probably already told him everything she'd crawled in there to discover.

"Yeah, yeah, fine. We can't all have your nose." She sighed and gave the rapidly disappearing sled a fond pat, which elicited a cough of laughter from him. "It worked well enough," she said defensively.

"Aye," he admitted. "It did."

Surprised by his admission, she gave *him* a fond pat as well, and began scrounging around for dead brush to use as a broom. Finding what she wanted, she swept the small space out, starting at the back and moving forward. When she got to the opening, she stepped out and gave Rhodry a gentle shove, indicating he should move out of the way so she could sweep the remnants out into the clear space between the stones.

"What're you doing?" he asked.

"Sweeping the house out. Women's work. You should be glad."

"I would be if I thought it would last."

"I could sweep it all back in," she threatened, holding her makeshift broom in the air.

"Did I mention what a great job you're doing?" he said with mock sincerity. "Truly. Can't think what I'd do without you."

She snorted. "I can." She brushed the unpleasant stuff well away from the "front door" of the cave and helped him finish off the sled, using her knife to weaken the long branches, breaking them into small pieces, which were then tossed into the cave for firewood. Their few supplies went next, and then she straightened, stretching her back as she looked around. "I am well and truly sick of rabbit. Any other suggestions?"

"Should be a diamondback lurking somewhere in these rocks." He drew in a deep breath, his head thrown back, eyes closed. When he opened them, he started off, and Amanda stepped in front of him.

"Just give me the direction. You should rest."

He drew up to his full height and scowled down his nose at her. It didn't faze her at all. "You did a lot of walking today," she said softly, moving in close. "And you'll need your strength." His eyes opened wide as her hand grazed up his thigh. He grinned and started to reach for her, then howled in outrage when she pressed her fingers directly into the still tender knife wound in his groin.

"Damn it, woman! What kind of healer are you?"

"No kind at all," she said smugly. "Now go inside and rest while I find us a snake for dinner."

"You could have just asked," he grumbled, crawling through the narrow opening and groaning loudly for effect as he spread out the sleeping bag and lay down on it.

She laughed, then turned away with a grimace. She'd never admit that she thoroughly detested hunting snake. Especially in the rocks like this. She didn't mind eating them. The snakes on Harp had a layer of fat that made them perfect for cooking over a campfire, and they could be roasted right in their skins. They were also sneaky, slithering creatures and a royal pain in the ass to catch.

There were times she wished she'd been born one of those helpless women who could sit back and wait for the menfolk to take care of everything. She sighed. This was definitely one of those times.

Chapter Twenty-Nine

"So how long will it take to cross the rest of this thing?" Amanda asked, referring to the Verge. She reached out and pulled a leg off the diamondback now sizzling over the fire. The joint came away easily, the meat tender and juicy. For all that she hated hunting the damn things, they sure were tasty.

"I told you, we'll sleep in the Green tomorrow," Rhodry said, wiping his hands on one of the strips of cloth they'd saved from the sled ties.

"And then maybe a week to the city," she mused out loud. "Assuming no more surprises." The fire popped and spat in the silence as grease dripped from the skewered snake, the light splashing orange against the dark stone walls and crawling toward the shadowed roof of the cave.

He paused briefly in the middle of cutting away a hunk of meat with one of her knives, and said casually, "You probably have some questions before then."

Finally. What she said was, "I *would* like to know why Serna's trying to kill you, and why Kane Daly went along with it. I know Kane. As shifters go, he's pretty easygoing."

Rhodry finished chewing, glancing at her before wiping his hands one more time and then leaning back against the rock wall behind him. "My grandfather was Brian de Mendoza."

Amanda nodded. "Brian de Mendoza tried to assassinate Cathal Martyn, and take the throne of Harp by force," she recited dutifully, scowling at his look of surprise. "I did a lot of reading over the winter. A society's history can tell a lot about its present, and its future. And I intend to be on Harp for a long time."

He raised an eyebrow at that, then continued. "I'm Brian's heir, his *only* direct shifter descendant in point of fact. I have plenty of shifter cousins on my father's side, the Devlins. For the de Mendozas, I'm it."

Suddenly Amanda understood. "And since the Ardrigh must also be a shifter, you're the only one who can carry on Brian's grudge against the Martyn regency."

Rhodry gave a sharp nod. "Not that I have any interest in doing so. Brian was a miserable, bitter old man who never pretended to have affection for any of us. His only son died long before I was born. He had four daughters. My mother being the only one who married a shifter, she was also the only one who could, and did, produce a shifter grandson for Brian.

"My father, Ennis Devlin, died in an accident when I was six years old, and my grandfather's only response was to demand that my mother and I leave the home she'd built with my father and come live with him as a proper de Mendoza. He was ambivalent about my two sisters, they could come or not. What he wanted was the raising of his only grandson. He considered me flawed, since I was a shifter by Devlin blood, rather than a true de Mendoza. Which only made him all the more determined to mold me into a proper heir, beginning with living in his house, under his thumb.

"My mother refused. Instead, she packed up all of us and moved in with my father's family. And I can never thank her enough for doing that. It can't have been easy for her to defy her own father, and yet that's what she did. And she did it for me, so that I wouldn't have to grow up with that hate-filled old man."

He threw the rest of the meat he'd cut off into the fire. "I've no interest in my grandfather's dream for the throne. No interest in anything to do with Harp politics, other than serving as the de Mendoza clan chief. Cristobal Martyn summoned me to serve in his guard, and I'll do my time. After that, I intend to return to my family and my clan, and do my best to forget the city even exists. Unfortunately, there are those who don't want to believe that."

"They think you've inherited your grandfather's ambitions."

"That's a big part of it. I'm here right now because of clan politics which followed me from the mountains and found common cause with my enemies in the city. Two separate factions who would normally work against each other united in their singular distrust of me."

"So Desmond Serna wants all the de Mendoza goodies. What does Kane want?"

He shrugged. "Hell if I know. I barely know the man. I assume he's one of those who think they're doing the Ardrigh a favor by getting rid of me. There are more than a few." He blew out a long breath and ran a hand over his face tiredly. "I'm sorry you were dragged into this. It seems a poor payment for saving my life."

Amanda brushed that away. "Will they come after you again?"

"They've no reason to think I'm still alive. Not yet anyway. The question is will anyone come looking for *you* and find *me*?"

"Why would anyone look for me?" she asked. "The only ones with reason to think I'm in danger are the ones who put me out here."

He regarded her silently, his catlike eyes eerily intent in the firelight. "What about Fionn? He might get suspicious if you're gone too long."

She considered sadly. "Maybe not if he knew they were going to drop me way the hell out on the glacier."

His lips tightened into a thin line. "In all fairness, I doubt Fionn knew. He cares about you."

"Fionn cares about his own pride. I wouldn't have thought he'd want me to get hurt. I *know,* however, that he doesn't want me to pass this trial, and he's angry I defied him. He thinks I should confine myself to more womanly pursuits; the two of you should get along great."

"I don't—"

She held up a hand to forestall his protest. "You didn't want me in the Guild either, Rhodry. You made that perfectly clear."

He grinned crookedly. "That was before you saved my prideful, ignorant male hide. Besides," he continued casually, "Fionn will no doubt change his mind once you return successfully. He'd love to lay claim to the first female Guild member."

"I'm not some sort of prize for claiming. And if I was, Fionn wouldn't be in the running. He likes his women more submissive than I'll ever be."

"He's a fool then. Though I'll not be the one to point out the error of his ways." He stretched back with a very satisfied smile.

"What about you?" she asked.

"Me? I'm no fool, Amanda."

"No, neither am I," she said. She leaned toward him, suddenly intent. "I've been working toward this trial for months, from almost the first day I landed on the planet. Half a year, Rhodry, spent planning every detail, studying, preparing. I've scoured the records of every trial undertaken in the last twenty years, and most of the ones before that, and not one shifter candidate, *not one,* has ever been dropped beyond the Verge."

Rhodry sat up again, suddenly focused on carving away the rest of the diamondback to save for tomorrow. "I told you, I wasn't on your escort," he said without looking at her.

"You were supposed to be, and I know what the Guild Hall's like. They gossip like old ladies. You must have heard something."

He pulled off the last of the meat and snapped the branch they'd used as a skewer in two, dropping the pieces into the fire. The smell of cooked snake sharpened as the fat-soaked sticks burned.

"Not until after it was done," he said in a quiet voice, his eyes riveted on the fire.

"What?"

His eyes met hers briefly across the fire, and looked

away again. "Nando and the others thought if they dropped you on the glacier's edge, they'd be seeing your rescue flare before the first day was over, and the trial would be done. Or if by some chance you managed to stick it out and find your way back without help, that you'd never take vows. They figured you'd be so glad to get back in one piece, you'd never want to leave the city again."

It was pretty much what she'd reasoned out for herself, and it still hurt. Something didn't add up, though. "How could they have known I'd draw the black stone for north? The odds didn't favor one over the others..." Her words faded away at his flat stare. "The stones," she breathed. She could hardly believe it. Had kindly Orrin Brady been a part of this too? Was that why he'd tried to talk her out of going ahead, not once but twice?

As if he could read her thoughts, Rhodry said, "I didn't hear any of this until you were gone, and I don't know how they did it. I don't think Brady was involved. For what it's worth, I don't think he'd have condoned such a thing."

"And you, Rhodry? Would you have gone along with it?"

"No!" he insisted vehemently, his golden eyes as bright as the fire. "How do you think my dear cousin persuaded me to go with him out onto the glacier? That was no hunting trip. I would never have gone hunting with him, and he knows it. Des came to me with the news that Nando and the others were back, that they were bragging about what they'd done to you, and he said we had to find you, that it was a matter of clan honor." He huffed a bitter laugh.

She frowned. "Why didn't you tell me this before?"

"I had only Serna's word that any of it was true," he insisted. "For all I knew, he'd made the whole thing up just to lure me out here."

"Well," she said mildly. "I guess I must have imagined it all then, huh?" She tossed down the rag she'd been using to wipe her hands and crawled out through the low cave entrance. It wasn't exactly a dignified exit. It didn't matter. She needed to get away from him, away from all of them.

Outside, she scrambled quickly to her feet, moving away until the faint glow of their fire was a wavering dab of orange light through the cave opening. She checked automatically for her belt knife. There were plenty of animals prowling the dark nights of Harp, and she had no intention of letting any of them prevent her from getting back to the Guild Hall and shoving her success right down their throats.

She leaned back, surprised by the warmth of the rock wall behind her, and stared up at the few stars. What would her life have been if she had never come down to the planet that day? Or if she'd left with all the others and gone back into space with Nakata and the fleet? She'd grown to hate living on that ship. Hated the sterile air, the narrow corridors, the hard surfaces everywhere. She'd wanted dirt beneath her feet, the wind on her face. The whisper of the trees.

"Amanda."

She jumped. Damn shifter. She hadn't heard him coming.

"Why?" she asked, without preamble. "I never asked for special treatment from anyone. If anything I had to work harder than any of you—being tested on things you all grew up knowing, passing physical trials designed for a shifter's physiology. And even if I get through this, and gain Guild membership, I'm no threat to any of you. So why do you hate me?"

"Damn it, Amanda. I don't hate you," he snarled angrily.

She gave him a weary look, knowing he could see her clearly even in the near darkness. Just one more shifter adaptation that she'd had to do without.

"Not now, you don't," she said. "You did, though. And you didn't even know me. It's the same thing as Cristobal's supporters hating you because of something your grandfather did before you were ever born. What is it about me — ?"

"I never hated you. That was the problem."

Her brow wrinkled in confusion. "I don't understand." He'd never hated her?

He stared at her, as if fighting the urge to explain. She wanted to thump his chest and demand he tell her, but that would only undo all of her hard work. And the stubborn ass probably wouldn't tell her anyway.

"It's not you," he said finally.

And she knew that wasn't what he'd wanted to say.

"It was never you," he continued. "It's what you represent."

"What?" she demanded in exasperation.

He was quiet for a few minutes. She could barely make out his features, only the spark of his eyes picking up the low starlight. Eventually, he said, "I've never been in space. *You* have. You know about other human hybrids, people modified for other environments. You've probably even seen some of them."

She nodded, curious now about what he was going to say. "A few. They're everywhere."

"And in most of those places, they're considered subhuman, aren't they? Useful, sure. Exotic, certainly. And not quite human anymore, even though without them and their modifications, most humans would still be trapped on Earth or cocooned in metal cylinders flying through space."

Embarrassment pricked her conscience for her fellow humans, and she didn't want to answer because what he said was true. He was waiting for her response, so she nodded reluctantly. "You're right. I *have* seen it. And I know that's not the case here on Harp. Hell, you guys run the whole damn planet."

"And that's my point," he told her. "Shifters were never meant to rule Harp. We were bred to be soldiers and hunters to keep the colony safe and fed, with just enough indigenous DNA so that the planet would recognize us as its own. Do you know what those long-ago scientists did when they realized what they'd created with the first generation of shifters? They killed them. And I'm not talking about embryos, either. These were children who'd just begun to manifest a shifter's natural, aggressive tendencies."

"That's impossible," she said, stunned. "There isn't any record—"

"There are records in the Guild Hall. Information that no one outside the Guild is permitted to see, things that every shifter is taught when he joins the Guild. Notes and diaries of the original scientists discussing those first nascent shifters in great clinical detail, how they were too smart, too aggressive. Our creators never intended to produce an entire breed of alpha males. When that's what they got, they made changes. Then, the second generation turned out to be even more dominant than the first, and it was too late to try again. Equipment was breaking down, human egg stocks were degenerating. Even if they'd had the time, they couldn't have started over again. And the struggle just to survive had become too great to throw away what they had.

"So they let us live. Not because they wanted to, but because the alternative was death for the entire colony."

She was appalled by his revelation. No wonder Cristobal had insisted the original records had been lost. "What does that have to do with me?" she asked. "I'm no threat to shifter dominance or—"

"Your very *existence* is a threat. You must see that. Norms outnumber us more than a hundred to one on the planet—"

"I'm *not* a norm!" she insisted. "I'm a freak who hears voices in her head. I wasn't even born here!"

"That makes it worse. You have to understand—" He gave a frustrated sigh. "What makes the shifters unique," he said slowly, "what lets us rule this fucking planet is our ability to commune with the forest. What if you're not the only non-shifter who can do that? What if you're the first of many? You don't only have to fail, Amanda, you have to fail spectacularly so that no norm will ever try again."

"That's the stupidest thing I've ever heard," she said in disgust. "If norms were going to line up to join the Guild, don't you think they'd have done it before now? And if that's the kind of thinking going on in the Guild, then I'm worried for the planet because it's being run by a bunch of furry idiots with dicks."

She saw the flash of his teeth when he smiled at her choice of words. She hadn't meant it to be funny, and she wanted to slug him for being so stupid. He seemed to sense her intent and sobered abruptly.

"You're right. I am an idiot with a dick who should have known better. My own mother is the strongest, most capable person I've ever known, and she'd be ashamed to know I had any part in what they did to you."

Amanda listened, her face turned away to the darkness so he wouldn't see the furious tears filling her eyes. She didn't even know why she was so angry, except that it was all so pointless. All she'd wanted was the freedom to roam the Green at will. Who could possibly be hurt by that?

"I *am* sorry, *acushla*," he said softly. He wrapped his arms around her from behind, pulling her back against his chest when she would have elbowed him away. "Truly I am."

He was so warm, so big and strong, and she was so tired of carrying all the worry alone. His arms tightened, holding her close, and she let him. Just for this moment, she wanted to let him be the strong one, let him worry that some vicious beast was about to pounce on them and make all of the Guild shifters' dreams come true.

"Promise me something," he said.

"What?" Her voice was thick with suspicion.

"Don't ever tell my mother what happened with you. She'll skin me alive and make a nice rug for the hearth."

Amanda laughed, knowing that was what he wanted, and unable to stop it. She straightened, feeling his arms resist for a second before letting her go. She turned and punched his chest lightly, careful to avoid hurting him. "You're an ass, de Mendoza."

"I am."

"I like you anyway," she said with a sigh. She rubbed her arms against the cold. "We should get back inside before some beastie undoes all my hard work saving your idiot life. I wouldn't want to lose you now."

"No," he murmured. "Not now." He dropped an arm over her shoulders, and they walked together back to the cave.

Chapter Thirty

Amanda's first thought on rolling out of the warm sleeping bag the next morning was that tonight she'd be sleeping on the soft ground of the Green. The night had been deeply cold, just as Rhodry had predicted. The fire had kept the cave fairly warm, and exhaustion had done the rest.

He murmured restlessly, and she tucked the covers back around him hoping he'd sleep longer. He'd fallen hard asleep the night before. Yesterday had probably been too much, walking as far as he did. On the other hand, the more exercise he got the faster the rockweed would be worked out of his system so he could reclaim his ability to shift. He still hadn't said anything about it, though Amanda knew it weighed on him that he couldn't take his animal form. And that weight grew heavier with each day that passed.

She pulled on her boots, which was much easier with both knife sheaths empty. She'd given Rhodry her spare blades, and kept the belt knife and the short bow for herself. He'd

tried to talk her out of the bow. Unsuccessfully, of course.
She wasn't even sure if he'd been serious about it, or if he'd
just been jerking her chain. It was hard to tell sometimes.

She picked up the arrow quiver and shook it unhappily.
Her supply of arrows was growing thin. That was something
else she'd have to work on once they got back to the trees.
Dropping to all fours, she threw the quiver and bow out
ahead of her and crawled through the cave opening.

The skies were clear and the wind completely still, with
the dawn air retaining a cold bite that sent a shiver down
her spine. She could appreciate the freshness of the morning, despite the cold, especially this close to the Green. With
no wind off the glacier, the fragrance of the distant forest
drifted in very faintly, full of the deep, earthy scent of the
trees and everything that dwelled beneath them. She drew
a full breath and exhaled on a long sigh. It was the smell of
home and it filled her with longing.

Telling herself the sooner they got started the better, she
hurried around the rock to take care of her morning needs,
her mind full of the pleasures waiting for her at the end of
this day's journey. She pulled her pants back up, rearranged
her clothes, and was just turning to go back to the cave when
a throaty cough sounded over the stones, carrying clearly
in the crisp air. She froze in place, even as her heart sped
up with fear. Stripping away her hood to hear better, she
slowly turned, searching for the source of the sound with
eyes and ears both. She couldn't see much from where she
was. The rocks were too tall and too tightly clustered, and
they blocked her view back toward the glacier.

She scrambled up the rocks, jamming her fingers into
tiny crevices, not caring about the blood and skin she left

behind. The top of the rock pile was precarious and uneven, perhaps twenty feet high. Leaping sure-footedly from stone to stone, she climbed rapidly until she reached the highest point.

She stilled, then stretched out her awareness and listened. The confirmation she sought was there in the trees they'd left behind, whispering to her of a fearsome creature from the darkward stalking the forest. Ice bear. They were deadly stalkers, their white coats making them hard to see, their eight-inch claws giving them the run of the trees despite their size. And they were fast, blindingly fast in the attack.

She had a moment's regret, wishing they'd gone only a little farther yesterday. The Verge was on the border of the bear's territory, just cold enough after a big storm for the creature to venture into for the hunt before retreating. So, was the bear hunting *them*? Or was she simply close enough to hear him hunting further north?

Either way, he was definitely hunting. That little cough she'd heard hadn't been an accident. It was designed to terrify the target, to flush it out, and make it more susceptible when the bear finally made its move.

It had worked. She was terrified. She could see the bear now, and what she saw made her heart trip before resuming its frantic rhythm in her chest. He was standing just inside the tree line, and he was huge, the granddaddy of ice bears. This monster was at least twelve feet tall and carrying well over the usual two thousand pounds of muscle and fat beneath a long, dreadlocked coat that was filthy and knotted with dirt and brambles. He was down on all fours, swaying on the edge of the Verge, his big head moving from side to side as if reluctant to go further. But then his nose came up and her heart stopped. He began running, lumbering across the open space of the Verge, untroubled by the same rock field that had so hindered her and Rhodry. Platter-sized paws stepped light as feathers, gliding over the rocky litter, growing closer and more terrifying by the second as he moved in a purposeful line toward her position, her scent clearly in his nose.

She spun around, jumping over rocks until she was right above their cave. She dropped down to her belly and leaned over the precipice to shout down a warning to Rhodry, just as a belling roar of discovery rolled over her. She looked up in shock to see the bear in full charge and heading straight for her. She scrambled to her feet, screaming Rhodry's name as she prepared to fight for her life.

Ignoring every instinct that told her to flee, she ran along the top of the rocks, leaping over boulders as fast as she dared, fighting for footing as she circled up one side of the horseshoe formation, angling for a bow shot. She heard Rhodry shout her name, saw him emerge head-first from the cave opening seconds later.

The bear's massive head swung around instantly, its nose lifting to the scent of shifter, and without ever slowing its lightning-fast speed, the beast altered its charge toward this new, more dangerous foe.

She shouted wordlessly, bringing her bow up to draw and fire in a single smooth movement. Her fingers stung as the arrows flew, as she reached for the next arrow and the one after that, aiming for the back of the bear's neck where its spinal cord met its vicious little brain. Her aim was true. Her arrows pierced the thick skin...and stuck there, unable to penetrate through the heavy layer of fat. The bear spun again, abandoning its efforts to reach Rhodry through the narrow cave opening, rearing up instead to meet her attack with a frenzied howl. She was ready. Her next arrows flew as true as the first, striking the beast just left of center mass where his five-chambered heart lay. Or so her studies had told her. She'd never faced an ice bear before, and could only hope the books were right. She loosed two more arrows, making a total of four lodged in the monster's chest and three sticking out of its thick neck. They seemed to have little effect, not even slowing the giant down.

Rhodry was shouting something that she was too distracted to hear. The bear was close enough to smell now, rank and disgusting, her arrows sticking out of his hide like quills, bobbing madly with the force of the animal's berserk rage. Tiny, nearly blind eyes glowed with fury, gleaming red orbs amid the dirty white of its fur, as it swung its head from side to side searching for her with its sensitive nose. She kept firing, afraid of revealing her location, even more afraid she would fail to put the creature down before it found her. She sent her last arrow flying with a hiss of a prayer, shuddering when those eyes focused suddenly and directly on her, pinning her in place with terror. The ice bear took a clumsy step forward and roared.

She stared in dread fascination as the monster opened a mouth as big as her head and let forth a howl of rage and pain. In a move too fast for her to follow, it flexed its hind legs and leaped onto the rocks, claws digging deep furrows into the stone with horrific shrieks that made it sound like what it was, a creature from hell itself.

She cried out and stumbled backward, stunned at this

new attack. She'd thought herself safe high above the ground. None of her books had said ice bears could jump like that.

Her hand shot down in a blind grab for her belt knife, her eyes searching frantically for someplace to hide. She was trapped on the rocks, treacherous underfoot and nowhere to run. If she could find a gap big enough to wedge herself in deep, she could use her belt knife to make the bear think twice about coming after her.

The bear was bellowing furiously as it came over the lip of stone, not even pausing before it charged. Wounded, bleeding from a half dozen different places, it was on her in seconds.

Her feet slid out from under her and she fell backward, the unforgiving stone slamming into her tailbone as she scrambled desperately to hold onto her knife. One giant paw swept in, raking down her thigh, shredding her leggings and tearing through muscle as she screamed in agony.

Chapter Thirty-One

Rhodry had heard the bear's victorious bellow and shot awake, jumping to his feet and nearly slamming his head against the sloped stone ceiling before remembering where he was. He looked around frantically for Amanda and heard her scream his name. Cursing his absence of claws, he grabbed the two knives she'd left him and scrambled out of the cave, snapping his head back in just before eight inches of ice bear claw nearly took off his face. Rocks tumbled from above and he heard the whisk of arrows.

"Amanda!" His shout was nearly drowned by the roar of the ice bear as it turned to deal with her attack.

Three bolts suddenly pierced the creature's neck, one right after the other, and Rhodry realized she was above him, up on the rocks and aiming for the back of the bear's neck, right where every Harp hunter would have aimed. And exactly the wrong spot to take down an ice bear. They had too much fat, hitting the spine was nearly impossible, especially on a monster like this one. The killing shot for an ice bear was through the eye into the brain. It was a difficult shot, not impossible for a trained Guild hunter. But did she know about it?

He yelled at her, knowing even if she could hear him, she'd be too consumed by the bear's attack to make sense of his words. The creature was wounded, her arrows had done that much. It was whipping itself from side to side, no longer interested in Rhodry, twisting around, searching for its tormentor, for Amanda. Another arrow flew, striking the thickly padded chest and sticking there. The bear reared up to a fearsome height, roaring, the percussion of sound sending rocks and dirt rattling down the stone face as one more arrow struck and the bear finally realized where the threat was coming from.

Beady eyes focused, powerful legs flexed and the screech of injured stone blended with Amanda's shriek of terror as the beast climbed upward. He shot out of the cave, forgetting his injuries, no longer feeling the pain. He rolled behind the huge animal and stood, knives thrusting upward, just in time to see the great creature make a final effortless leap to the top of the unforgiving stone. The bear howled in triumph and Amanda screamed.

Rhodry dropped the useless knives and shifted.

Chapter Thirty-Two

Amanda stabbed wildly with her belt knife, pressing herself back into the crevice, trying futilely to squeeze deeper into what was nothing more than a narrow seam between two giant boulders. The bear was maddened with pain and blood loss, wounded by her many arrows, one paw bleeding freely where she'd slashed it open with a lucky jab of her knife. Running on nothing more than instinct now, blinded by its own fury, the monster howled its defiance at the puny creature who'd dared to attack it, who smelled like prey, and yet fought like a shifter. It stuck its jaw forward, snapping at her arm as she drew back, sharp teeth barely grazing her forearm and yet slicing it wide open. She didn't have the breath left to scream. She could only choke out a silent sob and shift her knife to her left hand.

A savage scream suddenly ripped through the air, sending involuntary tremors through Amanda and spinning the ice bear around to face a new, far greater threat. A growling blur of black fur flew up and over the edge, and the two massive creatures collided, their mingled howls filling the air with rage and violence. She blinked through her tears, trying to make out what was happening, wondering what new hell had joined the fray. It was a huge beast, sleek and black with a mouth full of snarling teeth and eyes that spat gold fire as it grappled with the massive ice bear.

She gasped in shock. By all the gods, it was Rhodry. He had shifted at last.

The two great predators rolled back and forth over the uneven boulders, claws slicing flesh with terrifying ease, jaws ripping open bloody wounds as screams of fury and pain bounced off the surrounding stone.

She struggled to her feet, her leg barely holding her upright. There was little she could do. Her knife was useless for this, and she was out of arrows, though their bodies were so entwined, she would have been as likely to hit Rhodry as the ice bear even if she'd had them.

Rhodry's hind claws dug into the bear's belly as they rolled over and over, the bear trying to use its greater weight to crush the shifter, its huge jaws snapping at his throat. The bear gave a high-pitched shriek of pain as the cat's claws found purchase and ripped open a great gash in its gut.

Momentum shifted and now it was Rhodry who snapped at his attacker's throat, furious snarls tearing through the air. The bear wrapped its huge arms around the big cat and squeezed, trying to snap his spine, keeping its head tucked in to protect its vulnerable neck. They rolled perilously close to the edge, and Amanda cried out a wordless warning. The bear gave a powerful shrug and flung Rhodry away, then curled back to its feet and started forward after him.

Rhodry spun gracefully, all four feet leaving the ground as his body twisted in midair. He launched himself at the ice bear again, halting its forward momentum and shoving it backward until they were both poised at the very edge of the rock formation, twenty feet or more above the rough ground.

For a moment they hung there, balanced on the precipice.

Then she watched in horror as some infinitesimal balance shifted and they went over, falling with duplicate screams of outrage. She felt more than heard the impact shuddering up through the stone and then nothing.

She lunged forward with a shout of denial, her leg giving way beneath her, so that she half climbed, half fell down the rock face and landed with a shriek of pain. The two powerful creatures lay on the ground in front of the cave, neither one moving. Rhodry was barely visible behind the mountain of blood and fur that was the ice bear, the monster's neck twisted at an angle that left no doubt it was dead.

Stumbling and clawing her way over the bloody ground, she reached her shifter. His leg was trapped beneath the dead bear, and she threw herself at the thick body with a shout of defiance, shoving its great, lifeless bulk away until he was free.

"Rhodi." Her voice broke as she knelt over him, tears streaking down her face to fall on his blood-drenched fur. He was panting heavily, eyes closed, sides gusting as he struggled to breathe. She ran her hands down his sleek body, crying anew at every fresh wound, despairing of ever finding the skill to heal him this time. "Rhodi," she repeated, holding his head in her lap, stroking his face, not knowing what else to do.

She felt him stir, felt the shudder of flesh and muscle, and knew what it meant. She scooted away reluctantly, one hand trailing over his leg and paw. One moment there was a huge black cat lying before her, and then with a ripple of fur and popping bones, Rhodry lay sprawled naked, his golden skin torn and streaked with blood and sweat. He rose up on hands and knees, head hanging down, breath coming in great sucking gasps of air. He eyed her through half-closed lids and he shifted again, retaking his animal form.

She swallowed a wordless protest, knowing the effort it took for him to shift rapidly like this, knowing also that instinct was driving him now, pushing him to change, the shift finally undertaking the long-delayed healing of old wounds and new. The cat rose again on four wobbly legs, panting heavily. His big head swung over to regard the dead ice bear, and then back to stare unblinkingly at her once again. He took two faltering steps, closing the distance between them, and collapsed against her with a groan of effort.

A manda wasn't sure how much time passed as she sat there with Rhodry, the two of them slumped next to the dead ice bear. At some point, she slid to the ground, lying with one arm over his furred back, too weak to remain upright. She knew when he shifted again to human, could remember being relieved that he had his shifting ability back at last.

"You're bleeding." Rhodry's voice was low, with a note of panic she'd never heard from him before. "Damn it, Amanda, you're bleeding."

She smiled. Of course, she was bleeding. The bear had attacked her, hadn't it? She remembered pain…and fear. That was gone now. Everything was gone. She drifted away, coming back to feel a sharp ache around her upper thigh, something too tight. It hurt. She pushed ineffectively at the hands that were hurting her.

"Stop it," he said absently. "You're bleeding out here. Damn bear must have nicked an artery." That last was said more to himself than to her. His fingers dug into her leg and she screamed. "I'm sorry, I'm sorry," he muttered. "I've got to stop it."

"Amanda."

Her eyelids were impossibly heavy. Something in her responded to the urgency in his voice, and she forced them open, squinting as she tried to focus.

"Where's your flare, Amanda?"

She blinked at him in confusion, feeling sweet darkness pulling at her consciousness. She didn't want to be awake, why wouldn't he let her sleep? She shifted slightly and nearly screamed at the pain in her leg. Rhodry was holding her, forcing her to remain still, to look at him. "The flare, *acushla*."

She frowned. She didn't need the damn flare. It was all a trick anyway.

"Threw it away," she mumbled through dry lips. He swore viciously, and she felt laughter bubbling up. She'd fooled them all. She smiled and let her eyes close, and the pain went away.

When she woke next, his arms were around her and the ground was falling away. That wasn't right. She was too big. Men didn't sweep her off her feet like some dainty maiden.

"No," she protested fitfully. "Rhodry, no. I'm not—"

"What you're not is dying on me, damn it. Now hold still."

A manda's eyes opened slowly. Rhodry was sleeping next to her, his breath warm and steady, his arm lying across her body, his big hand draped protectively over her hip. She ached. Her hands, her arm, her leg more than anything, a deep pain that throbbed with every beat of her heart. *What?* Oh right, the ice bear. She doubted that particular memory would lose its potency any time soon.

Rhodry stirred, his arm tightening as he moved in his sleep. They were still in that damn cave. Or, no, not the same one, one just like it. He'd probably moved them, what with the big dead monster right outside the front door. She felt like giggling and recognized the touch of hysteria. She brought a hand up to cover her mouth, which didn't stop the tremble in her shoulders.

"Amanda?" His voice was rough with worry.

"I'm okay," she said, her voice shockingly scratchy. "It was just…" She closed her eyes, suddenly exhausted all over again, wishing they were waking up somewhere else, wishing things could be easier for a single gods-be-damned day.

He curled carefully around her, and his lips brushed her cheekbone. "When this is over, *acushla*, I'll take you to the mountains and show you my home. You'll see the Green like you never have before, rolling hills of it as far as the eye can see. There's beauty to be had in the darkward too. I'll show it to you."

She nodded silently, waiting until she knew she could speak without blubbering.

"What does '*acushla*' mean?" she asked, feeling overwhelmed by the sudden emotion of the moment. "You keep calling me that."

She felt his smile in the curve of his lips against her cheek.

"It's Irish Gaelic, from the Devlin half of my family. It means 'sweetheart.'"

"Oh," she whispered, wanting to cry all over again. What the hell was wrong with her? A little near death experience, and suddenly she was going all weepy. "Are you okay?" she asked hoarsely. "You shifted…"

"Shifted and healthy. It was you I was worried about this time. Damn bear ripped the hell out of your leg."

She mumbled something incoherent, already drifting off again.

"You threw your flare away," he said accusingly.

She answered without opening her eyes. "I wasn't going to use it."

"Amanda—"

"How long was I out? I mean since the bear attack," she asked, changing the subject.

He sighed. She could feel the vibration of his body, his heat against her chilled back. "The bear attacked yesterday morning, and today's sunset was about four hours ago."

Her heart fell. She wanted to be back among the trees *now*. She could taste it she wanted it so badly.

"We can start home again tomorrow. I'll go slowly—"

"Day after tomorrow, *acushla*. You haven't even been on your feet yet. And yes, we'll go slowly."

"I don't want—"

"Another day will give me some time to start curing the bear's pelt before we pack it out. It took most of today to strip it down. That was a fat bear."

"Pelt?" She opened her eyes and rolled over slightly to look at his face. His golden eyes were gazing down at her, glinting with humor. "You skinned the bear?"

"Aye, I thought that might get your interest. You didn't think I'd leave it behind, did you?"

"Who gets it?" she asked, eyes narrowing in suspicion.

"We'll talk about that later."

"Day after tomorrow then," she said, pushing her face against his chest to cover her yawn, finding it difficult to keep her eyes open. "We'll go slowly," she repeated, already asleep.

"Slowly," Rhodry agreed again, wrapping the tattered sleeping bag more securely around them both, and watching her sleep in the curve of his arm. He hadn't told her the whole truth. Hadn't told her how close she'd come to dying, her blood soaking into the dirt to mingle with the ice bear's. If he'd been even two minutes slower in recognizing the danger, it might have been too late, and she would have been gone forever. And in that brief instant when he'd thought he was losing her, he'd felt...empty. As if his own life was draining away instead of hers. It had surprised him.

It had scared the hell out of him.

All those oaths he'd sworn to himself to stay away from her, telling himself that she was a complication he didn't need. All of those excuses for ignoring the aching desire, the hunger that had consumed him from the moment they'd met... No more excuses, no more pretending. She was his, and he was going to fight for her whether she liked it or not. Because that moment of emptiness when he'd thought he'd lost her? It was something he never wanted to feel again.

Chapter Thirty-Three

Amanda half dragged the backpack behind her, suppressing a grimace of pain. Rhodry was in animal form, ranging out ahead somewhere. She knew he was keeping a close eye on her all the same. He'd watched her like a hawk ever since they'd started out from the cave this morning. She'd realized early on that if there was any hope of reaching the trees today, she was going to have to pretend to feel a whole lot better than she actually did. If it were up to him, she'd be sitting down and resting every time he went off on one of these scouting trips, and they'd have made only half the distance they'd covered so far.

Since there was nothing he could do to stop her, at least nothing he was willing to do, she thought with satisfaction, she just kept walking and pretended not to notice his displeasure.

Admittedly, she wasn't at her best right now. Her arm hurt, although she'd been lucky in that there didn't seem to be any nerve damage. Her leg, on the other hand, wanted to give out with every step, and she was pretty sure some of the local bacteria had taken up residence in the deep wound on her thigh. She had already begun taking the antibiotics that remained from her original stash. Rhodry no longer needed them. He was disgustingly healthy now that he could shift again. It hardly seemed fair.

Unfortunately, there was only a two-day supply of the pills left. Just enough to kick-start her immune system. If they reached the Green before then, she could find some coneflower, which might hold off the infection until they got back to the city, or until she reached one of her own caches. Unless it took weeks instead of days to get there. And that would only happen if they had bigger problems than her leg to worry about. Not that she planned to mention any of this to Rhodry. No need to borrow trouble.

It was sweet, really, the way he worried about her. And it was about to drive her absolutely mad. She'd camped alone in the Green plenty of times while preparing for her trial, even through the winter. She really didn't *need* him to light her fires, or help her over fallen tree trunks. Although, it was sort of nice that he did.

Part of it was guilt on his part. He still felt bad about not stopping Nando and the others from sabotaging her trial. Which was fine with her. He *should* feel bad about that. Even though he hadn't known about it until afterward, and he *had* come out here thinking to rescue her. It wasn't his fault that she'd rescued him instead. She smirked lightly.

That wasn't the only reason he was being so nice. The rest of it, and maybe even the bigger part, was lust. Her lovely, big shifter had finally admitted, to himself at least, that he wanted her. He hadn't said anything. The signs were there, though. In the way he looked at her, touched her. He wouldn't do anything about it as long as she was hurt. That would be too much like taking advantage, and Rhodry de Mendoza was not one to take advantage of a woman, she'd grant him that.

For her part, she wouldn't have minded a little hot, sweaty sex. She wasn't the one who'd spent months in denial. She'd been lusting after *him* from the first time he'd glowered at her in the forest. In fact, a *lot* of hot, sweaty sex might make her feel a whole lot better than she did right now, and if he didn't make the first move soon, she was going to make it for him. She wasn't some fading flower of Ciudad Vaquero, waiting for the big man to bestow his favors. She intended to have him sooner or later. She caught a glimpse of his powerful and sleek animal in the distance, and smiled grimly at the spike of pure desire that stabbed her belly, and a lot lower down, too. Forget the *later* part of that equation. They were damn well going to get together *sooner*.

Up ahead, Rhodry had stopped to stare back at her, his smooth head swiveling in her direction, the sun behind him making his eyes seem dark and penetrating. She sighed and started walking again before he could rush back to check on her. He'd only insist she needed to rest, and then they'd argue, and it would be even longer before they got where they were going.

The weather had finally changed for good the day after the ice bear attack. The northern winds had faded in the face of a determined, warm breeze from the Green. To Amanda, it had seemed as if the trees recognized their own in her and Rhodry, and were covering their return back to where they belonged.

The timing had been perfect. That first day after she woke, he'd bullied her into doing nothing more than sitting and resting inside by the fire, not letting her contribute to any of the necessary chores. Then he'd gathered wood and lit a second fire outside, so she could sit and watch him prepare the bear pelt without getting chilled.

And what a fine sight that had been. Rhodry stripped to the waist, black braid tied up and out of the way, his lovely skin glistening with sweat in the sun. The muscles in his chest and arms had flexed very nicely as he scraped away the remaining flesh and fat with edged stones before rubbing dirt into the skin as a temporary measure.

"Dirt?" she'd asked him when he'd begun pouring handfuls of the stuff onto the flattened-out pelt.

"Taste." He leaned toward her, holding out a handful.

Giving him a doubtful look, she wet a finger in her mouth, touched it to the dirt, and then to her tongue. Her gaze was on him as she tasted, *his* was glued to the path of her finger, from the dirt to her mouth, where it lingered hungrily. She smiled and his eyes flashed up to meet hers. He straightened abruptly and went back to work on the skin.

"What do you taste?" he asked without looking at her.

"Salt."

"Right. The local soil's full of it. It'll keep the skin from drying out too much before we get it back."

Amanda scooped up a handful and let it run through her fingers. "Probably a concentration of minerals from the ice," she commented, mostly to herself.

"That and the general increase in precipitation," he agreed. "The mountains where I live are in the same latitude as where we are now. And this close to the ice cap, we get three to four times more rain or snow as down in the city, plus a more direct run off. By the time it gets to the rest of you, most of the minerals have filtered out."

She smiled. She forgot sometimes that he just *looked* like a mountain man, an incredibly *sexy* mountain man. He'd been educated in a system not all that different from her own, except in the breadth and timeliness of the information.

"My mother sent me kicking and screaming to university classes," he said, as if reading her thoughts. "I could hardly wait to finish. You were fleet-educated, right? How far did you get?"

"I have university degrees in xenobiology and chemistry, double major. If I'd stayed, I would have gone on to graduate studies."

"You ever miss it? The fleet, I mean."

"Never," she said honestly.

He stopped what he was doing, sitting back on his heels and looking at her curiously, his chest heaving with the effort of trying to cure a bear pelt with dirt and stones. "Why insist on joining the Guild, though? I mean, there's no doubt you're qualified, but…" He gestured with one hand, clearly unable to think of the right words.

She broke away from admiring his chest to meet his golden stare. "Because the trees know me. This is where I belong, and nothing you do will change that."

"I wouldn't try, *acushla*," he said intently. "You can't still think that."

She studied him evenly. "No," she admitted softly, and then had to look away. It was either that, or jump him right then and there.

She glanced over and saw him smile before he swiveled around to throw more handfuls of dirt onto the skin. It gave Amanda a nice view of his broad back, not to mention his ass, which even in the loose trousers was well worth mentioning. She shifted her gaze again before he turned around. No need to encourage him.

"So, tell me," she said after a while. "Why do you think Cristobal brought you to the city? Why not leave you in the mountains?"

He shrugged. "Better to know your enemy, I suppose. It's what I'd do in the same situation. Leave me alone with the clans and for all he knows I'm planning a revolution. So he brings me in, sizes me up, maybe hopes to compel or connive my friendship and loyalty. I could have told him it was unnecessary. He already has my loyalty."

"Mmm." Amanda rubbed the muscles of her damaged thigh lightly beneath the heavy bandage. The bear had left four deep furrows in her leg, tearing into the muscle, and they'd had to bind it tightly to stop the bleeding. She probably could have used a few stitches, if she'd had the stomach to do it herself. Rhodry had never even seen a stitch until the ones she'd sewn into him. When they got back to the city, she'd have to see a real doctor. The last thing she needed was any kind of permanent injury for the Guild to use as an excuse to deny her, even *after* she passed her trial.

"Is your leg hurting?" He'd stopped working to eye her in concern.

She smiled. She wasn't the only one feeling the heat. He wanted her bad. "Just massaging, Rhodi, keeping it loose. Maybe I'll take a little walk—"

He jumped up. "I'll go with you. Just let me roll this up."

"W hat's wrong with your leg?"

Amanda blinked out of her memories and into the present, realizing she'd stopped walking and was rubbing her leg again. Rhodry was back in human form, his expression dark with worry as he came toward her with a long, rolling stride. He tied the loose waist of his pants around his hips, leaving his chest bare. His old shirt, already on its last legs, hadn't survived his sudden shift during the bear attack, and with the warmer weather, he was comfortable going shirtless. The pants hadn't fared much better. There was just enough for an illusion of modesty, which he seemed to require around her these days. She covered her grin.

"My leg's just a little tired," she said, answering his question. He was there in an instant, stripping away the backpack with its extra weight of the rolled-up pelt.

"You should let me bury the damn pelt. I can come back for it. For that matter, you shouldn't be walking—"

"I can't keep stopping all the time," she said stubbornly. "We'll never get there. And if you think I'm sleeping one more night on these rocks when I can see the Green from here, then you're as crazy as... Well, I don't know what, you're just crazy, okay?"

He swung the pack over one shoulder, with an easy gesture that belied its substantial weight, and glared down at her. Feeling wicked, she took a long step closer, until their bodies were very nearly touching. She drew a deep breath, inhaling the unique scent of shifter and Rhodry, the movement causing her breasts to brush lightly against his bare chest. Putting one hand on the smooth skin of his hip just above the cloth of his low-slung pants, she gazed up at him.

He seemed to stop breathing for a minute. His head came down until their faces were only inches apart, his warm mouth so close... Her stomach clenched in anticipation. And he stepped back, shaking his head as if clearing it of cobwebs.

Well, damn.

"There's a smooth trail up ahead," he said, his voice even deeper than usual. He gave a little shudder and continued more evenly. "The rocks pretty much clear out. We'll make better time after that, and you *will* sleep beneath the trees tonight, even if I have to carry you there."

That was the sweetest thing anyone had ever said to her. *That's it. Tonight, your ass is mine.*

Chapter Thirty-Four

He didn't have to carry her, though it was a close thing. The sun was already beginning its drop over the horizon by the time she registered the fact that her injured leg no longer jarred with fresh pain on every limping step, and the ground no longer consisted of hard dirt and rock. There were trees gathering around her, thick enough that she could see no more than a few yards in any direction and even then it wasn't a straight path. The last rays of mottled sunlight filtered down through a riot of branches in shades of gray and green, with the occasional splash of pure yellow from the fading sun. Beneath her feet, the forest floor was cool and moist, spongy with decades' worth of leafy decay and mossy growth, layer after layer building up to form a lush carpet. This close to the edge, it was probably only a few inches, not the several feet of depth that existed in the oldest parts of the Green. It was more than enough to make a huge difference to legs and feet worn out by days of travel through snow and ice followed by the hard scrabble of the Verge.

And for hearts and souls battered to exhaustion by the cold barrens of that hostile environment, the trees provided their own warm wash of serenity. There was life on the glacier. She knew that. Hell, they'd fought off some of that life to get this far. Compared to the burgeoning vitality of the Green, though, it was an empty place.

She relaxed step by step as the canopy thickened above her, even though the trees, too, were young by the standards of the deep Green. The truly ancient giants lay far into the forest, in the valleys and on the hillsides, nearly indistinguishable from a distance because of the verdant growth all around them. One had to stand at the feet of such a goliath to appreciate the full majesty of a tree that had been alive long before humans had taken their first fledgling steps into space.

She limped to a stop at the foot of a comparative youngling—barely a hundred, if that—and leaned against the trunk, her forehead touching the rough bark, her hands stretched out to either side, feeling the creases and grooves beneath her fingers.

"Thank you," she whispered.

"Amanda?"

Rhodry was right next to her, one hand trailing down over the back of her head and along her spine before falling away. He dropped the pack at the foot of the tree, and drew several deep breaths, as if cleansing his lungs of taint. She turned her head to watch him without lifting her forehead from the tree. It scraped her skin softly and she relished the gentle pain.

"Thank you, Rhodi."

He gave her a quizzical smile. "For what?"

"For putting up with me today, for not making me stop before we got here."

His smile gentled. "I wasn't looking forward to spending another night in dirt any more than you were."

"You didn't have to. You would have been here long ago if not for me."

He looked vaguely insulted and opened his mouth to protest. She took advantage of his outrage to push away from the tree and close the distance between them. With a quick move, she reached up and pulled his head down to hers, bringing their mouths together. She'd intended to kiss him hard and fast, more of a challenge than anything else. He called her bluff, his arms coming up to hold her as he deepened the kiss, his tongue circling hers in a sensuous exploration while their bodies melded together so perfectly, so naturally. She sighed as the kiss drifted into a soft, lingering touch of lips.

They stood that way for several minutes, neither one moving or talking, just holding each other, breath on breath, lips barely touching. She smiled and said softly, "I was planning on jumping your bones tonight."

"Was?"

"I'm not sure I'm capable of jumping anyone right now. Maybe never again."

His low laughter joined hers. "I must admit, I had better plans for us than this."

"That's good," she whispered. "As long as you've got plans."

He tightened his hold, using the effortless strength of a

shifter to lift her off her feet until she could feel the firmness of his erection between her legs. "Definite plans."

She made a soft sound of appreciation and raised her legs to circle his hips. He stroked his big hand along her thigh, and stopped what he was doing to frown at her. "Your leg's hot. The antibiotics aren't working?"

"They ran out last night."

He spat out a curse. "You never should have wasted any of them on me."

She glared up at him "Saving your life was not a waste. Besides—" She pushed away from him to stand alone. "There's bound to be some coneflower nearby. That'll hold off the infection until—"

He reached out, trying to stop her. "Sit down. Let me—"

"I'll find it, this is my trial. The last thing I need—"

"Fine," he snapped. "Do it your way." He let go of her and stomped away, quickly disappearing into the deepening shadows.

"Yeah, well, fine to you too, de Mendoza!" she shouted after him, then sank to the ground, muttering to herself. "I survived out here without you before, you stupid shifter."

"I heard that!"

She glared in his general direction and snapped her hand out in the one-fingered salute that had managed to survive over five hundred years of colonial separation from Earth. His only response was laughter drifting back through the trees.

Amanda tied off the last corner on the rather primitive lean-to she'd put together using their now sad-looking emergency blanket and some broad, waxy starfern leaves. The sleeping bag, which wasn't in much better shape, was spread out over the pile of moss that she'd gathered as a sort of mattress, although the forest floor all by itself was heavenly compared to the hard ground they'd been sleeping on for days.

The shelter wasn't pretty. It wasn't supposed to be. It was comfortable enough, and it would keep them dry during the night. She wasn't worried about rain. It was the other, far less savory things that fell from the trees on Harp. On her own, she'd have zipped the sleeping bag completely closed and skipped the shelter. With the two of them this would work better and, besides, Rhodry wasn't the only one with plans, even if he *was* a stupid shifter.

She already had a fire going, and had found a nearby water source. It was fresh and clean and just enough for her to finally wash away some of the grit and grime, and blood, of the last few days. Something she'd been desperate to do. A change of clothes would have been nice, too. She was pretty sure the dirt was the only thing holding hers together. And she couldn't help wondering how she smelled to Rhodry's shifter nose. Probably not good. It hadn't seemed to put him off before, though, and she was definitely fresher now. She'd even cleaned her teeth using some of the rough-edged piñata fern she'd found growing near the water, as always. Its strong minty flavor should make her definitely more kissable. She grinned at the thought.

Speak of the devil. She heard him approaching through the underbrush, which meant he was being intentionally noisy for her.

"What is it about you that brings out the worst in me, Amanda?"

She felt a little ripple of pleasure, but didn't acknowledge him, other than to say over her shoulder, "And here I thought I was seeing your *good* side." She turned around to find him slouched casually against a nearby tree wearing clean clothes, both shirt and pants, with his soft boots covering his feet. She gave him a quick look up and down and sighed to herself. She'd sort of gotten used to the half-naked look.

"You found a Guild cache."

"I did." He tossed her a bundle. "Not exactly the right fit. Better than what you have on."

She caught it automatically. "Aren't you sweet?"

He laughed. "I can be." He strolled over, leaned down, and sniffed the cup of hot water she had steeping next to the small fire. "You found some coneflower?"

"You mean the huge patch right over there? The one you stomped through on your way out, sending up a scent strong enough for even a dull human nose to find? That coneflower?"

He stood up with a crooked grin and came closer, one hand hidden behind his back.

She eyed him warily. "What do you have back there?"

"Something for you."

"What?" she asked suspiciously.

He came closer still, before whipping his hand around to wave a trail bar in front of her face. It was filled with nuts and fruit and was so sticky with honey she could see it gleaming in the faint afternoon light. Eyes wide, mouth watering, she managed through sheer willpower to keep from grabbing it from him. She looked up and met his laughing eyes.

"What's your price?"

"Price? Are you suggesting I'd take advantage of your situation to pry some favor from you in exchange for this trail bar, which by the way I can say from recent experience is quite delicious." He produced a small leather drawstring bag in his other hand. "There were several."

"Rhodi," she warned.

He closed the distance between them, circling her waist with one arm and yanking her up against his body. "A kiss, *acushla*. A sweet for a sweet."

"Why would I want to kiss *you*?"

"Because you want to jump my bones," he murmured as he nibbled the skin along her jawline.

"I'm not sure—"

"Yes, you are."

Trail bar forgotten, she feasted on his mouth instead. His lips were full and soft, and he tasted of honey as his tongue wound lazily around hers, belying the urgent hunger she knew they both felt for the touch of skin on skin, the glide of hard against soft. Amanda stretched up on her toes, wanting more, pressing her mouth against his, biting hard enough to draw blood, whimpering with need as the coppery taste flavored the kiss between them.

He growled, his big hands fisting in her shirt to tug it over her head and off, groaning with impatience when she had to help him with her bra—which was not one of her delicate, lacy ones. It was the sensible, tight-fitting kind she wore for traipsing through the forest. He threw it aside and his hands came back to cup her naked breasts, thumbs scraping roughly over her nipples, sending little shocks of desire skimming over her skin and charging the unbearable heat building between her legs.

Wanting him *now,* Amanda yanked at his fresh shirt, complaining when it resisted her efforts, and hissing with pleasure when her naked breasts finally met his chest. She rubbed her hardened nipples against the soft hairs sprinkled over his pectorals, and let the fingers of one hand follow the silky, dark line down his hard belly and below the waist of his pants.

He groaned, then grabbed her wrist, stopping her from going further. "Amanda," he said breathlessly.

She looked up and met his eyes, seeing the clear desire burning there. "Yes?" she asked in confusion. Had she misread the signals somehow?

"Birth control, *acushla.* I didn't bring—"

"I'm implanted," she said quickly, then seeing the puzzled look on his face, she explained further. "I have a birth control implant. Works like a charm." She slipped her wrist from his grasp and reached for him again, cupping his balls in her hand and squeezing gently before gliding her fingers up and over the hard length of him. "Any more questions?" she purred.

"Gods, no." Shoving his hands into the back of her pants, cupping her bare ass, he lifted her against his body until the ridge of his erection was nestled in the warm triangle between her thighs.

"Put your legs around me," he growled.

She laughed for the sheer joy of it. Jumping lightly, she wrapped her legs around his hips and her arms around his neck, then took his mouth once more.

"You have the sweetest, softest mouth," she murmured

in between kisses.

"It's the honey," he panted, his fingers dipping between her legs from behind, teasing into her wetness.

"No, honey," she whispered. "It's you. Why are you still wearing clothes?"

He laughed, holding her with one hand while he scrabbled ineffectively with the other, trying to undo the ties of his pants. Amanda tsked impatiently and slid down his body to do it herself, dragging his pants down over his hips, past his thighs, lingering to take him in her mouth and suck him in deeply until he curled both hands in her hair and gasped, "Gods, don't do that, I'll never last."

She looked up at him, her tongue swirling around his cock as she pulled it from her mouth enough to say, "I'll bring you back."

He growled and reached down to circle her arms with his strong fingers, holding her off long enough to let the loose pants drop to his ankles. He toed off pants and boots both, and she moved in closer, when he surprised her, sweeping her up into his arms and carrying her over to the lean-to.

Ducking inside, he settled her on the mossy bed and stretched out above her, whispering, "This isn't exactly what I had planned either."

"The hell with plans," she snarled. She spread her legs, hooked her good leg around his hip, then reached down and grasped his rock-hard length, and lifted herself just enough that the tip of his thick cock dipped into her aching sex.

He did the rest. With a hungry groan, he plunged deep inside her in a long, slow thrust, and then kissed her eyes, her mouth, her neck as he drove himself between her thighs over and over. *So big,* she thought blissfully. *So wonderfully big and hard.* She wound her fingers through his long black hair and yanked his mouth back to hers. She could kiss him forever, and never grow tired of it. He had the most exquisite mouth. And oh gods, what... He lifted her legs higher, opening her wider and granting him even deeper access to her needy core. She cried out at a stab of pain in her thigh, moaning instead as ripples of pleasure began rolling through her body, her nipples, so sensitive now, crushed against his massive chest, her inner walls beginning to clench against his shaft, trying to keep him inside her, because he felt so very good there.

He growled, a rumble of noise from deep in his chest. It was an animal sound that had shivers of desire racing down her body to her clit, making it ache with need. Desperate tremors of sheer pleasure shook every nerve and muscle of her body as his cock pounded into her.

Drowning in sensation, she tightened her arms around his neck. She crossed her ankles over his back, squeezing him between her legs, afraid she'd be swept away on the wave of ecstasy building higher and higher until it crashed into her, shoving her over the screaming edge of orgasm. Every muscle in her body contracted at once, the walls of her sheath convulsed, rippling along his hard length, sucking him deeper and deeper as she tugged his mouth back to hers once again, desperate for the taste of him, drinking in his roar of climax as he joined her, the two of them coming over and over until there was nothing left.

They lay together, limbs wound so tightly it was difficult to say where hers ended and his began. His face was in her neck, his breath almost cool against her overheated skin, as they both gasped for air, their chests expanding in sync, bodies coated with sweat. She stroked her hand down his strong back and firm ass, smiling to herself when he shuddered with renewed desire. She wanted to say something, to tell him how wonderful he felt inside her, how it had never been so good, so right.

She didn't say any of that. She didn't want to spoil the perfection of the moment with what she feared would be unwelcome emotion. So she lay beneath him, feeling his cock still firm inside her, still twitching with the aftereffect of his climax, his big heart thudding against her breasts.

He moved finally, turning slightly so she could stretch her leg out, murmuring softly about not wanting to hurt her. He wasn't. She didn't tell him that either. He rolled over, taking her with him, tucking her beneath his arm and against his chest, holding her close. And she dared to hope that maybe it had been good for him, too. And wasn't that just the worst cliché ever?

Neither one of them said anything for what seemed like a long time. They just lay in each other's arms, breathing.

Finally, when the air had begun to chill the sweat on their bodies, he said, "We should have done this a long time ago."

Amanda breathed a soft laugh, and let one teasing hand stroke down his chest to his groin and over his cock, her fingers stroking him into renewed hardness. "We'll just have to make up for lost time," she whispered.

He sucked in a breath, flexing his hips against her hand.

"I don't think there's enough time in the world, *acushla*."

"Then we better get started," she murmured, as she shifted to her side and began licking her way down his chest and over his hard belly. She would have taken him into her mouth again, but he fisted his hand in her hair with a growl, his strong arms pulling her up and under him in one smooth motion, sliding his fully-hardened shaft into her soaking wet sex and starting all over again.

Chapter Thirty-Five

Rhodry woke the next morning feeling lazy. No, not lazy, he realized at once. Peaceful. Relaxed. Something he hadn't felt since he'd left his mountain home, or maybe even before that. For the first time in too long he came awake without wondering if his enemy was close at hand, or if a new trap had been set for him.

Snugged against his chest, Amanda breathed out a long sigh of sleep, one arm resting along his ribs, her injured leg thrown over his hips so that he could still feel the slick heat between her thighs. He had a moment of guilt that he'd been so rough with her, that he'd forgotten about her leg in the urgency of taking her over and over again. Hell, just the thought of what they'd done had him hardening with need once more. He moved slightly, trying not to wake her, succeeding only in increasing the pressure of her full breasts against his chest. He stifled a groan as her lovely nipples grew to stiff peaks with the contact, and his shaft responded ever more eagerly, brushing against the soft skin of her thigh.

A low and sexy purr of sound washed over his skin as she laughed softly, letting him know she was awake. Without raising her head, she swirled her wet tongue against one of his flat nipples, undoing any good intentions he might have had about letting her sleep.

"You'll be the death of me."

She dismissed his words with a puff of breath. "Big strong shifter like you can handle it."

With no warning, she rolled over to straddle his hips, her short hiss of pain becoming a long sigh of pleasure as she began to rock gently back and forth, sliding his hard cock up and down along her silky crease. He placed a hand on each of her slender hips, enjoying the rhythm of her movement, the friction of her sleek skin beneath his rough hands. Her blond hair was free of its perpetual confinement, slightly damp, wavy from its braid, and hanging loose over her full breasts, which swung enticingly with every sway of her body, her pretty nipples surrounded by wide, pink areolas. She leaned forward to kiss him, and her breasts crushed against his chest as their mouths met in a hungry tasting of lips and tongue.

He held onto her when she would have sat back, raising his head to take each breast in turn into his mouth, sucking each nipple to a plump, rosy nub, then biting gently before letting go. He could feel her already wet center grow slicker and hotter as he suckled, heard her intake of breath as she ground herself against him, increasing the friction on her clit.

"Rhodi," she breathed, full of wanting. He felt his own hungry response to the need in her voice and tightened his fingers on her hips, lifting her enough to position his throbbing erection between her swollen lips, lowering her slowly to savor the feel of her tight heat against every inch of his cock, hearing her gasp of pleasure that matched his own groan of desire.

Needing to be closer, he sat up and wrapped his arms around her, gathering her softness against the hard muscles of his chest. Her breath was hot on his neck as she licked her way up to his mouth and he felt her smile against his lips. She began rocking faster, riding his cock with every stroke as he thrust against her, her breath coming in quick gasps of air until he heard her first cry of delight.

In a single swift movement, he rolled her beneath him so he could plunge deeper. Her legs tightened around him as her cries grew more frequent and more desperate, until her inner walls clenched and rippled along his cock. He swallowed her scream of climax, and thrust even harder, his own orgasm building until he came with a surge of release so powerful that it verged on pain. He hissed with desire, closing his eyes against the strength of it, wanting to roar with triumph as her body responded once again, milking the last of his seed as she cried out his name.

He collapsed, shifting his weight to one side and rolling them over again, so that she lay mostly on top of him. When she would have moved, he tightened his grip, not yet ready to let her go, to slide his shaft from inside her. She relaxed against him, and he slid his hands down to cup her sweet ass and hold her in place.

Her face was nestled beneath his jaw, and he tilted his head slightly, touching his lips to her sweat-warmed skin, finding her cheeks wet and salty with tears. He froze.

"Did I hurt you?"

She didn't answer, only shook her head and kissed his neck, her hair tickling his chest where it spread out over both of them. Rhodry shifted his arms up to her back, holding her tightly and wondering how he could ever go back to the city, with its politics and conspiracies, after this.

Chapter Thirty-Six

Amanda lay almost on top of Rhodry, soaking in the heat of his body. His heart beat hard and strong beneath her ear, his lungs a rush of sound deep within his chest. He'd almost undone her this time. When he'd asked if he'd hurt her, she couldn't have answered without sobbing, so she'd just shaken her head and snuggled closer. She was never this emotional about a man. Because no man had ever touched her soul before, made her *feel* the things that he did.

Maybe she was just tired. Overwrought, as her mother used to say. Every single day since she'd stood in the Guild Hall yard that morning before her trial began had been both emotionally and physically exhausting. Even so, it had been less than two weeks since she'd rescued Rhodry, so why did it seem as if she'd known him all her life? Sure, she'd wanted him, but this feeling was so much more than that. And how was that possible? How could Rhodry, of all people, have gotten to her? He was chauvinistic, old-fashioned, stubborn…

handsome, charming, smart, courageous and strong. She laughed silently and he patted her back, as if he thought she needed comforting. Maybe she did.

"Rhodi?"

"Aye?"

"Do you believe I can hear the trees?"

He gave a long-suffering sigh. He was probably wondering what the hell she was on about now. "I've said I'm sorry for that, Amanda. Of course I believe you."

She swallowed a laugh. It seemed he was the one who needed comforting this time. She stroked his chest dutifully, and thought about going back to the city and what it would mean. They would have to go back eventually. He had family who would be worried, and her mother would expect to hear something soon, even allowing for transmission delays. Elise knew about the trial, and knew when it had started. She'd worry if the silence dragged on too long.

And in addition to their families, there were their enemies, most of whom would be very surprised when the two of them showed up alive and well. Nando and his buddies clearly wouldn't have minded if she'd ended up as dinner for that ice bear. And Serna and Daly probably believed Rhodry to be long dead by now.

The memory of how they'd left him to die sparked a renewed flare of anger. *Damn right, we'll go back.* They had to deal with what had been done to them. Maybe they didn't need to go *right* back, however.

Her stomach growled suddenly, reminding her that they'd barely eaten the night before. They'd been too busy devouring each other. She smiled in memory, and her stomach growled again, louder this time, as if daring her to ignore it.

"I'm hungry." She sat up slowly and pushed her hair out of her face. "And you must be, too."

He gave her a very predatory look through half-lidded eyes, his stare lifting from a study of her breasts to her face with an appreciative grin. "Hungry," he agreed.

"Not for that, you goat. Feed me."

"Feed you?" He sat up, taking a playful nip at one rosy breast. "I wouldn't dare. This is *your* trial, Amanda," he said, throwing her words of yesterday afternoon back in her face.

"So it is," she agreed. "How about fish, then? If I'm right about our location—and you know I am—we should be less than a mile from the Leeward Stream. This time of year, the silvers are running fat and slow."

"Sounds like a plan."

She admired the graceful play of muscles as he rolled to his feet and held out a hand to help her up. She placed her fingers in his, giving a little yip of surprise when he pulled her up and tight against his chest, holding her securely with an arm across her back.

"You get dressed and gather our things," he said. "I'll break down the lean-to."

She nodded breathlessly, feeling his cock stir against her belly, watching his playful expression become something else, something... Her chest tightened at what she saw in his eyes as they stood there staring at each other.

Well. That was unexpected.

Rhodry blinked, seeming as stunned as she was at first. Then he grinned and slapped her ass.

"Get moving, woman, or you'll never get us fed."

She pushed away from him, away from the brink of the emotions hanging in the air, and started gathering their scattered clothes.

Chapter Thirty-Seven

Fat dripped on the fire, sparking hot pops of flame as Amanda turned the spitted fish. Satisfied it was cooking evenly, she banked the fire a little, then stood up and began stripping off her torn and filthy clothes, which were the same ones she'd been wearing when she and Rhodry had fallen into each other the night before.

Rhodry hadn't bothered to dress at all when they'd left the earlier campsite. He'd simply shifted into his animal form and taken to the trees. She didn't have that luxury. There were too many things in the forest that would find her sweet human flesh munchable. She wasn't worried about animals, not with her personal shifter around. It was the insects and certain breeds of carnivorous plants, too, that made it unwise for her to walk even a short distance naked.

All the same, she'd been loath to put on the clean clothes he'd brought for her, knowing she'd be cleaning fish before the morning was over. So instead, she'd pulled on the same leggings and shirt she'd worn for the past two weeks, and trudged the nearly three quarters of a mile to the Leeward Stream.

The stream was, in fact, a smallish river that cut across the Green in a long twisting route, starting from a spot somewhere in the glacier far to the north, then traveling through the Green and Ciudad Vaquero, until it disappeared again, swallowed up by the southern desert. Banks rose high on either side of the river to accommodate a water level that varied from a low of about two feet to a high, depending on run-off, of as much as eight feet.

In the aftermath of the recent storm and with the weather having warmed rather quickly, it was running just a little high today. If the mild weather held up, it would test its banks over the next several days.

Amanda lowered herself gingerly down the muddy bank, gasping as the icy cold water sucked every ounce of warmth from her body. One had to be desperate for a bath to venture into the damn thing so close to the glacial source. She closed her eyes, gritted her teeth, and bent her knees, dunking her entire body into the freezing stream and popping right back up again. Fuck, that was cold. She already couldn't even feel her toes.

She glanced over her shoulder at Rhodry. He'd dozed off on a wide, flat stone overlooking the river, and was peacefully unaware that she was freezing to death only a few feet away. He was still in cat form, lying on his side with all four legs stretched loosely in front of him, his black fur winking blue in the dappled sunlight. On a day like today, with the sun high in the sky and no clouds, the stone would be warm beneath him, and he was soaking it in.

Jealous, she snarled in his direction as she used wet sand from the river bottom to scrub her body quickly, being particularly careful of her various cuts and bruises, and especially the deep wounds on her arm and thigh. She'd taken the bandage off her arm. The wound was ugly, and already beginning to heal into an even uglier scar. Her thigh she'd left tightly wrapped, planning to exchange the bandage with something cleaner after she bathed.

She finished scrubbing, and braced herself against the need for a second dunking to rinse off. She really wanted to do something with her hair and scalp, even if she didn't have any real soap, much less shampoo. More dunking, damn it. She sighed. If they decided to head directly for the Guild Hall, it would make the most sense to shadow the stream all the way home. While the water would never get warm—not this time of year, even if the weather cooperated as it was doing today—it would eventually get less cold.

If they headed straight back, that is. An idea began percolating through her brain. Now she had to figure out a way to convince Rhodry of its worthiness.

She did a half-assed job of rinsing off, bending her knees enough to fully immerse her body and tipping back her head long enough for a quick scrub of her scalp. It left her hair thoroughly wet. Not clean, just not quite so dusty.

Her whole body was shaking with cold as she climbed out of the water and dressed in the fresh clothes from the cache. Sitting on a nearby log, she pulled on her own socks and boots, then finger-combed and braided her hair, thinking all the while of how to persuade him to her developing plan. If it worked, she'd be enjoying a steamy, *hot* bath before the end of the day. And with real soap. What bliss!

She crossed over to the base of the big rock where he was dozing and called up to him.

"Have you been topside today?" she asked, meaning had he climbed high enough into the canopy to take a bearing on their position.

He lifted his sleek head and blinked lazy golden eyes at her, apparently not inclined to shift in order to answer her question.

Oh, well. This *was* her trial. Sitting back down, she yanked off the boots and socks she'd just put on, walked barefoot over to the nearest canopy tree and began climbing. There were plenty of fingerholds in a tree this old, and her leg only hurt *a lot* when she pushed herself up.

Rhodry's roar of outrage sent birds shrieking from above and would have startled her from her perch had he not shifted to human at the same time, and moving faster than she'd have thought possible, plucked her bodily from the tree before she could fall.

"What in all the gods—"

"Let go of me!" she demanded, slapping his hands away. "What do you think you're doing—?"

"What am *I* doing? What the hell are *you* doing climbing a fucking tree with your leg torn up like that? Why are you climbing a tree at all? You could fall—"

"I've been climbing trees since I was a child! Those of us without claws and fur do figure out ways to go on living, you know. And how the hell do you think I navigate out here if I don't climb trees?"

He put her down and stared in genuine puzzlement. "I don't know. I just assumed you… Hell, I don't know. I never thought about it."

"Lucky you. Now, if you'll excuse me—"

He grabbed her with both arms before she could attack the tree again. "Please," he begged, holding her tight. "For me. I nearly had a heart attack when I saw you clinging to that thing. Just tell me what you want, *acushla*, please."

She studied her big, bad shifter, amused, and also touched by his concern. Her leg really did hurt like hell, and she wasn't exactly eager to find out if the long climb would start it bleeding again. Not that she'd tell *him* that. She smiled sweetly and patted his arm.

"Have you been topside today?" she repeated.

He inhaled deeply, blew out a relieved breath, and nodded. "On the way here."

"How far are we from the city?"

"Four days above," he said immediately, then thought about it. "So, maybe eight days below?"

"Hmmm, about what I thought. Tell me"—she wrapped both arms around his waist—"are you in a hurry to get back to the city? I mean I know you—"

He frowned suspiciously. "Why?"

She smiled. "Because I'm dying for a hot bath, and I know a place."

Chapter Thirty-Eight

The Green was deceptive in so many ways. From a distance, it was a huge, flat forest of almost identical trees. When one was deep in the heart of the Green, however, there was no uniformity. Every inch of it, high or low, was filled with trees in all shapes and sizes, intermingled with dense shrubs and clinging vines that twisted from tree to tree and climbed all the way to the canopy itself in search of sunshine. And the surface, which to the naked eye seemed completely flat from space, was in fact wrinkled and rippled, full of steep ravines and narrow, deep valleys which trapped heat and moisture and created almost jungle-like microclimates in certain places.

Her favorite hot spring was tucked into one of those hidden ravines. And it was only a short distance off their direct route to the city, which, she suspected, was why Rhodry had agreed to the detour. That and the fact that the antibiotics she needed were stashed there. And while the antibiotics may have been her trump card to persuade him, by midday she was convinced she really did need them.

They traveled steadily, eating fruit and trail bars along the way, making good time. The deeper they journeyed into the heart of the forest, the thicker the foliage became, and the more difficult it was to travel on the ground, climbing over and under, and detouring around, the riotous growth. Even so, she'd made this trip many times over the months she'd spent training, and she'd never found it this exhausting. Her leg hurt. Just plain *hurt*. And though she tried to conceal it, she was limping badly after the first two miles or so.

Rhodry had shifted and gone up into the trees after their last stop, wanting to get a better sense of where they were. When he dropped out of the trees this time, he shifted back to human, and watched critically as she hobbled toward him.

"We should stop for the day. There's no point in killing yourself for a hot bath."

"I don't want to stop," she said stubbornly, limping past him. "It's not that much farther, and if we get there *today*, I won't have to walk tomorrow at all."

He strode quickly past her and stopped, blocking her path. "Amanda."

She glared up at him. "Rhodry."

He blew out a frustrated breath and threw his hands into the air. "Stubborn, pigheaded *woman*," he muttered. He grabbed her backpack, pulled out his clothes and boots, and donned them quickly before stomping off through the trees ahead of her, clearing the trail so she wouldn't have to work so hard. She smiled. He really was a sweetie.

They reached a narrow valley not long after that, traveling down a gentle slope and pausing where it evened out to a broad plateau before dropping once again into a steep-sided ravine. It was late in the afternoon, the day still warm, the sun's heat trapped by a combination of heavy canopy and sloping terrain. She paused to rest briefly before the last push, half sitting on a fallen tree trunk. It was covered with lichen and crawling vines like everything else in the forest, its innards hollowed out long ago. Just another lump in the forest floor.

"This is it," she told him. She was puffing breathlessly, and fighting not to let him know it. She'd used up all her reserves of strength just to get this far. She'd lost at least ten pounds since the trial began, and it was weight she couldn't afford to lose since most of her body mass was muscle. Her shipboard training hadn't left much fat on her, and what there was had been whittled away by her training for the Guild trials.

"Are you all right?" He crouched next to her, his big hand a soothing warmth despite the heat of her sore leg.

"Just a little out of breath," she gasped, resting a hand on his shoulder and faking a grin. "I didn't get much sleep last night."

He stood, then sat next to her on the log, dropping an arm over her shoulder and encouraging her to lean against him. When she did, he kissed the top of her head. "I'll let you sleep tonight."

"You do, and you'll be sorry."

He gave a pleased laugh, and sat with her quietly until her breathing evened out. "So where's this hot spring?" he asked, inhaling deeply as he took in the forest's scent.

"Right in front of you," she said. "You shifters have your heads so far up" — he tightened his arm playfully and she laughed before continuing—"*in the trees* that you forget to look at what's on the ground."

She stood before her muscles could stiffen any further, and slowly started down the steep slope, pausing to give him an appraising glance over her shoulder. "You'll probably have to shift to get through here."

He shrugged, handed over their gear, and stripped efficiently. She caught the discarded pants he threw to her, then leaned back against the cool rocks to watch him shift. It was something she'd seen many times before, and it never ceased to amaze her. It was nothing like the old werewolf movies they had in the ship's vid library. There was no gush of fluid, no bursting skin. It was a graceful flow of flesh into fur, shimmering up his body until three hundred pounds of human became pure, sleek feline. Only his eyes stayed the same, slightly almond shaped, with a perfectly round iris of molten gold, giving him the same extraordinary vision in either form.

The huge black cat that was Rhodry arched his back against his front paws, hips held high to stretch his spine with a popping of vertebrae. He stood up and grinned at her, his long pink tongue licking his chops deliberately.

She laughed and wrapped her arms around his neck in a hug. "You're such a pretty kitty."

He growled and butted her with his big head, which only made her laugh more.

Straightening away from the rocks, she patted his shoulder, which sat just about level with her hip, and said, "Follow me."

The hot spring she wanted was very near the bottom of the deep ravine, buried in a jumble of rocks and boulders that was completely overgrown with moss and tangled vines. The dense umbrella of a giant urwillow concealed it even further, its fronds sweeping the ground with a thick and lacy curtain. She pushed aside several of the feather-like branches, and entered the labyrinth of stone that would take her to the heart of the hot spring.

She maneuvered easily through the twisting passage, snickering when Rhodry hissed with displeasure as he tried to fit through some of the narrower twists and turns. As she drew closer to the grotto at its heart, a few wisps of steam from the spring found their way through the maze of rocks to caress her face, letting her know the end of the passage was close. Not that she needed the reminder. Every turn was familiar to her. She'd considered marking the route after her first visit, wary of the many wrong turns that had left her with barely enough space to turn around and retrace her steps. In the end, she'd decided against it, not wanting to make it any easier for others to find. She turned sideways to ease through the last narrow gap, and stepped into a secret garden.

Twenty feet at its widest point and irregular in shape, the grotto was little more than a hollow within the stones, shaped over the millennia by the steady flow of hot water bubbling up from somewhere underground and emerging halfway up the wall on the far right. The spring tumbled over once-jagged rocks, now smoothed and rounded by the water's course, some pocked with small reservoirs along the way that constantly filled and overflowed as the water made its way to the larger pool at the opposite end.

The air was warm and steamy, and the uneven sunlight confused as much as it revealed as she made her way over the rough ground. Sunlight should have been hard to come by deep within the rocks like this. Luckily, the passage of time and pressure from the steam had joined to create a large daylight hole over the end of the grotto farthest from the pool. The hole was itself covered with a screen of tangled vines, its irregular opening providing at least partial light for most of the day, turning what would have been a dark, dank hole into a secret hideaway.

A stone skittered across the grotto floor as she kicked it. No matter how many times she did this, there was always a fresh batch of loose rock every time she returned. It worried her sometimes, the idea that the ceiling could give way at any moment, collapsing just as it had sometime before to create the daylight hole.

She passed under an overhang of several tons of rock and into a small alcove with a back wall that was riddled with crevices. It was here that she stored camping gear and supplies for her visits, zipping them into waterproof pouches and tucking them into the various cubbies. She located the big halogen flashlight stored there. It was much larger than the one she carried with her, and had a wide, flat base that permitted one to stand it on end as a lamp. Flicking it on, she searched through the cubbies, noting the extra quiver of arrows she'd stored here on her last visit, and finally pulling out a small case with a waterproof seal. She opened it quickly, and dug past the packages of sterile bandages and wraps until she caught the faint gleam of silver which denoted the sealed packs of antibiotic capsules her mother had provided for her treks into the forests.

"Yes," she whispered, half in relief and half in triumph, quickly tempered by disappointment when she saw that she'd already opened the package on one of her previous visits, leaving it a little more than half full. In addition to the partially used package of capsules, however, there was also a single pressure syringe of antibiotic. A quick calculation told her the syringe coupled with the remaining capsules would be enough to get her back to the city. Enough to knock the infection *back*, though not out. She peeled the syringe out of its sterile pack and pressed it against her leg, feeling a slight burn as the thick medicine spread into the muscle of her thigh. She shoved the empty tube back into the case before Rhodry could see it, not wanting him to know there was a problem. He'd just freak out, and there was nothing either one of them could do about it. She shrugged philosophically and swallowed two of the capsules, chasing them down with the water in her canteen.

An unhappy snarl had her stepping back to the main part of the grotto just in time to see her favorite shifter emerge into the mottled sunlight at last, twisting around to hiss viciously at the tight passage behind him. Tufts of black fur clung to the rocks and floated in the misty air, and she would have laughed, except for the unfriendly glare he was directing her way.

She covered her smile with a casual hand and pretended not to watch as he shook himself from head to toe in disgust, before beginning an immediate inspection of this new territory. Prowling from corner to corner, he snapped his tail back and forth in agitation, and stuck his nose into everything.

Knowing it could take a while for him to settle, she continued her inventory, occasionally crowing happily at what she found. For one thing, there was fresh clothing, including a clean pair of leggings which would actually fit her. The pants from the shifter cache had been too loose and too long, since the shifters were all big men. And she almost cheered out loud at the sight of several small waterproof bottles of body soap and moisturizer and…gods be praised, shampoo.

That was all the incentive she needed. She stripped off her clothes and bandages, loosened the tight braid of her hair, and grabbed the bottles of soap and shampoo. Sitting on the pool's edge, which was worn smooth by centuries of erosion, she eased herself into the water, mumbling word-lessly in a combination of pain and pleasure as the hot, hot water rolled over her skin, and stifling a shriek of real pain when it hit the still raw wound on her right thigh. The pain was brief, however, as her body quickly adapted, and before long, she was feeling wondrous heat all the way to her bones. She sank down with a groan of pleasure, letting her weight rest on one of the wide ledges beneath the edge of the pool.

Rhodry had ceased his prowling and was now perched on the rocks next to the waterfall on the other side of the grotto, staring daggers at her across the open space like some dark minion of vengeance. She smiled and blew him a cheerful kiss, then let herself slide even lower until the soothing waters were up to her chin, soaking away what felt like months of hard, cold weather.

Eventually, she dunked completely under and soaped her hair, thrilled to finally be able to scrub her scalp clean, loving the silky feel of each strand as the dirt washed away. She shampooed and rinsed again, just because it felt so good, then conditioned thoroughly before winding her hair up into a knot on top of her head, and sinking into the water once again, her eyes closed in utter satisfaction.

With her head resting against the lip of the pool, she let herself float, arms and legs rising to the surface, using the occasional light touch to keep herself from drifting too far.

A rush of familiar sound had her cracking one eye open to see Rhodry shifting form again, his animal flowing away to leave her gorgeous human lover standing in the thin light. He gave her a slow smile, then raised his arms over his head in a lazy stretch. Had she thought before that Rhodry would never preen? Because *that* move had been designed for one purpose only, to show off his beautiful body. Seeing her watching, he gave her a quick wink, then strolled the short distance to the pool and dropped over the edge, his powerful arms lowering his body slowly into the water.

"Shit!" he swore in surprise as the heat scorched his skin, then laughed. "Gods, that feels good." He submerged completely, and came up with a twist of his shoulders, his long hair flinging drops of water over the surface of the pool.

She floated, watching with hooded eyes as the water sluiced over his dark golden skin, muscles bunching and releasing before he dropped beneath the water once more and disappeared below the surface. A touch on her foot told her where he was seconds before he burst upward with an exultant shout. She laughed out loud, and swam forward to wrap her arms around his neck, tugging on his wet hair.

"Come on," she said, "I'll wash your hair for you."

"Only if you promise not to tie it in a knot," he said with a wary glance at hers.

"No promises." She pulled him through the water easily, turning him around with his back toward her, her legs wrapped around his waist to keep him in place. He let his head fall back comfortably as she lathered and shampooed, using her strong fingers to massage his scalp just as she had her own.

"This place is amazing. How'd you find it?"

"Serendipity," she said. "I had some time after I passed the written Guild exams—with a perfect score, by the way. I knew winter would be closing in before long, so I wanted to explore deeper into the Green while I could. I planned to be gone a couple of weeks, and Fionn had promised to come along—" She smiled at his growl. Shifters were so predictably territorial. "*But*," she continued, "he never liked going out into the Green with me, and especially not this far from the city."

"Has Fionn been to this place with you then?"

"Will you let me finish my story, please?"

He gave a little grunt of agreement, and she continued. "Anyway, Fionn didn't show, which wasn't all that unusual, so I went out alone."

"Fantastic. Why bother with those pesky Guild regulations, right?"

She knocked her knuckles on the top of his head. "Quiet, you." When he didn't say anything else, she went on. "Without really meaning to, I went farther than I'd ever gone before, especially alone. I saw plants and animals I'd only read about, and even more that I didn't recognize. I was sketching like crazy, determined to go back and find every one of them in the database."

"I hated people like you in school."

She laughed. "You weren't alone. I wanted to learn everything I could, though, so that I'd be ready for my final trial. Anyway, toward the end of my first week out, I was looking for a place to camp for the night. I climbed a tree to get my bearings, and I noticed a concentration of urwillows down in this ravine. I'd done a lot of hiking that day, a lot of ups and downs, and I was dying for a long soak. I knew urwillows were found near hot springs, so I went looking. Once I got into that rock passage back there…well, I couldn't find my way out. I hit so many dead ends and lost so much skin squeezing through tight places that by the time I finally stumbled onto this pool, I was thinking I'd never find my way out again."

"Probably easier for a shifter to come in over the top. Save some fur," he added darkly.

"Poor kitty," she soothed, brushing away suds to kiss the back of his neck. "I don't know if that would work. No one's ever tried. There's never been anyone here except me. Not that I know of."

"No one?"

"Nope."

"So Fionn *hasn't* been here?"

She rolled her eyes at the back of his head. "Especially not Fionn. I told you, he'd never come out this far with me." She tapped his shoulder. "Dunk."

He sank beneath the water, and she ran fingers through his hair, rinsing away the shampoo.

"Fionn's an ass," he commented after resurfacing.

"Don't be mean," she said, squirting more shampoo in his hair. "Besides, Fionn's all right. It's just that no one ever lets him forget that he's destined to be the next Ardrigh. I feel sorry for him sometimes."

His neck and shoulders bunched with tension beneath her fingers, and she wondered at how blind men could be sometimes. She leaned forward and whispered in his ear,

"There must have been one or two court ladies who fancied the de Mendoza clan chief, too."

He snorted dismissively. "Not a brain between them and they stank of perfume. It took days to get the smell out of my nostrils after one of the Ardrigh's social events, and I spent most of the evenings trying not to sneeze."

She felt his muscles relax again, and smiled. "You're such a charmer, de Mendoza. Dunk."

When he came up this time, he'd turned to face her, and she had to reach behind him to twist his hair, wringing out most of the water before letting her arms drop around his neck. She gazed up at him, and thought she'd never wanted anything more than to feel his mouth on her again, to have his body moving inside her, taking and giving pleasure. "Make love to me," she said simply.

He gave a rumbling purr of assent, and his arms closed around her. "So you've never had a man here with you before?"

"Never."

"Which means you've never had sex here before?"

"Nope. So you better make this one count."

"They all count," he murmured as his lips closed on hers. "Every time with you, Amanda. Every time."

Chapter Thirty-Nine

Amanda lay awake in the middle of the night, breathing in the warm moist air of the hot spring, wondering how long they could reasonably linger in this hideaway. She kept circling back to one concern. What would Rhodry's family do if he was reported dead? From what he'd told her of them, she didn't think they'd mourn quietly. They'd raise holy hell, maybe even challenge Cristobal's government. And who would that serve? Desmond Serna, probably. The very traitor who'd tried to murder Rhodry.

She frowned unhappily, and he reached out to pull her closer, somehow aware of her troubled thoughts. She let herself relax into his big body. Yes, they had to go back, she knew that absolutely. She was so reluctant to give this up, to give *him* up. Who knew what would happen when they returned, when obligations to family and crown laid their heavy hand on him again? Would he still acknowledge her? The de Mendoza clan chief and the unwanted Earther woman? There had to be a reason why he'd put her off for so long. Would she become his shameful secret once they returned to the city?

She laid a hand against his thickly-muscled chest, feeling the steady beat of his heart as she smoothed small circles with her fingers. His breath quickened, even in his sleep, and she smiled, letting her hand roam farther, down over his flat belly and lower still. His shaft rose eagerly at the touch of her hand, and she breathed a soft, delighted laugh. She pushed herself up and pressed her lips against his, sliding her tongue along the crease between his lips, teasing her way into his mouth.

He groaned and stilled her hips, holding onto her with both hands. "You keep this up, and there will be no sleeping tonight."

"Who needs sleep?" she murmured, kissing and licking his cheeks, his beautiful eyes, and then back to his delicious mouth. "Do your worst, de Mendoza."

"I'd rather my best."

The tender twining of their mouths became suddenly fierce as tongues fought and teeth bit into flesh. He growled low in his chest and flipped her beneath him, covering her body with his as he sampled first one breast, then the other, biting hard enough that she cried out, fisting her hands in his long dark hair and groaning as his mouth teased lower. His hands lifted her to him, spreading her thighs, letting his tongue glide into her slit to find her swollen clitoris and suck it into his mouth, his tongue working the sensitive nub until she screamed his name, begging him to release her. He made a rumbling, animal sound of hunger and rose onto his knees, wedging himself between her thighs and pulling her onto his cock as he thrust forward, his fingers digging into her hips as he drove deep into her body.

She clenched around him, holding him in her depths, trapping him with her legs as she reached up to pull him closer. He fell forward, his arms to either side of her as he slammed into her over and over again, the silky wetness of her arousal easing the way, creating a slick friction of heat as he pounded into her, as her sheath caressed his hard length. She felt his sac tighten against her ass, heard his breaths turn to gasps as he drove faster and deeper than she would have thought possible, deeper than any man had ever gone. Her own desire soared, every nerve in her body seeming to come alive at once, her breasts aching with the need to be crushed against him, her mouth hungry for another taste of his flesh. She tugged his head lower.

"Kiss me," she demanded.

He snarled his response, lowering his mouth to claim hers at the last minute, swallowing her scream of climax as he poured his own release deep into her body, filling her, shattering her, and making her whole.

They lay unmoving as breaths eased and hearts resumed a steady rhythm, listening to the trickle of water in the grotto, the rustle of small animals in the trees overhead. She licked dry lips, his and hers, and he responded, kissing her softly, tenderly, as if she was the most precious thing in the world to him, before wrapping her in his arms and rolling over.

"What are you thinking?" she asked eventually, already knowing his answer.

"We have to go back."

She sighed and rubbed her face against his shoulder in a way that always made him smile. He teased that she was becoming more of a cat than he was, that she was spending too much time around him. It hit her again that they might have less time together in the future, and her arms tightened around him possessively.

"How do you think Serna explained your disappearance? Especially to your family. And will Cristobal think you've deserted?"

"Regardless of what Cristobal thinks, my family would never believe I'd desert, and Serna's clever enough to know that. No, he'll have come up with a tragic tale. An accident or maybe even an ice bear," he said drily. "It doesn't matter. Whatever the claim, my cousins won't take Serna or anyone else's word on it, and I'm worried what they might do. I have to get back to the city before that happens."

"Serna and Daly will be surprised."

"It is my fondest wish to surprise them completely."

"In the morning, then?" she said quietly.

"Aye," he breathed, pulling her head onto his shoulder. "Get some sleep, *acushla*. We've a long, dangerous journey ahead of us yet."

Chapter Forty

Amanda watched Rhodry vault into the trees, his muscular legs and scythe-like claws powering up the thick trunk with ease. He paused at the first branching to crouch low and study her with a lazy, predatory stare, and, even knowing who he was, it gave her a little chill to be eyed like today's lunch. That is, until he opened his jaws in a big kitty grin, flicked his tail, and disappeared into the canopy's heavy growth.

She waited a while longer, thinking she could hear him moving through the upper branches, but decided it was just the wind. Then, eyeing her own clawless fingers with regret, she picked up her gear once again and, since he couldn't see her, limped in the general direction of Ciudad Vaquero. No gliding through the trees for her, she was earth-bound with a bad leg, making her way around thick clusters of undergrowth, running up against vines so intertwined among the trees that cutting through them would have added hours to her journey. Easier by far simply to walk around, no matter how far it took her from her path.

The hidden hot spring was already two days behind them, two days spent traveling ever closer to the city. The forest floor here was thick with old leaves and moss, layer upon layer of vegetation gone to mulch centuries ago, spongy and giving beneath her feet.

The usual small ground-bound creatures were scratching through the undergrowth and birds fluttered high above. The birds of Harp were generally a quiet bunch. One would occasionally burst into song, quickly answered from far away. And that was inevitably followed by a loud rush of wings as the whole flock took off for parts unknown, perhaps having been called to a better roosting by the distant advance scout.

The larger predators had stayed out of their path. Mostly, she knew, because of Rhodry drifting around above her. The animals had learned generations ago that shifters were vicious in protection of their human companions. Had she been alone, it would have been a very different story, and Amanda had to admit it was nice to walk through the Green without being constantly on the alert. She no sooner had that thought than she was scolding herself for it. It was dangerous to become too complacent on Harp, even with a shifter standing guard.

Far overhead the sun was shining brightly, sifting down through the trees to create a moving canvas of light. It took skill and experience to filter through the constantly shifting light and distinguish between fleeting shadow and real movement. She had long ago made that leap in ability, and on planets far away from Harp. It was almost like a dance to her, with the shifting light a silent symphony, twirling around a bramble, down a branch and up a vine. For all the encumbrance of traveling on the forest floor compared to weaving above it through the trees, she'd often thought that shifters missed the most basic song of the Green by not getting their paws dirty.

A rustle of leaves overhead drew her idle glance. There was always activity of some sort in the canopy. Any number of the animals who lived out here never touched the ground until death sent them to a final resting place on the forest floor. She continued on, pausing to pick some goldbud she found growing in a huge clump between the roots of a grandfather tree. This far south, the herb grew like a weed, its flavor stronger and more spicy than what she'd found growing near the glacier. She crouched down to pull the plant up carefully, leaving the dirt clinging to its threadlike roots as she rolled it in a broadleaf and tucked it into her pack. It would stay fresher, comforted by the presence of its home soil.

She slapped her hands together to get rid of the dirt, then brushed them down the front of her leggings. The pants had been clean when she and Rhodry had left the hot spring. After two days of travel, they were so filthy that the extra grime from her hands was hardly noticeable. Other than her cloak—and even that would need a thorough cleaning— there wasn't one thread of her clothing that would be usable after this. She'd probably end up throwing the whole bunch directly into the rag bag. On second thought, they might not even be usable as rags. Shaking her head, she kept walking.

There was that rustling again, distinct enough to draw her attention, and make her aware that she'd been hearing a steady movement overhead for some time. She stopped and leaned her head back, searching the canopy. Between the constantly shifting spectrum of light and the deep shadows of the higher branches, it was nearly impossible to see anything. She scanned slowly, listening as well as looking for anything out of place. Nothing stood out. She thought about calling Rhodry, unwilling to break the silence or even, she admitted, to act like a helpless female. With a last searching look overhead, she shrugged and kept going.

Another ten paces and a big bird took wing above her, its raucous caw of discontent punctuated by the snap of wings as it rose from its perch. She frowned and abruptly wondered where Rhodry was. A wayward breeze brought her the sound of claws on bark and she smiled. It was nearly time to stop for the day. She'd been angling toward the sound of running water for some time now in anticipation of their nighttime camp. She changed direction, aiming straight for the steady splash of water over rocks, wondering how cold it would be and whether she could manage a bath of some sort. What was it her mother always said? Beggars can't be choosers. And she certainly *looked* the part of a beggar.

She was chuckling at her own thoughts when a shadow fell over her shoulder, casting her into even deeper shade than the rapidly declining sun. She kept walking. Let Rhodi think his little ambush would work. Wouldn't he be surprised—

She stumbled, crying out in shock as a heavy weight laid a glancing blow across her back and knocked her to the ground. Her knees hit hard on a gnarled root, sending a jolt of agony up her injured thigh, snapping her teeth together to bite her tongue as she fell.

"Damn it, Rhodry," she snapped, and twisted around,

furious that he would try such a stupid stunt. She had only a moment to register the *tawny* cat's gold-flecked brown eyes before it yowled aggressively and launched itself at her, claws distended, mouth open to reveal very sharp, white fangs.

She shouted in surprise and rolled to one side, away from the tree and its massive roots. The cat's full weight missed her, with one heavy paw striking her lower back like a fist. She grunted in pain, recognizing in the same moment that he'd pulled his claws. That was curious, but the blow had still hit hard just above her kidney, and it hurt like hell.

She gathered her legs beneath her and pushed to her feet, pulling a knife as she did so. Whether or not he was trying to kill her, she had no intention of letting him beat her black and blue. She tried to scramble back against a tree as she searched for her attacker. The tawny cat hit her again before she'd regained her balance, this time from above, landing full on her back and shoulders and pushing her down into the smothering softness of the forest floor. Her nose and mouth filled with dead leaves and dirt, making it impossible to draw a breath. She fought back, fisting her knife and stabbing blindly backward, struggling to get enough leverage to use her full weight against him. He was heavy, though nowhere near as heavy as Rhodry would have been—younger probably, and definitely smaller.

Her attacker howled as her knife hit its target, the blow glancing off what felt like a rib. It was enough to distract him, and she lifted her face to suck in a breath of precious air. She managed only one, as the angry cat now doubled his efforts, using his greater weight and strength to hold her down while his nose burrowed into the space between her neck and shoulder. She could feel the heat of his breath, the hot wet spittle dripping from his fangs, and she knew if he succeeded in biting her there, he could kill her whether he intended to or not.

A roar of fury echoed through the forest, and her attacker howled in terror as Rhodry dropped out of the trees. The two cats rolled away across the forest floor, their sharp battle snarls punctuated by shrieks of pain as Rhodry tore into the smaller animal. Amanda shook her head, trying to focus. Her ears rang with her attacker's deafening cry of fear, which had been right next to her head when Rhodry attacked, and black spots danced in front of her eyes from her near suffocation on the forest floor. She spat wet dirt and moss out of her mouth, rubbing her lips vigorously to get rid of the disgusting taste. Lucky for her nothing in this area was poisonous or she'd have been dead.

She was convinced by now that her attacker didn't want her dead. He'd pulled his claws when he hit her, and even when he had her down on the ground, he hadn't bitten her, although there had been plenty of opportunity. Instead of pushing her face into the dirt, he could have severed her spine easily with a single snap of his jaws, or one swipe of those powerful claws. She blinked at the battling cats, one huge and black and the other…just a baby.

"Don't kill him," she shouted. She jumped up and ran toward the combatants, ducking behind a tree at the last minute to avoid being crushed by the tangle of snarling cats. "Don't kill him, Rhodi!"

He had the smaller cat at his mercy, bleeding profusely from several deep gashes in his muzzle, and one paw hanging limply as if broken. Her erstwhile attacker was on his back, belly bared, his mouth hanging open and gasping for breath, eyes rolling in fear as Rhodry's deadly fangs hovered above his throat.

"Rhodry!" Amanda shouted.

His massive head swung toward her, and he snarled angrily.

"Don't kill him. Please."

He stared at her for several heartbeats, then gave a disgusted snort and swiped one huge paw across the smaller cat's cheek, before flexing his powerful legs and jumping onto the branch just over her head. He stayed there, crouched protectively above her, his muzzle red with the tawny cat's blood, golden eyes watching every move.

She didn't move any closer to the injured cat. She didn't trust either her attacker's motives or Rhodry's patience that far.

"Go back and tell whoever sent you that we're coming home," she said flatly.

The tawny shifter wasn't paying any attention to her. He was staring at Rhodry who returned the gaze with fangs bared, a low growl rumbling steadily from within his deep chest. The younger cat finally dared to cut his eyes briefly in her direction, before snapping right back to Rhodry. Finally, with a pained grunt, he ventured a slow roll back to his feet where he immediately huddled into a tight ball, poised to run.

"Go on." The young cat seemed frozen by terror, and she blew an impatient breath. "If you've the brains of a houseplant," she snapped, "you'll leave while you can. He won't touch you as long as you leave us alone."

The attacker stood on shaky legs, his attention never

leaving the huge black shifter hulking overhead. Muscles bunched suddenly, and then he shot away, racing to the nearest tree only to howl in pain when he tried to climb it with his torn paw. Falling back to the ground, he slunk instead into the underbrush and disappeared from sight. Most likely, he'd stay on the ground until he felt safe, then shift a couple of times until he was healed enough to take to the trees again.

One thing was certain. When he got back to the Guild Hall, his masters would know that Amanda was on her way back, and that Rhodry de Mendoza was alive and well, and on his way home along with her.

Chapter Forty-One

Rhodry shifted in midair, dropping from the tree to crouch naked behind her. "Why the hell didn't you let me kill him?" he demanded.

He was obviously still pumping adrenaline from the fight — his chest heaving, body slick with sweat and streaked with the young cat's blood.

"I'm fine, thank you for asking," she said pointedly, standing with a grimace of pain.

He stalked over and began brushing the dirt and moss off her face and out of her hair with a gentleness that belied his temper, clucking in sympathy when he saw she'd bitten her tongue.

"Did he hurt you?" His strong hands ran carefully over her face and shoulders, down her body, pausing when she cried out. He lifted her shirt and turned her around, cursing when he saw the angry, dark bruise already blossoming over her kidney. "You should have let me kill the bastard," he snarled. "What happened?"

"I got careless. I thought it was you—" She fought back a hiccup of hysterical laughter at his look of offended outrage. "I didn't *see* him. He came from behind me. I heard him in the trees and thought it was you." She patted his chest with a shaky hand. "Once I got a look at his puny self, I knew it couldn't be you. By then, it was too late."

Feeling a sudden need to be closer to him, she moved in and snugged both arms around his waist. He wasn't the only one coming down from an adrenaline high. She was trembling, and not all of it was adrenaline. She'd been scared. His arms came up to hold her, one big, warm hand stroking gently up and down her back in a soothing motion.

"He wasn't trying to kill me," she insisted, having to fight to keep her voice even. "I'm not sure he even meant to hurt me. He just didn't know his own strength. He was so young. You must have noticed that."

Rhodry brushed his lips against her hair. "He wasn't *that* young. He should know better than to attack a norm, *any* norm. The bigger question is who the hell sent him out here? And why?"

"Someone who didn't expect *you* to be here, that's for sure. It was probably just a prank. Send the kid out to scout the incoming trails and if you spot the candidate, give her some grief. Like they haven't doled out enough already."

"I'll show *them* some grief," he growled. "And, damn it, now they'll know about me as soon as that idiot reports back. It might take them a while to figure out exactly who I am. I didn't recognize the boy, although he might know me. Either way, Serna and Daly will hear about it and *they'll* know that it has to be me."

"I know," she sighed softly. "The good times are over, I guess."

He laughed at the suggestion that their journey thus far had been good times. "We'll make better times in the future. We've just got to get home alive first."

"Hard to argue with that," she said, leaning back to admire his handsome face. "So, what's the plan?"

"You were right when you said shifters think in the treetops. They'll assume I'll be up there, even though they know you have to travel on the ground. They'll also expect us to stick to daylight, because you can't see in the dark. So we travel at night and on the ground. You'll just have to stay close to me."

She smiled. "Not a hardship. How long before the kid gets back to the Guild Hall?" she asked.

"Two, three days at best. He'll need to heal first, and he's rattled. And we'll be traveling at the same time he is, which means we'll also be closer to the city by the time he reports in. That's good in that there's at least *some* safety in the Guild Hall, and Cristobal wouldn't tolerate open warfare in the city. It's bad because our enemies will want to stop us from reaching that safety, and it won't take them as long to find us."

He kissed her forehead and stepped away. "I'm going to do a quick scout of the area to make sure our young visitor didn't bring any friends. I'll stay close. You keep going, and I'll join you before dark."

He shifted on the run, his sleek, black form vanishing into the shadows long before he was gone.

Three nights later, Amanda was following Rhodry's broad silhouette through the brush and not needing even her small flashlight to see. The forest around them was bright, and curiously monochrome, all color leeched out of the verdant growth by the overwhelming cool, blue glow of Fodla, the largest of Harp's three moons. It hung huge and full in the sky, appearing almost larger than the planet itself. Fodla showed her full face only once every seven months. Most of her uneven orbit around Harp was spent far away from the sun, and she seemed to bask in this brief reflection of warmth after her cold and solitary journey.

Back in the city, there would be celebrations. Families and friends would gather, starting with quiet, candlelit dinners and spilling out into the streets to dance under the blue moon. She thought about the parties now going on in the city, and knew she wouldn't have traded an invitation to *any* of them for the sight of Rhodry's strong back ahead of her in the moon-bright shadows of the Green.

By now, their teenage prankster had probably reached the city with his news. They were traveling fast, following the most direct route possible along the congested forest floor, trying to get back to the city before Serna and his allies could set out to stop them. Rhodry hadn't uttered a word of complaint, even though she knew it had to be torture for him, crawling over the ground with her. Alone, he could have taken to the trees and been at Guild Hall long ago, could even have outpaced the young shifter and reached the city *before* his enemies got word of his return.

She'd encouraged him to go ahead without her, had reminded him, for the umpteenth time, that this was her trial, that in point of fact she was *supposed* to be out here alone.

He hadn't argued with her, he'd just listened and kept going. It was like talking to a rock. A big, black, sometimes furry rock. They slept for a few hours every day, taking turns so that one of them was always awake and on guard. In the evening and through the night, they traveled, moving in silence—no joking, no conversation, not even a whisper—listening for that one sound, or absence of sound, that would give away the presence of an enemy—an enemy whose attack grew more likely with every passing hour.

And it wasn't just the night around them that they listened to. As she and Rhodry slid through the forest with its shades of gray, the hum of the trees was a constant in her head, more of a mood than a flow of information. Occasionally something would catch her attention and she'd dip deeper into the stream to listen more carefully.

When the threat finally came, it came without warning. The forest grew completely still—the trees, every living creature, seeming to freeze all at once, waiting, listening.

She automatically sank deep into the communal awareness, searching for the source of the danger. Nearly blind to the outside world, she didn't notice that Rhodry had stopped until she nearly ran into him, catching herself just in time. He raised his head, searching, then turned in a slow half circle, his nostrils flaring as he tasted the night air. Amanda didn't say a word, just watched him and waited. His senses were far keener than hers.

His head snapped around suddenly, and he seemed almost to be quivering with the force of his concentration. Then he dropped their backpack and began yanking off his boots. "You told me once you could climb," he said softly. "Did you mean it?"

"Yes, of course. What—"

His hand came up in warning and he said, "Listen."

She listened. And she heard…nothing. Absolute, dead silence. And then a high chittering noise, faint at first with distance, growing louder by the second. And she understood. "Dolans," she breathed in horror.

Rhodry was stripping off the rest of his clothes, shoving all of it haphazardly into the backpack while she stood and stared into the moonlit night, as if she could already see them coming. She gave a little yelp of surprise when he grabbed her arm and dragged her to the nearest canopy tree. "Climb. Now. I'll wait—"

"You don't need to wait, just give me the pack," she said instead, sitting down to remove her own boots.

"To hell with the pack, just climb."

She shoved her boots inside on top of his. "I've done this a million times," she said calmly, and took the time to buckle everything tightly before securing the backpack over her shoulders and turning toward the tree. She started to climb, then stopped when she saw he still hadn't moved.

"Rhodry?"

"I'll wait until you're up, I want to be—"

"The hell with that. What're you—"

"—ready to catch you just in case. I can shift and climb much faster than—"

"So shift, then."

"Damn it!" He strode over and took both her arms in his strong hands. "I can't help you once I shift, and I need to know you're safe. So, please, Amanda. Just this once. Do as I ask and climb the fucking tree."

She gave him an angry glare, then spun around and

began climbing, jamming her fingers and toes into the narrow runnels and grooves in the rough bark. "I swear," she muttered as she climbed, "if you allow one dolan to take a single bite from your smallest toe, I will rip you a new one."

"That would be somewhat counterproductive."

"Don't try to humor me, shifter, it won't—" She was forced to stop her harangue and pay attention to the climb, aware of the ever louder chittering coming closer, and now audible beneath it, the low thunder of ten thousand pairs of tiny feet crashing through the underbrush, destroying everything in their way. A tormented shriek filled the air as some poor forest dweller crossed paths with the swarm, and discovered the peril of not paying attention. She climbed faster.

As she climbed, she remembered what she'd read about dolans—tiny and four-legged, more insect than mammal despite their rodent-like appearance. They nested in large hive-like groups with a single matriarch at the center whose only job was adding to the hive. Fortunately, they were also highly competitive and cannibalistic which meant they were constantly fighting amongst themselves and eating the losers. It was certain death to step into a dolan nest. The good news was that they rarely stirred out of their home territory, unless something upset them enough to trigger a swarm. And when that happened, the first nest stirred up the next and the next until you had a veritable flood of ravenous dolans eating everything they could, and destroying what they couldn't. Even shifters could find themselves among the edible if they didn't move fast enough to keep from being overwhelmed by the swarm.

It was useless to try outrunning them—their path was too unpredictable, their shifts too rapid to move safely out of their way on the ground. The only way to avoid them was to climb above the fray and wait for the tide to pass. Dolans could climb, though rarely and not very well. Their primitive minds were incapable of the necessary complexity required for that kind of purposeful change.

She and Rhodry shouldn't have been in any danger of a swarm, however. Dolans were definitely *not* nocturnal, and rarely, if ever, swarmed at night. She reached the first branching on the big tree at about twenty feet, hoisted herself onto the thick arm, and paused to look down at him. "Okay. I've proved I can climb. Now shift, damn you."

"Keep going," he insisted. "You need another twenty feet at least."

She blew out a frustrated breath, stood up, and slid her fingers along the trunk, searching for the next handhold. She found it and began climbing once again, ignoring the growing weakness in her injured leg, knowing if he saw it, he'd delay his own safety even longer. When she reached the next fork, she turned and said, "Enough, Rhodi. You have to—"

He was gone.

"Rhodry?"

She searched the surrounding trees. He wasn't there and there was no sign of him on the ground. "Rhodry?" she shouted more loudly. There was no answer. Her brain conjured images of heroic last stands, of Rhodry trying to turn the swarm only to fall victim to a flood of greasy, brown fur and tiny, sharp teeth. Her heart was pounding a thousand beats a minute, tears of both anger and fear turning the moonlight to crystal against the black and white landscape.

"Climb!"

Amanda jerked her head to the right at the faint sound

of his voice.

She cursed him soundly under her breath, and kept climbing, not stopping until she was nearly fifty feet above the ground, and the branches around her were so thick and heavy, it was almost like standing on the ground. She dropped the backpack, and the attached bear pelt, into a secure branching of the tree, and made her way along a sturdy limb, scooting away from the trunk and over the forest floor where her view was better. She crawled as far as she dared, scanning the ground and the nearby trees.

Rhodry sped into sight without warning, whipping through the canopy in his cat form, nearly silent and yet with a speed and precision that took her breath away. It was as though gravity had no power over him. He launched himself at her tree from above, hitting it with enough force that it resonated down the trunk and its branches until she felt the wood beneath her shiver with the impact. Razor-sharp claws dug in and propelled him downward at a pace that made her own progress resemble tree sap on a cold day.

He stopped halfway down to locate her, then spun around the trunk like a snake, winding through overlapping branches until he was right next to the crevice with the backpack. And there he sat, lifting one paw for an utterly smug swipe with his tongue while eyeing her with reproach.

"Yeah, right. Kill me for caring," she muttered, making her slow, tree sap way back to the main trunk. Once there, he butted her carefully with his head, and she couldn't resist wrapping both arms around his neck for a hug. She didn't say anything, just held on while he purred comfortingly.

The chittering noise grew steadily louder as the swarm neared. A slender tree came crashing through the surrounding foliage, missing their own, sturdier haven by mere inches. Amanda surveyed the thick trunk nervously, comforting herself with the knowledge that it was strong enough to withstand the coming assault. As if reading her thoughts, Rhodry licked her face, then ducked away with a grin as she gave him a dirty look and rubbed her face vigorously with one shirtsleeve.

The wait was only minutes, and seemed to go on forever, until between one breath and the next, the swarm flowed into sight, leaving a gaping hole in the nearly solid wall of forest behind them. It was a heaving tide of bodies, more than twenty feet wide and with no end in sight. Oily fur gleamed wetly in the moon's cool light, the tiny creatures clawing their way over one another, a rolling wave of fur and teeth and claws, the leading edge constantly tumbled under and crushed as the swarm rolled inexorably forward. Their number seemed endless, and Amanda thought this was surely the largest swarm the forest had ever seen. There had to be hundreds of nests included, tens of thousands of the creatures in a wave more than a hundred yards long.

The surge of bodies rolled beneath them, flowing around anything it couldn't crush or eat, chewing a path through anything it could. A few hardy souls made halfhearted attempts to climb the bigger trees, some making it as much as twelve or thirteen feet from the ground before falling back to be crushed beneath the unstoppable swarm.

And the noise was incredible—a high-pitched squeal so loud that Rhodry buried his sensitive ears beneath his paws and she lay halfway on top of him, adding extra buffering while jamming her own ears with her fingers. The vibration of their passing traveled up the roots and through the tree trunk, and she could *feel* the tree bracing itself beneath the assault. She tried to concentrate, to listen to the forest song, wondering if the trees viewed this onslaught as an invasion or just a part of nature as they had the punishing storms. The noise was too great, the distraction too much. She just covered her head and waited for it to be over.

The forest was perfectly silent for some time after the dolans had passed, as if all the creatures in hiding feared making even the smallest noise lest the swarm be drawn back to wreak more destruction. She lifted her head, following the diminishing sounds of the invaders, hearing the awful, high-pitched squeals fade as they moved on to their own inevitable demise. The dolans would run until they met an obstacle they couldn't conquer—a steep drop off a cliff or a waterway too wide to cross—at which time they would lose tens of thousands of their own before finally grinding to a halt. Or sometimes, the swarm simply lost impetus when some indistinguishable signal known only to dolans called them to a halt. The swarm would then break apart, and the individual groups would move away to begin the formation of new nests, never to return again to their original nesting spot.

She sat up, one arm still looped around Rhodry's neck as he rose next to her, ears swiveling from side to side. His jaw opened and he yawned conspicuously. She laughed quietly. "I guess we're sleeping here today, huh?" she whispered, automatically adopting the silence of the forest around her.

He didn't shift, just settled back down on his belly, laid

his head on plate-sized paws and closed his eyes. She leaned into his warm weight, grateful for the sunlight just now beginning its rise, washing away even Fodla's bright glow.

She didn't try to sleep. Someone had to take the first watch and she didn't think she wanted to sleep right now even if she could. She had a feeling her dreams would be filled with gnashing teeth and small furry bodies.

It was dark when she woke. Pitch black. She couldn't see anything at all. And the darkness was purring.

She pushed herself away from Rhodry's warm flank with an appreciative pat, then sat up and squinted against the weak sunlight. He rotated his head to give her a single appraising look, then resumed his watchful position, sitting perfectly still except for his ears which twitched this way and that in response to noises she couldn't even hear.

"Good afternoon to you too, oh inscrutable one." She leaned back against the central trunk and began rummaging in her backpack for something to eat. She found her canteen first and slugged a drink of tepid water. If she ever got back to the city in one piece, she was going to turn on the hot water in her big, clean and fully accessorized bathtub and soak for a week. And then she was going to drink as much fresh fruit juice over ice as her stomach could handle. No, wait, she was going to put a big tub of ice right by the bath and fill it with containers of fruit juice so she could just reach out a hand and…

"Amanda!" Rhodry's voice jarred her out of the daydream.

"What?" She scanned the forest automatically, searching for some new threat. Finding nothing, she gave him a quizzical look, and registered in passing that he'd shifted to human at some point and she hadn't even noticed. Could that be why he was scowling at her so?

"Sorry," she said. "Daydreaming."

He raised his eyebrows inquisitively.

"A hot bath and fresh fruit juice." She waved her hand dismissively. "Never mind. What's up?"

He gave her a dark look, and she braced herself for a lecture on always being aware. Instead he drew a deep breath and said, "We need to decide where we're going from here."

"That depends on where our enemies will attack next, doesn't it? We both know dolans don't swarm at night. Not on their own anyway."

"They do, it's just not their usual pattern."

"Or maybe someone set them off."

"It's possible. Whoever did it would have to know that it wouldn't work, that we'd hear them coming and avoid the —"

"Maybe they figured I couldn't climb trees as well as I do. *You* were certainly surprised."

"I checked the swarm's back trail last night," he said somewhat irritably. "There wasn't anything suspicious. I think it was just coincidence. We need to focus on what happens next."

She eyed him curiously. He was awfully grumpy, and not being completely honest with her about the dolans, either. Clearly he'd already decided what they were going to do, and was trying to convince her that there *wasn't* a problem so she'd go along with his plan. Except there *was* a problem and that swarm *hadn't* been a coincidence. And he was way too clever not to have figured that out for himself. She decided to play along.

"What's to talk about?" she asked casually. "We'll reach the city before sunset. Unless you think someone will be waiting for us. Maybe the swarm was a delaying tactic."

"No," he said quickly, a little too quickly. "It's too late for them to try anything now. We're too close to the city, and they're probably too busy lining up allies and getting their stories straight for the Ardrigh. They know I'll go straight to the palace, even before the Guild Hall."

She tried not to react. The palace wouldn't be *her* first stop. Actually the palace wasn't on her schedule at all. She pretty much had to go to the Guild Hall first in order to verify the completion of her trial. And then, come hell or high water, she was going home to her bathtub. In fact, she'd kind of thought Rhodry would be joining her. It was a big tub. And it would be nice to make love in a bed for a change. She didn't say any of that.

"Okay," she agreed. "So what do you propose we do now?"

"We'll cross the perimeter patrols soon." He gave her a careful look. He was a smart man—most of the time, anyway—and he had to be wondering about her easy compliance. She just smiled and nodded amiably, waiting for his big plan.

"We should split up before then." He said it quickly, and immediately sucked in a breath, ready to counter her argument. And then couldn't conceal his look of surprise when she agreed with him.

"Good idea," she said. Although privately she wanted to

pummel him until he was nothing more than a wet lump of flesh with two golden eyes.

He narrowed those eyes at her now, openly suspicious. She wasn't sure she could fool him, so she buried her face in the backpack, digging out some battered pieces of fruit she'd picked up somewhere over the last couple of days. The days and nights all blurred together after a while. She eyed the fruit sorrowfully and took a bite. It might not look good, but it was tart and still juicy, and definitely better than nothing.

"You've no objection?" he asked.

"Not if you think it's best. It makes sense. If we split up, anybody waiting for us has to split up too, right?"

"Right," he said, then hurried to add, "not that I think anyone's waiting. We're just being careful. So, you should slip around the city and come in from the south, staying outside the perimeter as long as possible. It shouldn't take long. There are several day trails in that direction."

"Yes, I know." *I've probably traveled them more than you, you big, tree-climbing oaf.* She kept that thought private, too. "And you will be where?"

"I'll take to the trees and head straight for the palace."

And directly into any ambush, while I, useless female that I am, skip gaily along the path back to safety. We'll just see about that.

Chapter Forty-Two

Amanda shrugged her shoulders to settle the backpack more firmly. The bear pelt was tied below the pack, riding over her hips, since tying it anywhere else would have interfered with her ability to get to her short bow quickly. It was heavy, awkward, and more than a little fragrant, and she absolutely refused to leave it behind.

"I don't see why you can't bury that damn thing and come back for it. Or I could stash it for you up in the canopy in one of the caches."

"If it's way up there, I won't be able to reach it," she said reasonably. "Besides, I'm not in that big of a hurry. I've got nowhere to go, other than the Guild, and I don't think they're holding their breath waiting for me."

Rhodry's jaw tightened as she waited to see if he would try to come up with a reason for her to hurry. After all, there was no longer any danger of an attack, right? According to him, Serna and Daly were waiting politely at the Ardrigh's palace.

Clearly frustrated, he scowled at her and tried a different tack. "Your friends are probably worried, though. You've been out a long time."

Well, that was just pathetic. Couldn't he do any better? She didn't *have* any friends. "You might be right," she said, smiling sweetly. "I guess I could stop by Tonio's on my way to the Guild Hall. Just for a minute or two, so he'll know I'm back."

Rhodry scowled predictably at the mention of the other shifter, then eyed her oddly as if he didn't quite trust what she'd do next.

Gee. I wonder why?

She stretched her legs, lifting first one then the other, bending each knee up to her chest as she watched his face, hoping he'd come clean and tell her what was really going on. He wouldn't, of course. Big, strong shifter—he didn't need her help, did he? All the nightmares they'd been through together in the past weeks, all the times she'd saved his ass and he'd saved hers, and he still didn't understand who she was. *What* she was.

He waited until she had both feet back on the ground, then tightened his arms around her in what felt like a last, desperate embrace. She returned the hug, fighting the urge to pound her fists into his broad back and scream at him that she knew what he was doing, and she was *not* going to toddle off like a pliant female. She didn't bother, because it wouldn't have worked. He would simply deny everything, and then they'd argue again, and the result would be the same. Far better to let him think he'd fooled her, and prove to him later just how wrong he'd been.

She lifted her face to his, indulging herself in the touch of his sexy mouth one last time, sighing inwardly as the kiss deepened and became something more, a substitute for words they'd never said. And now maybe never would. Their mouths caressed each other, each of them reluctant to break away.

"Be careful, *acushla*," he whispered urgently.

She felt tears pressing against the back of her eyes and dug her fingers into the muscles of his back. "See you at the Guild Hall, shifter," she said with a tremulous smile.

"I'll be there before you," he lied.

She kissed him again, hard and fast, then stepped back and watched the shift sweep over his body. Those beautiful golden eyes gave her a last, lingering look and then the sleek, black cat launched gracefully into the nearest canopy tree.

She waited until he was gone, until she could no longer hear even the smallest sound of his passage. And then she stashed her backpack with its roll of heavy fur beneath a convenient deadfall, grabbed her weapons, and headed down the dolan swarm's back trail at a run.

Chapter Forty-Three

While it was never a good idea to run in the Green, sometimes it was necessary, and there was no better time or place than in the aftermath of a dolan swarm. Most of the wildlife had been temporarily displaced, and a dolan trail was like a highway through the forest. A sinuous line of crushed vegetation, it wound in and around the largest trees, even looping back onto itself at one point, and everywhere it touched had been laid utterly flat by the weight of those thousands of tiny feet and gnashing teeth. This trail was only hours old, and already the forest had begun to reclaim the devastated area.

The very act of destruction had released replacement seeds from their pods, and even now the first tender, green shoots could be seen in the rich loam of the flattened trail. Amanda felt almost guilty as they were knocked back once again beneath her feet. It wouldn't matter. In a few days, the new growth would thicken and within weeks, it would be

several feet tall and fighting for space against the encroach-
ment of older vegetation.

For now, it was a convenient path to take her to the exact
place she needed to go. If she hurried, she could confirm the
truth about what had caused the swarm, and still get back in
time to save Rhodry from his own chauvinist nobility.

In spite of the twists and turns, it took her less time
than she expected to reach the swarm's origin not far from
where they'd taken refuge last night. That explained why
they hadn't heard it sooner, and, to her mind, also made it
even more likely that the dolans had been stirred up on purpose. The originating point was an old, stable nest, familiar
to her from the months she'd spent wandering the areas of
the Green closest to the city. And if it was familiar to her, it
would definitely be known to every shifter in the Guild.

Staring at the emptied nest, she tried unsuccessfully
to shake off her irritation with Rhodry. He only wanted to
protect her, to keep his enemies from becoming her enemies,
and stop her from getting caught in the crossfire. He didn't
seem to understand that it was too late for that. Serna and
Daly had become her enemies the moment they decided to
kill the man she loved.

She froze in mid-stride and nearly fell, stumbling forward. Good gods, she loved him. A part of her had known
it was happening all along, and she'd ignored it, thinking,
half hoping, that the feelings would go away once they were
out of danger. The opposite had happened. The longer they
were together, the stronger her feelings for him had become.
And wasn't that a pain in the ass?

She was in love with a man who didn't trust her enough
to tell her the truth, and who sent her off into safety while he

went on to meet his enemies alone, because he was obviously convinced that she would be of no help.

How dumb was that? She wasn't sure if that last thought was for her or for Rhodry.

She took a few minutes to study the dolan nest, even though it was clear what had set it off. Now abandoned, it was situated between a huge grandfather tree and a cluster of several stumps left behind by loggers—maybe even the original builders of the city, judging by the age of the dried husks. Before the dolans had swarmed, the nest would have been no more than a slight up-swell on the forest floor, with most of the activity well underground. Given the panicked nature of their exodus, the tiny creatures had tunneled out every which way, leaving a churned up hollow of dirt and grass behind.

And tumbled in the middle of the disrupted nest was a dead banshee—or what was left of it after the dolans got finished. Banshees died all the time in the Green—of accident, old age, even mating battles. This particular banshee had an arrow lodged in its spine. It had probably been killed elsewhere, and thrown into the nest to start the stampede.

And gosh, maybe Rhodry had missed that little detail when he checked this place out. She snorted in disbelief.

Above her, a jaybird cawed stridently, warning off potential encroachers, marking his territory. Amanda glanced up, then looked back the way she had come. It took only seconds to make up her mind. Honestly, her mind had been made up before she'd kissed Rhodry good-bye. She was *not* going to stand by meekly while he hurried headlong into danger. She stepped carefully until she was free of the churned up and muddy nest, and then she ran.

Chapter Forty-Four

Amanda retraced her steps to the spot where she'd left her backpack, stopping only long enough to re-wrap the bandage on her leg, tightening it almost to the point of pain. It was going to hurt before this day was over. She hoped the bandage would at least keep it from tearing open, and maybe even give the still-healing muscles a little support. She grabbed her canteen for a quick sip of water, then left her pack hidden beneath the deadfall. It would be safe enough and besides, it would only slow her down. Rhodry would have been pleased by her decision, if not by her destination.

He was well ahead of her by now, especially with her detour to the nest. This was a big forest, however, and it might take him some time to *find* the ambush so that he could walk into it. She shook her head in disgust, and tried to reason out where the ambush was most likely to be.

If Serna and his pals thought she was still with Rhodry,

they'd target the ground routes, especially if there were any non-shifters among them, and she thought there might be. Rhodry had mentioned an abundance of non-shifter cousins in the de Mendoza clan, not all of them friendly, so it stood to reason that Serna might have some norm allies. Plus there was far more at stake now than old hatreds. They'd tried to assassinate their clan chief. What wouldn't they do to keep that from coming to light?

If she and Rhodry lived to bring their story to the Ardrigh, all of the conspirators would pay, shifter and norm alike.

Using that logic, she decided to focus on likely ambush spots along the established ground routes. Unfortunately, the closer she drew to the city, the more paths there were, since the norm population tended not to stray very far into the forest. This left her with a frustratingly large number of possibilities, though she still wasn't worried. Because while *she* might not know exactly where they were waiting, the *trees* would.

She followed a more or less direct line toward the Guild Hall, circling several old-growth giants blocking her path, and at one point giving a wide berth to a couple of breeding zillah lizards who'd posted a zealous guard over their nest of writhing offspring. It made her queasy to look at the slimy tangle of newborn zillahs, knowing that the next step in their development would involve a frenzy of fratricide in order to reduce the nest from several hundred to fewer than ten. She'd witnessed a birth frenzy once. It wasn't something she wanted to see again.

Upon reaching the outer edge of the Guild-patrolled area, she pulled up to catch her breath and take stock. While

Ciudad Vaquero was close, it was still far enough away that there would be hardly any foot traffic.

The trees here were farther apart and the undergrowth limited to the occasional stickberry bramble or tumble bush, which grew in large clumps before breaking up and rolling away. But while there weren't as *many* trees, they were bigger, taller and far, far older, making even some of the old-growth deep in the Green seem young by comparison. These were huge grandfather trees with trunks up to thirty-five feet around that soared higher than her eyes could see. Lichen and moss were thick around the exposed roots and trunk, especially on the northern face, and the absence of undergrowth made it seem as if the grandfathers had been granted greater living space in recognition of their ancient age and wisdom.

The ground was softened by a carpet of fallen leaves and needles, and the trees were mostly evergreen, thick overhead with loosely interlaced branches that still permitted light to filter through. The afternoon sun was warm on her head and radiated up from the ground beneath the soles of her soft boots. And when she spread her arms around one of the grandfather trees, the rough bark was just as warm against her cheek.

She gave herself a moment to enjoy the sensation of sinking into the tree's awareness, feeling the weight of its tremendous age, the reach of its roots as they tunneled unseen beneath the forest floor seeking water and sustenance. She felt the peace of the forest seep into her bones, the serenity that came from knowing time passed at its own pace regardless of the lives that might scurry by in their hurry to fill the few short decades allotted to them. The trees had always been here. They had been the first, and they would be the last.

She reluctantly dragged her awareness back to the present, tensing almost immediately as the urgency struck her once more. She kept her connection with the forest, pulling back to a surface awareness, sensing the sun in its pale sky, the lives of animals big and small moving through the trees, burrowing beneath the ground. At the very outer edge of the tree's perception was the city, a healthy gap in the whole of the forest, not a wound. There were trees aplenty even in the main square, and the people of Harp lived *with* the planet, not in spite of it.

Narrowing her search further, she concentrated on an area radiating out from the Guild Hall, which would almost certainly be the starting point of any shifter-led hunting party. The hall was easy enough to find. The forest saw the shifters as something special, like very favored children. They were always surrounded by a fond glow in the grandfathers' perception, each of the shifters a beacon of his own light. The Guild Hall and its concentrated number of shifters shined brighter than any single location in the Green, with the Ardrigh's palace and his shifter guards a close second.

By contrast, the deepest forest was cool and soothing and always made her think of great power concealed beneath a calm, unruffled exterior.

She'd often wondered if the shifters saw the forest the same way she did, if they were even aware of their rarified status. She'd never seen a shifter embrace the trees the way she did. Maybe because they didn't need to.

She forced her attention away from the fanciful and back to a practical search for Rhodry and, more importantly, those who waited for him. There weren't that many shifters out in the forest today. She identified the usual perimeter patrol by their predictable pattern of movement, then one or two others, clearly out for recreation.

Going back to the Guild Hall as a starting point, she searched outward, looking for a group of shifters, either stationary or traveling in a definite direction. When she found them, it was not so much the shifter presence that gave them away as it was the miasma of danger that they carried with them. They were angry, moving steadily out into the forest with murder on their minds. It was much the same dissonance she'd sensed from the trees before she'd found Rhodry way up north. At some level, the forest recognized the intent of these shifters and was troubled by it.

There were both shifters and norms in the hunting party, just as she'd expected. Only two shifters, probably Serna and Daly, so maybe the shifter part of the conspiracy was limited to those two. She couldn't tell how many norms traveled with them, only that they did. The forest barely registered the existence of non-shifter humans on Harp, as if they didn't matter.

Deep in fugue with the forest, she took a few seconds more, gathering information, then forced herself back into the real world. Normally, she took it slow, an easy drift back to awareness. Not this time. She was in a hurry, and the transition was like a sickening fall from a great height while the world spun around her, a jumble of color and light and sensation that left her reeling, barely able to remain upright. She leaned against the grandfather tree for support, swallowing several times against a nausea that threatened to relieve her of even the meager breakfast she'd managed to find.

"I'm sorry," she whispered to no one.

Then, shoving herself upright, she checked her weapons, swallowed hard one more time, and resumed her headlong run.

Chapter Forty-Five

The sounds of the fight came to her first. She couldn't run any faster, though she tried, racing toward the furious roars of enraged shifters, the shouts of humans who sounded as terrified of their allies as of their enemy, presumably Rhodry. She took to the heights when she got close enough, kicking off her boots and shimmying up the nearest tree, ignoring the growing weakness in her leg as the gaps and grooves beneath her questing fingers and toes proved deep and sure. Reaching several big branches, she moved with a reckless speed that would have impressed even a shifter. Unable to leap among the trees the way they did, she ran from tree to tree along the narrow, reaching branches of the upper levels, her lighter weight the only thing that made it possible.

As she drew closer to the fight, the trees thinned out even further to reveal a narrow clearing where one of the enemy shifters was already down, his belly scored in long bloody rows. She recognized Kane Daly, his unusual white-blond pelt streaked red as he leaned hard on the ground, struggling to shift and heal.

Rhodry and another shifter were fully engaged, snarling and slashing at one another in a blur of movement almost too fast for her human eye to follow. She didn't recognize the second shifter—he wasn't as big or as heavy as Rhodry, but his pelt was the same velvet black, and she assumed this was Desmond Serna.

They raged back and forth, dirt billowing around them in a golden cloud that hazed their movement while blood flew like raindrops. Furious snarls pounded the air, sending shivers up through the branches and leaves, the huge shifters slamming into one another, rolling across the small clearing with such force that Amanda imagined she could feel the tremors of their passing.

Her bow was in her hands, almost without conscious thought, an arrow nocked and drawn as she tracked the combatants, unwilling to risk hitting Rhodry in the tangle of bodies and speed. She caught a high-pitched whining sound and tilted her head, trying to isolate its location and figure out why it seemed so familiar. And vaguely threatening.

The whine changed pitch abruptly and a fine beam of light erupted from among the trees. A bright circle of fire blossomed suddenly on Rhodry's rear flank and the smell of seared flesh stung her nose. He howled in pain, digging his claws into Serna and using his greater weight to twist the other shifter into this unexpected line of fire.

From her perch in the trees, she swallowed a scream of outrage. A plasma rifle. Some idiot had violated the first law of Harp and brought a plasma rifle onto the planet. And he was trying to kill Rhodry with it.

She searched the gaps between the trees, thinking this new attack had to have come from one of Serna's norm allies. No shifter would be so stupid. Didn't the shooter realize what could happen if he discharged a weapon like that out here? Had he learned nothing from the disaster that had sent the fleet back into space? He was lucky the weapon hadn't already blown up in his hands and killed them all.

Kane Daly finally managed to shift back to human, and she caught a look of shock on his face when he stared at his norm allies. He was as surprised as she was by the rifle's appearance.

Her anger grew as she searched for the foolish shooter. She found the man lurking half behind a tree with the gun still butted up against his shoulder, waiting for another shot. Her arrow sped across the clearing, whispering past the heavy black rifle to pierce his right shoulder through and through. The man screamed, eyes rolling wide with shock as the illegal weapon fell from suddenly nerveless fingers.

A second man appeared from behind him, dashing forward with a shout to take up the rifle. Amanda fired two more arrows in succession, stopping him from reaching the deadly weapon. He fell, shrieking as much in surprise as pain, clutching at the wooden shafts sticking out of his leg. He crawled away, sobbing noisily as he heaved himself over knobby roots to take shelter behind a thick tree trunk.

Slinging her bow quickly over her shoulder, she shimmied to the ground and raced around the clearing until she reached the first injured norm. The plasma rifle lay only inches away from his groping fingers, and she picked it up reluctantly. She hadn't touched a powered weapon in a long time, not since she'd landed on Harp. She was surprised to note that it weighed little more than her solid wood bow. It should have been heavier, with its blocky construction and dull black finish, its ability to snuff out a life in seconds from afar. She carried it several feet away and laid it behind a tree, where neither of the injured men could reach it.

The shoulder-shot norm was swearing viciously at her, and she ignored him, only grateful that his aim was so poor. Rhodry would be dead otherwise. The more she thought about it, the more furious she became, until it took all of her restraint not to pick up his stupid rifle and beat him senseless with it.

Instead, she removed herself from the two norms by several feet and quickly regained the trees, climbing into the lower branches where she could see the entire clearing. Re-arming her bow, she studied the combatants over the arrow's smooth length of wood, sunlight winking off the metal tip as if to grant the magic of flight.

Movement drew her eye to the far left and Kane Daly. He was still in human form, half lying on the ground, his mouth open and panting with effort. His wounds were long streaks of angry, torn flesh, starkly visible against his pale, pale skin, and already they were better than they had been. He lifted his head briefly to stare at the ongoing battle between Rhodry and Serna, snarling as best he could with his human mouth, before closing his eyes, clearly intent on shifting yet again.

Amanda took aim on him, and then waited. While Rhodry and Serna continued to fight, both were clearly weakening from exhaustion and blood loss. If Daly managed to shift once more, he could change the balance of the fight. She'd shoot him if she had to, but only if it looked like he was stepping in to help Serna. She'd already taken the norms out of the fight. It was important that Rhodry be the one to defeat his shifter enemies.

A cat's howl of pain became a human scream as the tide of battle turned, and Desmond Serna surrendered his animal. His right shoulder was a gory mass of muscle and bone that was barely recognizable as human flesh, his arm dragging uselessly in the dirt. It was an injury even a shifter would have trouble healing, more than enough to take him out of the fight, and he lay on the ground, human belly bared, giving himself over to Rhodry's mercy.

Rhodry's cat loomed over him, his sides puffing like a bellows, his fur flat and dull with blood. A perfectly round hole of raw, burned flesh marred one flank. There was no blood to the wound, the veins having been cauterized even as the searing heat burrowed deep into muscle and bone. He lowered his head, massive jaws open and lips drawn back to reveal fangs hugely long and gleaming red with his enemy's blood. He roared once, then swung around to challenge Daly…who promptly gave up his attempts to shift and rolled belly up in submission.

Rhodry grunted his acceptance, then turned and looked directly at Amanda where she was perched in the lower branches, standing guard over the humans. He stared at her for several breaths, golden eyes dull and unblinking, his head drooping as if he was too weak to hold it up. He collapsed with no warning, falling heavily to the ground.

"Rhodi!" Her hands were shaking as she slung her bow and slid down the gnarled trunk, heedless of the bright pain in her injured leg as she clutched the rough bark. She was on the ground and running for him when a crashing overhead announced the presence of yet another shifter. Rhodry surged to his feet with a rumbling growl of warning, feet spread wide against the sway of exhaustion.

Bow once again drawn and nocked, she hurried to his side, pushing against him angrily when he tried to get in front of her, to stand between her and the coming threat.

"At your side, shifter," she snapped and turned her attention to the sleek, tawny cat dropping down from the trees far more gracefully than her own descent.

Rhodry yowled angrily, while she breathed a sigh of relief and let her bow fall to her side.

"It's okay, that's—"

He never let her finish, pushing in front of her and herding her away from the newcomer. She cried out when his big head butted against her injured thigh, and the new cat growled a low warning. His turquoise eyes shifted between Amanda and Rhodry and over to the two injured shifters, nostrils flaring when he caught scent of the two norms still hiding among the trees. He moved as if to interject himself between her and Rhodry, and Rhodry reacted immediately, his ruff standing nearly straight up, his powerful muscles bunched and lips peeled away from his teeth in a vicious snarl.

"Rhodry," she scolded impatiently. She stepped between the two giant cats and pushed him away, then turned to regard the other one. "Stop it, Fionn," she snapped.

The two men shifted almost simultaneously, and she found herself between two naked and very angry men.

"What the hell's going on, Amanda?" Fionn demanded, his gaze raking the clearing before coming back to her once again.

Rhodry was too busy glaring at her to say anything.

She looked from one to the other in disgust, then slung her bow over her shoulder with a sharp, irritated movement, slammed her unused arrow down into the quiver, and, without a word to either of them, strode back the way she'd come. She had a trial to complete.

She was twenty yards away before they realized she was leaving. Rhodry caught up to her a few strides later.

"What the fuck was that?" he growled, limping along with her.

She stopped and stared at him. "Do you believe Fionn was involved in this mess? Any of it?"

He frowned, obviously thinking about Fionn whose first reaction had been to protect Amanda from Rhodry himself. "No."

"Then what's the problem?"

"It wasn't Fionn you pushed away like a troublesome kitten," he muttered.

She thought he was joking, until she got a good look at his face and swallowed her laughter. He was jealous. Of Fionn. She shut her eyes for a minute, seeking her last scrap of patience, then walked over to him, not stopping until she was close enough to see precisely how deep the scratches were that crisscrossed his broad chest and arms, saw the thin runnels of bright red blood. She winced at the sight, then looked up and met his eyes.

"I pushed you because I knew you wouldn't hurt me. I couldn't be sure of Fionn. I trusted *you*." She paused to make sure he was paying attention. "You should have trusted *me*." Then she turned on her heel and strode away.

"Where are you going?" he called.

"To get that damned pelt," she said without breaking stride.

Chapter Forty-Six

Rhodry stared at Amanda's departing figure, not even turning when he heard Fionn approach.

"What the fuck," Fionn muttered. "Shouldn't one of us go with her?"

"I don't think she needs either one of us."

Fionn glanced at him, then at Amanda, and back to Rhodry. He scowled, then brightened almost immediately. "So she made it through. I told you she was remarkable, didn't I?"

Rhodry gave him a dark look as the two of them walked back to the clearing. "And you think that's any credit to you?"

Fionn's scowl returned. "What the *fuck* is going on around here anyway?" he snarled. "That was no friendly challenge. Those two are lucky to be alive. And, don't take this the wrong way, de Mendoza, but you're supposed to be dead."

Rhodry gave him a very unfriendly grin. "Sorry to

disappoint. So, you just happened to be in this particular clearing at the right time?"

Fionn shrugged. "Tonio and I were both sent south. I returned late last night, and this morning I discovered that Amanda was still out there somewhere. I sent for Tonio, and the two of us were going to go find her, except I decided I couldn't wait for him. I left him a message and was heading out alone when I heard the fighting."

They looked up in unison as another shifter arrived, circling through the trees several times before dropping to the ground with a soft growl. His fur was copper red and golden bright, and his hackles were standing straight up as he sniffed the air of the clearing. He immediately padded over to inspect the illegal plasma rifle and, nearby, the injured norms who cringed away from him. Pacing back to where Daly and Serna still lay recovering, he snarled menacingly, then shifted with sleek economy to reveal himself as Padraic Vaquero, first cousin to the Ardrigh and captain of his guard. Padraic was as close as anyone came to being in charge of the Guild shifters. Several inches shorter than Rhodry, he was just as broad, and hard with muscle. The silver winking among the gold in his bright red hair was the only obvious sign of his age. He faced Rhodry and Fionn, one side of his mouth lifting in a half smile.

"The Ardrigh will be pleased to see you alive, de Mendoza, not least because it will silence the hordes of Devlin cousins who've been plaguing the palace since your disappearance." His eyes slanted toward Fionn. "Fionn? I didn't expect to find you here."

"I heard the sounds of a fight and the discharge of a weapon. I came to investigate and found these two down," he indicated the injured shifters, "and the wounded norms back in the trees."

Rhodry lifted his brow in surprise that Fionn made no mention of Amanda.

Padraic eyed the two of them skeptically for several minutes before turning to study the various injured men once again. "This is for the Ardrigh to decide," he announced.

One of the norms struggled upright, bracing himself against the thick tree trunk behind which his skewered companion still lay moaning. "We need a doctor!" he demanded loudly. "That animal attacked us!" He pointed at Rhodry, who gave him a tooth-baring smile.

Padraic studied the two injured men, his attention lingering on the arrows still visible in both, before returning to Rhodry and Fionn, neither of whom was carrying a bow. He gave Rhodry a knowing look, then gestured at the two norms and said, "Are you acquainted with these fine gentlemen?"

Rhodry grimaced in distaste. "Both are de Mendoza, I'm ashamed to say. My cousins. The talkative one's Robbie, the other Zalmon. Not everyone was pleased with my grandfather's preference for his shifter offspring."

"Preference," Robbie spat. "He didn't give a damn for anyone else, you Devlin bastard. De Mendoza would be better off if you were dead."

"Unpleasant fellow," Padraic said drily. "Daly," he said over his shoulder. "You and Serna get your useless selves up off the ground, and help carry those two to the Guild Hall. We'll get them a cart from there to the palace.

"De Mendoza, you and Fionn come along. The Ardrigh will want to hear what you have to say."

Chapter Forty-Seven

Amanda stomped away, muttering imprecations against shifters in general, and Rhodry and Fionn in particular. Too soon, the adrenaline rush faded, and exhaustion overcame her anger. She slowed down, limping painfully. Now that the crisis was over, her leg was throbbing with every step, reminding her that there was a price to pay for shimmying up and down trees and running full out for miles. Her back still ached where the young shifter had hit her, and her hands and feet were scraped half raw from her precipitous slide down the tree to Rhodry's rescue.

And this day wasn't anywhere near over. She still needed to present herself at the Guild Hall, and deal with any challenges to her trial—and there were certain to be some of those, no matter that the whole thing had been rigged against her from the start.

Forget the iced fruit juice. When this was over, she was going to go home to her apartment, take a bath just long enough to get clean, then climb into bed and sleep for a week. Her original idea had been to include Rhodry in that bed. Now it seemed he'd be busy at the palace. He was the de Mendoza clan chief and someone had tried to kill him.

Besides, she was no longer sure he wanted to be in her bed with her.

She found the tree where she'd abandoned her boots, and sank down with a sigh, pulling on both socks and boots quickly. For a brief moment, she considered leaving the pelt in its hiding place. The long walk back to retrieve it was almost more than she could handle. The temptation was fleeting, however. If the Guild shifters didn't take her word for where she'd been dropped, and she knew many of them wouldn't, the fur would be proof that she'd been left on the edge of the glacier.

Rhodry could testify to that as well, if she only knew where he was or when he'd show up. If he ever did. He and Fionn were probably already settled within the cool confines of the palace, refreshing drinks at hand, maybe having already enjoyed a quick bath and a change of clothes before meeting the Ardrigh.

Amanda trudged along, hoping she was on the right heading, knowing she was, and that she was just feeling sorry for herself.

It almost surprised her when she looked up and found herself at the deadfall, her pack right where she'd left it. She'd been half afraid scavengers would have gotten to it by now. Gods knew the damn pelt had a smell strong enough to attract half the forest. That it was still there and unmolested was a bright spot in her otherwise crappy day. She dug for the crumpled half of a trail bar, which was all the food she had left, settled both pack and pelt on her back and limped off on the final leg of her trial.

O rrin Brady was waiting for her when she emerged from the trees, sitting on the back porch of the Guild Hall, his chair balanced on two legs. He was holding one of her arrows in his big hands, tapping it lightly against his knee as she drew close.

She stopped at the foot of the stairs and gave him an inquiring look.

"This yours?" he asked, regarding her from beneath bushy gray eyebrows.

She knew it was. And she had a good idea of where he'd gotten it. She made a show of climbing the stairs to take it from his gnarled fingers to examine carefully. "It is," she said.

He stood, careful not to crowd her on the narrow porch. "Thought so. Pulled it out of a norm just a bit ago, came through screaming about a shifter attack on him and his buddy."

She opened her mouth to respond angrily, realizing just in time that the old shifter was smiling.

"Bunch of shifters packed the two of them through here, and had a slightly different tale to tell. The whole lot of 'em went on up to the palace. Let the Ardrigh sort it out."

She waited.

He looked her over, his eyes widening when he saw the ice bear hide sticking out of her cloak where it was rolled beneath her pack. "You ready?"

"Ready and past ready, sir."

He smiled again and nodded. "Almost there, candidate."

He turned to go inside, gesturing for her to follow. She stopped him with a touch on his arm to ask, "Have any other candidates gone out since I left?"

He paused with one hand on the door handle, turning his head just enough to see her over his shoulder. "You've been gone for weeks, girl. But no, no others have gone out."

"And the jar?"

He took his hand from the door and turned around fully to frown at her.

"The jar with the stones," she clarified. "What happened to it after I left?"

Orrin's look turned thoughtful. "Should be in my room," he said, gaze sharpening. "Why?"

Amanda dug in her pocket for the black stone she'd retrieved on her way in, her arrow still marking the tree where it had fallen. "I think you'll find they all look like this." She held it out and dropped it into his open palm.

Orrin stared down at the smooth stone, then back up at Amanda, who nodded. His face darkened with anger. "Tiegan!" he shouted.

"Sir?" There was a shuffle of footsteps and a young shifter pushed open the door. He gave a little squeak when he saw Amanda standing there, and she realized he was the same teenager whose attack on her had gone so wrong for him.

Orrin pulled a small ring of keys from his pocket and held them out to the youngster who was staring at Amanda fearfully. "Pay attention, boy."

The boy in question jumped guiltily, and held out his hand for the keys.

"Go to my room, get the jar. You know which one, don't be ignorant," he snapped, when the young man opened his mouth to ask. "Don't open it, don't mess with it, don't even shake it. Just get it and bring it right back."

"Yes, sir," he said, nearly tripping over his own feet in his hurry to get away.

The judge watched the young shifter race off, his head tilted thoughtfully. "Tiegan's my youngest grandson," he said to her without turning. "A good boy. Foolish perhaps, as they all are at that age. A good boy nonetheless." His glance slid to her. "Funny thing is, he showed up a few days back, looked like he'd been in a fight. Claimed he fell out of a tree." The judge chuckled softly. "Never known that boy to fall; he was climbing before he could walk."

"You might ask him who suggested he climb that particular tree," she said.

Orrin stared at her a bit longer, then grunted. "Well, best get this finished. Come along, girl."

Young Tiegan must have passed the word as he'd hurried to do his grandfather's bidding. By the time she followed the judge into the Guild's great hall, and dropped her pack with its heavy load to the gleaming wood floor, shifters had already begun to gather. Some were in animal guise, their great, furred bodies lounging in improbable places, tails swishing in a mix of agitation or threat, depending on the shifter. Others wore their human form, a few only half clothed as if they'd pulled on the first thing that came to hand before rushing out to see. They emerged from the hallways and meeting rooms, lining the mezzanine overhead and crowding along the walls downstairs to stare at her.

Amanda knew how she looked. She hadn't had a proper bath in days. Her hair was filthy, pulled back in a braid that had started out tight, and by now had bits of leaf and bark clinging to it, with loose strands tickling her neck and hanging into her face. Her clothes were in worse shape—dirty, torn, streaked with blood, some of it fresh as her leg had begun bleeding again on the long walk back. On the plus side, she was alive, and still strong enough to enter the Hall on her own two feet. And only a short time ago she'd taken down two assailants with clean shots that had wounded, not killed. She had nothing to be ashamed of, and refused to let them think she did.

She straightened her spine and lifted her chin defiantly in the quiet room, the only sound the soft shuffle of feet, the gentle swish of tails along wood railings and posts. It was all vaguely ominous. She stood calmly and waited, her gaze circling the assembled shifters, never resting on anyone in particular, never meeting anyone's eyes.

With a clatter of clumsy feet and rattling stones, Tiegan came running back, shoving his way through the crowd to reach his grandfather's side. Clearly mindful of the many eyes watching him, the young shifter sucked in a breath, pulled his narrow shoulders back and presented the jar to Orrin with a solemn air. A ripple of tension ran through the room as the shifters saw what the boy had brought. That reaction told her that at least some of those present knew what Orrin would find. She managed to control the snarl that fought to reach her face as the judge took the jar.

Moving with a deliberate slowness, he set the ceramic container down on a table. He accepted his keys from Tiegan and slipped them back into his pocket, before placing his hand on the round lid. She experienced a fleeting panic. What would she do if it turned out she was wrong? He lifted the lid and upended the jar. She held her breath, half expecting to see a small flood of multicolored stones tumble out.

The flood was black. Shining, smooth and black. Orrin looked up with a thunderous expression, his glare falling first on Tiegan, who stepped back fearfully, then rising to spear every shifter in the great hall.

"Tiegan," he said softly.

"Grandfather?" the boy squeaked.

"Go fetch Evan Graham and Padraic Vaquero from the palace."

Tiegan's eyes widened, and he swallowed hard enough that she winced in sympathy. "Yes, sir!" he whispered, then spun on one foot and rushed for the doorway. Silence settled over the room, punctuated by the sharp crack of a slamming door as Tiegan ran for the city and the palace.

Both of the men Orrin had requested were shifters. Evan Graham was the other trial judge, and Padraic Vaquero was captain of the Ardrigh's guard. That Orrin was sending for them indicated he wanted more authority than his own for whatever happened next.

"Amanda."

It was the first time the old judge had used her name to address her, rather than the formal "candidate" or the dismissive "girl." She wondered what it meant that he used it now. Was he giving credence to her charges before hearing them? Acknowledging the successful completion of her trial? Or just treating her like a hysterical woman who could begin screaming at any moment?

"It will be some time before everyone gathers," he said gently. "And you must be tired. We've rooms if you'd like to rest or clean up."

She considered the offer. It didn't escape her notice that

she was being offered the hospitality of the Hall, which was strictly reserved for Guild members. Other guests, no matter how significant, were housed at the palace or elsewhere in the city. On the other hand, she wasn't quite comfortable enough to sleep or even shower surrounded by hostile shifters.

"I appreciate the offer, sir. I'd rather wait. I wouldn't mind a cup of hot tea, though. If I could use the kitchen?"

Orrin studied her for long enough that she wondered if he was trying to decide whether to be offended at her refusal. Finally one side of his mouth quirked up in a half grin. "I believe you know the way."

"Yes, sir," she acknowledged and hefted her pack onto her shoulder. "Thank you."

"Amanda," he said softly, when she started for the kitchen. "You can leave that here. On my honor."

She was loath to let the pack out of her sight, but there could be no doubt of the insult to Orrin this time if she refused. She drew a deep breath and let it out in a long sigh, then lowered her burden to the floor at his feet. She met his eyes directly, wanting him to know what this cost her. "Thank you, sir."

He nodded once, slowly. "There's fresh bread in the box, and some cold meats, or fruit preserves if you'd rather. Help yourself."

Her mouth already watering at the idea of anything fresh baked, she made her way out of the crowded room, shifters clearing a path ahead of her, then closing in again as she passed. She was painfully aware that for the first time in weeks, her back was bare to anyone who wished her harm.

And it made her wonder how Rhodry was faring, and who had his back as he confronted his enemies at last.

Chapter Forty-Eight

Rhodry followed Padraic Vaquero toward the palace, feeling the binds of civilization tightening around him. For all its dangers, his time in the forest with Amanda had been a welcome interlude. Already he could feel the suffocating hostility of the Ardrigh's court, the circling of old enmity.

Walking next to him, Fionn gave a mock bow to a group of women as they passed. The women giggled flirtatiously, and he tried to imagine Amanda standing around dressed and pampered within an inch of her life, having nothing better to do than flirt with passing shifters. Instead, he got a picture as he'd last seen her, angry with him, hurt even, because he'd tried to protect her, to keep her away from the attack he'd known was coming.

And what was wrong with that? He'd been raised to respect people with skills other than his own, taught to protect them as well, those who were weaker, less— He tripped on his own thought. Amanda wasn't less of anything, was she? She'd saved his life on the glacier, and who knew what might have happened just now if she hadn't been there to take out those two norms with their deadly plasma rifle. She had both the courage and the skills to match his own, as well as other abilities he'd never had to develop, relying instead on his physical prowess.

Certainly he was stronger than she was, because he was stronger than most people he knew, both norm and shifter. It was a simple matter of physical size and muscle mass, and he'd been born with that, it was hardly to his credit.

So, then maybe you shouldn't have treated her like one of those pampered females. He scowled at his own thoughts. He'd make it up to her later, after all of this was over. She was angry, so he'd talk to her. She'd understand. Wouldn't she? He thought about Fionn with his easy charm and good looks. Fionn who—

"If you please, Fionn," Padraic reprimanded over his shoulder, drawing both Fionn and Rhodry's attention back to the task at hand. Desmond Serna and Kane Daly, the two shifters who'd tried to kill Rhodry, *twice*, were walking just ahead, sandwiched between Padraic in the lead and Rhodry and Fionn behind. They were both worse for the wear, still visibly wounded and worn from carrying their injured norm allies back to the Guild Hall.

The norms had been given first aid, then sent on to the hospital with shifter guards and orders that no one was to see them until the Ardrigh or Padraic himself sent word. They'd complained loudly to anyone who would listen, though none of the shifters had given their whining much credence.

Daly and Serna walked with their heads down, feet

dragging, and Rhodry could almost pity them. He'd favored shifting and going around through the forest over this public parade on the streets. Padraic had overruled him, saying it would be too easy for the prisoners to slip away among the trees. He wasn't sure he agreed with that, doubting the two could have escaped in their current sad condition, and with so many healthy shifters on their trail. He wouldn't have been surprised if they'd tried anyway. There would be no good outcome for them from this affair.

Of course, since he'd been the object of their treachery, and since Amanda could have been killed in the course of it, whatever pity he felt was short-lived.

The palace loomed ahead, and he wished Padraic had at least permitted them to wash up before rushing over here. They were dressed at least, wearing typical loose shifter clothing with soft boots on their feet—Padraic had allowed that much, laughing at the idea of five naked shifters strolling through the city streets. Rhodry would have preferred to appear before his Ardrigh bathed and dressed. It was a matter of respect.

"Don't worry about it, de Mendoza," Fionn said in a low voice. "Everyone will be so shocked to see you alive, they won't even notice what we're wearing."

He looked over in surprise, not expecting any kind of empathy from Fionn. At that moment, the doors of the palace swung wide and a gust of perfumed air rushed out. He and Fionn exchanged identical grimaces of distaste, and Fionn laughed suddenly, reaching out to clap a hand on Rhodry's shoulder.

"Give me a bloody fight any day," he said softly.

Rhodry felt an answering grin tugging at his lips and

was startled to discover he was feeling something close to friendship for the Ardrigh's heir. He opened his mouth to agree, then spun around as a roar echoed down the hallway, a roar that resolved itself into his name.

"Rhodry, damn you!" Devlin cousins swarmed down the hallway to surround him, an unstoppable tide of meat and muscle. If the de Mendozas had a lack of male shifter offspring, the Devlins suffered no such shortage. The hallway was packed nearly wall to wall with his shifter cousins, every one of them well over six foot and solid as a tree trunk. He grinned as Cullen, his youngest cousin and a giant even among Devlins, crushed him in a bear hug that lifted him off his feet and threatened to steal the breath from his body, until a pair of massive fists crashed against Cullen's back, breaking his hold and yanking him away.

"Let go of him, you great oaf, we've just got him back and you're squeezing the life out of him!" Aidan Devlin pushed the young giant away, his blue eyes suspiciously wet as he embraced Rhodry in a bear hug of his own. "We thought you were dead, Rhodi," he whispered, as Rhodry returned the embrace. "They told us you were dead."

"Now, Aidan, don't go all maudlin on us." Aidan was yanked away in turn, replaced with yet another Devlin giant. "We never believed a word of it, did we, lads?" Gabriel, oldest by three years and thus in charge of the current Devlin crowd, did his best to crush what little breath Rhodry had left, then backed off and grabbed his shoulders hard enough to hurt. "Give us a target, Rhodi," he whispered fiercely, all signs of the crude mountain accent suddenly gone. "Give us a target and they're dead. No one fucks with a Devlin."

Padraic waded in, shoving Devlin cousins out of the

way like a pack of unruly kittens, despite their greater size. "There'll be no payback taken, Gabriel," he growled, not needing to hear the words to know what had been said. "Not from any of you." He glared all around, including each of them in his warning. "Rhodry's on his way to see the Ard-righ who'll listen to what he has to say and take whatever action's needed. We'll have no private vengeance. There's been enough of that."

That set off a low growl of disagreement from the Devlins, until Aidan stepped into the breach. "He's right, lads," he said, resting a lighter hand on Rhodry's shoulder. "We've got our Rhodi back. Let justice take its course. For now," he added with a dark look at Padraic. "You'll understand if we're a mite…anxious, Padraic? What with Rhodry here being dead and all?"

Padraic frowned, then nodded his head sharply. "I can see it, Aidan. As long as you and Gabe keep these boys in line. Don't make me do it."

Aidan was the most even-tempered of men, and even he bristled at the guard captain's words. Sensing disaster in the making, Rhodry threw an arm each around Aidan and Cullen, which was not an easy thing to do. He'd swear his younger cousin got bigger every time he saw him. Emotion swelled and he coughed before he embarrassed himself with an unseemly display.

"I've missed you, lads," he said gruffly, letting his eyes roam from cousin to cousin. He hadn't realized until this moment how very alone he'd felt over the few months without a single Devlin face for company.

"Now, Rhodi," Gabriel joked, "don't embarrass us." He rubbed at his own eyes surreptitiously. "You go on, talk to the Ardrigh. Aidan, you go with him while I ride herd on this bunch. Don't want to bloody these fine marble floors, do we?" He gave Rhodry a slight push. "We'll be waiting right here, lad. We'll not be leaving you alone again."

Padraic looked like he wanted to argue about Aidan coming along, at least until he shot a sudden look down the hall to where Fionn was herding the two accused shifters ahead of him. Rhodry had a pretty good idea of what Padraic was thinking. If the Devlins realized those two were the ones who'd tried to kill him, there'd be no stopping them. Easier by far to let Aidan come along before that happened.

Padraic gave him a grim look and hustled after Fionn, leaving him to follow with his lone cousin for escort.

"So what've we got here, Rhodi," Aidan murmured as they walked. He nodded at the two captive shifters shuffling ahead of them. "Des and his buddy there—they the ones?"

It was no surprise to him that Aidan had known what was going on, and had kept his mouth shut. He was always two steps ahead of everyone else, and he'd wanted to avoid a battle in the Ardrigh's palace.

He slung a companionable arm over Aidan's shoulder and leaned in conspiratorially. "It's been a long few weeks, cousin. Let's get to the Ardrigh, and I'll tell the story once for everyone."

Aidan gave a quiet nod. "For now, lad. Like I said, we'll give 'em a chance to do the right thing."

Chapter Forty-Nine

After weeks of subsistence living in the rough, Amanda managed to down only one thick slice of bread, well slathered with fruit preserves, before she felt full to bursting. Unable to eat anything else, she settled instead for the simple enjoyment of hot tea with honey, and the pleasure of sitting in a clean kitchen and drinking from a well-made ceramic mug rather than sharing a battered canteen cup with Rhodry. Though she wouldn't have minded the sharing part.

It had all seemed so easy out in the forest, with just the two of them and everything else so far away.

She drank down the last of her tea, washed her dishes quickly, and placed them in the drying rack on the counter. Glancing out the window over the sink, she saw young Tiegan loping back into the yard, his slim cat form emerging like some sort of fey creature from the shadows beneath the trees. He had obviously circled around the town, going through the forest to get to the palace. It was faster than walking the streets, and more fun for a young shifter.

He stopped short of the porch and shifted back to human, the process nowhere near as effortless as when Rhodry or Fionn did it. He was still panting a bit when he pulled on his trousers and, when he saw her watching, was young enough to blush with embarrassment.

She smiled and turned away, not wanting to discomfit the youngster any further. She still felt a little guilty over the scare Rhodry had given him, until the ache over her kidney reminded her it hadn't been fun and games for her either.

She heard Tiegan come through the door, and busied herself washing and drying her hands, waiting until his footsteps had passed into the main room, before turning to follow him. He went directly to his grandfather, Orrin, who was sitting on one of several huge sofas, deep in serious conversation with Evan Graham, who must have arrived through the other door while she was in the kitchen. The Guild Hall's ledger, the old-fashioned paperbound book that listed every shifter who had ever been a member of the Guild—as well as those candidates who had tried and failed—sat open on the table in front of them. The ceramic jar, once again capped and with its incriminating stones out of sight, stood next to it.

Evan Graham looked up when she stepped into the doorway, and while still listening to what Orrin was saying, acknowledged her with a short nod before returning his full attention to his fellow judge. Tiegan stood in front of them, dancing from foot to foot in youthful impatience.

Orrin looked up finally, and the young shifter bent forward to deliver his message. Orrin nodded at whatever was said, glanced at Graham, then stood and walked over to her.

While she'd been sitting in the kitchen, the big room had almost emptied out. Most of the shifters had drifted away, probably back to their own lodging or out into the forest to wait. Those who remained straightened attentively as Orrin approached her, and one or two streaked out the door, obviously intent on getting the word out to the others that the fun was about to begin.

She stood in the kitchen doorway, the towel she'd used to dry her hands knotted around her fingers as she forced them to remain still. She'd done what she could for her appearance, washing her face and hands, running wet fingers through her filthy hair and re-braiding it neatly. There was nothing she could do about her worn and dirty clothes, or her many cuts and scrapes.

She told herself it didn't matter. But it did. She was the lone woman in a room full of powerful men, and she looked like something a banshee had dropped half eaten from a tree.

"Amanda," Orrin said, drawing her attention. "Padraic has sent word from the palace, suggesting we proceed with your testimony and judgment. De Mendoza and Fionn are with the Ardrigh and, I suspect, relating much the same tale as you have for us."

"Most of it," she agreed. "Though I was out alone for a couple of days before I found Rhodry."

"Found him?" Orrin raised his eyebrows in surprise, then shook his head with a tight smile. "Never mind. We'll wait until everyone's assembled. I'm sure you'd prefer to tell it once and get it over with."

She looked up at him. "I would, thank you. Um, Orrin? How do we do this? I mean, I'm not sure…"

Orrin gave her a full grin. "We don't stand much on ceremony here at the Guild. You'll tell your story, and the floor will open to questions. Some will honestly dispute your claim, others will argue simply because it's in a shifter's nature to be fractious." He shrugged. "De Mendoza's corroboration won't hurt. He is well respected in the Guild, even by his enemies."

Orrin paused to look around the Guild Hall. "I think we can begin."

The room had filled with shifters in the short time she'd been talking to Orrin, more now than when she'd first arrived, and most of them in human form.

Easier to argue against me that way.

Evan Graham began the proceedings. "Candidate Amanda Sumner has returned to the Hall from her trial," he said loudly. The room quieted at once. "Are there any who would dispute her right to join our Guild?"

She looked at him in surprise. Apparently they weren't going to begin with a recitation of her ordeal, after all.

"I'll dispute it," someone called from high up on the mezzanine. She recognized the voice, and looked up anyway to find that bastard Nando staring down at her with hard eyes. How had she missed his hostility toward her all this time? Was she that blind? Or had Nando only pretended to like her because of Fionn?

"Nando," Orrin said, feigning surprise. "You were on candidate Sumner's escort, weren't you?"

"I was."

"She is here and alive, which would seem to prove her fitness. Unless you're saying that you did not deliver her darkward as required?"

Her stomach tightened as she shot a quick glance at Orrin. He didn't look back, didn't look at anyone. He was pretending to be concerned with something in the ledger in front of him, his hands busy turning pages. Rhodry must have said something on his way through earlier, must have told Orrin that her escort had dropped her out on the glacier. Maybe the judges were waiting for Nando and the others to incriminate themselves.

She swung her attention back to Nando who was standing on the second floor mezzanine, his hands gripping the thick wood railing, his expression perfectly still. He was an ass, but he wasn't stupid. He saw the trap in the question. Amanda wondered how he would manage to answer truthfully without incriminating himself.

"We took her darkward," he said.

"Where precisely?" Orrin pushed, his eyes now raised to Nando, reflecting only mild curiosity.

To his credit, Nando stood his ground. He glared back at Orrin with a low growl rumbling in his powerful chest, and didn't say a word.

"Evan," Orrin said, without taking his gaze off Nando. "Would you pour the stones, please?"

The unexpected request elicited a wave of murmured speculation from the gathered shifters. She glanced around the room, noting who was surprised, and who wasn't. She heard the slight scrape as Evan lifted the lid, followed by the clatter of stone on wood as the jar's contents were spilled onto the wide table. The sight of all those black stones set off a storm of reaction, and it did her heart good to see that most of the shifters around her were as shocked and angry as Orrin had been earlier.

"Beyond the Verge, Nando?" Orrin asked softly.

Nando tried to bluff it out, knowing it would be her word against his and the other three shifters of her escort.

"Is that what she's claiming?" he scoffed. "That would've put her nearly on the glacier. I doubt she'd be standing here if that was the case."

Her heart beat a little faster as the moment she'd been waiting for was suddenly upon her. All those hours and days of lugging that damn ice bear pelt around with her were finally going to pay off. Everyone watched curiously as she bent down and pulled her backpack out from under the table where Orrin had stashed it. There were a few impatient mutters as she untied her heavy cloak from where it hung in a neat bundle at the pack's bottom edge. The leather ties were stiff, and her fingers were sore, so it took longer than it should have. Eventually the last knot pulled free. She grabbed one end of the heavy material and gave it a jerk. The cloak, and the dirty, white pelt contained within, unrolled onto the floor.

The first reaction was the dead silence of stunned surprise, followed by scattered applause, and more than a few shouts of encouragement. Amanda's attention was only for Nando who stared down at her with bitter disappointment. He knew she'd been dumped half sick with a raging storm moving in off the glacier. Was he sorry she'd survived? Did he hate her that much?

The room grew quiet again, as everyone waited for a reaction from either Nando or the judges. Nando spoke first. "Very clever, Sumner," he sneered. "Did de Mendoza get that for you?"

Her nerves disappeared, replaced by a seething anger

that left her mind cold and clear. She blinked lazily, her mouth turning up in a slow smile.

"Rhodry helped," she said, with an agreeable nod. "Of course, that's not the point, is it, Nando? Ice bears rarely venture as far south as the Verge, though that's where this one found us. And that was more than a week's travel south from where you dropped me."

She cast her gaze around the room, challenging all of them, then knelt down to roll the pelt back up, tying it off with neat, efficient movements.

"Nando?" Orrin said.

"What difference does it make where they left her?" another shifter shouted. Amanda searched, unable to identify the speaker hidden in the crowd upstairs. "Five days or a hundred, the rules say the candidate must make his way back alone, and she admits de Mendoza was with her the whole time." There were mutters of agreement.

"Oh, not the *whole* time," she said loudly enough to silence them, before continuing. "It was a few days before I found him, and then he was unconscious for a couple more."

Orrin looked at her. "Found him," he repeated. "You said that before. What do you mean by that, lass?"

"Rhodry was half dead, surrounded by hycats and poisoned with rockweed so he couldn't shift and defend himself. He was attacked by his own, by shifters from this Guild, who left him to die in the middle of a raging blizzard."

All hell broke loose after that, questions were shouted at her, demanding answers, explanations, demanding Orrin do something, whether it was to stop her lies or to punish the offenders. It was Evan Graham who finally called for silence, his deep voice bellowing loudly enough to rise above the angry outburst.

"Enough!"

The noise shut off like a faucet, everyone turning to stare at her and the two judges who now stood to either side of her.

"Candidate Amanda Sumner has returned to the Hall from her trial," Graham repeated the ritual words. "Are there any who would dispute her right to join our Guild?"

No one said anything, until a single voice muttered from behind her. "I'll grant she wasn't treated fairly," the shifter said, sounding almost embarrassed by what he was saying. "The rules still say she must do it alone, and de Mendoza was with her," he said stubbornly.

"And should she have left him out there to die then?" a new voice asked.

Everyone spun to find Cristobal Martyn standing just inside the front doorway, his question still ringing in the silence that had greeted his arrival. Cristobal was only casually handsome—most of Fionn's beauty came from his mother—but the Ardrigh's authority hung over him like a spotlight, drawing every eye in the room.

Rhodry, Fionn and Padraic were at his back, and behind them, she assumed, were the Devlin cousins from the way they were clustered around Rhodry. She met Rhodry's eyes from across the room, and they were gleaming gold and fierce with a triumph that made her heart skip a beat. She fought to keep her expression even, letting her attention slide over to Fionn who was giving her a very pleased look that included more than a hint of pride.

"A Guild candidate"—Cristobal said, secure in the attention of everyone in the room as he strolled forward—

"abandoned on the glacier in violation of every rule of this Guild, much less the simple bonds of honor and duty, plucks a fellow guildsman from the very edge of death, nurses him back to health, and then, with him, survives to return to the Hall. And here she finds…what, gentlemen? Condemnation that she didn't leave him to die? Is that what the Guild has come to?"

"This is Guild business, not politics," an unwise someone muttered from far back in the crowd.

Cristobal's gaze sifted unerringly through the room, settling on a thick-chested shifter leaning against the wall in the deep shadows beneath the staircase. "And am I not a member of this Guild, Liam?" he asked with a deadly calm. His gold-flecked, turquoise eyes, so like Fionn's, glittered dangerously as he scanned the assembled shifters, scalding them with his judgment. "Attempted murder and assassination…is that what the Guild has come to?" he repeated.

No one moved, no one spoke. Some had the grace to look ashamed, while still others glared back defiantly, unmoved by the Ardrigh's words. After several minutes of silence, Cristobal said, "Evan? Orrin?"

Evan Graham spoke the ritual words for the third time. "Candidate Amanda Sumner has returned to the Hall from her trial. Are there any who would dispute her right to join our Guild?"

"Devlin stands for the candidate," a voice growled. A massive redheaded shifter stepped in front of Rhodry to stand next to Cristobal as an answering growl rumbled from several throats behind him.

"As does Martyn," Fionn agreed.

The room teetered on the brink of violence for several

seconds before the words were taken up by shifters from all over the Hall, and repeated until the rafters trembled with the massed roar of voices.

Orrin glanced down at her and grinned. "Welcome to the Guild, Amanda."

Chapter Fifty

It was fully dark by the time Amanda got out of the Guild Hall. Orrin Brady had invited her to stay and celebrate her success, but she'd had enough testosterone to last her a lifetime. She thanked him, and begged off, saying she wanted nothing more than a hot bath and a soft bed. He studied her for a moment, then nodded, clearly satisfied with whatever he found.

"You've three days to recover before reporting for assignment. I look forward to working with you. It should be interesting."

She smiled and headed for the front door, stopping only to exchange a brief word with Rhodry, who'd been deep in conversation with some of his cousins and the Ardrigh.

He made excuses to Cristobal when he saw her coming his way and stepped into her path, stopping her just inside the door. He was bathed and dressed in fresh clothes, his still-damp hair braided neatly down his back. She wondered if someone had done his hair for him, and felt a pang of jealousy for whoever it was. Standing next to his freshly-bathed self made her feel even grubbier. And the feeling only intensified when he reached out to take both of her hands in his—hers rough, scratched and grimy, and his clean and calloused, with no healing scratches marring the perfection of his shifter skin.

"You're not staying?" he asked.

"I need a bath," she joked halfheartedly, feeling inexplicably sad. "I stink."

He laughed, and seemed to agree, which didn't exactly make her feel better about things.

"I'm going home," she said abruptly, pulling her hands away. "You're welcome, if—"

"I'll be returning to the palace," he interrupted to say. "The Ardrigh has—"

"Of course," she said quickly, not wanting to hear whatever excuse he'd come up with. Hadn't she worked this out for herself earlier? He was a clan chief, and she was nobody.

She caught sight of the redheaded Devlin giant over Rhodry's shoulder. He was watching the two of them closely, as was the big blond, Aidan, whom she'd met at the dance that first night.

"You've got your cousins here now. You'll want time with them," she said, providing him with even more justification for avoiding her. She turned for the door.

"Amanda."

She stopped and looked back at him. He didn't say anything, just scowled at her.

"Take care of yourself, Rhodi," she said, then hurried out of the Guild Hall and down the stairs. She heard him swear behind her, followed by the rowdy laughter of someone who was probably one of his cousins. Apparently, she was a cause of some amusement among them. The Earther girl who'd fallen for the de Mendoza clan chief.

Of course, the Devlins had supported her at the critical moment, and probably turned the tide of opinion in her favor. She'd never forget that. On the other hand, she'd saved Rhodry's life, and the mountain clans were said to be very big on honor and obligation.

She couldn't get away from the Guild Hall fast enough.

Limping slowly down the empty streets of Ciudad Vaquero, she headed toward her apartment, while contemplating her absence of female friends. She could have used one right about now. How had it happened that the only people she knew really well on this planet were all shifters? It was a matter of circumstance rather than choice, she decided. She'd been so focused on qualifying for the Guild, spending all of her free time alone out among the trees, or hanging around the fringes of the Guild Hall, hoping to learn something. She hadn't had much time to make friends of the female variety, and it would seem not many of the male variety either.

Lost in thought, her weary legs stumbled around a newly installed planter and she stubbed her toe on the sharp edge. Talk about adding insult to injury. Like she wasn't already banged up enough. She leaned one hand against the side of a closed and shuttered store, rubbing the offended toe against the back of her calf and trying to massage away the pain. A soft foot scuffed on the dark street behind her, and she spun around, seeing no one there.

It was early evening, with tomorrow a regular work day, and, as always, the streets had rolled up at dusk. It was nearly as quiet here as out in the Green, with only the occasional loud voice from a nearby home or apartment to break the silence.

Amanda pretended to keep massaging her toe as she listened carefully. And there it was again. A movement so soft she never would have heard it if she hadn't been expecting it. Had one of the shifters decided to make sure she didn't make it to her first Guild assignment after all?

A quick survey of the street showed her a balcony overhang a couple of storefronts away. Quietly dropping her backpack into the shadows behind the planter, she slipped her bow over her shoulder and sprinted silently ahead, reaching her target with a few quick strides. The elaborately carved support posts were hardly a challenge to her tree-honed climbing skills, and she easily shimmied up to the balcony.

Once up top, she ducked down below the balustrade and waited. It didn't take long. Her shadow was a shifter. No surprise there. No one else could have moved that quietly. He was big, bigger even than Rhodry, with dark blond hair and enormous hands, his clothes neat and simple. He was frowning when he came into view, probably aware that he'd lost her somehow, and hurrying to catch up, too intent on his own irritation to use his nose to track her.

She waited until he'd passed by and she had his back in her arrow sights. "Whoever you are," she said grimly, "you should know I've about had my fill of shifters for the evening."

He froze in place before putting his hands out to the side and turning slowly, letting his gaze travel up until he found her staring down at him along the shaft of a drawn arrow.

"Ah, lass, don't shoot me," he said sorrowfully. "I'd never hear the end of it."

She blinked in confusion, but didn't drop her aim. "I don't know you," she said.

"I'm Cullen Devlin!" he announced brightly. "Rhodi sent me to watch over you while he meets with the Ardrigh and such, to make sure you get home safe and sound. Now, don't go off on me, lass," he hurried on before she could protest. "Rhodi says to tell you he knows you're not needing any protection. You saved one of our own, and the Devlins will have you safe."

She lowered the bow. How nice. Rhodry couldn't bother with her himself, so he'd sent his cousin to watch over her and fulfill his cursed sense of honor. Her lip curled in a snarl.

"You go back and tell Rhodry de Mendoza where he can shove his—"

"I'll not be doing any such thing. Despite he's my own dear cousin and all, I'm scared to death of the man. Besides, what can it hurt if I just follow you close-like for a bit?"

She let her arrow drop, catching it in her fingers and sliding it home in her quiver with a resigned sigh before skimming quickly back down the support post to the street.

"Now *that* was nicely done, lass. Don't think I've ever seen a norm climb quite like that," Cullen said in admiration.

"That's because I'm not quite a norm," she muttered, striding past him to recover her backpack. She took a good look at the enormous shifter, and decided it would be too much work to dissuade him from following her. "As long as you're here, you might as well make yourself useful," she said, and shoved the heavy backpack into his arms. She slung her bow over her shoulder and said, "I'm going home."

Rounding the next corner, she caught sight of the science center two blocks away. Normally, it would be as dark as the rest of the city. Tonight it was lit up like a Yule tree. Even the exterior lights were on, as if they were having a party. She frowned and tried to remember if today was an Earth holiday of some sort, and realized she wasn't even all that sure what day of the *week* it was, much less the date. And also...she didn't really care.

Cullen saw her staring at the brightly lit building and, ever helpful, volunteered the information she needed. "A shuttle came in yesterday." He sniffed, wrinkling his nose as if smelling something foul. "You can probably tell by the stink in the air. Hard to miss."

Amanda was reluctant to admit she was interested. "Was it a supply run?"

"Can't say, lass. I've never seen one before. There was a bit of a fuss down at the landing field when this one showed up. It wasn't really my concern, though, what with Rhodi being dead and all."

Amanda glanced over and found him watching her with a crooked grin. He winked. "We're sure glad you brought him home safe."

She managed to swallow her laugh, but the smile escaped. Cullen noticed and his grin widened. "You want to pay a visit?" he asked, jerking his chin at the brightly lit center. "Maybe you've got friends there?"

Her smile disappeared. Cheerful voices were coming

from the blocky building, like they really were having a party. Maybe the crew was about to change, and this was a farewell celebration. It all meant little to Amanda. Cullen was wrong. She didn't have any friends there either. Laughter drifted over the quiet night, floating above the hum of voices.

Amanda turned her head sharply to listen as a familiar voice followed on the laughter, and she began to run.

Chapter Fifty-One

"There's my girl!"

Amanda dropped her gear and ran to her mother, heedless of the hard-paved walkway jarring her already sore legs. Elise opened her arms and hugged her much taller daughter, laughing delightedly.

"If I'd known I'd get such a welcome, I'd have visited long ago!"

Amanda held on tightly, breathing in the familiar scent she didn't know she'd missed until now. It abruptly reminded her of her own rather fragrant state, and she stepped back. Elise's arms tightened briefly, and then let go.

"What are you doing here?"

Elise beamed up at her, lovely as always. "My only child is making history, and you think I won't want to be here? Really, Amanda," she teased. She ran a professional glance over her daughter's many injuries, and Amanda blushed, knowing what she must look like. She grabbed Cullen's arm, dragging the surprised shifter forward.

"Uh, this is Cullen," she said, trying to distract her mother's attention. "Cullen, say hello to my mother, Dr. Elise Sumner. Cullen's my new bodyguard," she explained.

"Cullen Devlin, ma'am," he said properly, giving Amanda a reproving glance. "It's a pleasure — "

"Bodyguard?" her mother exclaimed, interrupting Cullen. "Why do you need a bodyguard?"

"Amanda's having a bit of fun, Dr. Sumner," Cullen clarified. "Truth is, it's my cousin Rhodry who's been guarding her body. I'm just a poor substitute while Rhodi meets with the Ardrigh."

"Call me Elise," her mother said absently, turning to Amanda. "Who's Rhodry?"

She gave Cullen a dirty look, which he returned with a raised brow that said she'd started it all.

"It's a long story, Mom, and I'm — "

"Amanda!" Guy Wolfrum's booming voice announced his arrival a moment before he reached to embrace her.

"I really need a shower," she joked lamely, and shied away from him. They hadn't seen each other more than a handful of times in the last several months, and then only to nod hello in the corridor. So why the hell was he acting so friendly all of a sudden?

"I was telling your mother and Admiral Leveque how proud we all are of you."

Ah. Admiral Leveque was here, too. That explained the sudden effusiveness. He was under the mistaken impression that she and Leveque were close. Might as well disabuse him of *that* right now, and save them all the embarrassment.

Before she could say anything, Wolfrum moved in

uncomfortably close, and leaned in to whisper in her ear, "You'll have to brief us on everything you've learned about these shifters now that you're one of them."

She concealed her jolt of surprise. No one from the fleet was supposed to know about shifters. Sure as hell not Leveque, or even her mother. She stepped back, putting enough distance between them that she could study his face. The rumor had been that he'd stayed behind on Harp for love. Had it been for something else? She might have imagined the greedy undertone of his whispered words, but then again, there was no doubting the challenging stare he was aiming at her. Was he threatening to reveal everything if she didn't tell him what he wanted to know?

Stupid man to do that in front of Cullen, whose shifter hearing would have picked up the whisper. And he wouldn't have missed the implied threat either. Shifters were apex predators. They understood threats. And every word of this conversation would be reported back to Rhodry and the cousins.

"I'm not one of them," she demurred. "I'm simply a member of the Guild." She met his challenge head-on, daring him to make an issue of it.

Her mother interrupted the uncomfortable moment, taking her arm and steering her toward the science center. Wolfrum stirred, and would have come along, but Cullen blocked his path, demonstrating with a flat stare what a real threat looked like, and proving she'd been right about him picking up on the subtleties of the encounter.

"What you are, sweetling," Elise was saying, ignoring all of the byplay, "is coming right inside where I can take a proper look at you. You've been out in that wilderness for weeks with no word. Oh, yes," she added, seeing her look of surprise. "I know exactly how long you've been gone. Admiral Leveque and I had dinner with Cristobal Martyn—a lovely man, in more ways than one. So many of them are here, aren't they? Anyway, we heard all sorts of things. Randy wanted to do an overfly of that big forest you were lost in. We brought his pinnace down from orbit, of course. I said, no, my Amanda's just fine, you'll see."

Amanda's eyes misted up at her mom's vote of confidence, and she saw a matching shimmer of tears in Elise's dark eyes. "Thanks, Mom."

Elise sniffed. "I know my daughter. Now, come along. You must be starving."

"Mom, I'm filthy. I can't—"

"Cullen, could you?" Elise gestured with her chin at Amanda's gear, ignoring her protest.

Cullen picked up the worn gear, and followed her indomitable mother down the walk. "I could eat something, Elise," he chimed in, his cheer restored now that Wolfrum had departed without another word, hurrying back onto the street away from the science center.

"Excellent. I had Randy's chef pack a cooler," she confided. "I didn't want to trust what they had here at the center. Scientists can be so odd at times. You're limping, Amanda. Why are you limping?"

She laughed, and decided it was good to be back after all.

Chapter Fifty-Two

Elise had tried to persuade Amanda to return to the Leveque Industries starliner which was waiting in Harp orbit. Apparently *Randy* had commandeered the luxury ship for this trip to visit Amanda—one of the perks of belonging to a preeminent industrial family. From what she could gather, they'd been in orbit for more than a week, waiting for her return.

She had politely declined her mother's offer. The last thing she wanted was a return to space with its recycled air and claustrophobic environment. Not to mention water-saving showers. What she wanted was her comfortable, familiar apartment with its decadent bathtub, its big, soft bed, and Rhodry. She'd have to settle for two out of three, which wasn't bad.

Elise had put up only a token argument. In the final analysis, she really did know her daughter. She *had* insisted on medical treatment first, cleaning and bandaging Amanda's many injuries and pumping her full of antibiotics. The thigh injury was going to leave a terrible scar. As Elise had observed with some disgust, the healing process was already too far along for treatment to make a difference now. She was quick to point out, however, that reconstructive surgery would be an option in just a few months.

Personally, Amanda thought she'd leave it—a lasting memento of her first (and hopefully last) encounter with an ice bear.

While her mother worked, she delivered a decidedly censored recitation of her journey. Admiral Leveque made a brief appearance, mostly, she thought, to reassert his claim on Elise. Her mother didn't seem to mind, and since Elise's happiness was important to both Amanda and Leveque, they were both polite and something that resembled friendly.

By the time the visit was over, she was exhausted, with barely enough energy to walk the short distance to her apartment and climb the stairs. Cullen carried her gear without being asked, and dropped it just inside her door.

"I'll be downstairs for a bit, lass, if you need anything."

"Go home, Cullen," she said wearily. "Or wherever it is you're staying. I'm not going anywhere tonight, and besides I've lived in this apartment by myself for a long time. Trust me. I'm fine."

"Of course you are, lass. I'll just hang around for a bit."

She watched him glide down the stairs with shifter grace, and wondered what it was with these Devlin males that made them so damn certain of themselves all the time.

"And why are you wasting your time wondering about Devlins, when you could already be soaking in the tub?" she muttered, closing the door. If Cullen wanted to lurk in the shadows of her perfectly safe street, it was no skin off her nose.

She was drowning. The water was rising over her head, filling her nose, trickling down her throat to her lungs. It was cold and…it smelled like lavender?

Amanda sat up in the big tub, sputtering, choking on bath water. She'd fallen asleep, lulled by the hot, scented water, by the soft light of the candles she'd lit all around. And she'd been out long enough that her fingers and toes were wrinkled past the first knuckle, long enough that the soothing oil-scented water had turned cold and slimy. She grimaced at the greasy feel and knew she'd have to take a shower now, or she'd never feel clean. And she was determined to feel clean before going to sleep tonight in her very own bed with its heavenly soft sheets.

She stood carefully, flipping the drain open as she rose. Water began gurgling from the tub, probably causing a racket for her neighbors. What was a little running water between friends, right? Not that her neighbors were friends. She didn't even know their first names, just the last name on the listing downstairs, and the fact that they complained about how much noise she made.

Maybe she'd remedy that in the weeks to come, though definitely not tonight. She took a quick shower, just enough to rinse away the greasy feel of the cold bath water, and to be grateful for a return to that most basic amenity of modern life — hot water on demand. What a concept.

Stepping out of the shower, she dared to look in the

mirror for the first time. She'd lost a few pounds, her face looked drawn, and her skin was…awful. Red, dry, and chapped, it looked like something you'd scrub dirty pans with, and maybe worry about scratching the finish. The one good thing was that her hands matched her face. Delightful.

The next half hour was spent massaging mimseed oil into every inch of her body. It stung her many leftover cuts and scratches, the discomfort short-lived compared to her relief as parched skin drank in the much-needed moisture. Once that was done, her face received separate treatment — an assortment of creams and emollients supposedly tailored to her skin type that her mother had given her as a gift on her last birthday. She'd used them once and put them away. Now she was glad she had them. This was an emergency situation.

Properly oiled and soothed — or at least as proper as she could get in one night — she spent a few minutes blowing her hair dry and felt almost human again. Almost. Nothing that about twenty-four hours of sleep wouldn't cure anyway.

Wrapping herself in her big, fluffy robe, she opened the bathroom door and stepped out into a room that was fire-warmed and familiar…and occupied by Rhodry de Mendoza.

"I was about to come rescue you," he said, his perusal taking in the oversized robe with a crooked eyebrow and traveling up to meet her eyes. "Though I know how you hate to be cosseted."

She took a moment to be grateful she hadn't used the facial mud mask included in her mother's gift, then returned the favor, letting her gaze roam over his big body and up to those gorgeous eyes. He looked great. And her traitor heart was doing little handsprings in her chest because he was here.

His nostrils flared, and he grinned. "You smell nice."

She tried not to, but she laughed. It felt too right to have him here on what should have been the greatest night of her life. She was a fully-fledged and accepted member of the Guild. The goal she'd worked so hard for, for so long, was hers, and she'd refused to think of it all night. She'd even refused her mother's offer of celebratory champagne, saying she was too tired, and that they'd do something later. And now she knew why.

Because it wouldn't have felt like a celebration without Rhodry.

"Congratulations, Amanda. Welcome to the Guild." He held out a knife sheath, beautifully tooled, the brilliant red and gold Guild design worked into the gleaming leather.

She took a step closer, her hand shaking as she reached out to touch the leather sheath, not taking it from him right away, just letting her fingers glide over the dips and curves of the design as it lay in his wide palm. She glanced up at him quickly, as if asking for permission before she picked it up. It weighed almost nothing, yet it was good, solid leather, tightly stitched.

As she examined the gift, his fingers slipped beneath the knot of her robe and tugged her closer. He pushed aside the thick collar and buried his face in her neck, breathing in the scent of her hair and skin. "I can honestly say," he murmured, his breath warm against her ear, "that you're the only Guild member I've ever wanted to kiss."

Her laughter was smothered as his mouth came down over hers in a hard kiss full of passion and heat and desire.

She didn't need to think about her response. Her arms went around his neck, and she pressed her body in a tight line with his from chest to groin, wishing the bulky robe wasn't between them.

He growled against her lips, one hand dropping down to span her lower back and crush her close to him. The other cupped the back of her head, holding her in place as he delved deeper into her mouth, forcing her teeth apart to admit his probing tongue, bruising her lips with his need.

She tasted blood, felt his tongue slide along her lip, soothing and tasting in turn, and then the kiss softened, becoming something more than lust or simple passion. He explored her mouth, outlining her lips gently before dipping between them again to caress her tongue, sinking further with a tenderness that made her want to weep. His lips were so soft, his mouth so sensuous, his body so hard and familiar against hers.

And it was going to hurt so much when he left. She couldn't pretend anymore that it wouldn't. Just as she couldn't pretend that he wouldn't have to leave. His family, his home, were in the mountains. For all she knew, he had a woman there. He was probably pledged to someone already, just waiting until his stint in the city was up before going home to marry and raise a family with strong shifter sons to inherit the de Mendoza mantle.

She sighed into his mouth, letting her forehead rest against his for a moment before saying, "Thank you, Rhodi. It's beautiful." She swallowed hard and searched for something else to say, something to save her from the flood of emotion threatening to overwhelm her good sense. "Is Cullen still downstairs?"

He chuckled softly. "I sent the boy back to the palace. He'll only be in the city a short while. Let him enjoy it."

"Boy? He's as old as I am."

"Aye, and yet he's the baby of this batch of cousins. A few years younger than the rest of us, and too old to be permitted to bully the next generation down, so he's stuck being the baby forever."

She smiled, then frowned. "Speaking of which, I don't need a bodyguard. I'm perfectly capable —"

"I know that, *acushla*, don't be angry. And you were wrong before. I *do* trust you, how could I not after you saved my own hide more than once? It's still difficult for me to put you in danger."

"I'm not angry," she admitted grudgingly. "Not anymore. And Cullen was very charming, my mother loved him."

"Did she?" There was something in his voice when he said those two words. She couldn't quite figure out what. "I heard they were here, your mother and her admiral."

Elise would like that description. Randolph Leveque as her admiral.

"I guess everything went all right at the palace with Cristobal," she said. "I mean, at the Guild Hall, you two seemed very chummy."

"It was complicated," he admitted. "Harp doesn't have a death penalty. In the beginning, we needed everyone just to survive. And now, it's tradition."

"But they tried to kill you," she insisted, still angry on his behalf.

"And that's where the complication comes in. Des didn't only try to kill *me,* he tried to assassinate his clan leader. That puts him under clan law, and the penalty is clear. He fights me to the death, or accepts permanent banishment to the South. And since he already knows he can't defeat me in a physical challenge, he chose banishment."

"What's to stop him from coming back and trying again?"

"Clan law. If he returns, whether he moves against me or not, he'll be executed, and his entire family along with him, up to a second degree relationship."

"Eeesh. That'll do it."

Rhodry nodded. "Usually."

"And the others?"

"Kane Daly's a shifter, and under Guild law. It's not all that different from the clans, but without the family death sentence. Same choice, banishment or death challenge. He chose a challenge."

"Do you have to fight him?" she asked, worried even though she knew he could defeat that pale-haired bastard with one hand, er paw, tied behind his back.

Rhodry was shaking his head. "No, the Ardrigh leads the Guild. Kane made the mistake of thinking Cristobal's age and position had made him fat and slow. The fight was bloody and short, and Kane is no longer with us."

"They already fought," she said, stating the obvious. It was hard to believe it could be over so fast.

"They did. This afternoon, before we came over to the Guild Hall. That's why we were a little late getting there. That, and the need to stop by the jail to deal with the two civilians. They'll be staying there for a very long time, by the way."

"So, it's all done," she said, relief warring with sadness. With everything settled, there was no reason for him to stay in the capital.

"Mmm." Rhodry had pulled her close again. His voice vibrated against her temple, sending ripples of an entirely different sort down to pool warmly between her thighs, while his hands stroked down her naked back beneath the robe, which had somehow come completely untied.

She took a deep breath and asked the question she really didn't want answered. "Will you be staying in the city? I mean, they did try to kill you, and your cousins are all here now. Will you be going back with them?"

He didn't say anything at first, just tightened his hold on her, bringing her to her toes against him. "There's to be a wedding, so I'll go back with the cousins for a time anyway."

Wedding? Why was it suddenly so hard to breathe? Was he holding her too tightly? Or maybe it was just the tears swelling her sinuses until she couldn't draw a breath.

It all made perfect sense. Fionn had a sister. A couple of years older than Amanda, she was blond and lovely, just like Fionn. And how better to heal old wounds than to marry Cristobal Martyn's daughter to the de Mendoza heir?

Every inch, every bone, every muscle of her body ached at the thought.

"I thought your mother might want to come. I know she's not much for dirtside living, she might enjoy seeing Clanhome, though."

She blinked. "My mother?" she said in surprise.

"Unless you think she'd rather not." He frowned at her response. She could hear it in his voice. But why the hell would he think her mother would want to attend his damn wedding? Surely he didn't expect *her* to—

"Of course, maybe you'd rather not travel so far. It *is* a

fair distance to the mountains and you've just—"

"Me?" she choked. "You expect *me* to go to your wedding?"

He took hold of her shoulders and pushed her back so he could see her face. Her tear-streaked, swollen-nosed face.

"Amanda," he said, understanding softening his voice. "It's my cousin Gabriel who's getting married."

"Oh," she said, feeling stupid. "Which one was he?"

"The one with all the red hair. No one's quite sure where that came from, by the way."

"Well, sure, then, I'd love to go to his wedding, and I know my—"

He wasn't going to let her off that easily. "You think I'm the kind of man who'd dally with you in the forest if I had a woman waiting for me?"

"Well, no," she lied. "I thought maybe Cristobal had suggested a dynastic marriage or something."

"Fionn's sister? Not in this lifetime. Besides, what do I need a proper lady like that for when I've got you—"

"Are you saying I'm *not* a proper—"

"—the first woman ever to pass the trials and become a full-fledged member of the Guild. You'll go down in history, lass."

"Well," she said, pleased. "There is that."

"Besides, Cristobal wants me to take on the Guild, sort of a first among equals. It's a sad state when you've got shifters rigging the trial, and trying to kill one another. Something needs to be done. I'll divide my time between the city and Clanhome, but I can't imagine doing the job at all without you."

She waited for him to say something more. When he

didn't she scowled up at him. "That's it? You want me to make your job easier?"

His mouth twitched. "Well, that and I love you, and my life would be empty and, most especially, boring without you." He glanced around the small apartment, and then grinned down at her. "You think this place will hold two of us, *acushla*? Or will I be living a lonely existence at the Hall?"

She grinned back at him. He loved her. Her heart felt like it was too big for her chest. She was having trouble breathing again, and didn't know if she had enough air to tell him what needed to be said. Or hell, if she could get the words past the lump in her throat. She swallowed hard, ignoring the tears rolling down her cheeks, as she pulled his face down and kissed him. "I love you," she whispered against his lips. "And don't worry. Together we'll break down as many walls as we need to."

THE END

Acknowledgments

I want to thank Allison Collins for all her hard work in getting this story ready for my readers, and Theresa Marie Cole for falling in love with it in the first place. Thanks also to all of the people at Entangled who worked to make this book possible.

This story was a work of love for me, but a lot of people helped make it better along the way. In particular, my friends and fellow writers Steve McHugh and Michelle Muto have been there since I wrote the first paragraph, and they're always there to give a read, to share the triumphs, and to listen to me whine. They make everything easier. Another talented writer—my friend Angela Addams—was particularly supportive over the last year of this book's life, reading revisions, and cheering me on through the ups and downs of getting my story out there.

And finally, love always to my family, and to my wonderful husband, with whom I've shared so very many years of my life.

About the Author

D. B. Reynolds is the RT and EPIC Award-Winning author of the popular Vampires in America series of Paranormal Romance/Urban Fantasy and an Emmy-nominated television sound editor. She lives with her husband of many years in a flammable canyon near Los Angeles, and when she's not writing her own books, she can usually be found reading someone else's. Visit her blog at www.dbreynolds.com for details on all of her books, free stories, and more.

CPSIA information can be obtained
at www.ICGtesting.com
Printed in the USA
LVOW10s1516200117

521662LV00001B/56/P